Secrets Of The Tally

- Halie Fewkes -

To Autumn,

Never stop believing in magic. Enjoy!

- Stefl Se

Third Printing, 2019
Tally Ink Publishing

Cover Art by Ginger Anne London

ISBN 978-0-9961699-0-5

www.secretsofthetally.com

Tally
Book
1

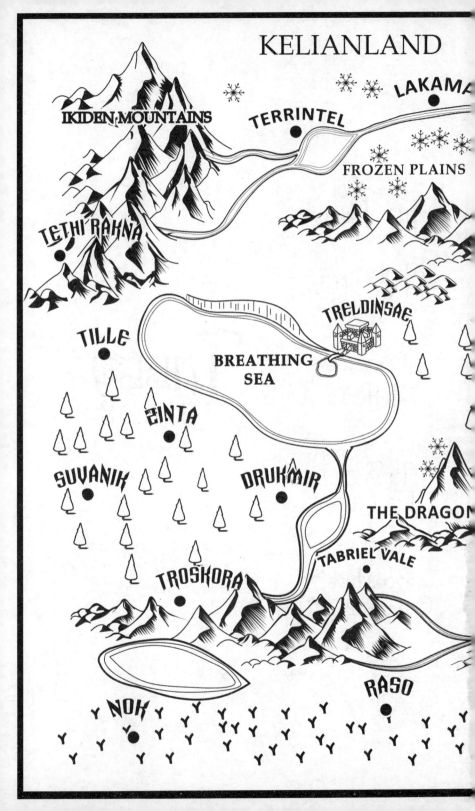

This book is dedicated to Amy Fewkes, who has taught me the meanings of bravery and strength without ever really meaning to.

And to the countless teachers who inspire creative dreams in their students. Without you, this story would have never been started, finished, or sent to print.

Thank you for all you do.

PROLOGUE

Sometimes when the sky was cloudless and the birds sang loudly enough, Margaret forgot that strolling wasn't allowed. A light breeze and a warm day were almost enough to make the forest seem harmless, and so she followed behind the two kids in her care without any sense of urgency. In fact, she found herself smiling when she realized they were holding hands. Eleven seemed a little young to her, but the kids had been best friends for years. She'd known this was coming.

All was peaceful until a shrieking scream echoed from ahead and froze all three of them to the trail. Margaret quickly hissed, "Back to town. Now!"

This was her worst nightmare, made even worse as her son took off *toward* the danger. His best friend, Ebby, darted after him, and Margaret was the only one left rooted to the ground in shock. *This couldn't be happening. If there was an Escali ahead, it would rip them apart.* "Ratuan, no, come back!" she cried, forcing her limbs to pursue, suddenly sprinting as only a panicked mother could.

A blonde teenaged girl sobbed and coughed in a patch of wildflowers ahead, writhing on the ground as she struggled to say something. The kids reached her first, and Ebby was on her knees in an instant, trying to figure out what was wrong when there was no blood.

Margaret skidded to a stop behind them, hauling each of the kids back to their feet. "Out of here. Now!"

"But I think she's a mage," Ebby protested. "We have to help her."

Margaret used all the strength in her arms to yank both kids back in the direction of safety. "Run now, and we'll send her help from town."

Margaret's forceful push suddenly became a restraint to pull them back to her as an Escali dropped down from a tree limb — a Human-like monster with wickedly black hair on his head and spikes of bone jutting from his elbows, now crouched with his sharp teeth bared.

The kids pressed themselves against Margaret from either side. It would only take the Escali seconds to kill all three of them.

CHAPTER ONE

Somebody had ripped my mind open and poured black ink inside. It was an all-consuming darkness, and when I woke I brought nothing with me except a sense of confused terror.

My legs were already working frantically beneath me, crashing through forest undergrowth for reasons unknown. I lurched involuntarily to one side and grabbed an ancient tree to steady myself, clinging to the damp moss with all the strength in my fingers as my knees threatened to collapse. My eyes stung and my head ached, so I smashed my face into the soft green life, and with the cool scent of rotting wood filling my nose and calming me down, I tried to think.

Something was wrong.

Everything was wrong.

I didn't know where I was. I didn't know what was happening. I didn't know if I was alone.

Two birds began to chatter to each other overhead, and I snapped my eyes open as blood's earthy scent hit me, a smell like steel and broken stones. My blurry vision sharpened as I pushed myself back from the thunderstruck tree, and I realized my hands had left crimson stains on the moss. Panicked, I whipped around to see an aging forest I had never laid eyes on before. A tangle of clovers and wild strawberry vines snagged my ankles as I spun, and I wrung my hands fiercely together in the nearest leafy bush to scrub the blood off.

Each breath became a shorter gasp as reality hit me and my weary lungs tried to match the accelerating pace of my heart.

I didn't know where I was from.

I didn't even know my own name.

Air scraped through my throat, and I clutched a shaky hand to my neck as I spun around again, trying to find signs of danger among the ferns and wildflowers.

Although I couldn't spot anything frightening in the dappled sunlight, I heard the shriek of a little girl in the distance and footsteps running toward me. My stomach twisted sharply and an overwhelming wave of frustration made me want to cry. I didn't know if friends or foes approached. I might be running from my saviors or waiting for my murderers if I chose wrong.

But even if they were coming to help, I couldn't explain why I had blood drying in the creases of my hands. I wasn't sure I had even seen these hands before, and I couldn't answer any questions. So in sheer panic, I bolted.

I didn't know what had happened, and I had no idea where I was going, but I tore through a blur of the deep green forest, trampling wildflowers and soft soil as my feet reveled in the discovery of running. My muscles seemed designed for this, propelling me forward with incredible speed, hurdling every mossy obstacle in my way.

The terror that drove me also reconnected something in my thoughts, and the last few minutes of my memory flooded back in a confusing jumble.

I remembered writhing in a patch of white ground flowers, unable to project more than one shriek in agony. Two kids running straight to me to help — a boy with acorn colored hair, not yet dyed crimson in his blood, and a smaller girl with a cascade of blonde. A woman — their mother? — sprinted close behind, hissing for them to leave me. Something was coming.

I remembered intense pain ripping through my entire body, preventing me from so much as getting to my knees. Even now, I could still feel my stomach churning, protesting the abuse as a makeshift marketplace came into view. My feet must have had a memory separate from my mind to carry me here, and my panic brought me to an immobilized stop right on the edge of what seemed to be a small village. A stranger brushed past me, and one almost bumped into me, but I couldn't recognize one face in the crowd of browsing locals.

Kids chased each other around carts filled with jewelry, clothes, instruments, and toys, but fear built in my chest the longer I stood still. I needed answers. I needed to feel safe, to figure out who I was and what was going on.

"Allie, you came back!" a man in a small hat exclaimed, sharing an aged smile that reached all the way to his large ears. He stood beneath a tent where a band of friends made a show of cooking breads and meats — juggling wads of dough and tossing pans to each other as they prepared food for a ring of onlookers.

I forced myself to rasp, "How do you know me?" wondering if I had just swallowed an entire briar patch. How else could speaking hurt so much?

His smile waned as he saw my anxious confusion, and I noticed a few cooks setting down their work to glance over as well. The short, wrinkled man in the hat said, "You were just here buying a roasted squirrel from us. I never forget a name. You said it was Allie."

Another of the cooks, a suntanned girl with tightly curled hair, abandoned her position to ask, "Are you alright? Do you need help?"

I replied, "I'm not… I just… Yes." I flung an arm over my mouth to muffle a hacking cough, a horrible bitter taste coming up with it.

5

Shouting drew the crowd's attention as a man with a bow arrived at the village's edge. "There's been an attack in the woods," he told the marketplace. "Margaret is dead, and her son badly hurt. We spotted a girl running from the scene, straight toward town. Tall with long blonde hair—"

That was me, and my face betrayed my terror as I scanned for the best route of escape. The curly haired girl grabbed my arm, boring her large eyes into mine. "Do you need somewhere to hide?" she asked.

As soon as I nodded, she pulled me beneath their baking tent with surprising strength to hide me under a cloth covered table. Completely concealed, I immediately pressed my face into the dusty grass and peered out to make sure nobody was pointing in my direction. I wasn't about to put total faith in the group of strangers. Not when I still had two legs and the ability to breathe.

The girl jumped into the air to catch a flying pan of food, and she emptied its contents onto a plate, laughing easily as though nothing was amiss. Maybe she could be trusted after all.

My entire body took advantage of the temporary safety and settled into the dirt. I was about to breathe a sigh of relief when my entire situation crashed down like old-growth timber in a storm. Branches of terror drove straight through me while a thousand suffocating leaves bore pressure on my ability to think.

How could I not know where I was? How could I not know *who* I was?

My heart hammered faster with the fear of uncertainty, and I tried to calm it. *Don't cry. Don't cry. Don't cry.* I squeezed my eyes shut so no tears could escape.

But how had I even gotten here?

I wracked my brain, looking for any tiny bit of information in the emptiness, but there was nothing to find that hadn't happened in the past hour. I curled my knees up to my chest and focused on my breathing.

I only knew two things. My name was Allie, and something horrible had just taken place. I grabbed the blonde tangle that reached to my waist and pulled it out of the dust so I could tug my fingers anxiously through the knots. Toying with it helped me feel real and kept me calm as I tried to at least piece the vicious attack back together.

The memory was dreamlike. Small details trickled through, but never the entire picture. The mother yanking the kids to their feet, telling them to leave me, to run back into town. Me trying to agree with her as I choked and squirmed. Run. Leave me. The panic in their faces as something terrifying stepped into sight.

I snapped my eyes open and focused on the stuffy warm air around me, pushing the image of the predator as far from my thoughts as I could. I twirled my fingers through the hair I had managed to detangle and used my other hand to poke at the rest of myself. Hard lean muscles all over. A few calluses on my palms. I wore soft leathers, probably to allow for ease of movement. Tight sandals wrapped the bottoms of my feet with leather soles, and the laces crisscrossed up my calves, built for running.

Had I been running all my life? Probably. And I would have to keep running if that thing in the woods ever appeared again. That Human-like creature with cloudy eyes and bared teeth, grinning wickedly at the sight of a woman, two children, and me. I shivered as I remembered the spikes of bone jutting from his elbows, jagged spines that could easily impale and kill someone standing behind him.

He had snapped his attention between the three standing over me with movements that were eerily jerky, like an insect. I shook my head, trying not to relive the moment when he slammed the little boy into the dirt. I tried to block the memory of a second monster ripping the woman's throat out — with his teeth. And that little girl... Screaming as they had taken her...

7

The cloth of the table rustled, startling me. Sunshine beamed inside, and I bolted upright as a small boy ducked into my fortress from the other side.

"Can I hide with you?" he asked, his eyes bright from the thrill of whatever game he was playing. His gleeful smile didn't sit well with me as I tried to overcome my crisis.

"No," I replied, wondering vaguely what he had done to cake so much mud into his hair and onto his face. The little boy looked like the lone survivor of a great battle, and like he had rolled in the aftermath.

I expected him to leave after my unwelcoming reply, but he settled onto his heels instead, frowning now. "Are you even playing?" he asked. I sank my palms into my eyes in disbelief.

"No."

"Well, what's wrong?" he asked, folding his legs across each other to make himself comfortable. "I don't recognize you. Are you one of the travelers coming through today?"

I let out a short laugh at the absurdity of his interest, but he wasn't about to leave. "I wish I knew," I told him. "But... something's wrong with me."

"Well?" he pushed. "What's wrong?"

I don't know *what* possessed me to tell this kid anything. Perhaps because of his large, inquisitive eyes, or my desperate need to simply talk to someone, I found myself explaining, "I just, sort of woke up out in the woods, without any idea who I am. And I don't know where I'm from. I don't know what happened, and I don't know what to do." Getting those words off my chest gave me room to finally take a deep breath, but I felt strangely uneasy. It wasn't this kid's age that bothered me, it was the fact that I had just opened up to him. I was putting my trust in someone I didn't know, and everything about that felt wrong. Like I was breaking a sacred value.

The boy nodded, giving me more attention than I thought possible for his age. "Well, why are you hiding?"

"Because... Something bad happened in the forest, and I think I might be blamed for it."

His eyes grew wider, and he exclaimed, "You're the girl the mages came looking for!"

Oh *wonderful*. Now I had to figure out how to keep him from revealing me. "Tell me about these mages," I said, hoping to keep him talking while I figured out what to do, apart from tackling him.

The boy was entirely too happy to know something I didn't, and said, "Those are two of the mages who keep Tabriel Vale safe from monsters. I don't know their names, but one of them has the power to use fire, and the other is an ice mage."

I knew mages could only have one power. So if these two wielded fire and ice, they wouldn't have any magical ability to track me down. I knew that like I knew a rock would fall if I dropped it. It was the way things were.

"Are there other mages around... what did you call this place?"

The boy scrunched his eyebrows, confused. "There are mages everywhere with the Eclipsival tomorrow. And this is Tabriel Vale. Don't you..." He gasped as understanding finally reached his eyes. "You've really forgotten everything!"

"Just about," I said, not loving to admit it. "But I think there's a difference between knowledge and memory. I've only forgotten names and events. Faces and places, you know?"

But I suspected I hadn't *entirely* forgotten them. In the midst of confusion and terror, my feet had brought me to Tabriel Vale, my best bet of finding safety and answers. My survival instincts had simply kicked in to save me, and that thought was intriguing. I wondered if that was all I needed to jog my memory, a little life threatening danger.

The noise from the market began to trickle in to me, and I heard the old man beneath the tent call, "One Baking Show Special, sweet sauce and sliced roast!" and the whole crew answered back, "All grilled to perfection, then served on wheat toast!"

Every order had a prearranged call and a specific response, but I focused on the conversations outside to see if I was likely to escape the town unnoticed. Most discussed money or longed for the items on display, but I also heard several kids talking. A little girl said, "We haven't found Leaf yet," and a boy answered, "Good. Let's just leave him."

I glanced at the mud monster beside me and said, "I'm told my name is Allie. What's yours?"

"Leaf," he replied, smiling as though the name itself made him happy. I felt an immediate irritation with the kids outside for leaving him out of their fun. "What else do you know about yourself?" Leaf asked.

"Nothing really."

"Did you find anything when you searched your pockets?"

Pockets! Why hadn't they crossed my mind yet?

I plunged my hands into the small pockets on each pant leg. One came up empty. The other closed around a folded scrap of paper, worth more to me than gold. I jerked each fold apart in haste, ready to find incredible knowledge between the creases. As I undid the last doubling in the paper, the dim light only illuminated a few sloppy and disappointing lines.

Leaf got anxiously to his knees and exclaimed, "I'm too little to read! What does it say?"

"It says: *Allie, I'm volunteering for the Eclipsival setup today with West, and I probly wont be back to the Dragona till its dark. Your sister, Liz.*" I set the paper down and said, "Well, at least I know I have a sister. One who has clearly never held a pen before."

"And you're from the Dragona!" Leaf exclaimed. "That's where they train kids to become mages. They just recruited me too! And if you live at the Dragona, you must have a power — or you will someday. Do you know what yours is?"

10

"I barely know my name," I replied. "So, no." I fixed my gaze on the note in my hand, trying to connect the names with faces, or images of any kind. Liz? West? The Dragona? Nothing. Empty thoughts about my home and my sister just didn't jog my memories like overwhelming fear had.

"Leaf, when are you going to the Dragona? And how are you getting—"

I froze as a large pair of boots stopped next to the table. A hand lifted the cloth covering, and sunshine from outside momentarily blinded me.

Chapter Two

tale, muggy heat escaped from beneath our table into the wind, and the old man of a thousand smiles ducked down to peer in. "The mages and search parties are all in the woods looking for you now. It's safe to come out of this furnace Corliss stuffed you into."

Leaf leapt into the fresh air. "She's a mage! She's going to the Dragona, just like I am."

I pushed myself into the sunshine and grabbed the table edge to get to my feet, thankful to be standing again, but feeling skittish now that I was in the open. I glanced over my shoulder to make sure nobody lurked behind me. "Which way is the Dragona from here?" I asked.

"Why, so you can travel there by yourself?" The old man chuckled. "Come with us. We're leaving for the Dragona in a matter of hours, and we've got extra room on the cart."

Though I was desperate, his offer made me uncomfortable. I couldn't accept more charity, not when I already owed them for hiding me. I was *not* helpless. "I really appreciate the offer, but I'm sure I can find a way there." I threw in a casual shrug to hide my distress and added, "*Accepting help when you can help yourself is the surest sign of a thief.*" The saying came to mind easily, like something said a thousand times before.

"Well that's cow dung," he said, waving a hand as though to clear the smelly air. "Nobody travels alone. There are Escalis in the woods."

That word stopped my heart mid-beat. It represented the vile creatures that had shed so much blood earlier in the day, and I immediately found myself searching for a diplomatic way to accept their company on the trip after all.

"I'll tell you what, I have a whole basin full of dishes that need to be washed before we can leave," the old man said. "You look like you have a good pair of arms on you. Are you a good throw? A good catch?"

"I... what? I don't know," I replied. This was the perfect solution, but it still set me on edge. I didn't know why. I could help for a few hours, and they could get me back to the Dragona. I needed to say yes. "I'm sure I can learn quickly though."

"Excellent! Come over here, and we'll show you how to do it. And by the way, you can call me Osty."

The old man, Osty, turned to lead the way, and I put a hand on Leaf's shoulder before he took off to join the kids' next game.

"Listen," I said, crouching down. "You can't tell anybody what we were talking about. Got it?"

"I wasn't going to," he said, already astonished that I might doubt his loyalty. "Because we're friends, right? You'll be one of the only people I know when we get to the Dragona."

"Sounds good to me. You'll be the only friend I have too."

The old man turned back to me and exclaimed, "Allie! Quit slacking!" Leaf smiled before running off, and I almost smiled back as I dodged between two cooks on my way to the old wash basin.

"The Travelling Baking Show only has one rule you'll need to follow — throw everything," said the old man. "When the cooks need something washed, they'll toss it to you. You can throw the

13

clean dishes to Corliss and she'll dry them." I broke my gaze away from the basin as he flung a cup at the curly-haired Corliss, who wasn't even facing us. She caught it behind her head and tossed it onto the stack next to her station, never looking up from the vegetables she chopped.

"Bravo!" old man Osty said. "So you think you're ready?"

"Yes," I said, unable to fake enthusiasm when I felt so empty. Stacks of breakable dishes lay submerged in the murky water, but I could only really focus on the settling ripples above them. An echo of my identity rested upon the water's surface, reflecting brown eyes set into the angular face I couldn't recognize. Seventeen years old, perhaps? I tilted my head a bit to the side to see my smooth skin in a different light, then snatched one of the ceramic dishes uncomfortably and attacked it with a scrub brush, distorting the reflection.

Burning anger flared up in my chest as I assaulted the old bowl. How could this have happened? I had the overwhelming sense that I should be doing something important right now, not scrubbing dishes. But I had no idea what, and being so helpless, so useless, made my insides churn. What if my memories were permanently missing?

The ceramic bowl shattered against the side of the washbasin. *Oh no.* I glanced quickly around to make sure nobody had noticed, waited ten seconds, then slipped away to discard the bowl's remnants beneath a prickly bush. Returning with nobody the wiser, I picked up a new cup to clean. I scrubbed this one a little more carefully and began to rehash the past hour of my life, trying to reach further back in time and remember more.

I had already run out of details to recall concerning the attack in the woods, and I only had a few other scraps of myself to cling to while investigating every corner of my mind. Liz, West, and the Dragona were the only leads I could explore, but their names remained faceless and the Dragona remained an unimaginable

14

building. I mindlessly tossed and caught dishes from the singing and dancing crew, far too preoccupied to take part in the comradery or poke fun at Osty like the rest of the bakers. Time slipped by surprisingly fast as I toiled with my thoughts, scrubbing at ceramic and wood until my hands wrinkled from the water and the crowd began thinning.

"What happened out in the forest?" asked Corliss, the only member of the crew who looked to be my age. The other cooks began to tear down the operation, and although I didn't really care about the dishes, the fact remained that I hadn't finished them.

Knowing that I owed her an explanation after she had helped me, I shrugged and gave her the same short version I had given Leaf. I left the predators, the Escalis, out of my retelling because a lump rose in my throat when I tried to think about them, but I truthfully recalled the rest of it. At the end of my story, Corliss squinted incredulously and answered with a flat, "Uh-huh."

"I know," I sighed, tossing three wooden spoons to her. "I'm having a hard time believing it myself." She dried each one thoughtfully on a towel and set them on the table beside her as I clenched my teeth and gathered my thoughts. "All I know right now is that I need to get to the Dragona."

"We caught you at a good time then. We're getting excited to head up there and sell to tomorrow's Eclipsival crowds."

"What is Eclipsival?" I asked as I neared the bottom of the wash basin.

She peered at me, as though amused. "The Dragona has been preparing for this for the past six months, Allie. Don't you think you're taking this memory thing a little far, claiming you can't remember the biggest celebration on the continent?"

"I'm not lying about this," I snapped, throwing a heavy cutting board to her with more force than necessary. I knew I needed to calm down, but my frustration would dissolve me into a blubbering fool if I didn't keep a strong front.

15

She caught it easily as a short balding man approached our tent, looking at me as though memorizing my every feature.

"You look like the girl the mages are searching for," he said. I should have been scared sick by the thought of being turned in, but with so many crises already torturing me, I just felt incredibly annoyed.

"I hope you're not talking about my daughter," Osty intervened on my behalf. Osty's wispy white hair made him far too old to be my father, but I appreciated the thought.

The nosy skeptic didn't believe it either and repeated, "Your daughter? What's her name then?"

"I don't believe that's any business of yours, and you don't have any business being here. We're closing up."

I picked up one side of my wash basin and shot Corliss a look that said *help me*. She promptly grabbed the opposite handhold, and we lugged the heavy bucket to the trees to dump it.

"I might have to run," I told her as dish water cascaded into the grass. I was equally willing to fight the guy, but that was a dead-end option.

"Just wait first. Old Osty is better with words than you would believe."

We returned to the tent where nearly ten people had slowed their pace to watch the argument. Leaf watched with the most intensity, as though learning all he could from the interaction.

Every time the short man tried to speak, Osty cut him off. It was almost comical, and I realized Osty's goal — to make the bystanders laugh rather than take this man seriously.

Shorty was trying to say, "She has blonde hair, exactly the length—"

"And she's the only one!" Osty interrupted, drawing his voice out to sound elderly. "No other girls with blonde hair even walked by today."

"The mages also said she was wearing calf-lacing sandals—"

"Will you stop looking at my daughter's legs already? We're just trying to wrap up an honest day's work out here."

"Quit talking over me!" the flustered man exclaimed.

Instead of talking over him, Osty called to the crew like he would any order, "I've... Got... One nosey customer, being quite rude!"

The crew responded, "Invite him to come back, we'll *spit* in his food!" When the entire Travelling Baking Show spit on the ground, I had to cover my mouth to hide my first true smile of the day — the first true smile of my new life. The people who had stopped to watch began to leave with grins as well.

The short man took off in a huff, and I muttered to his back, "And that's why you never make an enemy of entertainers."

As soon as he was out of our sight, Osty said, "Let's get the cart loaded and hit the woods. We should leave before he sends the mages to ask questions. And we definitely don't want to be out after dark."

I thought of a pitch black forest where treetops blocked the stars, and the memory of Escalis constricted my chest again. I needed to know more about them. How to avoid them, how to kill them. But such a question was difficult to bring up.

"Don't rush for my sake," I said, baiting them into an explanation. "I don't mind if we have to travel in the dark."

All packing stopped as the entire Travelling Baking Show turned to stare, like every last baker thought they'd heard me wrong.

Corliss only scoffed. "And how would you like your corpse found? Arms torn off, throat ripped out, or with a punctured lung where you took an elbow spike through your ribcage?"

"Corliss," Osty scolded her as Leaf's eyes grew gigantic. Osty pointed at Leaf and whispered, *"Parents!"* She immediately folded her arms and closed her mouth.

17

I didn't want to stir up anyone's emotional hardships, but I needed more information. "I'm only saying it shouldn't make a difference whether it's daylight or not. If anything, it should be harder for something to track us down in the dark."

Corliss just squinted with disbelief. Osty was the one who said, "You know Escalis are built for tracking, right? They can see in the dark and follow scent trails. And they hear *everything*."

"Well I'm sure we have enough of us to fight one off if it finds us," I said.

Corliss broke into laughter and I felt my face heat with frustration. "Fight one off? An Escali?" She took heart in the joke until she suddenly gasped and pursed her lips. "You weren't kidding, were you? What you told me?"

I took a slow breath to calm myself before saying, "I swear on my dead memories that I do not know anything about my past life. I don't know what this Eclipsival is. I don't know what the Dragona looks like. I wouldn't know my name if you hadn't told me."

The bakers caught on to the situation quickly, but their sympathetic looks and sighs made me want to bolt away. I wasn't weak. I didn't want their pity.

"Before we leave, will somebody just tell me how to kill an Escali?" I asked.

The lively group became even more solemn. "You just have to hope there are mages nearby," Osty said. "Because you don't stand a chance otherwise. An Escali's skin is impenetrable. No matter how sharp of a knife you hold or how fast of an arrow you shoot, you can't cut through their hides. So to kill them, you either have to burn them, or drown them, or crush them or something. And even then, they can shake off injuries unbelievably fast."

I thought Leaf might burst into tears as some old past tormented him, but he looked straight at me. "They're fast and strong, and they live to hunt people," he said, as though warning me was

18

suddenly the single reason he existed. "Everybody's lost someone to the Escalis. In a way, you're lucky you don't have to remember."

I felt a new pit sink into my stomach, wondering who I'd lost, and whether I'd ever remember them. I hadn't even been able to keep their memory alive, all because of the Escalis.

Osty pulled Leaf over to give him a hug as he said, "That's why we're leaving together, in the daylight, when the mages are guarding the trails. Travelling is perfectly safe when you do it right."

Leaf completely ignored the attempt to cheer him up and wiped his eyes before adding, "You're better off dead than in the Escalis' hands. If you ever know you're about to be captured, remember that."

"I will," I said, looking into his large dark eyes to acknowledge his warning. Something awful had happened to his parents, and keeping others from the same fate was probably his only way of honoring their memory. In one look, I tried to tell him that I knew his story as well as he knew mine, and by the way the kid smiled gratefully, I think he understood.

Corliss startled me by pushing a large chunk of bread into my hand. "We need to go. Daylight's fading," she said, clapping me on the shoulder. "And lighten up a little. We'll be at the Dragona in no time." I allowed my tense shoulders to slouch just a fraction, but true relaxation was beyond me. They might be heading straight for the Dragona, but I had different plans.

Their one horse even had a sense of humor, stealing Osty's small hat off his head before leaving. Then the wheels hit the trail, and the Travelling Baking Show began their journey with a loud chorus of *Why is the Pear in the Pickle Plum Tree?* I lagged at the back of the lively procession to watch for danger and the chance to disappear unnoticed.

I had known I'd be returning to the wildflower patch since I first remembered the brutal attack. Seeing the last place I'd been to

19

before my crisis might just jog my memory, and even if it didn't, I had to pay some sort of respect to the mother and two kids.

A massive cedar tree leaned over the path ahead, and I made sure everybody was preoccupied before dreadful guilt forced me to step out of sight behind it. Was it my fault the Escalis had gotten to them? I scolded myself for making that a question when I already knew the answer. They had been running straight to me to help. The *real* question was, why had I been alone in the woods to begin with?

As the boisterous voices of the Travelling Baking Show died away, I trod across the soft ground and found the patch of white flowers from my memory, many of which had been crushed or bore flecks of blood on their petals. The flattened foliage showed exactly where two bodies had been lying, one significantly smaller than the other. Mother and son.

Standing among the wildflowers didn't stir any more of my past, so I scoured the area for the little girl, finding only a shred of her hair on a scorched branch where the leaves had been ripped off, as though she had tried to hold on. I didn't wonder where she was. I didn't want to know.

Better off dead than in the Escalis' hands...

Overcome with guilt and frustration, I smashed a cluster of flowers into the ground with my heel and kicked the heads off several others, stopping as the whistle of a bird resonated through the dimming forest. Instead of twitters and chirps of no meaning, the duskflyer whistled a full melody, a tune of mourning.

I knew the bird was called a duskflyer like I knew a tree was a tree, or a foot was a foot. It was knowledge, not memory, and the calming simplicity of the song allowed me to realize that two moons now glowed brighter than the pink clouds in the sky. Although the forest hadn't grown dark enough to steal my shadow, the evening gave me a sense of unease.

I retreated to the trail and put my runner's legs back to use to overtake the Travelling Baking Show. Long minutes dragged by as I ran, and I picked up speed after I felt I should have reached them. I knew they wouldn't have stepped off the trail, but I couldn't believe how quickly they covered ground.

The beautiful birdsong died away, leaving the forest entirely silent. My ragged breathing only had to compete with a few crickets in the distance, so I didn't miss the flapping of powerful wings above me as a bird of prey swooped in the dark. Even the crickets ceased chirping when the falcon pierced the night with a screech that clearly meant, *Come here, I found it.*

As fear lurched through me again, my instincts slammed me with the awareness that Humans didn't hunt with falcons. Escalis did.

CHAPTER THREE

s I tore down the dirt path, my survival instincts briefed me on everything I needed to know. I needed to find a leafy bush with purple — there! I snatched a handful of leaves and purple berries as I sprinted past, knowing that their crushed scent could hinder an Escali's senses. I rubbed the bitterly potent juice on my arms as maps flashed through my mind, telling me the distance between Tabriel Vale and the Dragona. I had a chance of making it back to the Dragona as long as nothing caught up to me first.

I caught a glimpse of something running to my left, but the blur was so fast it was able to spring through the air and knock me to the ground before I could even react. My momentum hurtled me into the base of a tree while the Escali rolled back onto his feet, crouching to growl at me.

My right knee took most of the impact in a sickening crunch, causing more than enough pain to curl up and cry over. Despite my certainty that it was broken, I only lay still for a few seconds of shock before I grabbed the tree beside me and pulled myself back up. My instincts screamed to not appear cowardly, even if my eyes watered and I had to put all my weight on my left leg to stay up. The Escali kept his stance and assessed everything about me as I shot a stare back at him, holding his gaze.

22

His bared teeth, the wide angles of his face, and the set of his eyes all made him seem wolf-like. His green irises were clouded with undefined pupils, and the staff he carried on his back gleamed with blades on both ends. The spikes of bone jutting from his elbows alarmed me more than the conventional weapon.

All of my limbs shook violently, filled with adrenaline for which I had no direction. What options did I have?

"This one is *fast*," an Escali woman said as she caught up and abruptly stopped. She had the same alarming look about her, as though mostly person yet part monster, but the protruding bones of her forearms rested against her upper arms since she held her hands loosely at her sides. Every time she switched her attention to something new, whether it was my injury or the other Escali, her movements were quick and her gaze intensive.

"She shouldn't have been running," he growled, crouching over the stump in front of him to distribute some of his weight to his hands. I got the impression he was comfortable on all fours, and possibly about to spring.

The cloudy eyed woman replied, "She's done running. Let's take her before those mages get here."

The male Escali pulled out his bladed staff and I cringed against the massive tree, aware that I had nothing I could grab to prevent them from dragging me off.

"Do you not speak?" He took a step closer, head cocked to the side. "Say something."

My inner mind pounded on my awareness, demanding that I match their aggression with my own pride. "I'm not afraid of you," I snarled, surprising myself with how convincing my lie sounded. "What do you want?"

The Escali's eyes narrowed as though he found my question humorous, and he put the blade of his staff to my throat. "You have a lot to atone for. We're taking you back to Dekaron."

The brown flecked falcon swooped down and landed on the staff, inquisitively watching me.

"Atone for?" I repeated, trying to keep my voice from trembling. "What did I do?"

I angered him by asking, and he said, "Your stupid questions aren't fooling anyone. You're the Tally we were told to pursue."

The woman crouched defensively, and with her eyes on the trees behind me, she hissed, "Their mages are almost here."

When the male froze to listen as well, I thrust the blade away from my neck, grabbed the falcon, and dashed back from his irate response.

He bared his teeth and leapt toward me. "What are you doing?" He only stopped because I was ready to break the falcon's neck. "I swear to you, girl, if you kill my bird you'll follow it straight into oblivion!"

The falcon shrieked and flailed, trying to free itself, but I kept my grip on it through the talons and snapping beak. My knee still bellowed agony to me, begging me to sit down, but I shoved the pain from my mind.

The woman said, "We need to go. Now! We'll send someone else out for her later."

"Not if she's dead," he growled back.

"You know we can't kill her," the woman replied. "Not this one."

"Nobody said I had to bring her back with both her arms," he said, but I heard another tiny voice whisper to me.

"Duck." The voice was a woman's, but nobody else was near me. "Get on the ground. Now!"

I had no idea who was instructing me, but I dropped the falcon and flung myself down as a wave of fire slammed into the two Escalis. I could hear the footsteps of a half-dozen mages who guarded the woods.

Gravity pushed me into the dirt harder than ever before, and I saw the same pressure hindering the Escalis as vines sprang up to entangle them. Both attempted to remain on their feet, and I used a strange combination of rolling and crawling to get myself away from the snarling predators.

"Is that Allie?" one of the women asked as the pressure lessened and I got painfully to my knees.

"It figures she's the one in trouble again," another man answered, his arms stretched toward the Escalis with an orange glow in his hands. I didn't even look back to see what magic they used to combat the monsters now. As soon as I had my feet beneath me, I took off.

I favored one leg over the other, resulting in a weird skipping run, but it was enough to get me away from the danger. I could still hear shouting behind me as I stopped to lean against a tree, pulling my knee in close. Gripping it tightly with both hands kept the pain at bay and gave me a chance to catch my breath.

I looked back just in time to see the entire sky dim as two black lightning bolts struck near the conflict. A crack of thunder rumbled through me, rattling needles free from the branches overhead, and I ran again.

I was almost to the Dragona, so I ignored the pain in my knee and picked up as much speed as I could. I came out to a grassy clearing near the base of a massive, snow-capped mountain, but I saw no buildings. The Dragona had been right here on the map in my mind. I was sure of it. Yet I couldn't find any evidence of life in the empty field. Had I been horribly wrong? I didn't want to retreat to the mages to ask, and I stuck a fist in my mouth to keep from whimpering, wishing with my entire being to just be home and safe.

"Allie!" a guy who looked my age shouted, running toward me. Paranoia had me on the verge of fleeing again, but he was clearly Human and knew my name. "What's going on? We heard something about your memory, but it's a joke right? You do know who I am?"

Taller than me, he had messy brown hair and handsome dark eyes I couldn't remember seeing before.

And though it was entirely irrational, I flung my arms up and grabbed his shoulders with a grip that could crush rocks. "Who are you, and how do you know about my memory?" I had to be suspicious of everyone. There was a chance he could read my mind, after all.

His eyes were wide with disbelief and only a hand's-breadth away from my face. "I'm West. I'm one of your friends. Allie, this crazy troop of bakers just came stampeding through the Dragona, saying they'd found you. They said something about your memory, but that they lost you again."

I responded with a choked mix between a laugh and a sob, picturing the bakers flailing their arms and exclaiming they had lost me. I glanced around again and let go of him. "Where is the Dragona?"

"You're at the Dragona."

I gestured frantically to the empty evening. "Then what? It's invisible?"

"No," he replied, "It's underground in the caves. This really is bad, isn't it? Do you even remember who Liz is?"

"I know she's my sister," I said. I quickly squashed the hope in his eyes as I added, "But only because I found a scrap of paper that said so. West, can you tell me who I am? What was I doing that made me lose my memory? Why are the Escalis targeting me?"

He had to process the shock of everything I said before replying, "I don't think the Escalis are after you specifically, Allie. They just like to hunt people in general."

"They just told me I have something to atone for. They were trying to take me alive."

"*What?*" West said. "Allie, Escalis can't speak our language."

26

"These ones could!"

West must have run out of logical reasoning for me, because he said, "We need to get you to Anna. Come on, one of the Dragona's entrances is hidden in the rocks over here."

My knee still hurt, but I was already able to hide my hobble as I followed West. I must have seriously overreacted to the injury, thinking it was broken. It definitely wasn't.

"Who's Anna?" I asked as we climbed over a mossy jumble of stones to enter the concealed tunnel system.

"Anna and Sir Darius are the Dragona's leaders," West replied. "Anna's a fire mage, and I know she's probably the more dangerous of the two, but she'll be the better one to talk to. Trust me."

I wouldn't be following him through an underground maze if I hadn't placed some sort of trust in him. The rock walls of the tunnel were rough and jagged while the floors had been smoothed by years of foot-traffic, and I followed West blindly as the sight of the Escalis flashed across my mind. As terrifying as they were, the mages were just as dangerous. I was lucky they were on my side and not suspicious of me.

When the cave forked we took a right, and then we headed left as it split into two more tunnels. West and I approached the wooden door of Anna's study, and it opened before we had a chance to knock. When we entered a small room, which smelled like the aged pages of a book, I needed a second to absorb the peculiar appearance of the woman who let us in. Taller than me and with bright green eyes, she retreated behind a desk littered with scrolls and leather bound tomes. I didn't need an intact memory to know staring wasn't polite, but still…

Red as a hair color?

It was an abnormality that distracted me from launching immediately into my saga.

27

Anna raised her eyebrows and said, "You should probably stop staring at the red hair, Allie, and tell me what's going on."

I only felt a tinge of embarrassment as she called me out, but my cheeks flushed as though I bore the shame of a coward. I swallowed and said, "Where do I start? I just woke up in Tabriel Vale, and I literally know nothing. I was chased down by these two Escalis on my way back here. They were specifically after me, saying I had something to atone for."

Anna remained composed, but the squint of her eyes gave away her concern.

"I told her they can't speak our language," West said. "Maybe that's Allie's power? She can understand other languages?"

"Some Escalis can speak our language," Anna said. "They train a select few to do it, and it's no coincidence that those are the ones who found you and let you live. That never happens. It's possible they were trying to plant false information with you. Did they give you a message? Or seemingly let something slip?"

"No..." I said. "I don't think they did."

"Think! Think of any way they tried to mislead you."

I wrung my hands as I tried to recall their words. "I don't know. They were calling me a Tally and saying I was in trouble. They were going to take me somewhere. I don't remember the name of it, but they would have dragged me off if the mages hadn't come."

Anna nodded solemnly. "They are good at carrying people off."

A quick knock preceded a frazzled woman bursting into the room, declaring, "I've got a minor emergency with the Eclipsival setup."

Anna folded her arms and tipped her head to the side before she replied, "I'm in the middle of one that is much more important right now, so I suggest you either solve it, find Sir Darius, or wait until I'm through here."

The woman glanced around at the three of us, backed out of the room again, and softly closed the door. I wasn't sure which element of the situation convinced me I liked Anna, but I knew that I did.

Her theory also made sense in every way except the lack of any message from the Escalis. They hadn't told me anything except that somebody would come after me later.

"Allie," she said, moving past the interruption, "Do you have any idea what happened to your memory?"

"None," I replied. I proceeded to tell her about coming to my senses in the woods and meeting the Travelling Baking Show, but she agreed through the unease on her face that none of it was useful information. I ended by asking, "Why was I in Tabriel Vale?"

"You shouldn't have been," she said. "Nobody is supposed to leave the Dragona without permission, but that's never been a rule you've followed. This isn't the first time our mages have saved you from Escalis in the woods, and word has already reached me that your attackers got away, so we won't know what they wanted."

"They got away?" I repeated, unable to believe it. "But the mages were incredible."

"And the Escalis are incredibly resilient," Anna replied. "Knock them down, and they'll get right back up to bite you."

"They're going to send more after me," I told her. "They said they would. What should I do?"

"As long as you're in the Dragona, you don't need to worry," Anna said. "We keep the Escalis fooled into thinking this is a mountain of wild dragons, so they won't know to look for you here. We also patrol the woods often in case one strays this way."

I asked, "How can you be sure—" but was interrupted when the door to the study flung open again. I only had a fraction of a second to see the running girl, with dark hair and brown eyes on a face about five years younger than mine, before she collided barreled into me, almost knocking me over.

CHAPTER FOUR

I saw how closely her face resembled mine right before she flung her arms around me. I could guess exactly who she was, but I held my hands awkwardly away from her, not ready to return the hug or stroke her straight hair like a sister probably should. She pressed her face into my shoulder and squeezed her arms tightly around my middle.

"Liz?" I didn't say her name as a question of her identity; I just hoped I might find familiarity somewhere in the name, the hug, or her response.

"I told them you wouldn't forget me," she replied into the base of my neck.

I clenched my hands together as guilt wound into my stomach, even though nothing was my fault. I opened them again and set my palms on Liz's shoulders to push her back from me, trying to match her face with some sort of memory.

Liz stared straight back at me, and her voice shook as she said, "This isn't funny."

"Believe me, I know," I said, searching her eyes. Devastation and terror widened them as tears collected in the corners, giving me a sense of how close we had been. All it took was that one look, her eyes telling me that I meant the entire world to her, and I knew with

30

all my soul that I would do anything for this girl. I would kill without remorse if she was ever in danger and give up everything dear just to see her laugh. All this I knew, but I couldn't *remember* anything about her.

"Liz..." The wrenching sadness and guilt were worse than the fear that had twisted my guts all day long. "I'm sorry. I thought I would be able to recognize you when I saw you, but I can't."

She squinted to watch me closely, and then a scornful smile played at the edge of her lips. "I just heard you use my name. What are you trying to pull?"

"I only know your name because I've already heard it. And it's not just my memories of you, Liz. It's everything. It's as though my whole life has never been lived. Everything I used to know is gone."

Liz wrenched herself away from me, as though I was suddenly offensive and Anna was more worthy of her attention. "How can we fix her?"

I felt like my heart was being crushed as Anna replied, "I think we just need to give her time."

Liz flicked her gaze back to me and said, "I don't want to give her time. I need Allie. The real Allie. What about the mind mages? One of them can help her, right?"

Anna replied, "Liz, you need to calm down and quit acting like this is her fault. There are four mind mages in Kelianland who should be able to help, but none of them are here. The irony is, they were all here this morning for the Eclipsival, but Sir Avery came in this afternoon with a special assignment for them. As soon as they get back, Allie, one of them will be happy to look into your lost memory. I'm sure they'll be able to help you get it back."

"That would be fantastic," I said, feeling relief on one small level. Knowing I had hope made a world of difference, but Liz's words still stung. I wanted so badly to hold her and declare it all a joke.

31

"Why can't Sir Avery help her?" Liz demanded. "He could probably fix her problems in less than a minute."

All Anna had to do was look at Liz. She didn't frown, didn't raise her eyebrows, and didn't even need to deviate from her stern gaze. "You can ask him if you'd like."

Liz's demeanor shifted quickly from demanding to resigned, and she muttered, "I know, we can't go asking personal favors of him. Shouldn't have asked."

"Who is Sir Avery?" I asked. I was ready to march up to anybody who could possibly salvage my memories and ask for help. The very worst they could do was say no. I didn't have much else to lose.

I watched three jaws drop around me, which was probably a response I needed to get used to. West muttered, "Oh holy life, you really did forget everything."

It visibly pained Liz to tell me, "He's our Epic. The hero born with every mage power in existence? He's probably too busy to help though."

Anna said, "Give it time. Tomorrow is the Eclipsival, so let's just get you through that first. There isn't much else we can do right now, and I should probably tend to this Eclipsival crisis waiting patiently outside my door. Elira, you can come in."

The eager woman was back inside the room within seconds and had already launched into the details of the catastrophe before we could leave. We heard all about how the ice mages and water mages had been practicing when one of the water mages broke her leg, and even though they were able to fix it, she was afraid to be thrown in the air which was keeping the entire team from practicing — and the high-strung woman hadn't even stopped for breath by the time we were out the door.

West had just barely pulled it shut when Liz lunged at me, demanding, "How could you do this to me?" I lurched back to avoid her clawing hands, West grabbing her arm as she tried to take a swing. "You know how much I need you!" she shouted.

"How could I... to *you?*" I repeated. I needed *her.* I needed her more than my memories, more than my identity, and more than anything else important in the world. To have her spit accusations at me when I was vulnerable was beyond cruel. "I am the one who can't remember anything. And I didn't purposely forget my life to spite you! Do you hear yourself?"

Liz wrenched her shoulders to either side to make West let go, then clasped her arms across her chest in a huff. "You just can't do this," she said to the ground. "You're all I have."

The despair in her scrunched eyes made my whole chest ache even worse, as if this really was my fault. "Don't we have any other family?" I asked.

"No. We were the only ones left. The Escalis killed everyone else, and let me guess. They're probably the ones who took you from me too."

"I'm right here, Liz. Not dead," I said, resenting the implication.

"Well the Escalis will be when I get my hands on them!" she exclaimed with fiery hatred. She spun on one foot and took off down the tunnel, apparently beginning her vendetta right on the spot.

"And how are you going to do that?" I asked to her back as she marched away.

"I don't know!" she replied, rounding a corner and disappearing from sight.

With wide eyes, I looked to West and asked, "Is she always like this?"

Looking equally startled, West replied, "We usually joke about how fast her mood changes, but I've never seen her so upset. I can go talk to her."

"No. Thanks, but I need to," I said, taking off after Liz. I glanced back to see West setting his hands restlessly in his pockets. He seemed uncomfortable leaving us to settle our own differences, but I was glad he didn't attempt to tag along.

"Where are you going?" I asked as I caught up and matched Liz's pace. The tunnel comfortably accommodated the two of us side by side.

"To your room," she replied, avoiding eye contact as she strode. "Somebody has to show you where it is."

The flat tone of her voice gave me no inclination to thank her. "And then what? Are you going to leave and refuse to talk to me until I'm normal again? Because I don't know when that will happen."

Liz finally took her eyes off her feet to meet my gaze. "But you do think it will happen?"

Now it was my turn to fixate on each rock along the path beneath me. "I think it will," I said as we began to pass wooden doors embedded in the cave walls. "I know that some of my past is still in here, at least. I can remember things when my life depends on remembering them."

The tunnel cut to the right, and Liz grabbed my arm to steer me into the narrower branch of the cave. "That's the only time you remember anything?" she asked.

"So far, yes. Maybe something else will be able to trigger it though. Maybe something we aren't expecting. I don't know."

"Sparring," she said with sudden certainty. "You fight like you were born with a stick in your hand, and I swear it pains you to put it down. We have lessons every morning. Come tomorrow."

"I'll be there if you think it will help. Is that my power then? The ability to fight?"

"No," she replied. "We haven't found our gifts yet. West and I have been betting lately about which power you'll get, because you're good at everything, but we don't know."

I could inherently remember which gifts were most common. Fire, ice, water, speed, light, and jumping into the air to disappear

34

and reappear in entirely new places. Other mages could make illusions, read people's minds, shield themselves, turn invisible… The possibilities were endless.

"Maybe I'll get more than one power," I said, knowing it wasn't possible, but wanting to argue it anyway. "I mean, if Sir Avery can have all of them, what's to stop me from having two?"

Liz took a deep breath, like explaining to a child that they couldn't fly. "It doesn't work like that. Epics are the *only* ones with more than one power. That's why Sir Avery's always so busy. He's either defending cities from the Escalis, infiltrating enemy territory, saving lives, or stopping Prince Avalask."

"And who's that? Another Epic?"

"The only other Epic. There are two bloodlines that carry the Epic genes, and only the firstborn son in each family inherits the power. So in every new generation we get a new Epic from Sir Avery's bloodline to defend us, and the second Epic comes from the Escali royal family. They call him Prince Avalask, and he's the worst form of evil that's ever set foot in the world, a murderer you can't lift a finger against. We would all be worse than dead if Sir Avery wasn't here to defend us from him."

That was a chilling thought, an Escali that was already wickedly fast, strong, and aggressive, with the added advantage of every power in existence. "Do either of them have kids yet?"

Liz nodded quickly, and I finally saw excitement chase the gloom from her face. "Sir Avery does. He's kept him hidden since birth to let him grow up and train, but I keep hearing they're going to introduce him at the Eclipsival. The unveiling of our new Epic is tomorrow, Allie! When people look back, they'll remember our generation by his name."

"How do you know it won't be a girl?" I asked as Liz stopped walking, setting her hand on the smooth dark wood of a door.

She scoffed as though my question squashed her excitement. "They've always been the first born sons. That's just the way it is. And this is your room," she added, pushing the door open.

I liked the scent of pine and the simplicity of the layout, but hated the unfamiliarity of it. A white pine bed ran along the right wall with three books stacked on a wooden chest at the foot. A small fireplace had been carved into the wall with a slatted pine bench and wardrobe on either side, and a belt of two swords hung from the wardrobe. I stepped inside as Liz remained in the doorway.

"I'll be back in the morning to get you for sparring," she said. She was about to leave, and I only had a broken second to decide if I wanted her to stay.

"Wait," I said, not ready to be alone just yet. "I thought Humans were the only ones who had magic. How can an Escali be an Epic then?"

Liz gave me a half-smile. She knew I didn't want her to go. "We're the only ones who can become mages, but the Escalis... They're made of magic. Kind of... I don't know much about it, but I know that's why they're so vicious, and it's why their skin can't be cut. They're like Humans gone bad."

"But if they're as strong as everyone says, what's stopped them from destroying us? I mean... mages are rare." I couldn't remember exact numbers, but I knew rare was an understatement. "It doesn't seem like there would be enough mages to keep us all safe."

"Not on our continent, maybe, but we also get all the kids from Tekada who have the potential for magic. You and I are from Tekada. Can you remember living there?"

I matched her half smile and said, "No."

"Oh. Well, I guess if you can't remember my name, you wouldn't be able to remember King Kelian. He rules over our home continent, Tekada, but all he really does there is banish people. If anybody shows signs of magic or commits a displeasing crime, he sends them here, which is supposed to be more humane than a death sentence. What a joke."

"You mean *we* were banished?" I raised my eyebrows, amused. "Was it because we could use magic, or were we criminals?"

Liz breathed a short laugh. "You used to joke that they sent us here because you started a Tekadan uprising. I guess I wouldn't be surprised if you had."

I liked the thought that I had once been able to lead and inspire, and hoped it was more than a joke. Liz yawned and added, "I should probably go. Maybe you can try to remember something while you're sleeping. I really do want my sister back."

Implying what? That my current state made us suddenly not sisters? Liz noticed me recoil from the comment and added, "I don't mean it in a cruel way, Allie. You were just so brave and you always knew what to say. I need you."

"Yep," I replied, concentrating on my breathing, "and I'll let you know in the morning if I remember anything. Goodnight."

I could see that Liz regretted her choice of words, but she made no move to stop me from closing the door. I leaned back against it and waited until I heard her amble away.

Of course the old Allie had been brave. She wouldn't have hid under a table, knowing that a little girl had just been carried off. She was the one everybody wanted to come home.

I was just Allie's worthless shadow now, holding on to her body until she could find her way back to it. But I hadn't chosen for this to happen! I wanted to be back to my normal, accepted self.

Growling in frustration, I slammed my fists onto the door behind me. I crossed my arms tightly across my chest and heaved a few deep breaths before stepping forward to grab the belt of swords from the wardrobe. I hurled them onto the ground in a clatter and kicked my heel into the wooden bench, only stopping because the first two slats splintered apart beneath my foot.

The crunch of the breaking wood was accompanied by tinkling of metal on the rock floor, and I dropped to my hands and knees to see a ringed key with two teeth at the end. It had been hidden on the lip of wood under the bench.

I picked it up and flipped it over a few times, hoping to find some sort of engraving. None existed. Obviously it used to be mine, but I didn't see any locks around me.

In an attempt to make sense of just one facet in my confusing life, I upended my entire room. I still couldn't find any fits for my key. Anywhere. The chest only had a simple latch with clothing inside. I even flipped my bed over and shoved my wardrobe out of place. I checked every dent in the floor for secrets, and found none.

I stomped on the ground, not wanting to break anything else in my frustration, then lay on my bed to fume. I wasn't about to fall asleep with so many questions struggling for my attention, and I covered my face with both hands to exhale an angry sigh.

How was I expected to take this all in at once? My mind needed to be fixed, both because of the lack of memories and the newly found chaos of information. Mages defended our cities with one power each. Epics were the heroes born with all the powers. An uncaring king had exiled us to this continent where vicious predators threatened our very survival. And I only knew a few things about where I fit among the chaos.

One. My name was Allie. My memory was gone, but I was finally at home where I had friends to help me to recover it, assuming Liz would ever look at me again without disappointment.

Two. The Escalis. I was safe from them now, but no closer to knowing what they wanted from me. I hadn't heard them wrong. They wanted me in particular, and I needed to know why. Why had I left the Dragona without telling anyone? What had I done to anger them?

Three. My knee was definitely feeling better. I removed one hand from my face to rap my knuckles against it, but it only twanged with a slight ache. I wished my memory could have healed as quickly as my dumb knee.

Hours seeped through the cave floors unnoticed as I lay on my bed, trying to pull memories from an empty brain, denying that I might possibly fail. As sleep finally began to tug at my eyelids, I rolled over and slid heavy hands beneath my pillow to grasp it tightly, like it was hope itself. My hands crinkled a piece of parchment inside the pillow, and I reached into the case to grab what seemed to be an old list of tally marks. In my former life, I had titled it *Deaths That Were My Fault*, and scribbled fourteen hashes beneath the words. Fourteen lives had been destroyed because of me.

What?

Had I actually, *physically*, killed them? Would I ever even know?

I frowned and blinked my sleepy eyes to make sure I was seeing clearly. Fourteen lives. I had the feeling that Liz, West, and Anna didn't know this. Wouldn't they have mentioned it?

I flipped the page over on a whim, only to find that the top read *Lives I've Saved*, and hundreds of tally marks covered the entire second side. I flung the paper like it was dangerous and scooted to a sitting position as it fluttered to the floor, hash marks glaring up from the ground where I couldn't avoid them.

What had I been doing?

Something incredibly important, judging by the amount of ink slashed across this side of the page. Something secret, judging by the way I had tucked it out of sight. Something that I needed to figure out very quickly.

If danger was the only thing that could bring back my memories, then I was going to seek it. This list was the key to my identity, and to everything that mattered.

I picked the list back up, feeling like the hash marks might jump off the page and strangle me if I didn't reveal their meaning. It would be better to die, trying to recover this important life I used to lead, than to live as an echo of my former self.

With that resolve in mind, I began to count how many tally marks had been scrawled over an undetermined number of years. I fell asleep somewhere between three and four hundred with the parchment still clutched in my hand.

CHAPTER FIVE

I bolted upright in my bed, startled by an abrasive trumpet call echoing down the corridors. It wailed its morning greeting for no more than three seconds before my door burst open, kicked in by someone with far too much enthusiasm.

"Good morning!" Liz bellowed.

I flopped back down beneath my covers to keep the cold out and moaned, "What is wrong with you? I thought you were supposed to be upset." My list sat safely beneath my pillow.

"Well, it's a new day, and it's time to get your memory back."

"You're always like this, aren't you?" I peered at her with my covers pulled to my chin. "A new mood every five minutes?"

"Yes, and it keeps my life interesting," she replied. "You also tell me that I'm easily distracted and talk too fast."

"I've only known you for a few hours and I already know that's true."

"Well sorry if I'm not good enough for you." She left in a dramatic huff and closed the door behind her, which at least muffled a bit of the wakeup call.

I knew she wouldn't be far. I would kill her if she left. None of my memories had returned during the night, and I couldn't just get myself to the sparring field.

I ripped my covers off in one inconsiderate swipe, then slunk to my wardrobe. One freezing jerkin and two pant-legs later, I threw my hair into a long ponytail. Holy life, it was cold! Could the sun really be up already?

I stood again and picked up the belt of swords I had flung. Each pommel had a simple sun engraved in the metal, but my throw had dented the carved light rays on one. Sorry to see the damage, I put the belt on, and lastly I tied my mysterious key around my neck, tucking it away as Liz invited herself back into my room.

"Shut the door," I chattered, "you're letting all the heat out."

"What heat?" Liz asked, leaning against the rock wall. "You didn't light a fire last night."

"Didn't think about it," I shivered. Stupid me, I should have taken notice of the fireplace.

"Well, put a coat on." She walked to my wardrobe, flung it open, and threw one to me. Even though it was freezing too, I felt warmer as soon as I pulled it on. "Remember anything new last night?" Liz asked.

"I don't think so."

"Well, sparring practice should fix everything. Now come on, the sun's almost up. Do you want it to beat you to practice?"

"No, we wouldn't want that," I replied grumpily. "Why aren't you wearing a coat?"

"Because I feel fine. It's not that cold. Now let's go." We left my room, and to my dismay it got progressively colder as we neared the end of the tunnels. Finally we were outside, where we barely had enough light to see the frosty glitter on the grass. My breath lingered in the frigid air and my nose felt numb already.

Liz maintained an absurd smile as though the temperature had no effect on her. We made our way down a hill to a flat field ringed by trees, where a shivering group had gathered around two supply shed doors that opened from the ground. The people toward the back of the crowd noticed me and immediately decided I needed to be swarmed.

"Allie! We heard what happened! How are you feeling?" a short boy asked.

"I'm fine. I feel alright," I replied.

"What happened to you?" another girl asked.

"I don't know. I was —"

"How much can you remember?"

"Can you recognize me at all?"

"Hey, Allie, we used to work with the combat dragons together. Do you remember me?"

"Where were you?"

"Do you know how it happened?"

I couldn't even attempt to answer one question before they'd asked three more. People at the back of the group, who didn't have a clear view of me, filed around the sides and then crowded in behind me to hear, so I was soon enclosed by an inquisitive horde. An instinctual voice in my head said, *get out of here, too many people*, but I also knew shoving them away from me wasn't my best option.

"Alright, alright," I said, holding my hands up, which actually quieted everybody for a strange moment. "This giant *mob* thing is not getting us anywhere." I gestured to the pack around me, and after a second, they loosened to give me a little breathing room. "Now, I am heading this way. Please do not stand in my path."

I cut straight through them toward an underground supply shed, and nobody closed back in around me. Taking a moment to observe all my own body language, I noticed myself walking with what had to look like confidence. My voice was also something I liked — loud when I needed it to be, and a little on the aggressive side.

A hearty bald man with dark eyes and an untrimmed beard stood on the steps into the supply shed. Behind him I could see the interior lined with wooden weapons while piles of junk and broken equipment littered the floor next to brimming bins.

"Allie, this is Sir Bruscan," Liz said as she caught up.

"And I already know who you are," he said, climbing out of the stash to shake my hand. "I heard what happened, but I just didn't believe it till now. You were always my best fighter, Allie. Let's hope you've still got it in you."

"I'm feeling confident I do," I replied for the sake of the crowd watching us, although *confident* may have been an overstatement. He grinned and then turned to the rest of the group.

"Good morning everybody! As you've probably noticed, the temperature this morning is as cold as Izfazara's heart, so let's not waste time. The sooner we get moving, the warmer we're going to be. Who wants to make the first challenge?" Sir Bruscan asked as a ring of light appeared on the ground before us. A light-mage for sure.

A few people chatted about who they'd like to challenge, but since nobody was speaking up and I was ready to get warm, I said, "I'd like to challenge Liz."

"Battle of the sisters?" Sir Bruscan said with a smirk. "It's fine by me, although we all know who will win. Go ahead and pick your swords."

Liz climbed into the ground-shed and I followed her to look through the racks of wooden weapons on every wall.

"West... If I use these shorter swords, I can use one in each hand, right?" I asked, feeling pulled toward two pseudo-blades that were barely as long as my forearms.

"You bet," he said, pulling them down for me. "You've just got to disarm your opponent or get your tip pointed at them to win, so doubles are great for sparring."

I stole a glance at Liz to see her grab wooden short swords as well, and she stepped back into the freezing morning, still not bothered by the cold.

"It's interesting. Even without memory, you're still drawn to the type of weapon you used to use," West said. He handed me the wooden blades, and their weight in my hands made me feel instantly more secure, like I had just gained a little control over the shifting sands of my life. "How was last night?" he asked.

"It could have gone better," I replied. "And Liz didn't tell me much about myself. West, what sort of person am I? Am I just like everybody else here?"

West shrugged one shoulder and replied, "Yeah, you're like everyone else, just a little better." *My list was definitely a secret then.* "And honestly, I think you might scare people. You like to work with the murderous combat dragons, whereas I'd rather do any other chore in the Dragona. Maybe that's just me though, valuing personal safety and such nonsense."

I smiled because the idea of personal safety *did* seem like a joke, and I also liked the sound of combat dragons. If sparring didn't jog my memory, I'd be signing up to work with them as soon as I could.

"Are you going to take all day?" Liz asked impatiently.

"No, I'm here," I said, joining her in the ring of light.

I tossed one of my wooden swords into the air, caught it, spun it, and knew this was going to be easy. Liz lunged straight for me and I easily sidestepped to avoid her. She recovered quickly and stabbed straight for my face, a move I blocked as an afterthought. She clearly wanted to win, but she was off balance and reckless.

I struck to see how she'd react, but she parried me and went for my throat. With my right hand I took a risk and swiped both of her swords away in one swift movement while I brought my left blade up to point at her neck.

As quickly as it had started, it was over. Sir Bruscan gaped at me, and the rest of the group stared as well.

"You just beat Liz in less than seven seconds," he said in amazement. "I mean, it usually takes you about twelve, but *still…*"

Fighting felt like running or speaking, a skill so engrained that I had woken up with it. Unfortunately, this meant I hadn't recalled any of my past in the effort.

"Ready to take on two at a time?" Sir Bruscan asked.

"Two? Can I do that?"

Everybody laughed at my question. "We might have to make it three if they're not hard enough," he replied.

West had already jumped into the shed and come back out with a long blade and no need for an invitation. It was him and Liz against me, and I was ready.

"Go!" Sir Bruscan shouted. In less than a second, West and Liz both came at me and I had no time to think. Three swords against my two — I dodged one of Liz's and parried the other two from her and West combined. The fight still wasn't necessarily hard; it just required a little more involvement from the rest of my body.

I bent over backwards to avoid a blow from West and kicked one of Liz's swords from her hands when I saw the opportunity. It probably wouldn't have worked in a real battle, but oh well. West was unbalanced after his blow missed, and I took no hesitation in jumping back up and maneuvering my blade around his to touch him with the tip.

He stepped out of the circle, distracting Liz just enough. I got a parry with one sword and then victory with the other as I held it to her once again. As our audience applauded, she smiled and asked, "Do you remember something now?"

With my sword still poised over her neck, I replied, "No," and withdrew it. Liz didn't stop smiling, and I wondered if she even heard me.

"And *that*, boys and girls, is how it's done," Sir Bruscan rounded off the applause with a final few loud claps. I was relieved to step out of the circle. Not that the fighting wasn't fun, I just didn't adore the attention from all sides.

46

Sir Bruscan called a girl with frizzy dark hair out to fight and I sat down with Liz and West to watch as a shorter boy stepped up against her, his sword on fire. Now that I was out of the action, I had to bite back the irritation I felt for not recovering any of my past. Sparring didn't scare me, and I guessed that was why it didn't jog my memory either. I needed real danger, it seemed; practice-danger wasn't enough.

"That was really good, Allie," Liz said. "Even after you lose your mind, you can still annihilate us all in sparring."

"It's fun," I replied, trying not to see fun as a waste of my time. "Actually, that was a lot of fun," I admitted. "Do we practice every morning?"

"Yes," West replied, "and tonight at the Eclipsival, we get to fight with the real swords, sharpened and everything."

The notion of danger perked my attention, but that sounded like too much danger. Play-fighting with sharpened swords? "Don't we run the risk of dying?" I asked.

"I thought I told you about the Eclipsival last night," Liz said. "Nobody can get hurt during the Eclipse of the three moons, so we get to play in fire and fight with sharp swords. I was wondering why you wore your good clothes. You should have worn something you don't mind destroying."

"You definitely didn't mention that," I said.

The fighting girl with the frizzy hair surprised me when she flung out a hand and blasted her fire-wielding opponent out of the circle.

"And if we can't be killed, why are we wasting our time celebrating?" I asked. "Shouldn't we be out attacking the Escalis?"

"The Escalis can't be killed during the eclipse either," West said. "So, we could knock down some of their buildings, but I think it's better that we take a break from them. A break from the constant fear."

47

"I heard that Dincara will be attacking the Escalis during the eclipse," Liz said.

"Well that's not a surprise," West replied. Seeing the blank look on my face, he added, "Dincara is our fortress on the coast. They've got the best non-mage fighters, and that's where the ships from Tekada dock."

A loud whack from the ring interrupted our conversation, but I could only see one person swinging his sword foolishly around, fighting someone invisible.

"Where are we going after this?" I asked Liz, beginning to feel restless.

"West and I still have chores to do before the Eclipsival tonight," Liz said.

"We could take you to the Wreck first," West said.

I smiled, wondering when anybody was going to catch on that I couldn't remember anything. "I don't know what that is."

Liz said, "It's where people go when they aren't working. There's food, and games, and other people. It's basically where you spend any free time. *And* it's like a circus right now with everybody here for the Eclipsival. They've been selling things and doing crazy tricks in there for weeks."

"Great, I'm ready to go," I said, anxious to charge forward with my day.

I was going to be able to put myself into as much danger as I wanted as soon as the moons eclipsed each other, and with all the Eclipsival chaos, I could find a way to stay in danger after the moons' safety had vanished. By the end of the night, I might know why the Escalis hated me and why I had once hidden a list of so many tally marks.

CHAPTER SIX

I was itching to leave by the time we headed to the Wreck. Liz turned to look at me as we climbed a grassy hill near the base of the mountain. "Guess what, Allie. There's a new guy who just showed up at the Dragona. From what I hear, he's your age and extremely good-looking." She nudged me in the side an excessive amount of times.

"Liz... I have a lot of other things on my mind right now," I smiled. "Why is this relevant?"

"Well! I was just thinking that he's going to be new, and you're sort of feeling like you're new. You could be friends."

"Thanks, but I'll be alright."

I just then realized the racket taking place ahead, and we came over the grassy knoll to see hundreds of people set out in front of us. If the market from Tabriel Vale had grown ten times in size and added jugglers and fiddlers, it might have barely compared to what we were seeing now.

"This is just the spillover of people who couldn't fit in the Wreck," West said, raising his voice to compete with the event as we approached. "Keep in mind when we get inside that this isn't how it normally looks!"

"Come on!" Liz grabbed my shoulder as one of the people-streams moved us toward a pile of boulders. Thrilling music behind the rocks sparked excitement in me, and we climbed between them to reach an enormous cavern filled with shouting, laughter, and chatter. Half the continent's population seemed to be packed in to see it all, and the cavern's sheer size took my breath away. Three fiddlers and a drummer played upbeat jigs immediately to our right while a troop of bounding dancers took up the space to our left, putting smiles on every watching face.

"Back here is where you get food when you're hungry," West shouted over the celebration, leading the way through the crowd. He laughed. "There isn't usually quite so much though." I could see the blaze of cooking ovens taking up an entire wall, all making bread from the smell of it, while three enormous bears roasted on turning-spits. Smoke escaped through a skylight, but the wonderful smell remained to make my mouth water.

Another source of entertainment from across the Wreck reached me over the music — one calling voice, answered by a chorus of others.

"Two roasted stuffed peppers, sing hey hidey hey!"
"Hey hey two stuffed peppers to roast right away!"

I looked quickly to Liz just as she made a one-footed turn, dropped to her knees, and crawled beneath a table to get to a pile of brightly colored undershirts.

"Liz," I said, snagging her attention as she stood with the table between us. "We've got to see the Travelling Baking Show." Their calls already felt like a familiar pull.

The fiddlers finished a song, but Liz didn't lower her voice appropriately. "Go on without me!" Her face reddened slightly as she realized she wasn't competing with the music anymore and had drawn attention. She lifted an ugly pink undershirt in front of her face, pretending it had her full focus. "West and I have to get our chores done anyway, so we should probably go."

50

"Alright, then I'll meet you at the Eclipsival tonight?" I asked.

"Sounds good." She set the shirt back down to feel the soft fabric of a different blue one. "And the tunnel back to your room is over there." She stood on her toes and pointed. "You'll just need to take a left and then a right, and then you go up into the tunnel above and take a right and then a left, and you'll be at your room."

"Thanks Liz. I'll see you both later."

"Have a good life," she said, a phrase that seemed to be of her own making.

I engrained *left, right, up, right, left* in my mind as I turned to push through the crowd, then turned around to walk backwards. "You have a good life too, Liz." My use of her words made her smile, filling me with the kind of warmth that made me smile back.

The Baking Show had thrown a makeshift wooden structure over their heads, and Corliss stood on top with her mass of curly hair, taking orders from the giant ring of spectators and relaying them to the crew below.

I was almost to them when I noticed a curious group of girls point me out, whisper to each other, and begin to make their way over. The crowd was so dense that I knew I would never make it to the Travelling Baking Show in time to avoid the girls' questions. As the only option I could think of, I cupped my hands to my mouth and shouted, *"One Baking Show Special, sweet sauce and sliced roast!"*

Half of the Travelling Baking Show began their reply automatically, but the other half found me among the crowd and Old Osty shouted. "Allie! Great to see you!"

I battled my way through the people and Corliss crouched from on top of the structure to say, "Best seat in the house is up here! I'll pull you up."

"Alright," I agreed with a smile, feeling truly welcome as Corliss extended a hand down to me and I jumped.

I was surprised she was strong enough to pull me onto the wooden roof, but she did it effortlessly, and I sat down as the next customer shouted an order to her. She entertained the entire crowd with her energy, confident voice, and ability to twist anything into a joke. And during her short breaks from interacting with the spectators, I told her about what had happened since yesterday.

"It's absurd that there isn't a single mind mage around with the Eclipsival tonight," Corliss said.

"I know. It's just my luck."

The bakers below groaned at something that hadn't turned out right, and Corliss leaned half her body over the side of the roof. "Osty! I can still hear you messing up the calls from up here. How long have you been doing this?"

"It isn't my fault," he called back. "You guys change the order calls on me every other week. I'm elderly!"

"Osty. We only changed it a week ago because we ran out of wheat toast. Now we've changed it back. Adjust!"

Another of the bakers below defended him. "Come on, Corliss. How many years did it take you to get *sweet sauce and sliced roast* right?"

"Hardly any," she replied, pulling herself back up to stand again.

The guy below asked, "How many poor customers thought their Baking Show Schpecial had sleet sauce, and sweet swauce, and swiced woast—"

I saw Corliss grinning as she shot back, "And how many dishes did you break the first day you started?"

"Nearly all of them? I told you, it was on purpose. I was starting a new theme, and the customers loved it."

"Who is that?" I asked, wanting a face to put with the quick-witted voice below.

"That's just Archie," she said, waving her hand dismissively. "He wasn't with us yesterday when you met the troop, but he's a friend of ours. And he *apparently* has the potential to become a mage, so he's been invited to stay here at the Dragona. That lucky bat."

She took a few more orders, and I faintly heard the Archie guy from below say he was heading out to find his room. "I think I'm going to go, Corliss," I said, curious to catch a glimpse of the stranger before he left.

"Alright, let me know how the memory stuff turns out for you," she replied.

I swung my feet off the wooden roof and dropped to the ground, accidentally smashing into the person beneath me along the way. I knocked a load of things from his hands and caused him to drop a bag full of loud clanking items. I was back on my feet in a second, face flushed like a boiling lobster.

"I am so sorry!" I immediately crouched to help him pick it all up, my self-esteem refusing to let me look anywhere but at the objects I hastily grabbed. "I don't know why I didn't look—"

"It's fine," he assured me. "I needed to sort through it all anyway. Now I won't be so shocked at what I find."

"Well I guess that's a good way to look at it," I mumbled as I stacked a couple rolls of paper on top of each other. One of them had been open when I ran into him, a map of the whole Dragona.

Corliss stifled her howling laughter from the top of the wooden structure, and although the gathered crowd wasn't quite as ruthless as Corliss, they still had the pointing and snickering bit down. Corliss finally took her hands off her mouth, wiped a tear from her eye, and asked, "All part of the show then? Sing hey hidey hey?"

"Yes, all part of my theme," the guy named Archie replied. He took one step closer to her to add, "Next theme day, I'm breaking more than just your dishes."

"Right, right, you break all sorts of things," Corliss agreed. "You break dishes and equipment, now you break falls. Go break a leg finding your room!" She broke back into laughter, and when I finally felt brave enough to look at Archie, I saw he wore the grin most people reserved for old and good friends.

It suddenly donned on me that this was the same new guy Liz had mentioned earlier in the day. She had gotten *something* right. He had straw-blond hair, and beneath his several-shades-darker eyebrows were blue eyes that I immediately feared I would be caught looking at.

"Hey, are you alright?" he asked, picking up the last of his things.

I handed everything back to him, unable to say anything except, "I am so sorry."

"Really, it's fine. You know how you can make it up to me though? This map." He waved the roll of map I had just given him. "I don't understand it at all. Would you mind helping me out?"

"I could try," I said, still horrifically aware of the ring of onlookers. "We should walk though."

"Alright."

I promptly took off to escape the watching crowd, which of course, involved entering into the crowd itself, but Archie was right behind me until I stopped. "Alright," I started off. "Again, I'm really sorry —"

"Sorry about what? There's nothing to apologize for." He unrolled the map and tapped it three times. "Do you have *any* idea how this mess of squiggling lines is going to get me to my room?"

I took the map from him and then stared it down, trying to understand the chaos of tunnels that looped over each other, split apart then reconnected, and dead-ended unexpectedly. "This really *doesn't* make sense. I hoped I might find my room on it too, but I can't even find the Wreck."

I handed it back to him as he sighed. "Whoever decided to throw noodles at a piece of paper and call it a map should be shot. I doubt anyone can read it." He tilted it drastically to the side. "Although, maybe if we had a new angle..." I let a sharp laugh escape as he smiled and rolled it up. "Well, you know my name, but you haven't told me yours."

"I guess I haven't. I'm Allie. The assaulter of newcomers."

"What a title. I guess I'll see you at the Eclipsival tonight?" he asked.

"Yeah, I'll be there."

"Great. I'm going to start wandering aimlessly and hope I can find my room in time to make it down. With any luck, I'll see you there."

"Yeah, hopefully." I replied. He started toward one of the caves, and after a few seconds I realized I hadn't moved. I needed to get a grip, so I shook off everything that was wrong with me and proceeded into the next tunnel over to find my room before the festival of the decade. Maybe I could be friends with the new stranger after all.

Chapter Seven

My gravelly tunnel almost immediately split into two more. Liz had said left and then right. Did that mean left as soon as I stepped inside? I hoped so. I turned left and then as soon as the cave forked, I took a right. I wasn't exactly sure what she had meant by *go up*, and I was still wondering minutes later when I saw a hole in the roof of the cave above me. Was that up? Must be.

Two or three turns later, I knew I was lost. I just couldn't tell which fissures in the wall counted as places to turn and which would compress into crevices I couldn't fit through.

The entire place looked abandoned as my current choice of tunnel cut steeply upward then spiraled back down. A gaping hole swallowed the rocky path in front of me, and I knew it was time to give up and backtrack. Except when I turned around and climbed back up the spiraled gap in the rocks, I came into a spacious new tunnel that hadn't existed before, and neither direction held any familiarity.

Oh no.

I couldn't even get myself back to the Wreck. Each new fork in the tunnels forced me to make my best guess, and my guesses swallowed the next hours of my life. For as long as I wandered, I never came back across another hole in the floor and never recognized a single rock. I couldn't even fathom how I had gotten so deeply lost.

I knew the mages of the Dragona would track me down if I went missing, but I needed to find my way out before the Eclipsival began. Maybe it already had. Time passed strangely underground, leaving me unsure of how many hours I lost in the rocky depths.

I tried to induce a sense of panic in myself, hoping some instinct would kick in and show me the way out. Any memory at all would have been appreciated, yet I got nothing. My life didn't depend on escaping, and so my instincts weren't rising to this occasion. This was just dumb. The old Allie would have never wasted her time getting lost in her own home.

I heard a faint *Allie* echoing through the tunnel, and the first thing I shouted back was, "I'm lost!"

A guy halted his momentum next to me within the next second, so fast I knew he had to be a mage. Built lightly for speed with thick and steep eyebrows, he shouted, "I found her first!" He glanced at me cautiously and said, "I'm Michael. Your next door neighbor?"

"Right. Hi." Without anything else to say, I stretched my hand out to shake his. I needed some sort of protocol to follow for reintroductions, because this speechless handshake went beyond awkward.

I hadn't met many girls taller than me yet, but one appeared in the air and landed both feet beside me. "Hey, Allie. We heard about what happened. How are you feeling?" She had a hoarse voice that sounded seasoned by years of yelling.

"I've had better times," I said, this time leaving the handshake out. "Sorry... but I can't remember who you are."

"Terry." Based on appearance and muscle mass alone, I would guess this rugged girl would be more eager to wrestle a hog than receive a compliment. She wore her dark hair tied back like I did. "Michael and I live on either side of you."

"Ok, but how did you find me down here?"

Terry grinned and said, "The second we found out you had taken Liz's directional advice, we knew you'd be lost."

"So we had a race to find you," Michael said. "Which I won. Because I'm awesome."

Terry raised her eyebrows at him to let him know his ego wasn't as impressive as he thought. To me she asked, "Were you trying to get to the Eclipsival? Because they've already started on the tower building, and Shadar the storyteller has got everybody laughing and crying at his tales."

"I was trying to get to my room first, but never mind that. Yes. I don't want to miss it."

Michael and Terry glanced at each other, clearly wanting to ask more questions before offering to help get me there. I sighed and asked, "How much have you heard about me?"

"Well, the entire Dragona knows what's happened by now," Terry said. "Word spreads fast, but we don't have any details."

Michael said, "West has threatened half our lives for bothering you with questions, but we figured you might make an exception for your neighbors and tell us what happened?"

I smiled hopelessly and told Terry and Michael the briefest of tales. I ended by saying, "Sorry, but I don't remember a thing about either of you. I have absolutely no idea what's happened, why I was in Tabriel Vale, or what I did to gain the Escalis' attention."

I noticed Michael peek behind himself, as though making sure Escalis hadn't invaded our abandoned tunnel. "Do you think we should be on the lookout for danger?" Michael asked. "We do live right next to you."

I shrugged and found myself gripping one hand with the other as I replied, "Maybe. The Escalis made it clear that I've angered them, but Anna says they don't know where we are."

"They don't," Terry said, "so how can the Escalis know of you?"

"It's killing me that I don't know that," I said, feeling my nails biting into my fingers. I pulled my hands apart and fidgeted with the ends of my hair instead. "I must have done something. I'm told I used to wander off a lot, but I don't know what I was doing in the woods. Alone."

"We could ask around and see if anyone knows why you traveled to Tabriel Vale," Terry suggested. "We really should get to the Eclipsival before we miss half of it though."

"Race you there?" Michael asked, already gone by the time his challenge reached our ears.

"Here, take my hand," Terry said, extending hers to me.

"Umm... Why?"

"Because the Eclipsival is a fair distance from the Dragona, and we certainly aren't walking all the way there." I still had my hand reluctantly in the ends of my hair, so Terry grabbed it from me. "Now, when I say so, you're going to jump forward with me and we'll be there. Don't feel silly about it, because if I jump and you don't, I'll probably take your arm off. Ready?"

"I guess."

"Go."

I jumped forward, feeling ridiculous, but instead of landing a cubit away, my feet hit the ground on a crowded hillside. Thousands upon thousands had gathered on the hills of a valley, around the tables and massive stumps with incredible food spread across every surface. Our appearance caught the attention of those sitting on logs and on the ground around us, but they turned their eyes back to the dead field below, watching a spectacle which caused my jaw to drop.

Nearly fifteen mages in the center of the field combined the powers of water, freezing, flying, and maybe levitation to build a massive tower of ice over a base pyramid of logs. The logs alone nearly reached the sky, but the ice reached far higher, and I watched as two mages leapt from the top, plummeting toward the ground. One mage streamed water as he fell, and the second froze the stream into another icy spindle, connected to the delicate masterpiece.

"There you are, Allie," I heard Liz say, but I couldn't take my eyes off the mages who slammed onto the ground. The pair stood unharmed to add more supporting ice to the tower's foundation, and another pair of mages leapt from halfway up to add more intricacy.

Shadar the storyteller stood in the very top spire, telling the crowd an amplified story I had missed half of already. His face was so animated I could see his smile from the hillside as he said, "Then I told the Tekadan, *Sir, you're in Dincara now!*" The entire valley howled with laughter, and I moved over to sit by Liz, knowing the joke was lost.

"You got here right at the boring part," Liz said. "They've already spent ten minutes building this ice block."

"Boring?" I watched the team spiral glittering frost down the tower's edges. In ten minutes, our mages had built a tower fit for royalty, tall enough to scrape the bellies of low-drifting clouds.

Liz replied, "There are more exciting things we could be doing. I already got to fly a dragon without a saddle before everybody stopped to watch the tower building. It threw me right off, and I was fine. And I got to pet a bear!"

"Can't believe I missed it."

The whole crowd cheered and stomped on the valley's hills, stifling their enthusiasm because the man on the ice balcony in the sky had started a new story, apparently a world favorite.

"Nobody can fathom the power of an Everarc Crystal," he began. "Nobody…"

The entire valley fell silent in anticipation. "With more magic than the three moons combined, so condensed that brushing against a chipped shard could bring dreams and nightmares into reality, Humanity was warned never to go near the Everarcs. Some say they remained buried for thousands of years, encased in a rock

60

their magic couldn't escape, but Humanity was too curious. Never has a rule remained unbroken in time, and *so we dug them up."*

As Shadar spoke, three gigantic red crystals dislodged themselves from the ground and rose into the air. "The illusion mages almost make them look real," Liz whispered as the hovering Everarcs began to circle the tower.

"The unearthing of the first Everarc Crystal, some say thousands of years ago, cursed our world with Escalis." Brutal shadows of the monsters with spiked arms leapt across the clouds, and from the way they jerked and moved, I imagined their snarls and growls. "More predatory than the fiercest animals and with added intelligence, Humanity stood no chance against them. They tore throats open, ripped the limbs off their victims, and chased Humanity from this continent. We were forced to live on Tekada for hundreds of years afterward.

"Not much is known about the second Everarc, only that it was unearthed in the middle of the Breathing Sea. Some say that only one shard of the crystal fell into the water, which is why the entire Sea now teems with eels and Sirens and all sorts of horrific monsters. Yes, you could breathe the water if you stuck your head in, but doing so would be a forfeit of your life.

"Then a band of adventurers found the third and last Everarc Crystal within the last century, in the heart of the Dragona. Humanity was gifted with the mages, our first real defense against the Escalis, and so we were finally able to leave Tekada and return to this land, whether by choice or by exile." The shadows of Escalis fled from the sky as the images of mages appeared, flashing their different powers across the faces of the clouds. "And of course, with the creation of the mages, we witnessed the rise of the Epics. First came Wikferl, the greatest hero we've ever known!"

"WIKFERL!" The entire crowd shouted and whistled as the gigantic face of the legend reflected off every side of the ice tower — bald with dark eyes that spoke of accomplishment.

"But, of course, Wikferl soon met his wicked Escali counterpart, Juhdect." A giant Escali, clad in black, appeared near the tower to the crowd's vocalized dismay. His hands and eyes glowed with a sickly green magic, with his hair so dark that I couldn't call it black. It was the opposite of all colors. The opposite of light. "Juhdect stole more lives, inspired more terror, and destroyed more in his path than any other Escali ever had, and as a result, the Escalis crowned him king of their race." The recreation of Juhdect began to dart about and viciously assault the ice tower with magic, but the flat image of Wikferl reached out a giant hand to shield the work of art from every attack.

"As Wikferl battled to keep Juhdect from destroying us entirely, it became apparent that the Escalis were growing interested in the Everarc Crystals. If the Escalis gained their own mages, they would destroy Humanity for certain, so the leaders of the day turned to Wikferl to conceal the three crystals for the rest of time."

The gigantic reflection of Wikferl materialized off the face of the tower, reached out both arms, and slammed Juhdect onto the ground. The Everarc Crystals joined together in front of Wikferl's glowing hands while Juhdect remained motionless.

"Wikferl quickly found and bound the three Everarcs. He concealed them in a place where neither Escalis nor mankind would ever find them, and there they remain to this day — the source of all magic in the world, never to be found again."

The giant Wikferl forced the three Everarc Crystals into the ground and vanished from sight as two new Epics clashed in the air above him, their colliding magic blinding.

"We all know how the story went from then on. The firstborn son of each Epic inherited their respective legacies, either as a royal weapon for the Escalis or a defender of Humanity. And then their first born sons after them, and so on." Each pair of fighting Epics was replaced by a new set, but they always looked similar. The

Human of the pair always stood tall and protective. The Escali always wore black, but it was never as dark as his hair.

"And the fifth generation of Epics is almost upon us."

An anxious murmur rose around us, and Liz whispered to me, "They're going to reveal him!"

"I doubt it," I whispered, prompted by the strange gut feeling that he wouldn't be unveiled tonight.

Shadar's smile became apologetic, and he said, "I know how long we've all been waiting to meet Sir Avery's son, but we've still got a bit of a wait ahead of us." The entire continent released bated breaths in disappointment. "We all know the boy is hidden for his protection and ours, but believe me, it won't be long until he is ready to join us.

"Wikferl's descendants have protected us for generations, and perhaps Wikferl's great-great-grandson will bring an end to the Escali torment in our lives. He may be far away, training to be our sentinel someday. He could be out among you, listening. But rest assured that when he joins us, his name will shine in the sky with the light of a thousand *fires*."

The center of the ice tower began to flicker dimly, and I noticed a slow drumbeat resonating, though I couldn't remember hearing it begin. The drumbeat gained momentum while the flicker grew brighter, until the entire structure seemed to be alive. The blazes inside the ice exploded outward to the cheers of the crowd. Birds of flame flew into the sky as the beautiful tower of frost collapsed, and exciting music joined the drumbeat.

"You have about ten minutes left of immortality!" Shadar hollered. "Enjoy it while it's here!"

The falling ice flashed into steam as it crumpled onto the heat of the great bonfire. On top of the burning mountain stood Anna, her hands outstretched, and joyful power burning in her eyes. She shot flames into the field, exploding into all colors. Other mages sent flaming snakes across the sky and created waves of green and purple fire. They were doing a fine job of lighting the field on fire by themselves, yet several bolts of lightning struck the ground, on cue with the music, as though to help.

It seemed to me that people should have fled as the dead field ignited, but instead they all rushed toward it. "I think I've been waiting my whole life for these fire dances!" Liz said as she attempted to pull me down to the field.

"Ummm," I said, "I know we're immortal right now, but I don't think our clothes are."

"Didn't I tell you to wear clothes you didn't mind destroying?" Liz asked.

"I never made it back to my room to get them. Look, you go have fun. I have something I've got to do."

Liz shrugged and took off to join the jumping and hollering in the wildfire. On the crest of the valley hills, I saw my danger of choice — the dragons Liz had mentioned flying and falling from. Tethered outside a ground cave, I could see people taking off and landing the horse-sized beasts, but never flying above the tree tops. If I could grab one now, then I could keep it for ten minutes until the danger became truly life threatening.

Despite my fixation on the scaled creatures, reflecting every color on the forest spectrum, a group of kids still caught my eye, probably because Leaf played among them. Except, I realized he was in the center and not happy about it.

I found myself stopped, torn between the danger of the dragons ahead and the anger that rose in my chest as the kids I recognized from Tabriel Vale had their fun. Leaf had clamped his hands tightly over his hat, but one of the boys was still trying to steal it from him, laughing as though it was harmless.

"Come on, Jog, leave him alone," one of the little girls said, but her added giggle rendered her words meaningless.

As soon as I saw tears in Leaf's reddening eyes, the idea of dragons fled my mind and I veered off my path. Jog, the largest of the kids with a round face and strong arms, was still only half my size. He had Leaf's hat halfway off when I grabbed the front of his leather jerkin and found him light enough to lift with one hand, an act which terrified the rest of the kids. Leaf jerked his hat back down, almost to his eyes, but I had already seen the shock of orange hair he was trying to hide.

"Listen," I said, holding Jog at eye level as he gripped my hands and tried to squirm free, "you are going to stop being a mean little brat, right now. Got it?"

Jog nodded wildly, and his feet were ready to tear into the ground the second they could touch it again. He fled from the group of friends, and the other kids retreated to follow him, frightened that I might do the same to them.

Leaf wiped tears from his eyes and fixed them on the ground. "Thank you."

"Look," I said, sitting just above him on the steep hill, putting us face to face, "you can't let people treat you like that."

"It doesn't matter," he said, sniffling. "I've always been different. I just didn't want you to see."

"Leaf, you're at the Dragona now. Nobody here is going to be mean because you have orange hair. Haven't you seen Anna? She doesn't hide beneath a hat."

"Yeah, but Anna and I are the only ones," Leaf said. "And I'm not powerful like she is. I'm just weird."

"You might not be powerful yet, Leaf, but I bet that someday you will be. So be proud to be different."

Leaf took a deep breath, then said, "I'd rather have friends."

His longing saddened me, but I smiled anyway. "You've already got one, right here, because I know you're going to do amazing things."

Leaf pulled the hat from his head, and said, "I guess I can try." His messy hair had the vibrancy of deep orange flames, which no longer seemed strange to me. It fit his lively personality. "I guess I just have to find something great to do."

"You could help me, if you wanted," I said, noticing no more dragons leaping into the sky. "See where they're starting to land the dragons? I need a distraction so I can sneak into the cave and steal one."

"What are you going to do with it?" Leaf asked, eyes wide.

I laughed and said, "I just want to fly on it. I'll put it back."

"But the magic of the eclipse is about to wear off."

"Then we should move fast!"

Leaf nodded as I stood up, and he ran ahead of me to the group removing the saddles. The sight of him was peculiar enough to catch their attention, and just as he began to ask them questions, his voice was drowned out by Shadar the storyteller, who told the valley, "It's time to come out of the flames and stop jumping from treetops. Yes, you, with the sharpened swords, you're about to severely regret playing with those! Happy Eclipsival! See you again in seventeen years!"

I grabbed the closest saddle and slipped into the gaping cave as the valley cheered for the end of the festivities. Accomplishment burned in my chest, just from helping Leaf. The cave dropped abruptly into a pit, and I climbed down the jagged handholds with a smile lightening my life. If saving a kid from a bully rewarded me with this much warmth and purpose, I could hardly fathom the fulfillment of saving a life.

Two dragons rested in the cavern depths, each the size of a gigantic horse with talons and teeth longer than my fingers. The dragon with deep red scales was curled up, sleeping, while the second raised his head and snorted smoke at me. With brown, green, and black patterns swirled over his back, he stood stock still with alert eyes.

I took a careful step forward, and the dragon simply watched me, as though daring me to take another. When I stepped to the side of him and threw the bulk of the saddle onto his back, he snapped his head back to glare fiercely.

It took a few minutes to secure every strap and buckle on the saddle, and the dragon watched every step of the process through angry eyes. I had plenty of time to question my insane motives as I double checked my work. Maybe danger could bring my memories back, but those memories wouldn't do me any good if this dragon killed me.

The list of tally marks from my room wandered back to my mind, reminding me of how important it was to recover my memories. I had saved *so* many lives. What if people were dying right now because I wasn't doing whatever I was supposed to be? And I might still need redemption for the fourteen tally marks on the other side of the list. I didn't even deserve to call myself Allie when I didn't understand what they meant.

I bent to undo a thick linked chain from around the dragon's leg. I hadn't lost the feeling that he was about to turn and attack me, but I was determined to use that fear to my advantage so I jumped on the dragons back, feeling shaky in the saddle. The dragon unfurled its wings and stretched each as far as it would reach, shaking its head as though waking from hibernation. I took a few deep breaths, not sure how to take off, and not sure the dragon was going to wait for my signal.

"Is that you, Allie? What are you doing?" a man asked from the mouth of the cave.

"Flying a dragon," I replied, trying to keep my voice from shaking. We both knew the magic from the eclipse would no longer protect me.

"I thought you couldn't remember anything. Do you remember how to fly?"

I dug my knees into the dragon's sides, and he leapt up with amazing force to land on the mouth of the cave, next to the man asking the question.

"No!" I shouted, my answer drowned out by the deafening roar the dragon let out before jumping up to catch the wind under his wings. I held tightly to the saddle, sure I was going to fall off as each wing stroke jumped us higher, and the dragon seemed eager to scrape me off in the clouds. Either I was about to remember how this worked, or I was probably going to die.

CHAPTER EIGHT

*oly life, I was reckless!*

The dragon streaked through the clouds, thrilled to be out of the cave below. Too thrilled. I clung to the manic beast with every limb, and my plan wasn't sounding brilliant anymore. If I didn't figure out how to control him fast, he was going to throw me off in his excitement.

I let go of the saddle to grab the reins in one unbalanced swipe, yanking them back. The dragon slowed to glide on the wind currents, no longer racing ahead. I remembered! I also realized that leaning forward would make him dip lower, and I directed him to skim around the treetops as small flashes of past trials and errors reminded me of my favorite flight tricks.

I could make him do a backward flip without being thrown off, although I knew a forward flip would be too much to ask for. The sensations of rising and plummeting in the air were fantastic, but also familiar. I could remember them.

I wanted to return to the ground to tell Liz of my revelations, but I loved flying. Maybe my past would have an easier time returning while I was in the air anyway. The dragon seemed to love the sky as much as I did, so we watched as the crowd of thousands vacated the valley and the fire in the middle burned down to glowing embers.

I had hoped for a flood of memories to wash in with the recollection of flying, but I had no such luck. I had thought that at least a small stream of the past would reward my risk-taking, but I didn't even get a puddle of my old identity. If memories were like water, mine were all secluded in lonely buckets. I had remembered how to fly, and that was all.

We stayed in the sky for hours, but not near the festivities. Instead, the dragon and I flew over moonlit streams and the gigantic needled cedars that grew around the Dragona. I even saw a muscular tama cat, with short golden hair and black-tipped ears, hunkered among dark branches.

I had plenty of time to think with only the wind whistling past my ears, and I knew for certain that my survival instincts were pulling up memories from the past to save me. By getting lost earlier, I had learned that this phenomenon only worked when my life was truly in danger. Now I also knew that I could only remember things directly related to the danger. I remembered how to fly a dragon when my life depended on it. I had only remembered how to hinder an Escali's senses because they were chasing me, and I only remembered the importance of bravery when they caught me. I probably wouldn't have remembered anything about the first Escali attack if I hadn't been scared stiff by the sound of distant shrieks and approaching footsteps.

Then what did I need to do to remember my secret past? I would have to be in some danger related to it, but I had no idea how I had saved so many lives. I only knew that my life-saving secrets had somehow angered the Escalis, which brought to mind an idea I wished I could unthink.

The only danger that would make me remember that past would involve the Escalis. The idea of Escali-related peril terrified me, but the torment of the tally marks in my room may have been even worse.

The dragon beneath my legs finally began to tire and glided to the entrance of its cave as I decided to ask Anna about joining some sort of mission against the Escalis. I needed to figure out what I had been doing, no matter the risk.

The dragon plunged into its steep pit in a startling nose dive. I thought we were going to crash and die until he pulled up, skipped across the ground like a stone, and skidded to a stop before slamming into the back wall.

"Good to see you're still alive," I heard from Liz, who was leaning against a rock in clear irritation.

"Liz," I said with a smile, leaping from the saddle. "I thought you would be in bed."

"How would I be able to sleep when you're in the sky on a dragon you don't know how to fly? One of the reckless ones too."

The dragon and I had a reckless streak in common. "Well, thanks for waiting," I said as I stroked his green and black nose, realizing he wasn't really glaring at me. "So, you can tell these dragons apart?"

"Sometimes, but I know this one in particular. I actually remember bottle feeding him when he was a baby. Can you believe that? I feel like he and I grew up together. I even gave him a name once, but I won't tell you what it is."

"Interesting," I said, failing to have any interest in what Liz had named the thing. "We should probably get to bed soon."

"Alright, here, let me help you get the saddle off," she said stepping forward to help loosen the straps. "And make sure you put the chain back on him. You can get Time if you let one of the dragons loose."

"Time?" I repeated.

"Come on, you know what Time is. The kind that's a punishment."

71

"Trying to have you explain things is a punishment," I groaned.

She pulled her lip back in an exaggerated, sisterly sneer to let me know what she thought of my complaint. "*Time* speeds your mind up so fast that you get tons of time to think things over. There's absolutely nothing to do but think. If you accidentally lose one of the dragons or something, then you get a month in your own mind to wish you hadn't. But only seconds pass in real time."

"That sounds harsh. An entire month of nothing but thought..."

"You think a month is harsh? The penalty for treason is ten thousand years."

I thought about the severity of ten thousand years and found myself nodding slightly. "I'm guessing nobody commits treason anymore."

"Never."

"Then maybe it's not such a bad rule."

"I agree, but can you imagine? Ten thousand years, and you couldn't end it for anything, not even to die. You would go crazy... literally."

I would rather die than endure such a torture, and I wondered briefly if I would even wish such a punishment upon my greatest enemy.

I triple checked that I had the dragon secured properly. I didn't know what I would do with myself if I had a month of just thought. I never wanted to find out. "Let's stop thinking about it. I'd like to sleep tonight."

"Me too, so let's go and I'll see you tomorrow."

"I need you to get me to my room, Liz. I don't know how to find it yet."

"That's easy. From here, you'll need to take a right," she gestured with her hands as though the cave system was in the air and I could see where she was directing me. "And then—"

"Liz, I'm not about to follow your directions again. You take me there, or I'm sleeping in your room."

She snorted and said, "Fine, I'll take you. You are the most violent sleeper in the entire world, thrashing around all the time and throwing blankets. You're crazy."

"I already knew that," I said, smiling because I had been brave enough to jump on a dragon and recover a piece of my memory. "It must run in the family."

I woke from a vivid nightmare the next morning, kicking a wad of blankets across the room in a panicked sweat. My dreaming self had crawled beneath a collapsed building to pull two injured kids into a dark night, lit only by building fires and the destructive magic of mages who had arrived too late. I had hurried the kids to the edge of the massacre, amidst clanging metal and screaming, and their fear filled faces were so clear to me, I wasn't entirely sure it had been a dream. It might have been a memory.

An Escali had darted from the woods and picked up the younger brother as his sister shrieked and I shouted something unintelligible. I couldn't remember what I said, but something about it had caused the predator to pause, and when he jerked his focus to me, the piercing gaze of his cloudy eyes terrified me into waking up.

I squeezed my eyes shut now, trying desperately to determine if the dream had been a memory or wishful thinking. Saving kids and battling Escalis sounded too fantastic to be real.

Since I had nowhere to be, and no knowledge of the tunnel system anyway, I deliberated on the matter and rifled through my existing thoughts as my morning time hunger turned into starvation over the course of a few hours. I didn't expect to remember anything while safely in my room, but that didn't keep me from trying.

Loneliness was also beginning to set in when somebody knocked on my door. I leapt from my bed to fling it open with a bit more excitement than necessary. "West! What can I do for you?"

My greeting startled him. "I was just wondering if you wanted to take a trip to the Wreck."

"Yes, I do. The Wreck is where the food is. Let's go!" I was already out the door and had started down the tunnel by the time I finished my sentence.

"No, Allie, it's this way," West said, holding back a grin.

"Right you are," I replied, turning on my heel to head the opposite direction. West was kind enough to explain the tunnel system to me as we walked, pointing out distinctive marks and main tunnels so I could finally find my own way.

When we got to the Wreck, I was shocked to find it so empty. It was still filled with the chatter and laughter of people sitting around octagon tables, or getting up to get their dinner, but wasn't comparable to how full it had been the previous day. Most of the venders had either left, or were just finishing their packing, and I liked this atmosphere much better.

"Allie," Liz waved to me from one of the tables. "Come sit with us."

"Not a chance. I'm getting food," I replied, having no difficulty smelling exactly which way the meal was. One corner of the Wreck housed tables full of meats, an assortment of breads, a stand of vegetables, and a pile of tableware to dish up on. A pit of coals burned close by, where a few people roasted more trays of roots or birds on spits, loading them onto the table when they were done. As I piled meats onto my plate, I also kept an eye open to see if anyone else I recognized was in the Wreck.

I set my steak-dominated plate back down as I spotted Archie with Anna, just about to leave. She was the person I wanted to see most at the Dragona, with the exception of possibly Sir Avery, so I reluctantly abandoned my plate to integrate myself into their

74

conversation. Anna had a gigantic sheathed sword slung over her shoulder as they walked.

"And you say Sir Darius recruited you?" she asked Archie, as though the massive sword didn't burden her.

"Yeah, he said he was going to talk to you—"

"He probably already did. I've just been too busy to be bothered," Anna said. "And Allie, I was just coming to find you," she said to me. "I've spoken with Sir Darius, and he says he didn't send you to Tabriel Vale, nor does he know what you were doing there. I also have bad news on the mind mages. Sir Avery still has them out on some assignment he's calling the 'Utmost Priority.' I don't know what he's doing, but he's ignoring our every attempt to contact him."

"Alright," I said, already resigned to believe I would have to get my memory back on my own. Then, feeling no lead-in required, I told her, "Anna, I think I remember things when I'm in danger."

Anna heaved the sword off her back and rested it on the ground, considering my words. When she finally spoke, she said, "I have plenty of dangerous missions I can send you on. Is that what you're asking for?"

That *was* what I was asking, but the blatant proposition took me strangely by surprise. "Yes," I replied. "But ones that I'll live through... preferably." I noticed a smile flicker on her lips, as though my daring encouraged her.

"I'll find you something. Until then, why don't you sign up for your normal chore rotations? You can start with the baby dragons in the hatchery tomorrow."

"The hatchery?" I repeated. Bottle feeding babies had to be the safest job in the entire Dragona, a complete waste of valuable time. "I was hoping to sign up for something like the combat dragons."

"I don't doubt your bravery, Allie. We're just training Leaf out there, and he's been talking about you all morning, asking if you can come out and help him."

75

"Alright then, I guess I can. I've also been wondering actually, is he..." I only realized the question might be inappropriate halfway through, and by then, I had to finish it. "Yours?"

"No," Anna replied, "although I wish he was. He thinks his parents were killed by Escalis, but they're alive and well on Tekada. They abandoned him the day his hair came in orange, and Tekada exiled him to our war zone."

I frowned in disbelief and said, "The more I hear about Tekada, the less I like it."

Anna assured me, "On Tekada's great list of offenses, this one rates near the bottom. I need to leave, but I'll let you know if I find a mission for you. Or if one of our mind mages returns."

"And I can show you how to sign up for chores," Archie said. "Sir Darius just put me on the list earlier today."

"Yes, do that," Anna said, heaving the great sword back onto her shoulder to leave. I'll keep trying to get a mind mage back here for you, Allie, but in the meantime just let me know if you're ever in need of anything. You were important to the Dragona before your incident, and I'd much rather get the old you back than have you as a new recruit to train."

Her comment stung as she left us, but I knew it shouldn't. She'd meant to give me a compliment by telling me how important I was... *was* being the key term though. *Used to be.* The same as how I used to be the sister Liz relied on. I allowed my shoulders to slouch, resenting my empty mind and directionless heart more than anyone else ever could. Didn't anyone know I would trade my right arm to recover my past? I used to have a purpose. I used to save lives. I would ache to have that meaning back, even without their reminders.

I thought I kept my contemplations concealed behind a blank expression, but Archie picked up on them. As we watched Anna exit the Wreck, he said, "You know, my sister used to tell me that some compliments are like a hug and a backstab at the same time.

76

I wouldn't worry too much about that one. You seem to have plenty going for you, just the way you are."

"Well, thanks," I said, a bit taken aback. Sometimes it was nice to have a friend who hadn't known the old me. "What are you, a mind reader?" I added.

Archie laughed and replied, "Naw, but I hear you're looking for one. I'm just here to help you sign up for chores tomorrow. The sheet is here on the wall."

A massive chart of chores, weekdays, and names covered a sheet so large I could barely reach the top rows. People had signed up for a chore every day, and I scrawled my name in tomorrow's box for the hatchery, where Liz was also scheduled to work. I saw to my disappointment, "The slots to work with the combat dragons are full for the next five days."

Archie pulled the quill from my hand. "You should come help me out then, so I don't have to be the only clueless one showing up to these things."

Archie scribbled my name next to *shipment receiving* and *chopping firewood.* "You signed up for all the awful ones," I protested as my name also landed next to *wreck cleaning* and *daily cooking.* "Why don't you just add our names next to *paper making* and *blanket weaving* while you're at it?"

I snatched the quill back to scratch my name next to *combat dragons* on the first day it was available, at a time when Archie was signed up to be shadowing and learning from the mages in the woods.

"You call that handwriting?" Archie asked. Even with a task as mundane as signing up for chores, he was able to put a smile on my face.

"I'm sorry," I grinned, "I didn't realize I needed to be a calligrapher to sign up."

"You at least need to know which end of the quill to use! Let's pretend *that* never happened." He tore a neat little hole in the paper and essentially removed my name from existence, then rewrote it beneath.

I laughed when he finished. "Mine was at least legible! Whoever reads that is going to think a bear stumbled in and tried to sign up."

"It *clearly* says Allie. You poor girl, can't write *or* read, can you?"

"Must have lost the ability with the rest of my memory." I took myself by surprise, joking about the loss of my past. Up until now, it had been a serious matter.

Archie studied me for a hesitant second. "I've… heard a bit about your incident from other people, but I know you probably tell it best. Can I ask what happened?"

"Actually, you can," I replied. I felt comfortable telling him what I knew, but I left out the part about the Escalis. I knew I shouldn't worry, but the thought of scaring him off bothered me. As I wrapped up what was a fairly short explanation, Liz found us and squinted skeptically between us. "Allie, how do you know somebody I don't?"

"I'm new here," Archie offered.

"Oh! I've heard about you," she said, turning big *I-told-you-so* eyes toward me. "You know, you and Allie are going to get along great, getting to know everything and such. Come on, West and I can show you guys how to play chips."

We followed Liz back to her group at the game table and sat down to a conversation already in progress. I studied several games until I felt that I knew how to play; I listened intently to every joke and piece of information spoken throughout the evening; and Liz and West introduced us to about fifty mages-in-training. I would be lucky to remember half their names by morning, but it was important to try. The key to my past could be hidden anywhere, and I needed as much knowledge as I could get.

"My friends and I were idiots, thinking we could steal firehoney," Archie said later in the evening as he walked me back

78

to my room. Something about his random stories gave me a sense of comfort, like a short break from the pressing need to recover my secrets. "Two of the farmers were on the porch talking to each other when we realized we had found the dog-pen instead of the firebees. The dogs, of course, went ballistic when they heard us, so we tried to escape through the grass fields, and go figure, *that* was where we found the firebee hives. The bees lit up and attacked us, and as soon as we got away from the light of one nest, the next one would swarm us, showing the entire world our failed escape attempt. We ended up with a few hundred stings and didn't get to try a lick of firehoney."

I found myself laughing, realizing how refreshing his stories were after so many great legends and world concepts. "I wish I had stories to share," I said. "I'll bet I had some good ones."

"I'm sure you'll remember them someday," he said, stopping next to a wooden door. "Well, thanks for walking me home," he teased, and I stopped as well.

"So this is your room?" I asked. "Let's see it then."

"I don't think so," he said, setting his hand on the brass knob.

"Are you serious? What are you trying to hide in there?" I tried to give him an intensive stare, but I tainted it with a smirk I couldn't keep under wraps.

"I'll tell you what," he said, holding his hands out like I might run at him without warning. "Give me ten seconds. I'll be right back." He cracked the door to his room open and slipped inside, shutting it before I could get so much as a peek.

I stared at the wooden door, bewildered, and realized how much I needed him to reemerge. Everything in me started to ache again as my chronic fear of uncertainty crept back in. The possibility of not remembering myself, of living empty and alone, didn't plague me when I had Archie's distraction. Something about him made me feel safer.

He barely nudged the door open to come back out, and carried two broadswords with him, one of which he held out to me. I took it uncertainly as he said, "Here's the deal. If you can get past me, you can come in. What's it worth to you?"

"Not my life!" I exclaimed, holding up the metal blade. *"Are you here to assassinate me?"*

"No. They aren't sharpened. And what's this sudden worry with being careful? Careful is for beginners." He ran his hand down the side of the blade to prove it was dull.

I held the heavy sword up, and the weight in my hands felt good rather than awkward, though it was much bigger than my usual short swords.

He said, "I know you usually carry short swords, but they're not to your advantage unless you're faster than your opponent."

"I doubt you're faster than me," I said, challenging him with a squint and wondering vaguely how he knew I was thinking about my short swords. Did he know me so well already?

"Alright, hang on," he said, stepping back into his room. He emerged this time with three wooden sparring swords. A long one for him, two shorts for me.

"Archie, I do want to warn you. I'm pretty good," I said as I swung both arms out in a quick stretch and flipped both blades around my hands.

"Well, I'm decent too, so don't go too easy on me."

He looked like he had the potential to be fast, but he held his sword in nothing more than a casual stance, making me wonder if he even knew how to use it.

"It's your job to get to the door," he reminded me.

"Thanks." I struck at him, and he swiftly parried, almost too fast to see.

I went for him again, but he simply leapt back without the slightest effort, still blocking my way to the door. I tried striking with both swords, aiming for his legs, lunging then disengaging, feigning then striking — I tried getting the upper hand any way I could, but nothing worked.

"You're not fighting back!" I barked through my rising irritation.

He went on the offensive like a striking snake, throwing attacks in such rapid succession that I could barely get my blades up to defend myself, let alone strike back. He was able to spin around, kick at my feet, and take them out from beneath me, knocking me flat on my back.

I gasped and then stood back up to gape at him in furious disbelief.

Archie opened his mouth to say something but I flung a finger up to point at him, cutting him off. "Again." I threw down my wooden weapons and picked up one of the metal broadswords.

"Ok," he agreed, surprised. I didn't even wait for him to pick the second sword up. As soon as he touched it, I lunged straight for him and swung downward with everything I had. He crouched and held his sword up, brushing mine to the side. Before the clang of colliding metal even reached my ears, he rolled past me and onto his feet, his sword pressed to my back. I threw my blade down and spun around to confront him.

"How are you doing that?" I snarled with a piercing glare. My reaction had him laughing lightly to himself. I had yet to catch my breath, but he still looked as calm and relaxed as before we started.

"I told you I was good. I don't think you're supposed to hate me for that."

"No, you said you were decent!"

I glanced quickly around to find where my surroundings might give me an advantage over my admittedly superior opponent. Our cave was only separated from the next tunnel over by a rock wall about twice my height.

"And I don't hate you," I said, rather unkindly.

81

He tossed his sword from one hand to the other. "Then what do you call that look you're shooting me? Friendship?"

I lunged unexpectedly at Archie as I got an idea. The flick of his wrist caused our blades to collide with a resounding clang as I turned around, got a running start, and jumped up to grab the narrow crest of the cave wall. I pulled myself up until the ground was far beneath me, and I was standing on a jagged balance beam of rock, no wider than my hand.

Archie took a few suspicious paces toward me, studying the situation silently from the ground.

"I'm just wondering how good your balance is," I said innocently, testing my weight on precariously poised feet.

"Alright then," he said.

He leapt up to take hold of the rock wall with both hands, and had only pulled himself halfway up when I went on the offensive — a dirty tactic I was willing to stoop to. I tried to knock him off the wall before he got any bearing, but was forced to jump as he looped an arm over the rocky edge and swung at my feet with his blade.

As soon as my feet touched back down, he knocked my legs out from under me with the arm still holding the sword. I landed on the cave's rocky teeth with a yelp as Archie pulled himself up onto the wall, his eyes suddenly wide with concern.

Still on the ground, I growled as I gripped my sword with both hands and swung to hit him in the ankle, feeling the brutal thud of my blade making contact. I was instantly terrified I may have done real damage, but it wasn't so bad that Archie was willing to end the duel over it.

It took him a second to process what had happened, but even as he recoiled onto his good foot, he lunged forward and flung me over the side of the wall. I shrieked and had to drop my sword in order to reach up and grab the edge, dangling over the side with my feet still far from the ground.

He crouched to tilt his head and give me a *this-is-your-own-fault* squint. "Now are we done?" he asked as I held on.

"Yeah, I think I'm good." He reached down and grabbed one of my hands to pull me up. Before I had half my body on the wall, I asked, "Is your ankle alright."

"Of course, it's fine." He was, however, very careful not to stand on it.

I sat on a smooth section of the stone feeling rather guilty, but I shifted my eyes up and admitted, "That was kind of fun," concealing a grin until I knew how he would react.

"Of course it was," Archie replied, sitting next to me, his smirk returning. "It's sparring." I leaned over to look at the sword I had dropped as Archie pulled his ankle in to examine it. "I might be done for the night though."

"Right... I'm really sorry," I said again. "I didn't mean to hit you that hard."

"Naw, it's fine. I'll be ok in a few minutes." I still felt bad, regardless. I hadn't held anything back. His ankle had to be broken. "Next time though, you're dead," he added.

I was about to reply that I was ready to go now, but I shook my head instead, smiling at the thought of beating him another day — when he wasn't handicapped.

"I guess these swords *can* cause damage when they aren't sharp, can't they?" I said. I wished he wasn't wearing boots so I could see how ugly of a mark I had left. That wasn't wrong of me, was it?

"They're just as good as any sharpened swords when it comes to Escalis," Archie said, twisting his foot in a circle. "Once Escalis become adults, you can't cut through their skin with anything."

"I've been wondering about that," I said, looking at the blunt blade. "Why do we use swords then? Is the point just to hit them hard enough to cripple them?"

"Well, King Kelian reasons that if the Escalis find us, we're dead no matter what weapon we have. So he was going to ban weapons on our continent altogether, but ended up being *gracious* enough to allow us swords in case of animal attacks. Of course, the rest of the continent doesn't care what he decrees and trains with weapons that can harm Escalis, but it's all technically illegal."

"Well, you sure got good with a sword," I said. "Where did you learn to be so quick?"

"I used to spar with my friends all the time," he replied.

"Where did you guys live?" I asked. "And what did you do before you came here?"

"Actually, I used to live on the outskirts of the Daarago."

"The what?"

"It's the giant Escali forest, east of here. That's where their capitol city is."

"Why were you living out there?" I asked, swinging my legs in the air as he thought about his answer. "There must have been Escalis everywhere."

"There were. Their royal family even lived out there. But, I don't know, we just… had to live somewhere, I guess."

I could tell he had no interest in discussing the details, which was fine. If we were going to be friends, he would tell me eventually.

"Have you heard about Prince Avalask?" he asked me.

"Yes. He's one person I've been educated about."

"What are you two doing?" West had clearly sprinted to reach us, and bent forward to catch his breath.

"We were just—" I stammered as Liz caught up to him and sucked in the stale cave air as well, resting an arm on his shoulder to recover as she saw we weren't being killed.

West shook his head and gaped at us like we were unbelievable. "How did you even get up there?"

Archie and I exchanged puzzled glances. "We jumped?" Archie offered. I glanced at the ground. It wasn't *that* far.

"*Were you two sparring?*" Liz demanded. "In the middle of the night? You have chores in the morning!"

I burst into laughter, because she was scolding me over chorework. "Alright, and do tell, Liz, why are the two of you up so late?"

Liz glared coldly in response, and I locked eyes with her until the edges of her lips twitched into a sly grin.

"Let's all get some sleep," I said, jumping off the wall and bending my knees to absorb the impact of hitting the ground. I threw an arm around Liz's shoulders as Archie landed behind me, and I whispered, "Thanks for coming to save me," as we started walking. Just before we rounded the corner, when Archie thought I wasn't looking, I threw a glance back and saw him exchanging quiet remarks with West, but he didn't show a hint of a limp in his stride.

His ankle should be broken. Something was wrong.

CHAPTER NINE

Sparring flew by every morning because Liz and West began practicing together to make a formidable team, almost a challenge to fight, and the mages made incredible matches. When I faced Terry, the rough-around-the-edges girl who could jump, I had to be constantly ready for her to reappear right behind me. With super-speed Michael, I just had to accept that he was undefeated and too fast to compete with. I was secretly waiting for the day when Archie had to face Michael, because I needed to see him lose, and he hadn't so far.

Unlike Archie, I could only hold my own against a few of the mages. I just couldn't get used to lifting my sword for a parry and watching my opponents' blade pass straight through it, or sometimes even melt it. My mornings were never boring when I was blasted across a field or nearly lit on fire, and after sparring, Archie kept even the most miserable of chores entertaining with his love for competition, a trait I shared despite my losing streak.

When we had to haul carts of disgusting dragon food up hills, Archie would say, "Race you to the top?" and even after I faked disinterest and jumped ahead of him, he would reach the hillcrest first. When we competed to see who could chop the most firewood, he could get an extra twenty logs split per my one hundred. When we had to cook food in the Wreck, he distracted me on purpose so my venison came out charred. I don't know what witchcraft he used to keep my bread from rising too, but I felt entirely comfortable blaming him for sabotage, which he protested with a grin.

Today I would be handling the combat dragons without him, but the best of our chore-times still had me smiling as I sat on the sidelines of morning sparring, watching the battles and reliving how we cleaned the entire wreck in the dead of the night.

Everybody had gone to bed and Archie had stolen wooden swords from the supply shed. We made a competition of picking up fallen and forgotten food in the midst of lunges, parries, and foul play, and we fought each other between the chairs and on top of the tables as we picked up the day's filth. Of course, Archie ended up picking up more than I did.

My ideas about him were ludicrous, but it was the most ludicrous of them all that I came back to every night before I fell asleep.

Could he possibly be the new Epic?

Archie faked a limp over the next few days, but I knew if he took his boots off, there would be no swelling or bruising to justify it. He also rarely talked about his life. Archie would tell me stories of his friends' adventures, but he never mentioned his childhood or his parents, even when I asked. I knew strange little things about him, like his fighting tendencies and his favorite part of the duskflyer song, since he would occasionally whistle it when he thought nobody else was around, but I knew nothing of his past.

His incredible talent for sparring was another factor playing on my mind. He was so accomplished and *so* fast. Realistically, I knew I just wanted him to be an Epic so I could piece my pride back together. I still felt like a stupid dandelion whenever I fought against Archie — so fragile that a light breeze was fatal. At least if he was an Epic, I could justify my endless losing streak.

I had gotten *one* good kick that took him by surprise on our cleaning-night. With a rag in one hand and a sword in the other, I had knocked him off a table-top, accidentally shattering a chair as a result. He had taken it to his room, claiming he could fix it and put it back with nobody the wiser, but I had my doubts.

"What are you smiling about?" Archie asked, joining me on the edge of Sir Bruscan's maze of light. The goal had been to reach the middle of the maze while fighting everybody we came across, and losers could leave to start their day's work.

Instead of answering, I exclaimed. "You're out of the maze! What happened?"

He shook his head and simply said, "Liz and West."

"Same here. West came at me from the front, and Liz threw both of her swords at me from behind while I was distracted. Is that how they got you?"

"No, it was more of a flying tackle, and then Sir Bruscan called foul on me for crossing over the boundaries."

Liz grabbed West's arm to slow him down as she noticed Archie and me talking. The two stopped running just long enough to give us mocking salutes, then they carried on conquering the maze.

Archie and I exchanged a slight laugh to cover the fact that we were actually sore losers, and Archie said, "I'm heading back to the Wreck before I go out with the mages today. You want to come?"

"Yes. I still have a few hours before I get to meet the Dragona's combat dragons." We headed for the Wreck, knowing that Liz and West would catch up with us, and I asked Archie, "How is that chair doing?"

"Well," he replied, blue eyes looking into mine as though they held tragic news, "I'm doing all I can, but the chair just might not make it."

"Let's just not tell anybody," I said, laughing as we stepped into the Wreck and sat at a chips table with a full complement of chairs.

I only recognized Michael among the players, laying his chips down so fast that I could hardly tell where they landed.

I joined the next game, but soon Liz came running to sit with us. "Sir Avery's back!" She must have left West far behind, which wasn't like her.

"The Epic? Are you sure?" I asked, never convinced that Liz was entirely reliable.

"I'm positive about this one," she assured me. "He just got here. I also heard he's staying for a few days, which is great news for you, Allie!"

"Where is he?" Archie asked.

"He's talking to Anna and Sir Darius, and then I think he's coming down here."

"Really?" I found myself attentive now. Maybe I could talk to him. Was it actually possible that my problems could be solved within the next few hours?

"I think I have to go," Archie said, standing up just as West reached our table.

"Why?"

"I forgot to… I don't know. I'll see you later." He swung his legs quickly off the bench and left, the three of us puzzling after him.

"What's wrong with him?" West asked as soon as he was out of sight.

"I don't know. I'll go see," I replied, getting up to follow him into the living tunnels.

I had hardly taken a step before I heard, "Allie!" and I saw Anna approach our table. "Consider your chores cancelled. You wanted a mission, and I've got one for you."

"You found one?" I repeated. "What is it?"

"Dincara sent out a raid on the Escali city of Treldinsae during the Eclipsival," Anna said, "but nobody has returned. Since Prince Avalask is keeping our mages from seeing the area, we need a team to actually get close and tell us what happened. This is one of our less dangerous missions, and Sir Avery will be here in about ten minutes to give you more details, so quickly pick who you'd like to come with you."

I had barely opened my mouth to respond when Michael said, "I'll go." Of course he was eager to get in on the action. His incredible speed could keep him safe. "West and Jesse both want to come too." Michael pointed out West and the guy next to him, whose dark bangs hung nearly into his eyes.

West agreed, "Definitely. I need to find my power before old age kills me."

"And I make a good leader," Michael said.

I saw Liz about to open her mouth, and I shook my head to cut her off. There wasn't a chance she was allowed to come. "I need to go find Archie," I said. He was the team member I needed most of all.

"Alright, but be back in ten minutes," Anna said. "You don't want to keep Sir Avery waiting."

I darted into the tunnels and only slowed when I caught up to Archie, taking care not to tread too lightly so he would be forced to acknowledge I had followed him. I wasn't sure why he was so hesitant to talk to me, but he only stopped walking because we reached the door to his room. He took such an immense time to turn around that I grew impatient and asked, "What's wrong?" before he faced me.

"Nothing," he replied, his gaze on his door. "I just needed to come back to my room. This chair isn't going to fix itself."

I tilted my head just a bit to the side and gave him my *I'm-no-fool* frown. "Why don't you like Sir Avery?"

Archie sighed and finally returned my eye contact. "It's not so much that I don't like him."

"Then what?"

"I just don't want to be around him."

90

I wasn't interested in ambiguous half-answers, so I asked the very pointed question, "Why don't you want to be around Sir Avery?"

"It's... I don't know. He's an Epic, so he can see into the minds of everyone within shouting distance of him."

"I don't think it's a big deal," I reasoned. I also didn't think it was the truth. "If he can hear all of us, then why does it matter that he can hear you?"

"Well... I don't know. It's complicated."

"I'll understand."

Archie watched me undecidedly, then said, "I have to tell you something, Allie. Mind mages can't hear my thoughts. Whenever I walk into a room I instantly have their full attention, and I do not need Sir Avery's attention right now."

I found that interesting to hear, not because I believed it was the real issue, but because having a blocked mind sounded like another power. I needed to start making a list. "I don't think it's anything you have to worry about," I repeated.

"Doesn't matter. I'm just going to avoid him."

"Why? Do you have something to hide?" Archie either didn't catch my sarcasm, or just didn't find it funny. He was deep in thought. "Look," I said, slipping back into a serious tone, "you should come back to the Wreck. Anna has this mission —"

Somebody landed with a startling thud behind me, and I had already whipped around and pulled out a short sword by the time I realized Sir Darius, the second of the Dragona's leaders, was a friend rather than a foe.

A bit startled himself, he said, "Good reflexes, and I appreciate that you identified your target before striking. Both of you need to be in the Wreck, right now. Sir Avery isn't going to wait to explain this mission to you."

Sir Darius leapt back into the air, and I said, "Just forget about Sir Avery. He won't be worried about you. I need to go on this mission, and I need you to come with me."

"I know."

"You can't just leave me because you're afraid of your own leader. What kind of coward does that?" Archie's expression took a proud and irritated turn with the simple downward tilt of his head. I had touched a nerve.

A few people passed us, and Archie waited until they were gone to repeat, "Coward?"

"You heard me."

Archie folded his arms, and I watched as he took a contemplative breath, obviously deciding what to do. I think I *saw* him make up his mind as he simply shook the irritation off. "I'm not going," he said, opening his door and stepping into his room.

"Are you kidding?" I entered after him, uninvited, and shut the door so nobody in the hall would have to hear the coming dispute. His room was fairly unadorned, just a wooden chest at the foot of his neatly made bed and a few swords in the corner. There was nothing in here worth hiding. "Why can't you go near Sir Avery? Did you do something?"

He exclaimed with his hands, "No! I never did anything."

"Then *what?*"

Archie jumped onto his bed and said, "Then *nothing*. When you meet Sir Avery, you'll understand. He's been stretched beyond his limits for his entire life, he's volatile, and he's dangerous. Any tiny thing you do can set him off."

I had to unclench my teeth to say, "How would you even know that?"

Archie simply shrugged and said, "I'll come on the mission with you, Allie. I just can't come to the Wreck right now."

I raised my eyebrows and said, "If I tell Sir Avery, *the Epic*, that I have one more person who wants to come, won't he read my mind and know exactly who you are?"

Archie laced his fingers tightly together before he let his breath out. I added, "You won't be able to hide from him if he knows you're trying to," and Archie nodded, still thinking to himself.

"You're probably right," he finally said, pushing himself to his feet with clenched fists. "Alright, let's go."

It was amazing how quickly the Wreck filled with people keen to see Sir Avery. When Archie and I entered, the Epic of the legends was standing on a sturdy wooden platform at the far end, speaking urgently with Anna and Sir Darius.

Sir Avery was everything I had pictured — taller than both of them and with a noble air about him. Brown scruffy hair curled to his shoulders as though he hadn't found the time to cut it in years, and the way he held himself spoke of resilience, as though he could take on the world at any moment. As though he knew he had to.

I turned to Archie, about to say *I told you there was no reason to worry*, when I saw he was actually quite pale. Frozen in place and staring straight ahead in concentration, his jaw was the only part of him that moved when he said, "I told you this would happen."

"What's going on?"

I flicked my gaze to Sir Avery to see him watching me and Archie, unhappy with our arrival — well, Archie's arrival. I hadn't imagined his problems with Sir Avery would actually be serious, but the strain on Archie's face showed that they were.

"Are you ok?" I asked.

Entirely too calmly, Archie replied, "No, I don't think I will be."

People quieted and followed Sir Avery's gaze until they spotted us still standing in the doorway. They could tell something was wrong and whispers rose as the whole cavern took notice.

"Archie, why is he doing this? Just tell me, and I'll try to get you out of here."

Archie's hollow stare gave me the feeling he hadn't heard the question, and I really began to worry. I tried to snare Sir Avery's gaze, but he was watching Archie too intently to be interested in me.

I watched Archie's knees threaten to buckle, and then every part of him collapsed backward as his stony expression broke and he yelped in pain. I was able to catch him before he hit the floor, and I shouted to Sir Avery, "Hey! Knock it off!"

He flicked his glare of determination momentarily to me, then jumped into the air and disappeared as Archie muttered, "I can't feel my hands." The Epic's feet hit the ground in front of us, and he grabbed Archie from me.

"You're next," he barked, briefly meeting my eyes before he and Archie vanished. I crouched, frozen to the spot, not knowing what to do. His gaze had bored through my every defense in our split second of eye contact. Everybody watched me now, but with only a fraction of the shock I felt. Nobody spoke.

CHAPTER TEN

iz gripped my shoulders an eternity later. "Allie! Come on, let's get out of here." She tried to pull me from everybody's sight, but I was too far in shock to move, and she couldn't persuade me otherwise. It took West ramming into my other shoulder to get me into the tunnel, away from my gaping audience.

"What just happened?" West asked.

"I don't know," I barely choked out.

"Where's Archie?"

"I don't know."

"What did you two do?" Liz demanded.

"I don't — we didn't do anything!"

"Then what's going on?" West asked again.

"I don't *know!* Archie was afraid of Sir Avery for some reason, but I didn't know it was serious! I didn't think—"

"Calm down," West said, keeping his own voice even to offset mine.

"Didn't you hear Sir Avery?" Liz piped up. "He said she was next!"

"You calm down too. Listen, both of you. Everything is ok. I'm sure Sir Avery—"

Everything around me — Liz, West, and the tunnel walls — suddenly vanished and my feet dropped onto the hard rock of a new cave. The new location startled me, and I saw Archie huddled against the wall with his hands pressed against either side of his head, eyes clamped shut. Between him and me stood Sir Avery.

"Did you know he was here?" Sir Avery demanded, pointing at Archie, who was unresponsive.

"What? Of course I know he's here!" I retorted, angered by everything Sir Avery was doing.

"And you just let him into the Dragona?"

"I had nothing to do with him coming to the Dragona. What's wrong with him? What did he do?"

Sir Avery shook his head several times and paced, fuming. He halted and peered down at Archie, deep in thought. Then he abruptly asked, "Why can't you remember?"

"I don't know! Should I know what your problem with Archie is?"

"You should know a lot more than that." This time when Sir Avery switched his gaze to me, his angry features also leaked concern. "I know you don't remember much, but do you know what happened to you?"

I folded my arms, not ready to respond kindly just yet. "No. I don't."

Sir Avery spoke as though he knew me.

"I thought your memories would come back in a day or two, but you still haven't recovered any, have you?"

"No. Why does it matter to you?"

Sir Avery dragged his hands over his eyes, as if it mattered quite a bit. "You *have* to remember. You knew things, Allie. Important things." He took a deep breath and looked at me apologetically, his expression glazed with sadness. "I just wish you would have told me you were going to Tabriel Vale."

"Told *you*? Why would— Wait... You know what I was doing in Tabriel Vale?" My voice shot up and my eyes widened. Here were the answers!

"Only vaguely. You have to remember it on your own."

"Why can't you just tell me what you know?" I demanded.

Sir Avery seemed suddenly distracted, frowning at a piece of the wall as though he saw something else through it.

And Archie began talking to himself on the ground. It freaked me out to see him in such a state, and I wanted to punch Sir Avery to make him stop. I would have if I didn't suspect it would end badly for me

"It isn't my fault," Archie muttered in distress, "and why does it matter if I'm here? She gets to live here."

I knew this wasn't something I was supposed to hear. I disregarded Sir Avery and knelt down to snap Archie out of it — even though I would probably wonder what he was saying forevermore. I shook him, but when that didn't do anything I grabbed both of his hands and pulled them away from his face. Sir Avery disappeared from the room and Archie's eyes snapped open with dangerous intentions before realizing who I was.

"You need to tell me what's going on!" I said, letting go and maneuvering myself away from his threatening glare.

"How long have you been here?" he asked, disoriented and defensive. "Where's Sir Avery?"

"He just left."

Archie looked around the room anyway to make sure, then back at me, this time without the frightening eyes. "What just happened?"

"That's what you're going to explain to me!"

He checked around one more time and took a deep breath. "Sir Avery's trying to punish me. Didn't want me here."

"Why?" I asked, always coming back to the same question. "What did you do?"

"I've never done anything! It's just... family, you know?"

"No! I do not understand, Archie!"

"His family... my family... they've just got some issues. Sir Avery told me I was never welcome at the Dragona. That's why I didn't want to go near him. I didn't want him to know I was here."

"He's coming back, you know. What do you think he's going to do?"

"I don't know. Whatever he wants, I guess. Epics know no bounds," he said, getting to his feet slowly. I stood too and felt the blood return to my legs.

"Before Sir Avery comes back, can you tell me what I mean to him?" I asked.

"What makes you think I know?"

"I don't know, but he makes it sound like I'm important. Why should he care if I get my memory back?"

Sir Avery reappeared in the room, startling both of us, and answered, "Allie, you used to know things nobody else in the world knew. I need for you to remember what they are. Your mind used to be so ridiculously guarded, only a fool would try to pry anything from it. A lot has been ruined now that it's in shambles."

I scowled, still unwilling to accept anybody insulting my intellect. "If it's in such shambles, why don't you try helping me? I won't mind sharing my memories with you if you help me find them."

Within a second, every aspect of my consciousness felt different — like a headache had plagued my entire life and suddenly been lifted. I should have been startled by his sudden compliance, but cares, worries, and the burden of existence itself was immediately gone as warmth seeped into the corners that made up my mind. I didn't particularly know what Sir Avery was doing, or how long he scanned through my recent memories, nor did I care in any way.

Returning to reality was like being doused in icy water. Realizing my feet were still on the ground was a sharp and unpleasant shock as the weight of thoughts and senses returned. It didn't take long to readjust, but the real world seemed harsh. Sir Avery stared at me, deep in thought, and Archie glanced eagerly between both of us.

"Well?" Archie asked, clearly hoping for me to have made revolutionary progress. I couldn't remember anything from my past life right away. I thought hard, looking for a childhood memory or something, but still had nothing to recall.

"I still couldn't find anything," Sir Avery answered before I could ask the question. The lack of success visibly disheartened him. "I'm not sure if the memories are gone, or if they're just blocked. It's so strange. I don't know why I can't tell."

"Can I ever get them back?" I asked.

"You just might. You've got an instinct to survive that's as strong as any magic I have, so I think you've reached the right conclusions about putting yourself in danger. This mission could be one of your best opportunities."

Realization hit Archie's eyes. "You're risking death to get your memories back?"

"I'm... Well, yes," I said. It hadn't occurred to me that he didn't know that. Not wanting to discuss my reasoning, I said rather unkindly to Sir Avery, "I still don't understand why we're the ones going. Shouldn't you have the real adult mages looking into this, or maybe even you?"

"I would be able to scout Treldinsae easily if I was the only Epic in the world, but I'm not. Prince Avalask is keeping me from seeing anything in the area, and we often allow older members of the Dragona to take on missions if they choose to. They usually go in search of their powers, the same way you're searching for your memories."

"What time will we leave?" I asked, setting my hand on the door to let him know I had no intention of talking with him any longer.

"You will need to leave shortly before dark."

I glanced at Archie to see if he was coming with me, and he said, "I'll just be a minute. I think Sir Avery and I need to talk."

"Great. See you soon," I said to the empty hallway as I left. I would have been lost, except I heard the echoes of the Wreck and followed them.

I had hoped to find Sir Avery a noble and respectable man, but the famous defender of Humanity was nearly the opposite, and I had no desire to ever talk to him again.

The second I set foot in the Wreck, Liz abandoned an oven she was tending so we could sit at an empty table.

"Are you alright?" she asked.

"Yeah. Just not very fond of this Epic we've got."

"We can talk about him later. Allie, I've been thinking…" She laced her fingers together and set them hesitantly on the table. "I've heard enough bad news for one day. Please tell me you're not going on this mission."

I sat back and studied her face, surprised to hear opposition. "We're leaving before dark," I told her, wrapping an arm over the back of my chair. "But this is a good thing, Liz. I'm going so I can get my old self back."

Liz stared at the table and swallowed nothingness before saying, "It won't do you any good if you're dead."

A part of me wanted to scream at her, to ask why she acted like I was worthless, yet discouraged me now. The sisterly part, however, realized that she didn't think I was worthless at all, which was why she didn't want me to go. This ordeal of my life was hard on her too.

"It'll be dangerous, Allie. Treldinsae is on the coast of the Breathing Sea, where the monsters can be worse than the Escalis."

I sighed. "I might as well go though, since somebody has to. I might also find my power while I'm out there, you never know."

"I guess. Plus you couldn't be with anybody better than Archie, Michael, and West. Just make sure you get home safely, alright?"

"You know we will," I said, feeling strangely sentimental. We'd be alright, surely. "And what were you saying about bad news, Liz?" I asked, trying to shake off the strange sting behind my eyes before I let a tear into the world.

She crouched over the table and whispered, "Allie... I heard today that Sir Avery never actually had a son."

I wrapped my feet around the legs of the chair beneath me and immediately refused to believe that Liz knew what she was talking about. Sir Avery knew how important it was to pass his genes on. I didn't like the guy, but he wouldn't have doomed our whole race by neglecting to have a kid, leaving the next Escali Epic unopposed. I felt justified in pushing the terrifying thought from my mind since I had so much to focus on already.

"I have to go back to cooking," Liz said. "Stay safe tonight. And let Archie know if he doesn't have you safely home by midnight, I'll kill him."

Her timing was perfect, because Archie had just stepped into the Wreck.

"I'll let him know," I told Liz as she returned to her oven and I headed straight toward him.

"Shall we get ready?" he asked, stepping to the side of the tunnel entrance to let me through first.

"Archie," I said as we headed to our rooms, "*what* is going on between you and Sir Avery?"

"I already told you—"

"You didn't tell me enough! Family issues? What does that mean? What happened? How long ago did this feud start?"

"I don't even know," he said. "It had nothing to do with me, much less anything to do with you, so can we drop it?"

"Of course we can't. Why would he be so angry if you'd never done anything?"

"That's the whole issue. He has no reason—" Archie stopped mid-sentence as a few of the Dragona's adult mages walked past us. "Can we talk about this later?"

"When is later?" I asked him as he stopped at his room. "Because I'm worried about this mission tonight. There's a real chance we could be caught."

"I know… I'm worried too. I ran into Michael on my way to talk to you, and he wants us to split into two groups to scout the area, so the chances that both groups will come away unseen… Our odds aren't great. And I hate the Breathing Sea. I don't know why the Escalis had to build their stupid city next to it."

I found a mocking grin tugging at the corner of my lips, making the situation seem a little less daunting. "I didn't expect you to be afraid of the Sea," I said.

"You can make fun of me all you want, but everything about it scares me. That's where the second Everarc was found, and everything beneath the surface wants to kill you."

"Great," I said, not sure if I wanted to think about the Sea or the Escalis. "And all I have are swords, which won't do anything against the Escalis if we're caught. Are we bringing some other kind of weapons along?"

Archie bit his lip for just a second before saying, "Everybody's doing something different. Michael and Jesse are carrying maces. West really wants to find his power, so he's not bringing a weapon at all. I'll try to convince him to change his mind, but I don't think he's going to. I'm bringing a sword, since I think I'm good enough to hold my own against them. You're probably good enough too, but it's up to you."

"Alright, I'll bring mine," I said, since swords were the only weapons I had laid hands on since waking up. I turned to head for my room, then flipped back around to walk backwards as I remembered, "Liz wants you to know that if the Escalis get me, you'll have her to answer to."

102

Archie smiled and said, "We're going to be fine. I'll see you at the dragon stables."

I rounded the corner as he softly said, "And the Escalis would have me to answer to first."

I glanced over my shoulder at the black tunnel rock that resonated so clearly, glad to have a moment to myself to think. What had *that* meant?

CHAPTER ELEVEN

I shouldn't have let my imagination run wild, wondering what would happen if we were caught, assuming we weren't immediately killed. The gruesome outcomes I pictured left me even more nervous, and my stomach twisted into a horrible knot, knowing what we were about to attempt. My fingers shook with anticipation as I tried to decipher the complicated mess of a draconic saddle in front of me, and the horse-sized beast eyed me skeptically. We had to fly because nobody could jump in or out of the Escali city, but I already foresaw problems getting back to the dragons during our escape.

I had braided all my hair together so it didn't snag anything, pulled on my darkest deerskin clothes, and filled my pockets with soot from my fireplace. Now I could only get my mind off our dangerous undertaking by asking myself the unanswerable questions. How had I known Sir Avery? And what could I have known in the past that even he didn't? And why in the world was he so at odds with Archie's family? If that was even the truth of the matter.

The new member in our group, Jesse with the dark hair and prominent nose, asked, "Is there any way to tell if one of the Escalis happens to be an Epic?" He spoke with the same volume we did,

104

but his voice sounded whiney and hollow, as though he needed to clear his throat.

"Yes," West said, "you'll know Prince Avalask if you see him. He's the one with the fangs and the long hair, so black it can make a dent in the daytime sunlight."

"Thanks, but I wasn't looking to hear a horror story," Jesse said. "I'm worried that we could run across Prince Avalask's son and not even know it. Is there any way to tell the Epic Escali apart from the rest?"

"If you see one using magic," Archie replied, tightening the straps on his own saddle, "then that's the new Epic."

"Something I've actually wondered," West said, "is how you tell Humans and Escalis apart? Obviously you look for the arm spikes. But what if they broke them off? Would you even be able to tell they were Escalis?"

"You would still be able to," I said. "They don't move the same way we do. Their actions are quick, and they jerk their attention around."

"But that's all learned," West said. "They could probably teach themselves to move smoothly like we do."

"They'd still have the cloudy eyes," Archie said. "Once you've seen them, you can't mistake them for anything else. Now let's quit wasting time and go."

My scrawny dragon with sickly green scales worried me from the second he leapt into the air. He struggled to stay aloft, beating his wings three times faster than any of the other four in the troupe. He slowed the entire group down, but he did at least get me there faster than I could have on a horse. Barely any light remained by the time we landed, and I welcomed the ground beneath my feet.

"How long of a walk is this going to be?" I asked, with the dragons secure in the dense brush.

"We'll probably get there around complete darkness," Michael replied. "And as soon as we leave here, there's no more talking, period. Is there anything else we need to get out of the way before we go?"

"Yeah, are we looking for anything in particular?" West asked. He had truly come with no weapons, only a leather bag slung over his back.

"Just general recon of the area. See if there are many Escalis left, how the battle went, *who won...*"

"I think we already know who won," Jesse said. I couldn't pin down what about Jesse bothered me, but my deep instincts told me I needed to watch out for him.

"Nothing's for sure," Archie answered, "and that's why we're here. Now let's go." He left the dragons, and the rest of us followed without further discussion.

Within about twenty minutes we began to slow our pace, and I was the first to spot the walls of Treldinsae just beyond the tall pines. The solid barrier stood at least three times taller than I did, built from jagged stone to warn intruders away. We hardly had any light left to see by; still we hunkered down in the bushes to wait until the sun was completely gone with only moonlight left. I pulled the soot from my pocket and put some on my face as Michael gave us silent instructions, his voice less than a whisper.

We were splitting into two groups and circling around the city to get any information we could. Nothing new.

"See the tallest tree on the other side of the city?" Michael breathed, "We'll meet there and then make another sweep around. Allie and Archie, I'm assuming the two of you want to go together, so take Jesse with you and circle around the west side. I want to head around the east side with West. *You* should change your name so it's not one of my directions," he added.

"Look at the sky," Archie whispered. We lifted our eyes to see three falcons circling over the top of the city, lit by a flickering glow from beneath and silhouetted against two moons.

"Stay out of sight," West said to all of us. "And good luck." We all stood up silently. Archie, Jesse, and I made to go left along the wall while Michael and West turned right.

"Let's stick to the trees," I whispered as I saw an Escali sentry prowling along the top of the wall with a light in hand. He had the same appearance as the ones I had seen in the woods — gleaming sharp teeth and lethal spurs growing from his elbows. Archie nodded when he saw the Escali and we silently pushed ourselves closer to the underbrush. Jesse followed our every move without comment as we stayed crouched and crept around the outer wall. We heard occasional shouts and yells from inside the city, but we couldn't see a single thing.

"We're not getting any information like this!" I whispered as another sentry came patrolling along the wall.

"We definitely know who won the battle..." Jesse said for the second time in low spirits. As soon as no sentries could be seen in either direction, I crept quickly to the wall and felt it. It had been weathered away and the protruding stones looked almost—

"What are you doing?!" Archie whispered frantically as I jumped up and found that it was, indeed, climbable.

"Getting information," I whispered back as I approached the top. I made sure the falcons weren't straight overhead, pulled myself up, and then gazed upon the wreckage of the city.

I could imagine what everything would have looked like before the attack. The stone buildings would have been all different shapes, large and majestic towers would have stood tall, and the trees growing throughout the city wouldn't have been burning. Now however, fires blazed through everything not made of stone, the far walls had crumbled, many of the buildings had been demolished, and I could see Escalis darting like ants whose hill had been disturbed. Some were clearly searching for survivors, others were clearing debris from paths, and a few were piling their dead to be buried — or whatever Escalis did with their dead. Who knew, maybe they ate them.

I looked off to my right and saw the light of another sentry along the wall, so I leapt back down and returned to the trees.

Archie glared at me for my reckless actions. "Well?" he said.

"The whole northern and eastern sides of the wall are knocked down. We definitely got in and did some damage. A whole lot of people and Escalis are dead, but I guess the Escalis still managed to hold the city…"

"Ok, well let's keep going. We have to meet up on the other side."

We crept through the trees until I heard crashing water ahead, clearly in waves rather than currents. The wall came to an abrupt end, opening to what looked like a harbor with two Escali sentries speaking to each other at the end.

"That's the Breathing Sea," Archie whispered.

"So what, this is the harbor or something?"

"It can't be. Nobody can touch the water. The Escalis wouldn't be able to build boats. But the legend of Treldinsae says it has a bridge to the middle of the Breathing Sea, built before the Sea was filled with monsters. If you look closely, you can see it out on the waterfront."

We were too far to make it out clearly, but I could see the tide crashing into some sort of a structure every ten seconds, exploding in white spray.

Jesse asked, "How will we get to the other side of the city to meet up? We'll never pass by that giant gap in the wall."

"What if we swim out a ways, cross beneath the bridge, and come back to shore on the other side?" I said quietly.

Archie gasped a laugh. "Have you been listening? We can't just get in the Breathing Sea. We'd be better off cutting straight through the city."

"Is that *your* brilliant idea? I'm open to hearing a better one."

I didn't get to hear his idea, because just then an Escali shouted from inside the city and both sentries left their posts in response. I looked at Archie and Jesse, thanking our luck, and we crept quietly to their abandoned positions to see the commotion.

Someone shouted out in agony as we peered around the corner of the wall. The Escalis had found a man — a Human man — half buried in a pile of debris. The sentries had left the other edge of the wall to assist also, and I saw it as our best chance of crossing unseen.

Jesse was hesitant, so I pulled him down to the wet sand — as far from the light as possible — and we ran to the other side. We lingered at the other corner in hopes of seeing where they would take him once they got him free, but they still had a ways to go in pulling him out.

Even though his legs were still half buried, they grabbed him and heaved him up as he yelled and struggled against them. He was already injured, and now the skin on his legs had been severely mangled as well. Two of the Escalis tried to tie something to one of his wrists while the others watched, but he fought against them, swearing loudly.

The two snarled and threw him onto the ground. One jumped on him and viciously bit into the back of his neck while the other one backed off.

I could feel my blood begin to boil as we were forced to retreat from our vantage point, hearing screams and what was unmistakable laughter from the Escalis.

Archie's face was frozen in horror. I couldn't find my own breath to say anything, and Jesse simply bolted ahead toward the meeting point. We ran until we saw West and Michael, where Jesse frantically started in on the story.

"We just saw a—"

"Shhhhh," Michael shushed him.

"But we just saw—"

"Shhhhh. We need to fall back to a place where we can talk."

We retreated deep into the forest before Jesse turned on Michael and exclaimed, "You didn't warn me about anything like this when you convinced me to come along!"

"Keep your voice low," Michael warned.

West asked, "What happened?"

I quickly explained, "The three of us saw a man dragged out from under a collapsed building."

Jesse added, "He wouldn't let them tie him up so they bit him, and he was bleeding, and screaming, and I never wanted to see something like that!"

"At least they didn't kill him," Archie said.

"Actually, they've taken a lot of people alive," West said, "and we saw where they're putting them. They're near the western wall in one of the remaining buildings, where you guys were."

Archie said, "We could get to them if we had a good enough distraction."

"There are about a hundred horses tethered right outside the northeastern wall. Cutting them loose would be a good distraction," West said.

"Wait…" Jesse interrupted the planning. "We don't have to save anybody." He stopped talking when he realized we were all watching him.

He was right, of course. We *would* have better chances of making it home if we didn't try to save them. But I wasn't sure if I could live with the guilt of leaving them to the Escalis.

So for me, this was a defining moment. For the first time since waking up in the woods, I didn't care how my former self would have chosen to proceed. I was done trying to identify with Old Allie, trying to make the decisions she would have made. I was

New Allie now, and I had to choose what I wanted to do, not for the sake of recovering who I used to be, but for the sake of moving on.

I met the gaze of every person in the circle and said, "Let's do this."

I locked eyes with Archie last. He didn't smile at me, but his eyes held a proud grin of their own, as though my bravery was worthy of admiration. "Alright," he said, turning his conspiring gaze to the rest of the group. "There are five of us. Two people can free the horses, two can get in to let the prisoners out, and somebody else can start running right now, get back to the dragons, and fly them over to meet the people on the horses."

"Great idea," Michael said. "And the people on the horses can lead the Escalis in the exact opposite direction of the Dragona. This might work."

Archie said, "Jesse, are you going to be able to get on the horses to cause a distraction?"

Jesse gawked at Archie. "As bait so the Escalis can chase after me? I don't want to *die*! I didn't sign up for this."

"Then you can go with West to grab the dragons for us, right?" Michael said.

Jesse said, "I'll go grab the dragons, but I'm taking mine straight home. Look, we did what we came here to do. I'm not going on this suicide run with the rest of you."

West said, "I'll go with Jesse to grab the dragons, and I'll convince him to quit being a coward along the way. Once we have them, where should we meet you?"

Michael replied, "Meet us on the top of that hill. I'll be the one to spook the horses so Allie and Archie can stay together. My chances are best when I don't have anybody slowing me down, and if any of us has to fight the Escalis, those two probably have the best hope of living through it."

"You want Allie and me to go into the city?" Archie asked. I thought I sensed disbelief, but I wasn't sure why. That wouldn't be any more dangerous than Michael's role in the plan.

"It makes the most sense," Michael said.

"The people you're going in to rescue are in the giant dome building near the wall," West told us. "The doors are a very dark wood, and one of them has been torn halfway off. Hopefully Michael can draw enough attention with the horses to keep the guards from noticing you. The whole city is thick with patrols, which you won't be able to kill or escape if they see you."

"Actually, look what I found," Archie said, pulling out a bundle of arrows with a piece of cloth wrapped around the heads. "We have a defense against them now." He unwrapped the cloth to reveal the strangest arrowheads I had ever seen. They were each a swirling glow of neon colors, shining brightly in the dark.

"Escali stunners!" Michael's face lit up. "Where did you get them?"

"Yeah, where did you get those?" Jesse asked.

"They were right next to the wall at the harbor, where the sentries abandoned their posts for a second," Archie said. "Didn't you see me grab them?"

"No, but oh well. How do they work?" I asked.

"The tips are made of some kind of Escali magic, and when they touch living flesh they disappear, leaving the victim incapacitated."

"So they work on Escalis too?" I asked.

"They work on everybody."

"You guys can take the bow then," Michael said, handing it over.

"Ok. We have sixteen arrows, so once we're in, we can only be seen by sixteen Escalis before we're done for," Archie said. "We'll go back down to the wall and climb into the city as soon as you take the horses."

"I'm not helping with this," Jesse said one last time.

"Don't worry, Jesse, we'll be fine without you," Archie said. "I think we're ready."

Jesse turned and left us. Before West followed him, he said, "Good luck to all three of you. And don't worry — I'll change his mind."

He took off after Jesse; then Archie, Michael, and I met each other's nervous glances.

"I can't believe we're doing this," I said.

"Best of luck," Michael said. "I'll be riding for my life until the horse gets tired, then I'll be running. Don't go in until you hear the horses making noise. And if the Escalis don't fall for the distraction, don't go in at all."

"Alright, just stay alive," Archie said.

"Don't let them catch you," I added.

Michael turned very slowly toward his edge of the city, then took off at his incredible sprint. Archie and I departed a few seconds later to find the building West had described.

We treaded lightly to where the northern gates of the city had been reduced to rubble and the inner buildings were visible. Archie pointed to the dome West had mentioned, and I nodded. Escalis were scattered everywhere, still pulling away at the remnants of buildings, but they all froze to listen at exactly the same moment, alert to the sound of at least a hundred spooked horses.

CHAPTER TWELVE

A sentry right inside the ruined wall had crouched into a ready stance to watch the commotion. Archie shot him with one of the arrows, and we watched him slowly keel off a small pile of debris. We climbed silently through the gaping wound in the wall, able to see Michael take off at a full gallop, and the Escalis immediately sprinted after him, truly as fast as he was.

We climbed down the wall unseen as even more chaos and snarling ensued among those who had seen him escape. West and Jesse needed to be quick getting those dragons because I could hear the Escalis strategizing group tactics to cut Michael off.

"Archie," I whispered, pointing to the smooth inside of the wall as we moved to where it was still intact. "We can't climb back out."

"Don't worry about it. I've got an idea," he replied, stealing forward to the cover of the buildings.

I followed Archie around a few corners, and the only Escali to see us was quickly sent into unconsciousness. We stopped at the edge of what seemed to be a house, and I could see two Escalis guarding the entrance of the domed building. Archie paused.

"If I shoot one of them, the other one will react faster than anything..." he said.

"Here, give me an arrow," I said, reaching to grab one.

"What are you doing?"

"I'll take out the one on the left. You get the one on the right."

"You're going to sneak up and touch him?" Archie whispered.

"Yes. Be ready."

I was extremely careful to check for Escali patrols before I circled back around our building and darted across the dirt road. Now I was on the back side of the structure we were trying to get into. I slowly edged to the corner, where I knew the sentries stood guard. Archie, reading my thoughts, had already drawn an arrow, ready to step into the open to join me.

I whipped myself around the corner and jabbed at the closest Escali as Archie shot the other. The arrowheads dissipated and both monsters fell where they stood.

"Hurry, grab them and drag them inside!" he said, running over to grab one. The Escali I tried to move was unimaginably heavy, but I managed to drag him through the busted doors. Inside we found a great spacious ceiling, grey stone walls, and the entrance to a hallway on the other end of the floor.

"Are you sure this is the right place?" I asked dropping the Escali with an echoing thud.

"This is where West told us to go… They must be down that hallway." For being so sure, I saw concern on his face.

We skittishly crossed the floor, entered the passage, and still saw no one. The hallway turned into a steep winding staircase. We both hesitantly descended, seeing no one until we got to the bottom.

About fifty people sat along the ground, their wrists tied together. Instead of being alone like we hoped, at least ten Escalis were in the room, a few of them sharpening their blades to pass the time.

We jerked back around the last bend before any of them had seen us and exchanged looks of worry.

"I didn't know there would be that many Escalis," Archie breathed.

"What are we going to do? If we shoot them all, we'll only have two or three arrows left."

"You assume we *could* shoot them all."

Footsteps approached from the room and we started backing silently up the staircase. Archie handed me half of the arrows, and when two Escalis came around the bend they didn't have the chance to see us before we touched them with the tips and they crumpled.

"I don't see any other choice," I said as the Escalis toppled down a couple stairs before coming to a rest. Surely none of the other monsters had heard with all the commotion outside.

Archie said, "Here, you take the bow and shoot at them from the doorway. I'll take a few arrows and stop anyone who tries to get to you."

"Ok," I said, taking the bow from him. Having the bow in my hand was a familiar feeling, and I knew I could use it. We edged back down to the doorway and I took aim toward the Escali closest to us to get him out of the way first.

As soon as I fired, I had the next arrow ready and flying without looking to see if they were hitting. It only felt like five seconds before the pile was gone and I had hit every Escali in the room.

Archie gaped at me. "Are you serious? Here you've been letting *me* do the shooting?"

I smiled and shrugged it off as I pulled out one of my swords and cut the ropes off a rugged woman's hands.

The overbearing man whom Archie had just cut free stood up, rubbing his wrists. He had a large head with the strangest facial piercings I had ever seen — jewelry protruded from between his eyes and next to his nose, among other places. He said, "Thanks kids. We can take it from here now."

Archie and I exchanged brief glances. *Kids?*

"Ok," Archie said, clearly irritated, "but let us show you the way out. The wall is —"

116

"Really son, I thank you for coming in here and helping, but now that we're free, you had better let the adults do the thinking." Archie raised his eyebrows, not about to accept the man's supposed authority.

"Do you want our help at all?"

"Well, now that you mention it, those arrows you're holding would—"

"Here, take them," Archie said. He promptly handed over his remaining arrows. "And why don't you take Allie's bow too?" I was appalled to have to give it up, and I couldn't believe Archie had just… *volunteered* it like that. I felt my sense of security leave as soon as it left my hands.

"You don't know what's going on out there," I tried to reason. "We can tell you where is safe and where isn't. When you get outside—"

"Listen, sweet, we killed the majority of the Escalis when we came in, so trust me when I say I can lead us—"

"You're from Tekada, aren't you?" Archie asked abruptly. "You're one of the commanders Kelian appointed."

"That's King Kelian to you, boy."

I felt Archie surreptitiously reach over and grab my hand. "Our military would be twice what it is now if Kelian would leave it to the competent leaders. If this lot wants to follow you, you can go ahead and get them killed any way you like. We're going to make it out of here alive."

The man was just about to retort when Archie jerked my arm with him — we were making a run for it back up the stairs. We jumped over the sleeping bodies of the two we had downed in the hallway and ran all the way up to the room above. The man we had left behind wasn't stupid. He didn't shout after us or even come chasing. He had realized too late that we weren't sticking around.

"Shanking Tekadans," Archie muttered. "The Dincarans should have already overthrown anybody appointed by Kelian. Dincarans are always the strong fighters, the intelligent ones. I can't believe they let a Tekadan take charge!"

Archie's hatred for King Kelian just didn't matter to me at the moment, so I ignored the rant. The Escalis we had dragged inside earlier were still void of consciousness, and we left them that way as we peeked out the doorway to make sure all was clear.

The biggest moon illuminated the whole world with its greenish glow, and we pulled back to avoid a large group of Escalis sprinting by. As soon as they passed, we started making our way back to the destroyed section of the wall. "Oh no," I said, seeing at least five new brutes next to our escape route.

Before Archie could respond, a grey flecked falcon swooped down and landed on a charred window frame very close to us. It watched us with a cocked head, not yet making noise.

"Don't move," Archie said, almost so quietly that I couldn't hear him. I didn't need him to tell me. I was frozen. The falcon watched us for about a minute until another one screeched within the city and this one took off to join it.

Maybe the falcon also thought we were too young to be a threat?

I stared after it, open-mouthed, until Archie grabbed my attention. "We need to get out of sight and lay low until that bird forgets us," he said. I was in total agreement until I realized he meant *let's hide in this building.* He pushed a door open and I dashed inside with him, although I felt certain that entering an Escali's home was an awful idea. How did we even know it would be empty?

A minor corner of the room had crumbled apart during the attack, right next to an ascending staircase. I immediately found myself hunched next to the chink in the wall, peering out to see three more Escalis running past.

"That was too close," I whispered. I glanced over my shoulder to see Archie staring hard at the door. Redwood tables of many levels were arranged about the room, and one wall held an array of

118

Escali knives, swords, and staves. Nothing else resided in the stone chamber. "How do we get out of here?" I asked him. "This house, the whole city…"

He took his eyes off the door to look at me, and then several things happened as he began to say, "Allie, I think I have to tell you something."

Please be an Epic, I thought as he spoke. *Say you can get us out of here.*

And *BRUM! BRUM! BRUM! BRUM!* at the door cut him off.

The thunderous hammering terrified me as the Escali outside snarled, "Get out here, Tally!"

I should wonder what *Tally* meant, but I didn't have time.

Archie shook his head and took a short breath. "It doesn't matter right now. There's a second door here behind the staircase. Let's get out of here."

We exited within seconds, before the predators got the chance to surround the house, and my voice squeaked embarrassingly as I asked, "Where are we going to go?"

"I don't know," Archie said as we darted behind a building and pressed ourselves against it. I pointed out a dim crevice where a chunk of demolished roof rested against the crumbling structure it had previously topped. We both sped into the hiding place and crouched in the shadows.

"What are we going to do?" I asked, trying to keep the panic from my voice.

The stress on his face was equally worrisome. "I don't know. They've got too many guards near the destroyed section of the wall."

"They've only got a couple next to the Breathing Sea," I said. "And we have to get out before the Dincarans do something stupid and the Escalis swarm this area."

"You want to go to the harbor of the Breathing Sea?" he said in dismay.

Instead of answering aloud, I peeked around the corner of our hideout and dashed into the next shadowy crevice of the city, glad we hadn't come to Treldinsae in the light of day, but still wishing the moon wasn't quite so full. Archie came with me, and we hopped between a few more buildings before I heard a rough call from behind us. "They're over here, trying to escape."

This Escali didn't seem particularly bloodthirsty. He just followed after us as though keeping track of an annoyance, waiting for somebody else. I, on the other hand, adopted a dead sprint toward the split in the wall where I knew the Breathing Sea crashed upon the shore. Archie kept up with me, and we caught the attention of every Escali we flew past, practically gone by the time they comprehended the instinct to chase us. I did flick my head around long enough to see the quick pursuit of a new enemy, but I then had to leap over a pile of fallen bricks and my next three steps fell on a rough gash in the road. I almost tripped in the rubble, so I kept my eyes ahead of me, horrified to know that I recognized one of the pursuers.

We rapidly came to the wide opening of Treldinsae's wall where the water lapped at the bridge, rocks, and sand.

"Don't touch the water!" Archie exclaimed. We both skidded to a full stop, mere cubits from the foam of the last wave. The bridge was attached to a few of the larger jagged rocks, but the waves came far past where the structure met the land, leaving water between us and the bridge. The Escalis on each side of the open walls regarded us with eyes that wanted to kill as our pursuers arrived behind us. No dead end had ever been as dire, with Escalis on three sides and the Breathing Sea.

I could tell by the way the wall guards hesitated that the two Escalis tailing us were highly regarded, even though they seemed younger than the rest. Each had hair darker than a moonless midnight, as Prince Avalask himself was rumored to have. The one with hair spiked at all angles atop his thin face stepped toward us, his knees bent, ready to spring. He looked exactly the same as he had the day he attacked us in the woods. The second Escali, burly with tied back hair, the one who had ripped the woman's throat out, stood behind him.

Without moving his mouth, Archie breathed, "Allie, you can draw blood from Escalis if they're not adults yet. We have a chance."

CHAPTER THIRTEEN

he bristle-haired Escali pulled his upper lip back into a vicious grin. "Tallies don't deserve to live in this world," he said. Most Escalis spoke roughly, probably from their years of snarling, but his voice was lethally sharp — leaving a razor-thin cut in my heart where panic could leak in. I wasn't even sure when I had pulled my short swords out, but I had them ready.

I noticed from the corner of my eye that the last wave from the Breathing Sea had receded particularly far. The bridge was within jumping distance!

"Archie, come on!" I said, grabbing his arm just long enough to get him moving with me. I got as much of a running start as I could manage before leaping over the remaining water.

I barely heard Archie warn, "No, we can't!" before I landed with a thud on the speckled granite face of the bridge. He landed next to me within the next few seconds, all objections forgotten. The edge of the bridge was lined with piers taller than I was, but in the great space between them, one could easily step right over the edge and fall into the Sea.

My first few steps slipped beneath me in my haste to take off, even though the stone bridge was completely dry. Archie and I only made it as far as the third pillar before the two Escalis with the unnaturally dark hair thudded onto the granite behind us. Archie grabbed my arm to stop me. "We don't have a chance of outrunning them."

I had my short swords at the ready, but I expected to have a spare second of panic before the Escalis jumped us. I didn't get one.

The growling Escali with the spiked hair pulled a bladed staff from his back and collided with Archie, but I had no idea what happened to him past that because the burlier of the two monsters made a grab for me, not even holding a weapon. I ducked into a crouch with surprising speed, using the blade in my right hand to slash at the monster with his hair tied roughly back. He darted to the side to avoid my swipe, then lowered his shoulder and charged straight into me, catching me in the middle and crushing me into one of the pillars lining the bridge.

The bone-crunching crash knocked hope itself out of me, and I hunched immediately forward against him, unable to even gasp for air. One of my swords hit the ground with a devastating clink, but I drew my other arm above my head to get the tip of my remaining blade to the Escali's neck. I drove it forward, hoping to kill the beast, but he jerked himself quickly back from me. Even without his weight pinning me, I still couldn't draw a breath.

My opponent was merciless, dashing to the side and lunging forward. Instead of crashing into me again, he grabbed my wrists, twisting my hands sharply to make me drop the second blade. In the same motion, he turned to the side and used his momentum and brute strength to flip me over, slamming me onto my back and rattling my very thoughts. I rolled quickly away from him and onto my feet, but before I could even begin to stand he tackled me back to the granite.

I wasn't fast enough to be considered the slightest threat.

The Escali was so close I could see the dark storm clouds in his irises and feel his spit as he snarled at me and clamped his hands around my neck. I still couldn't breathe from being crushed — he

123

didn't need to strangle me too.

I had my hands wrapped around his, trying to pull the pressure from my throat, aware that I didn't have a chance. All I could muster was a pathetic gasp as he murdered me. I could see Archie still locked in combat with the other Escali, his eyes alive with a hatred I had never seen in them. I was starting to notice the noises around me dimming, and then I saw Archie kick his enemy back into one of the bridge columns. Seeing the action was becoming a strain on my eyes as well.

Archie abandoned that fight long enough to take a stab at the Escali holding me down as I noticed two dragons approaching us in the starry sky. The burly Escali I hadn't been able to deal with let go of me and instantly brought one of my forgotten swords up to parry Archie's attack. The thinner monster then jumped back onto Archie from behind and knocked him to the ground. They both struggled to get back to their feet and keep the other down, and I had already twisted myself onto my stomach and dug my elbows into the chinks between granite blocks, dragging myself away from the Escali so I could get up again.

I expected to be crushed within the next second, but Archie got the upper hand against his opponent, and all commotion suddenly stopped. They were standing again, and Archie was holding him against one of the pillars, blade at his throat, spitting through his teeth as he growled a hateful warning at the monster.

The Escali was muttering something, getting louder each time he repeated it. "Kill the dragons, kill the dragons, KILL THE DRAGONS!"

The thicker Escali finally took the hint and launched my blade like a javelin at the dragons just as they reached us. No longer watching, I grabbed the edge of the bridge to pull myself on my belly toward my other dropped sword, but I knew the Escali's throw struck true. A distressed roar ripped through the air and the entire structure beneath me shook as something large crashed onto it.

I had just grabbed my sword and pulled my knees beneath me into a crawling position when I saw the pony-tailed Escali leap for me again. This time when he knocked me back down, I threw all my weight in the same direction as his momentum and succeeded in rolling him over and landing on top. Never had a victory been so short lived. I growled through my teeth at him and he snarled back, grabbing my weapon arm and then throwing me back down beneath him. My head and shoulders were off the edge of the bridge now. He wrenched the sword from my hand and dug the tip of it into my neck, making me crane my head back and grit my teeth together.

At least four voices exclaimed "WATCH THE HAIR!" in multiple languages.

I snapped my head sideways to see the water beneath me, and the motion pulled my braid up just in time to miss a passing wave from the Breathing Sea.

The Escali jerked his attention over his shoulder, and I struggled to keep my head high and my hair out of the water as an invisible force blasted him off of me. I was quick to sit up and push myself back to my feet. Although my mind spun and compressed in response to the sudden stand, I was still able to see West next to a dead dragon, his hands outstretched. He and Michael had shown up. The Escali who had been suffocating me leapt back to his feet, but was flung backward again at the flick of West's hands.

I wanted to exclaim, *you found your power!* but I had to take a second to hunch over with my hands on my knees and gasp air into my lungs.

The Escali landed roughly and rolled past where Archie and the spikey-haired villain were dueling once again. Now Michael had joined Archie as well, and the combined speed and skill of the two of them was enough to push the Escali back toward land. The pony-tailed Escali West had just thrown off me bared his teeth in a livid rage, and he snarled over his shoulder, "Shoot them! Shoot!"

I saw two Escalis from across the water take aim. "Look out!" I shrieked, finally at the point of forming words again. West ran forward and flicked his hands out, knocking the arrows straight off their courses, but he missed one. Michael's scream turned into a string of obscene curses as the arrow hit him in the side and West's power knocked the Escali violently back. Michael dropped back from the fight, clutching his side as blood began to stain the ripped hole, and I dashed forward to help hold him up. The spiky haired one disengaged from his furious battle with Archie and shouted, "Just get back! Their mages won't be able to find them if they cross the bridge."

Both Escalis turned in a flash and leapt back to land, and Archie took no hesitation in grabbing Michael to help hold him up as well. West used his newfound power to deflect the next arrows shot at us as we helped Michael hobble farther from the predators. Michael exclaimed through a grimace, "That coward of a dragon left us here!"

"And the other one's dead! We're going to have to retreat across this bridge," West yelled over the crashing of the waves beneath us and the taunting from the Escalis on the shore. "We don't have another choice."

Archie told West, "We're going. Just blast them back again if they try to follow." I retreated with them and hardly had a split second to cringe as I wrenched my sword out of the dead dragon's side, letting go of Michael since Archie had him.

I whispered "I'm sorry" to the dragon as I sheathed the sword. I grabbed Michael's other side again to help him move faster, and the four of us beat a hasty retreat.

The Escalis didn't follow us — one of the first things to go right in a night of failures.

So many thoughts whirred through my head that I was taken aback to see the bridge connecting to moonlit land ahead of us.

Treldinsae had already vanished behind us in the dark.

"Is this an island?" I asked, still holding Michael up. West still followed behind us to make sure the Escalis couldn't pursue, and none had.

Archie said, "This is the Everarc island, where they found the crystal that cursed the entire Sea."

The end of the bridge was buried in what would have been a golden beach if we weren't seeing it in the dead of night. A sandy slope led from the bridge to higher elevations, and the rest of the island seemed to be bordered by a giant cliff that walled off the Breathing Sea waves. A few trees had grown scattered in the sand, and the ground was dotted with tough clumps of grass.

"We need to figure out what else is on this island," Archie said as we stepped into the fine sand.

"I think I'll stay here and hold the crossing," Michael groaned, breaking away from us to sit against one of the trees.

"I'll stay with him," West said, "since I can keep the Escalis from getting across the bridge. Allie and Archie, you two had better come back as soon as you can. We're going to need the world's two greatest fighters here if anything shows up to kill us."

"Just keep the Escalis back," Archie said. "Nothing from the Sea should bother us as long as we don't touch the water."

"And we'll be back as soon as we can," I said, turning to climb the sandy embankment.

I added quietly to myself, "Although, calling us both the best fighters may be an overstatement."

"I heard that," Archie said, stepping only on the clumps of grass in the sand to get traction. "Allie, you were incredible against those Escalis. Don't you dare think otherwise."

"You actually defeated yours at one point," I said, rather than argue that I wasn't as competent as I had hoped. "*And* you managed to keep the second one from killing me."

"My Escali wasn't as good of a fighter, and Allie, that's what friends are for. Had we switched opponents, you would have been saving me from that bigger one too."

"Yeah, I guess so," I said, feeling strangely better. We reached the top of the island, and I held on to a tree near the cliff's edge where I could see a huge stretch of the bridge. I breathed a sigh of relief when I found no Escalis trying to cross, and I turned back to Archie to see that he was already reliving the fight in his mind. Hatred began sinking into his eyes as he explored, so I left him alone for a little while.

We moved north, following the cliff, but within ten minutes we'd circled to the south side of the small island. Even with the terror of being pursued, I couldn't help but catch my breath at the sight of ten thousand stars overhead, resilient enough to shine despite having two brilliant moons to compete against. I hoped the beauty of the sky would never be lost on me, no matter my situation.

Archie had also used the silence to calm down, and when he glanced back to make sure I was coming, I asked, "Do you think we can find where the Everarc Crystal used to be?"

"Probably," Archie said, climbing a small rock pile to see over the short trees around us. "There would have been a cave left behind from where the crystal was excavated."

"How big of a cave?" I asked, walking along the southern cliff line. "Are we talking a little rabbit hole, or a tama cat den?"

"I don't know," he said as he pushed through a large growth of brush. "But I don't think we should go looking for it." Rather than ask why, I just shot Archie a questioning look, and he sighed when he saw it. "You remember the story about the Everarcs, and how they give magic to the world, right?"

"Yes."

"Shadar mentioned that there was barely any magic in the land before the Everarcs, because they were encased in magic-resistant rock. When they took the Everarcs out, everything became the exact

128

opposite. The magic was out in the world then, while the excavations where the crystals *used to be* became void of magic. Does that make sense?"

"It does," I said. "And I could see how that would be dangerous, since we're both going to be mages and the caves would be void of magic. But could it really be worse than crossing back over the Escali bridge or trying to swim across the Breathing Sea?" I asked.

Archie gave me a smirk in response. "Maybe not, but it isn't going to get us off this island either."

"I know what might," I said, climbing onto a large boulder embedded along the edge of the cliff. Archie came over to join me and saw the same moonlit land I could see across the water. Trees, sand, bushes with old silvery mosses hanging from the branches — it was the way to get off the island. The strait of water was no wider than a small river, which somebody could swim across in about two minutes without a current. Not me, but somebody.

"It's almost cruel how close that land is," Archie said. "I know it looks like hope, but we still can't touch the water."

"We may not have to," I said, pointing to a cove at the bottom of the rocky cliff, sheltering a pocket of water from the Sea. It even had a steep trail leading down to it and a patch of sand and trees nearby that almost glittered beneath the stars.

"That's got to be the cave where they dug out the Everarc Crystal," Archie said, seeing the same hope I did, bobbing in the water as a wave swept past. "That's the only way there could be a boat in the water."

I skidded down the sandy slope near the bridge with more optimism than I had left with. Archie wanted us to forget about the small carved boat, but I was eager to get back to Michael and West to tell them the news.

West met us before we got to Michael and immediately said, "You guys, I pulled the arrow out and wrapped his side as tightly

129

as I could, but I don't know anything else about healing. I just know he looks awful. We need to get him out of here."

"We might be able to," I said, but Archie cut me off before I could mention the narrow strait of water.

"Jesse will be getting back to the Dragona sometime soon," Archie said. "As soon as he does, the mages will know to look for us and bring us home."

"The mages won't find us out here," I said. "That Escali said so. That's the only reason they didn't follow us."

"What do you mean he said so?" West asked. "You must have the power to understand other languages, Allie. They were definitely speaking Escalira."

"Maybe it is my power," I said, "because I have no doubt that's what I heard."

We all whipped our heads back toward the beach as Michael shouted, "ESCALIS ON THE BRIDGE!"

The three of us swore quietly and ran back toward Michael to help. Archie was the only one with a real sword left. I didn't know what I was going to do with just one short sword. I saw Michael, still against the tree, but I didn't see any Escalis on the bridge. West quickly pulled a sheathed dagger from his pack and handed it to me. "You need it more than I do," he said.

"Where are they?" I asked, quickly flinging the sheath to the ground.

"They're not here," Michael replied, holding his side. "I just don't want you guys talking about me while I'm not there."

I leaned against a tree and waited for my pulse to calm. West, however, shouted, "I hate you! Do that again, and I will push you into the water!"

"We found a boat," I said before somebody else could make a retort. "And this island comes really close to the main shore on the south end."

West, Michael, and Archie turned to look at me, instantly

130

focused on my news. I could tell Archie still didn't want to consider it a possibility, but West squinted skeptically and said, "I thought nobody could build boats in the Breathing Sea."

"It's in a cove," Archie said. "We think it's the Everarc Cave, otherwise the boat would have been demolished when something in the water caught sight of it."

"But the fact that a boat is down there must mean something," West said, sounding hopeful.

"Look look look look look!" Michael said, pointing back to where we had come from. This time when we looked, we actually saw a black falcon swiftly tearing through the air over the bridge, only visible because its wings blacked out a few stars at a time. It reached the island where it clearly saw us, then swept in a tight circle to fly back toward land on exactly the same route.

Archie said, "Do you see that? The Escali falcons won't even *fly* over the water of the Breathing Sea. Trying to get in a boat will be suicide."

"What about Michael?" I asked. "We can't just wait out here for help."

"He's fine. Just look at him," West said, brushing that to the side. "He'll die of starvation before that wound kills him. Trust me." I knew West didn't believe that for a second.

Michael said, "If this gets infected and spreads, I may never be able to run again. I would rather be dead, so we need to get off this island. Now."

"We will be dead if we try to cross the Breathing Sea," Archie repeated. "Let's just give it until morning. Please. If nobody from the Dragona comes to get us by then, we'll reconsider."

"Fine," Michael said, wincing as he tried to get to his feet. "Now somebody help me to the top of the cliff."

I kept a close eye on the bridge while Archie and West carried Michael to the higher elevations, but I also couldn't help glancing at West's dagger in my hand. The blade had wolves, falcons, and a rabbit carved in among the detailed foliage. I had never seen anything like it.

I climbed the hill minutes later, still watching for Escalis, and at the top I heard West asking, "Should we build a fire?"

"No reason not to," Archie said. "The Escalis already know exactly where we are."

I tried to hand West's dagger back as we began our search for sticks to burn, but he said, "Hold onto it. Tightly. My grandfather gave it to me. He said he killed an Escali once and took the dagger from its dead hands."

"Was he a mage?" I asked, tucking the dagger into the lacing of my sandals.

"No," West replied, pulling flint and steel from his bag. "I just happen to be from a long line of Dincaran Escali killers."

That caught Archie's attention as he dropped an armload of sticks he'd already gathered. "You're from Dincara?"

"Did I never mention that?" West asked, seeming genuinely surprised. "I usually flaunt it whenever I can. Couldn't be prouder."

"I have friends from Dincara," Archie said, his voice taking on new life at the mention of his friends. "Best fighters I've ever met in my life. They taught me most of what I know."

"Well of course they were," West said, stacking the twigs into a pyramid. "Did they ever show you their tattoos?"

Archie laughed. "I'm not sure a day ever went by *without* them showing their tattoos."

"You have a tattoo?" I asked, my voice flat with disbelief.

West didn't wear an undershirt beneath his sleeveless jerkin like the rest of us, so he easily pulled the leather aside to reveal a black spider painted on his shoulder. "It's just the Dincaran spider, everybody has one," he said, striking flint and steel together to make a shower of sparks. "And let me tell you, I've never regretted coming to the Dragona," his pile of sticks began smoking and a

132

small flame came to life beneath them, "but there are times when I see a body of water that isn't my ocean, and it sure makes me miss home."

The fire warmed my cold hands and was perfectly positioned for us to keep watch over the waterfront, but it gave me little comfort. I couldn't gaze at the popping and crackling driftwood for more than five seconds without turning to check the bridge again. No Escalis.

The silence had drawn on for long enough. I called, "First watch," and moved away from the fire so I could keep my eyes on the bridge without getting too cozy.

I ended up on my stomach, resting my chin on folded hands where I could see the granite walkway below. Archie and West stretched out next to the fire and Michael curled in against himself. I heard a venomous hiss resonate from the Breathing Sea, and I hoped nobody else had heard it. Sleeping would be even harder with the sounds of danger playing amidst our dreams.

Time ebbed away as I watched the foamy waves slam against sharp black rocks, and I lamented the fact that none of my old memories had come back. If being chased down and pummeled by Escalis wasn't dangerous enough to reawaken my past, nothing was. *Except maybe the Breathing Sea*, I thought, watching the water explode into mist. We still had to escape *it*.

I didn't know if Archie woke up or had never fallen asleep, but after a few hours he joined me on the cliff to watch the empty bridge.

"I know what those Escalis said," I told Archie. "They said our mages wouldn't be able to find us on this island."

"I know," he said. "I believe you. The Dragona's mages would already be here if they were coming."

I readjusted my hands so the rocks no longer jabbed them as sharply. "Isn't the Escali Epic blocking all of Treldinsae from the mages? Maybe he's blocking this island from being seen as well."

"Could be. Let's just hope our mages can track us down as soon as we get to the mainland."

"You're considering crossing the Sea then?" I asked, glancing up at him.

"I'm equally considering cutting back across the bridge," he replied flatly.

"Can the monsters in the Breathing Sea really be as bad as the Escalis?"

"Worse. I'll bet you can't even hear the Sirens out there, can you?"

I listened closely but shook my head. I could only hear waves crashing into the rocks. "What are Sirens?"

"Beautiful sea women," Archie replied, staring vacantly ahead. "And they sing. I heard one singing a little while ago, the most beautiful songs you could imagine."

"I don't think I heard any songs," I said, feeling left out and curious.

"The singing doesn't affect girls, but for us, a Siren song makes us want to jump into the Sea, swim down to the depths, and stay there forever. Lucky you, you don't have to resist it."

"So I'll probably be the safest getting in the boat then?"

"No, because the Sirens are vile, made entirely of jealousy. They kill any girl they find simply so no other man can ever fall in love with her. That's one of the reasons we're not supposed to go near the Breathing Sea. Guys are put under the spell of a false, never-ending love, and girls are murdered for being anywhere near the water."

The beginnings of daylight started creeping up the horizon ahead of us. I said, "They still don't sound worse than the Escalis."

Archie laughed and said, "The Sirens are just one monster in the Breathing Sea. I've heard so many stories. About snaky fish called eels that can swarm out and shock you. Clear jellyfish with tentacles that sting you until you die. Something called an octopus, with eight arms to strangle you. Fish that look like dogs and rip you apart because they like carrying around the limbs. And those are just some of the small ones."

"How big are the big ones?"

Archie's thoughtful frown told me he wasn't sure he even believed what he was telling me. "When the Breathing Sea was first tainted, they say the ships in the water were swallowed whole by gigantic water lizards with plated armor on their backs. I think they're still in the depths. And there were water dragons, like gigantic snakes, that were able to breathe fire underwater. The tiniest drop of blood in the water would send them into a frenzy from a mile away. Even the plants down there want to kill you. The shores are lined with thistleweed. If you touch so much as one leaf, you come down with a delusional fever for three days and die."

"Alright, alright," I said. "It's dangerous. That boat has to be there for a reason though."

"And I'm still hoping our mages get here so we don't have to find out," Archie said. "Why don't you get an hour of sleep and I can watch the bridge."

"I could probably use it," I said, moving back to the fire. "Wake me up if you need anything." I threw another dried chunk of wood on the coals and settled in.

Of course, falling asleep was nearly impossible with such a beehive of thoughts buzzing about, so I just lay thinking. Thinking about Treldinsae, wondering if the Dincarans made it out of the city, thinking about every monster I had just heard of, along with the ones I had so recently faced.

When Archie thought we were all asleep, I heard him softly whistling the part of the duskflyer song he liked so much. Nothing bad could be happening as long as I could hear it, so I was finally able to drift off.

I woke to find daylight blazing through the branches of the one leafy tree above me, and I blinked my eyes several times. Michael and West slept soundly, but Archie had disappeared. I double checked the bridge for Escalis, squinting against the bright reflection coming off the water, and Archie showed up seconds later to sit on a mossy rock next to me.

He gazed silently over the water as I rubbed the sleep out of my eyes and asked, "What's the plan?"

Archie shook his head slowly, fixing his eyes on the bridge. "I don't know… We might as well go now if we're going to do it. No sense waiting until we're all faint from thirst."

My neck was stiff from sleeping on the ground, a discomfort I was reminded of as I nodded in agreement. "What have you got there?" I pointed at Archie's closed fist.

He held up the dozen brightly colored flowers and said, "These are for you."

I was awake now!

"Oh," I said, closing my fingers slowly around the stems. I wanted to scream at him, *you're doing this now?* Instead, I stammered, "Well… thank you."

He smiled at my attempt to avoid blushing and saved me the trouble. "They're breakfast," he said. "They only grow around the Sea."

"Well then, thanks for breakfast," I said, holding them up in a toast. If this had been anyone but Archie, the moment would have been fantastically awkward. But all was fine among friends. Right?

I bit into one of the small buds and found it sweet and rosy.

Archie shook West to wake him, but West didn't take kindly to the bright light and almost knocked Archie into the fizzled fire before realizing where he was. I had a small laugh and was glad to see the commotion wake Michael. Archie had breakfast for them as well, but neither seemed particularly hungry.

"Guys," Michael said, setting his brunch bouquet in the dirt.

"Why don't you just put me in the boat and give me a good push into the water. Somebody's got to try to get across. I have the least to lose right now."

"And then you get to the other side and hobble back to the Dragona alone?" I asked. "I don't think so. I'll go."

"How about we all go," West said. "Nobody wants to be left behind on this island. Will the boat hold all of us?"

Archie and I looked at each other and said, "Maybe."

"We're not far from the south side of the island," I said. "Come see for yourselves."

We all left the vantage point to head for the boat, and although we risked having the Escalis come while nobody watched, it was a risk we had to take. West and Archie helped Michael, and as soon as we got to the southern cliff, West said, "That can hold four people."

"I'll go down and get it," Archie said, stepping onto the narrow zigzagging trail. The beginning of the trail was no more than two hands wide, carved into the eroding stone and in great disrepair. He had walked an entire three cubits and turned around one corner before the precarious trail gave way, sliding him down to the next level of the path and sending little amounts of debris into the Sea. I couldn't believe he was lucky enough to land on the next narrow piece of ledge.

"Maybe this isn't a good idea," I said, clenching my fists.

"Not at all," he called back up, eyes wide in fear as well, "but at the rate it's eroding, it's going to be safer to climb down now than in an hour." He pushed forward to the next turn, and I followed after him. I jumped over his excavation before making my first turn in the trail, thankful for my exceptional sense of balance since I found no handholds whatsoever.

From above, I heard West say, "Looks steep," and I looked up just in time to see Michael cuff him on the back of the head, flinching from his own movement.

Archie had already found the boat's chain and pulled the craft over to the sandy beach by the time we safely reached him. Only two trees grew in this sand, and Michael immediately sat against the bigger of the two, breathing heavily.

"Before we all get in this boat, I just want to try something," Archie said. He tossed the chain to West and said, "Tie this around the tree trunk?"

As West did so, I nodded in understanding. "You're sending it into the water on its own first, aren't you?"

"Yes," Archie replied. "Look how long the chain is. I just want to make sure nothing happens to it, and then we can pull it back in."

West finished tying it securely to the tree, and I stepped carefully into the wet sand to help Archie give the boat a great shove. I only had a second to admire the ornate carvings on the exterior of the wood, like intertwined ropes, before the boat drifted into deep water.

"Back up," Archie said quietly, and we both took slow steps back from the wet sand. My heart beat quickly, but nothing happened. The bobbing carrier peacefully reached the end of its chain length, but I heard the beginnings of an earth-rumbling growl and the water began to churn.

The greatest leviathan of a mouth I had ever seen erupted upward from the water, and the boat was immediately swallowed whole between teeth larger than me. One black eye, set among sickly brown scales, emerged from the waves but sank immediately back into the Sea, blasting water up to us on the shore. The boat was gone.

I was about to say how lucky we were when the chain snapped tight with a twang and the entire tree behind us was wrenched from the ground in one swift motion. Its winding root system slammed into us from behind and I found myself ensnared in the tangle just about to crash into the Breathing Sea.

CHAPTER FOURTEEN

We plunged into the dreaded tide within a second, and a horrific scream ripped through the waters as the herculean monster pulled us under. Water rushed by so forcefully that I had to press my arm over my eyes for fear they might be torn out and float away. When our movement slowed, I whipped around to see that the others had been ripped free from the roots. I was alone, in deep murky water where light barely filtered down to me.

I could hardly hold my breath anymore, and had yet to even disentangle myself from the root system. I hoped the legends of the Breathing Sea would prove true in one more way as I released the air in my lungs and watched my bubbles tear toward the surface.

Drawing my next breath felt like an offense to my very Humanity. I was clearly dragging water into my lungs, but I didn't feel the sting in my nose of drowning. I was almost free of the roots when a net settled onto the entanglement. From between the roots I saw the slimy face of the Siren who had thrown it. She held a golden trident in her webbed green hands. Everything about her was eerily green, from her glimmering tail to her long seaweed hair, fanning from her head in every direction. The tree I was stuck in floated slowly toward the surface of the Sea, and she swam effortlessly up to stay even with it. She kept her entirely white eyes fixed on me while each flick of her tail moved her one drift closer.

"Well hi," I said, my voiced suppressed and barely audible in the water.

I almost made the mistake of thinking she was beautiful until she flung her jaw open wide. What sounded like a hiss from between her four rows of teeth turned into an ear-searing scream, forcing me to clamp my hands to my head to block out the noise.

She stopped her screaming as six slimy eels snaked up to us from the darker depths. They easily passed through the holes in the net around me, and I recoiled from a sharp shock as one of them brushed against my neck. Another jolt struck my right leg, and I jerked my sword from my side as another one zapped my arm.

The Siren barked another short scream, as though concerned about her precious vermin, and they darted away from me before I could cut one in half. The wicked Siren swam up beneath the overturned tree, grabbed the chain still tied around the trunk, and struggled to pull the entire thing down to deeper water.

I immediately turned to the net in front of me and attempted to pull it from the root system, but it was already entangled and snagged on every tendril of wood. I started sawing at the rope with my one sword, but the strands had been densely hardened by years in the water. I had barely cut through one strand by the time I looked down and saw jellyfish drifting below.

My instincts screamed that those would kill me.

But why was she going through the trouble of dragging me down to them? Why send eels after me when she had a trident that could easily do the job? I realized why she looked so frightened seeing my sword — she didn't want any blood in the water.

Whatever this Siren feared seemed like hope to me, and I quickly pricked the back of my arm with my blade. A tiny wisp of blood flowed into the water where it was pulled apart and thinned until I couldn't see it. The Siren smelled it within a second, however, and let go of the tree to look fearfully in every direction.

I heard a roar and snapped quickly around to see a gigantic blue snake, easily big enough to swallow me whole, cutting through the water faster than an arrow. The Siren immediately took off, and given the choice between pursuing her or trying to dislodge me from the tree roots, the massive snake thankfully bolted after her.

Cutting through the remaining ropes took time, but soon I was free and swimming for the surface.

I had no idea when I had lost my hair ties, but my long hair had been freed and obstructed my vision every time I tried to turn my head now. I also found that I was an awful swimmer as I made my way upward. I kicked hard with my legs and tried to pull myself through the water with my arms, but I barely felt as though I was moving.

When I finally breached the surface, I immediately heard, "ALLIE!" and saw Archie running along the shoreline. The southern shoreline — he had made it across!

I swam toward him and tried to speak, but water spilled from my mouth instead of words.

"This whole shore is solid thistleweed!" he shouted to me. I saw the thorny vines and red leaves between us. "You've got to come about fifty cubits south, and there's a place you can climb out!"

I nodded and turned the direction he said I'd have to swim, but something grabbed my foot and water surged back over my head as it jerked me under again. It was another Siren, even greener and fiercer than the last. This one jabbed the back end of her trident into my stomach and then charged forward, pushing me through the water until I landed in the patch of thistleweed.

Every leaf and broken thorn felt like a tiny shock, a pricking burn, and a biting sting all at once. A poisonous fever raced into my mind, and I could feel my awareness clouding as I brandished my sword at the Siren to ward her away.

Her trident was far longer than my blade, and she plunged the prongs into my flowing mass of hair, twisting sharply. Despite all my thrashing, I couldn't pull myself free or move my head, nor could I reach her with my own blade. She tried to pull me to the ground by my hair, but I fought to stay standing, arched at an angle where I could see the sparkle of sunlight on the water just above my eyes. I thrashed more and tore at my hair, but I couldn't pull it free.

The Siren kept me just below the surface as every thistleweed leaf around me burned and stung against my skin. My arms, my neck, my face, my legs — the smarting seeped deeper the longer I struggled to get free.

I could hear muffled shouts from Archie on the shore ahead. He was so close! I just had to get to him through the thistleweed.

It dawned on me that I had one desperate measure to break me free from the Siren — and I was willing to take it. In one swift swipe I cut through all my hair and dashed forward. The Siren wasn't about to follow me into the thistleweed, and I lunged straight into the thick of it, bursting from the water to grab Archie's outstretched hand.

A hundred thorns scraped my arms and legs, leaving tiny bleeding trails that would surely have the Siren fleeing for her life. Archie pulled me onto the shore where I crumpled to the ground and heaved water out of my lungs. Air had never tasted sweeter.

"Allie! Are you alright? Can you hear me?"

I coughed and nodded quickly. Nauseating clouds were beginning to set in, and I thought sputtering more water up might help to clear my head, but my mind just began spinning one way and my stomach another. Even with most of the water spat onto the ground, the spinning only picked up speed.

"West and Michael?" I asked.

"I'm sure West escaped somewhere down the shoreline," Archie said. "I got Michael out, but he's bleeding everywhere. He's just past that tree down there. I'm going to grab him and be right back. Don't move, alright?"

"Yeah, sure," I said, holding one hand to my forehead. "Where are you going again?"

"Just past that tree down there," he repeated, pointing. It shouldn't have been so hard to find a tree, but I just couldn't focus clearly enough to figure out where it was. "Allie, just don't move for a minute. I'll be right back."

I curled into a ball and heaved a big sigh. "Alright, Allie, you know that you've been poisoned, right?" Archie hadn't come back. The voice whispering to me was my own, and I felt obligated to answer it. "I know, so now I have this fever. It can't kill me though. No way, not with all our healing mages at the Dragona. It's just going to make me crazy." I laughed shortly to myself, "It's already started! At least I know it. Archie will get us help. Except the Dragona is days away from here. And Archie has to carry Michael too. We'll never get there."

I continued muttering to myself, but even I couldn't understand what I was saying. I heard something rustle the leafy bushes behind me, but when I snapped my head around I didn't see anything.

Then I saw Archie setting Michael against a tree trunk so he could come speak quickly to me. I hadn't actually noticed them arriving. Maybe they had just appeared! "Allie, do you know who I am?" was the first thing he asked me.

"You're Archie," I replied with a scowl.

"Ok, that's a good start. Listen, you're about to start seeing things, and everything is going to be more confusing than you know, but I need you to stay with us. No matter what happens, you have to stay close to me and Michael. Can you do that?"

I closed my eyes and nodded a few times. "Mmmmhmmm."

"Allie, what's my name?"

"You're... Wait, you're..." I knew! I did know who he was. I also understood the severity of the situation when his name didn't come to me in a split second. I couldn't handle more memory issues.

"Archie!" I spat out.

"And you'll stay with us, no matter what happens?"

"Yes. I promith," I said.

"Good. Let's go." Archie slung the arm of the second guy over his shoulder and started off.

I followed them sleepily.

I followed them dreamily. Then the dreams became real.

Falcons swooped over top of us, talking about the weather. Leaf walked next to me for a little while, telling me about baby dragons. A few of the trees danced to Eclipsival music as we walked by, and I craned my head back to keep watching them.

The dreams grew scarier. The Sirens had followed me out of the Sea. They kept their distance, but they slithered along behind, watching. A tama cat pounced between me and the two guys ahead, and I was forced to stop as it eyed me dangerously. Golden fur, lean muscles, black tipped ears, almost the size of a bear, it was going to kill me. With my attention on the cat, the Siren grabbed me from behind, and I screamed as she shook me by the shoulders.

"Allie! It's just me!"

The Siren holding me flickered and turned into the guy who had been carrying the other.

"Allie, none of it's real. I promise, nothing you're seeing is the truth. You have to keep walking."

"Alright," I said, shaking my head to hold onto the moment of clarity.

"Do you still know who I am?" he asked.

"No," I said, wanting to cry. "But I know I trust you."

He smiled and squeezed my shoulder. "We're almost there."

I was pretty sure I hadn't lost consciousness at any point... But if I hadn't, I had to admit that my memory of the entire walk was riddled with holes. I couldn't tell how much time had elapsed, but there was no way we could already be at the Dragona.

"Mizelga's cabin is out here," I blurted unexpectedly as the image of a strange old woman surfaced in my mind. "Maybe she can help us."

Guy-one studied me with concerned interest. "That's where we're going… But how did you know that?"

"I think my life might depend on us getting there," I mumbled to the ground as the leading guy veered onto a barely noticeable animal trail.

The earth rumbled and split apart before my eyes, forming a gaping fissure I couldn't possibly jump over, and I managed to stop myself right before I fell into it. Someone said, "Come on Allie, keep walking."

I closed my eyes and whispered, "It's not real." I took a careful step forward, and actually, it was real. As soon as I stepped into the fissure, I fell an impossible deadly distance, so fast I couldn't even scream as the wind ripped past me and I hurtled to the rocky depths.

"Allie, it's not real," the blue-eyed one said, pulling me to my feet again.

I locked gazes with him, suddenly suspicious of where I was being taken. "Where are we going?" I demanded. The stranger still had a hold of my hands, and I yanked one free so I could jab a finger into his chest. "And *why* are you so ridiculously attractive?"

"Can we talk about this at a later time?" he asked as I glared and tried to figure out why he was suppressing a laugh. "We're there. I just need you to look ahead and walk. Ten more paces, come on."

"Fine, but it's just ridiculous," I muttered straight to his face. I felt my mind begin to wander again, but something about his eyes anchored me in the present, the way they truly seemed to see me, and know me, and care. He gave me just enough clarity that I could see a rotting cabin ahead of us, at the end of a stone path suddenly beneath my feet. I asked, "Is that real?"

"Yes, that's Lady Mizelga's cabin," he said as he let go of me, passed the second guy now sitting on the ground, and stepped onto the porch. He knocked loudly with no response.

"Be careful, she's crazy," I said loudly from the pathway.

"Yes," he answered, turning away from the door, "but please don't say so around her. Lady Mizelga!" he yelled. "We need your help!" The door opened a crack as I staggered onto the porch, and a tiny decrepit woman peered through the opening.

"I don't do medicine anymore," she croaked, about to shut us out.

I stumbled forward quickly enough to stick my hand in the closing door. Didn't even feel it! "Please?" I pleaded with her. "We'll do anything if you —" she tore the rotting wood back open on its rusting hinges, saw me, and gestured for us to enter. I stepped inside, and then watched as suspicious-guy dragged half-conscious-guy through the door as well.

"You," she said pointing to someone in the room, "put the one you're carrying in the room behind me. You'll find a table. And you," she said, now approaching me. The woman was tiny and reached up to grab my eyelids. "What have you done to yourself?"

"She got into a huge patch of thistleweed," someone called back to her.

The tiny, small, old old old woman thrust a triangular bottle into my hands and said, "Drink this. You'll recover." Then she retreated back into the enclosed room.

I followed her to find a table in the middle, with the injured one already on it, and I noticed the walls were covered in various jars and cages full of creeping bugs and scary concoctions.

"Get out, get out!" she shooed us from the room.

"Wait," the blue-eyed one said, "wouldn't it be best if we —"

"You want me to help him or not? Get out." She hobbled toward us and we backed out of the door, which was then shut lightly in our faces.

146

"Come on, Allie, drink it," he said, pulling the stopper from the bottle.

I peeked into the depths, and saw — "Worms." I cringed.

He checked in the bottle and assured me, "No, no worms in it." I tipped it back and swallowed the two gulps it contained with a shudder. Dead grass and bitter tree bark.

"How do you feel?" Archie asked.

I was instantly aware of where I was and who was around me, but all I could mutter was, "Exhausted," before I stumbled toward a wooden bench and Archie grabbed me to keep me from careening into it.

I woke later to the noise of someone moving around the room and found I had a comfortable wool blanket thrown over me. My first thought was that I needed a weapon, but a flickering lantern only illuminated Mizelga hunched over her desk.

"Your friend is doing all better now," she whispered. She still had her back to me as she mumbled to herself, and I barely picked up the words, "Follow me," as she left the room, holding onto the doorframe to support her movement. Archie slept on a second wooden sofa, sitting with his legs pulled in like a tight ball, and I laid the blanket across the front of him before I went anywhere.

"I can't believe we both survived," I whispered, not sure what I had ever done to deserve Archie in my life. I was beyond relieved to see he didn't have a scratch on him.

I turned to follow Mizelga into a musty dark kitchen, and she closed the door behind me, which set me on edge. She whispered, "I have been waiting for you for a very long time, Allie."

"Who are you?" I asked, my words sounding slurred.

"Who I am is not important. You knew me once, and someday, you shall know me again. Right now, I need to give you something that belongs to you. I took it a very long time ago, in a time when I understood very little." She handed me a small wooden box, about

147

the size of my two fists held together, decorated with intricate carvings across the faces. "Someday, when you remember, return here please? I would enjoy the company, and we could catch up on a few things."

"Sure," I replied dumbly, "I'll... come back to visit."

"Good. Now go back to sleep. It is late."

"But, wait. Can you please tell me how you used to know me? I am so desperate to—"

"After you remember, we'll speak."

"No, I really need to know why the Escalis want me. I need you to tell me."

She nodded to herself, said "Goodnight," and then walked through a different door to go to bed. I was a little puzzled, but I returned to Archie's sofa in the main room and leaned back against him with my feet kicked up on the bench. *Why was nobody ever any help?* I blew out the lantern and fell back asleep.

When the twittering of birds was finally loud enough to wake me up, I opened one bleary eye and saw the box I had received on the table next to me, proof I hadn't dreamt the whole thing. I picked it up and thought of opening it as Archie came in through the front door, letting in a warm shaft of sunlight.

"I looked everywhere," he said brightly. "No Escalis, no falcons, I think we lost everything that was after us. How do you feel?"

"I feel normal," I said, relieved. "How's Michael doing?"

"Lady Mizelga says we'll be good to take him home today."

"Already? How can he be better already? Actually, I don't care! When do we leave?"

He laughed. "You anxious to get out of here?"

I held up my thumb and finger to say a little bit as Mizelga came out of Michael's room. I saw to my surprise that he was sitting up on the table, his entire torso wrapped from his waist nearly to his shoulders. I was pretty sure it was an excessive amount, but I was no expert to be talking.

"You are able to walk now," Mizelga told him quietly. He jumped off the table and exited the room at a quick stagger, holding the wall for support as soon as he reached us.

"How are you feeling?" Archie asked.

"Lousy," he replied, the squint of his eyes showing a clear irritation with his condition. He did look pretty lousy. He picked up his deerskin jerkin to pull it over the bandages, and I could see at least six holes that had been torn clear through it. His bandaged side actually looked better than the rest of him, which was covered in scratches and trails of dried blood from getting out of the Breathing Sea. Michael rubbed his hand over his side once he got the jerkin on.

"I can't run like this," he scowled, cringing as he hit a particularly sore spot.

Mizelga picked up the box she had given me from off the table, handed it to me, and then opened the door to send us outside. "It is time for you to go," she said in her decrepit old voice, motioning for all of us to exit. She followed us out to the porch, carrying a brown linen bag and a large wooden bowl full of some sort of liquid.

"Can you take care of this for me?" she asked Archie, handing the bag to him. "I found it in the forest next to my favorite patch of toadstools. The nerve of the creature!" I definitely saw something squirm inside, and when he opened it I peeked in to see a fluffy brown rabbit.

I glanced at Archie to see that he wasn't thrilled to accept such a gift, but he replied, "Sure thing." Then something more worrisome caught my attention.

"That's a gigantic snake!" I exclaimed, jumping back from the scaly green mass of muscle slithering alongside the cabin.

149

Michael narrowed his unhappy eyes even further and said, "Allie, there's nothing there."

The old woman laughed to herself and said, "You'll still be seeing things until the fever fully wears off. And well, this could help, but you probably won't want it." She turned to retreat back into her cabin, but I stopped her:

"What do you mean? What's in the bowl?" I asked.

She stood with her back to us, thinking to herself, then I saw her nod as though agreeing with something. She returned to me, stepped very close, and tipped the bowl to the side so the contents spilled onto my sandal-laced feet. I felt my shoulders immediately tighten from the splash of cold water, but I remained otherwise frozen in bewilderment. In all seriousness and with her eyes gazing up to mine, she said, "Water. For luck." Then she stepped back through her door and shut it, no further explanation on the way.

Michael's expression mirrored my befuddlement, and I saw Archie trying with all his will to keep from bursting into laughter.

I flatly said, "We should go," as multiple locks scraped into place. We walked down the steps and onto the stone path, slowly I might add, because of Michael.

Archie had his hand over his mouth as though he still couldn't restrain himself from grinning at the absurdity that was Mizelga. I knew he wasn't directly laughing at me, but the action still irritated me to no end. I tried not to overreact, but I didn't come across kindly as I asked, "Did you know her?"

Archie, his smirk coming to a conclusion, thought quickly over his answer. "Know her? I don't think so. I mean, no, I haven't met her, but we've all heard the stories, haven't we?"

"Sure," I said, still feeling like I was missing something important. "Then, does she know you?"

Archie shrugged and replied, "I don't think so. What's with all these questions?"

"I don't know. What's with the rabbit in the bag?"

150

Archie held the bag up at eye level, but the bunny inside had settled down for the ride. "Didn't you hear?" he asked. "I'm supposed to take care of it. And we should probably slow down. We're leaving Michael behind."

"It's more than just the wound that hurts," Michael complained as we slowed to wait for him. "I'm sore all over from those tree roots slamming into us. And Archie practically dragged us through a briar patch to avoid the thistleweed. Why are neither of you shredded up like I am?"

"Well, we kind of are," I said, trying to make him feel better. "I have a bunch of holes in my clothes like you do…"

"And I'm sorry for pulling you through the blackberries," Archie said. "We were a bit limited for options."

"Yeah, I guess," Michael grumbled.

The trip back to the Dragona wouldn't have taken so long if we could have gone normal speed, but with Michael carefully choosing every step he took, it dragged for endless hours.

Archie and I both offered to carry him, but he flatly refused and hobbled along by himself. We stopped many times to let him rest, and while we waited on the edge of a field of crab-grass, I tried to strike up a new conversation.

"Why do Escalis call us Tallies?" I asked Archie as Michael sat on a log across from us, not paying any attention. "Like the ones on the bridge. I heard them say it."

"Tallies?" Archie repeated. I saw that he found the strangeness of the name amusing. "It's just their name for Humans. They call us all Tallies."

"How come?"

"I don't know." The question didn't seem to be one that he found interesting, so I didn't dwell on it further. I decided to pull out the box Mizelga had given me so I could inspect it while we waited.

151

The outside had been engraved with symbols and delicate flowers twisting around every side. Their colorless petals seemed to shimmer in the sun even though they were only carved from wood. The vines of the flowers were intertwined with the markings and symbols across the faces, and each symbol glowed with an unknown meaning, as though burning to be heard.

"What's that?" Archie asked. Michael stood to look too.

"I don't really know. Mizelga gave it to me last night while you were sleeping."

"What's inside?"

"I was just about to open it."

"I'll bet it's something useful. Even the box looks like it's got some magic in it," Archie said. I lifted the lid and saw nothing spectacular, just fine black sand and a small note that read, "This will stay where you leave it." I sifted my fingers through to see what the sand concealed, but I couldn't find anything. Had it been stolen?

I passed the box to Archie, who observed it skeptically, scanned through the sand as well, and handed it to Michael, who also found nothing of significance.

"Pour a couple grains out and see if they do anything," Archie suggested.

I got up and tilted the box over the stump. The sand rolled to the edge, but as soon as it left the confines of the box, it hung suspended in midair, unsupported. I poked it with my fingers and it moved in the direction I pushed it, but stayed floating. I poured a little more out and swirled it around in the air.

"That's sort of awesome," Michael said, which was impressive because I had the feeling that not many things amazed him. He poked at it, but for some reason, it wouldn't budge for him. He pushed harder using his whole fist, but the sand remained stationary, hovering where I had left it. He withdrew his hand, which was then peppered with tiny bleeding holes in his skin. *Of course, he needed more wounds.* Archie tried to push it as well while Michael walked slowly away, but he didn't have any luck either. It wouldn't move for anyone but me.

Michael came back carrying a dead log, and without saying a word he smashed it onto the hovering sand, favoring one side of his body in doing so. Every single grain was immoveable and the wood got stuck in the air, held up by nothing but the grains embedded in the bottom.

"Why would it only move for you?" he asked, the unfairness clearly bothering him.

"I don't know... Maybe because it belonged to me?"

"If it's yours, why did Mizelga have it?" Archie wondered.

"I think I might have known her before. She told me to come talk to her once I remembered. It's weird."

"It is." Archie picked up the box and ran it over the sand to scoop it up. As soon as the sand passed into the confines of the box, it fell to the bottom and looked normal once again.

We walked for hours more before Archie released the rabbit from his bag, and I was about to start off again when I saw West. I blinked my eyes to make sure I was seeing clearly, but it was definitely him, staring straight at me with solemn eyes. He stood beneath a distant, leafy maple tree that was tilting at an alarming speed, surely about to crush him. My heart stopped, and I screamed, "LOOK OUT!" but he didn't move.

I looked quickly to Archie and Michael as the tree crashed its rustling leaves into the ground, snapping the bottommost branches.

I saw worry in their eyes, but they were looking at me rather than the fallen maple. Archie asked, "Are you seeing things again?"

"Wait... You didn't — the tree?" I put my hand to my forehead and turned back around to see the forest undisturbed. "I'm sorry. I... I thought I saw West."

Archie and Michael glanced at each other, and Michael said, "I'm sure he's back at the Dragona already. He'll probably laugh at us for taking so long."

"Right," I said, taking a shaky breath as my heartbeat began to calm. "I'm sure he is."

I didn't see anything frightening the rest of the journey until the Dragona came into view, and Archie startled me by abruptly stopping, peering ahead with a concentration that meant he heard something in the bushes too.

CHAPTER FIFTEEN

I calmed down as I noticed his intrigued grin, and he asked, "Smell that?"

I glanced around and sniffed at the air, my mind automatically registering the scent as a tama cat. No question. *That*, I could remember.

"It's up ahead of us," Archie said. "We're going to run into it."

"Good," I replied. "I'm starving."

Archie pulled out a hunting knife and disappeared into the bushes. The intensity of his attention and the silence he moved with gave away that he was a practiced hunter. That tama cat would never know he was coming.

Michael sat down to rest, and I followed stealthily after Archie, stopping at precisely the right angle to see him throw his hunting knife with impressive speed. The large cat died almost instantly as it sliced into her neck. Her paws were the size of my hands, her golden shoulders easily stood taller than the alpha male of any wolf-pack, and she was very leanly cut — meaning she had been hungry too.

"Is there anything you can't do?" I asked, gesturing to Archie's killer aim.

"Actually, yes," he said, approaching the cat to withdraw the knife. "I've never been very good at skinning animals. Would you do the honors for me?"

"Um, no?" I replied, folding my arms with a grin. "Hunting rule number one: you kill it, you gut it."

"I was hoping you had forgotten that with the rest of your memories."

I dropped my jaw, but couldn't keep from smiling as I exclaimed, "That's horrible! You can't say that to somebody like me."

Archie only shrugged as he started on the cat's hide. "It's the truth."

My delicate mental state never stopped Archie if he had a joke to make, and that was one of the reasons I liked having him around.

"You know what else is the truth?" I asked, knowing my retort was a bit late. "You really aren't any good at skinning that thing. Here, give me the knife so we don't have to wait three days to leave."

I opened and closed my hand several times. Archie just flipped the knife blade up toward his arm so as not to brandish it, and then he held it behind him to say I couldn't have it. "For one, Allie, I can't believe it took you that long to think up an insult so unimpressive. For two, there's no way you could get this done faster than me. I'll just be a minute. If you get a quick fire going, we can eat this and leave."

"Take your time," Michael called from behind us, sprawled across a moss covered log to catch his breath.

In the late afternoon, we reached the Dragona with full stomachs. Archie went straight to find Anna and Sir Darius while I took Michael to the medical wing. I found myself too stubborn to

156

ask the healing mages to look at me too, and simply headed back to my room where I hoped to crash into my bed.

Liz busted my door in as soon as I had my eyes closed. "I'm glad you're back!" she exclaimed, pulling me from my bed with a hug tight enough to mirror her relief. "My hero of a sister, you are!"

I smiled to myself, glad to have Liz to come home to. "You don't even know how glad I am to be here. Why call me a hero though?"

"Because you guys helped the Dincarans escape! You made such a commotion on the west side of the city, they managed to escape over one of the walls unseen. Most of them are here now, and they've told Anna and Sir Darius all about the battle. It's still horrible, of course. They left half of their wounded behind so they could get out, but you gave them the chance."

"They left half behind?" I exclaimed before realizing, "It was that shanking Tekadan leader! He made them leave their wounded."

"It's alright, we'll get them out. Sir Darius is briefing a team of mages right now who should be able to jump in and free them. This is what the Dragona does. But anyway! Allie, are you alright?"

"Getting better at least," I said, running my fingers over my temples and through the roots of my now shoulder-length hair. "I touched a patch of thistleweed, and the fever I got—"

"I know the feeling," she cut me off. "I've had it before! I touched one leaf and I—"

A knock at the door interrupted Liz's story, and she frowned dramatically before pulling it open.

Before Archie could say anything or even come inside, I saw a dreadful sadness in the slouch of his shoulders and asked, "Is West alright?"

I had never seen Liz shift moods so quickly, nor had I ever seen her eyes so deathly serious as she turned on me and asked, "Why, what would be wrong with him?"

"Nothing, I just wanted to make sure he made it out of the Breathing Sea."

She exclaimed to me, "*What?* I thought you all came back together. Archie, he's alright, isn't he?"

I shouldn't have ambushed him so quickly. I should have let him start the conversation. Liz also saw the bad news in his eyes as he struggled for the right words.

"Archie!" Liz said, as though he had the power to change the outcome with his response.

"I... I never saw him, and Anna says our mages can't find him either. I didn't want to say anything when we still had hope," he looked sorrowfully at me, "but I think the Siren songs got him. I know I had to fight to keep Michael from jumping back in after them. Nobody would have been there to stop West."

I felt water in my eyes with the realization of what that meant. Liz still didn't comprehend.

"So how do we get him back?" she pressed.

I could see on Archie's face that he was afraid to tell her the truth. Liz's breathing began to quicken. In the highest octave of the Human register, she asked, "Archie?"

"I don't think we... Liz, there's nothing any of us—" Archie was unable to finish as Liz turned around and stormed off to her room in a mess of devastation. "That's what I thought," he said to himself.

I stepped hesitantly out into the tunnel to watch Liz disappear, her sobs echoing back to us.

"She's not... mad at you," I told Archie, turning my eyes to the ground as breathing became nearly impossible. This couldn't be happening.

"I know, she's just upset with the world," he said. "This isn't fair."

I leaned against the wall and tried to keep from breaking down, from crying, from collapsing to the floor. And at precisely the worst possible moment, Jesse the coward rounded the corner.

He sneered when he saw us. "And here you two are, safe as worms in the dirt. I tried to tell you this would happen! Your stubbornness just cost West—"

I instantly had a rock in my hand from the cave floor, and I hurled it at Jesse, pulling West's dagger from my calf in the same motion.

"HOLY LIFE, ALLIE!" Archie shouted as my rock shot past the instigator. I hadn't meant to hit him, just to express the violent anger I couldn't convey with words.

As Jesse bolted, I immediately wished I hadn't done it. Now I was furious with myself, and I had a dagger in my hand.

"I wasn't trying to hit him — I just hate him!" I said as Archie yanked the blade away from me. West was gone. My hair was gone. Nothing was right, and I shouldn't have reacted so violently.

"You can't just threaten to kill people!" Archie shouted.

"Shanking life, I know!" I said, unable to vocalize the regret already sinking in. Far angrier with myself than anybody else, I turned and thundered off toward my room, distancing myself from Archie, from Jesse, and from my outburst of rage. I quickly grabbed my hairbrush from my room then stomped back into the tunnels, amazed I didn't run into anyone as I strode moodily through the Dragona. Still no one as I got outside and into the trees, and still nobody all the way down to the lake.

I threw my head in the water and sat angrily on a nearby boulder as I pulled my brush through hair that wouldn't reach my waist again for years to come. My half-wet tangles fought against every stroke, and I cursed everything in sight. The boulder beneath me probably received the worst as I punched and kicked and vented on it.

An overhead screech suddenly tore through the air, and I looked to see a falcon circling before it flew off over the lake. The thistleweed fever must still be in my mind. I was clearly imagining things.

Although, in case that really was a falcon, I needed to leave.

"Stay where you are," a deep and coarse voice said from behind me. My anger vanished as I turned to see a massive sharp-toothed Escali pointing a bow at me, his strong arms holding it still so he had perfect focus on his aim. In one fluid motion, I swung my legs to the backside of the boulder and dropped to a crouch behind it. An arrow screamed over my head, and my incredible reflexes were the only reason it hadn't struck my heart.

My feet rested on the ledge where the shore plummeted into deep water, so I was truly stuck.

"Why don't you come out, Allie? We both know nobody is close enough to hear you," he said. I was startled to hear my name, and he hissed a chuckle as I held my breath. A blade thudded softly into the grass where I could see its pommel of dented sun rays. My blade. The second one I had brought to Treldinsae and dropped on the bridge. "Come out and we can talk."

"I can talk from here," I said, knowing I was about to find out what I meant to the Escalis, one way or another. "Just tell me what you want."

He was almost to me, and I could sense him pulling back on the bow again—

He snarled a loud curse in Escalira, and I peered around the rock to see he had somehow caught fire. *What?* Flames scorched his entire body as he leapt quickly into the water, surfacing with a furious snarl that caused a woman behind us to laugh.

"If you don't want to burn to death," Anna stooped to pick up the bow and arrow he had dropped, her red hair literally flaming, "then enjoy drowning." I could see the blisters on his skin already magically healing themselves when Anna shot him with his own arrow.

As soon as it made contact, the Escali froze and lost his grip on the edge of the lake. Anna and I watched his motionless body drift backwards and slowly sink. Anna said nothing, but her hair slowly stopped flaming as the Escali dropped from sight.

"Thank you," I said, unsure of what else to say.

She remained silent as she bent and picked up the arrow shaft from the surface of the water. "Was he trying to shoot you with this?" She held it up, but the head was missing.

"Yes," I answered, "Why? Does it mean something?"

"Yes," she answered as she picked the one out of the water that hadn't hit me. She held it up and I could see that the arrowhead consisted of swirling neon colors. I knew exactly what that was. "He was trying to take you alive."

"And I still don't know why," I said, glad that somebody else could finally confirm I wasn't imagining this. "Sir Avery does. Can't you make him tell me why I'm in so much trouble with the Escalis?"

"I can't make Sir Avery do anything."

"They know my name, Anna. That Escali had the blade I dropped in Treldinsae. He was here specifically to find me. They recognize my face. They're trying to get something from me, or make me pay for something I once did. I don't know."

"Then it was awfully foolish for you to come here by yourself, Allie. Use some common sense! If you're being targeted, you can't wander around outside — especially alone." Now her face betrayed the fear she was trying to hide.

"I know. I'm sorry. I wasn't thinking." I felt suddenly guilty.

"Don't let there be a next time, because I probably won't be down here."

"Why are you down here?" I asked.

161

"It's a good place to come and think, and I've got a lot of thinking to do after what happened in the Sea…"

I folded my arms over my chest, as though to shield my heart. I wasn't sure if I'd ever reach a point when it didn't ache. "It's my fault. I pushed us to go in after the Dincarans." I clenched my teeth together and tried to swallow the lump in my throat.

"I'm not about to argue with you, if that's what you want," she replied, her green eyes filled with understanding and strength, from which I couldn't break my gaze. "That was your decision, and this is your fault. All you can do is own it."

I only nodded in response, unable to reply. Anna turned her eyes out over the water and said, "I see a lot of myself in you, Allie. And I want to tell you something I wish someone had told me before I became a leader… The decisions you make… they'll hurt you more often than you want, but that doesn't mean they were wrong."

I nodded again, thinking of tally marks. West was just one more hash to add to my list, on the side I wished to avoid. Had all fourteen of those death marks hurt this much?

"I think I know what my power is," I said quietly. "I can understand the Escalis. Every time we run into them, I know what they're saying."

Anna nodded wordlessly as the sun sank lower in the sky and pink clouds reflected off the water. "You must just have incredible luck then, since you keep escaping impossible odds." At last she sighed and said, "Let's go back to the Dragona. We'll get you paired up with another mage of languages to train with soon." Anna picked up the Escali bow and neon tipped arrow and followed me through the trees as I led the way back to the Dragona. We were quiet the whole way back until we were about to part ways, and she stopped me.

"I've been wondering, Allie, what in the world happened to your hair?"

I grimaced. "Goodnight," I said, heading to Liz's room rather than my own. I needed to make sure Liz was alright before I went to bed to face my own emotional firestorm, but I only found her door blocked shut with all sorts of junk.

"Can I come in?" I asked her. When I heard a small moan of agreement, I pushed past the barrier. Lying on her bed with the blanket pulled over her head, not moving or making any sound, she stirred when I sat next to her. From under the covers I heard her mutter, "Everything's over."

I felt the same inside, but in seeing her suffer, I gained the strength to disagree. "Everything isn't over," I told her.

"Everything's over," she repeated. I heard her relapse into sobs and I rubbed her shoulder through the blankets. A part of me wished I could be out escaping from Escalis again, rather than comforting my sister as she sat up with puffy red eyes. I didn't know what to do. I wasn't good at this.

"It's my fault," she said, her lip quivering on the brink of more sobs.

I put a hand on her shoulder and told her, "Liz, there's no way this is your fault."

"It is. You were putting yourself in that danger because I wanted the old you back, but I didn't want this. I never want you to risk yourself again. I don't know what I'll do if I lose you too."

Unexpected and unannounced, the door opened and Leaf entered, shutting it softly behind himself. I couldn't imagine why he had shown up, but he had brought a tiny red dragon with him. He crossed the room, set the dragon on Liz's lap, and jumped up on the bed between me and her. He wrapped his little arms around her as Liz hugged him back and just cried. The baby dragon nuzzled against her tummy, then released a contented cross between a squeak and a sigh before curling into a sleepy ball in her lap.

Everything stayed that way for a while. Liz held Leaf as though he was the only thing left in the world, and Leaf didn't seem to mind. After a little while, Liz quieted down again and even let a laugh escape as the baby dragon hiccupped and choked on a wisp of smoke.

"He isn't gone until you let go of him," I heard Leaf tell her.

"No, Leaf, he's gone," Liz said, wiping her eyes.

"We'll get him back someday. You'll be the one to find a way, *unless* you lose hope. Losing hope is always the first step in losing everything."

Liz and I both looked at him in surprise. I never expected to hear something so meaningful come from little Leaf. "I think he's right," I said, meeting Liz's gaze.

"Yeah," she hiccupped too. "Maybe he is."

I stayed for hours before retreating to my room, giving Liz time to process the situation alone. I tied my annoyingly short hair back before bed because it bothered me. Every part of me was tired, and I still felt sick from seeing Liz in such a state.

My pre-sleep thinking time that I usually valued so highly was nothing more than distressing. If I wasn't thinking about the Escali, I was thinking about West. Thoughts of West put me back in Liz's room. I refused to cry, but a few stray tears did find their way down my face. It was strange to know he might still be alive and we would all have to hold on to hope.

I barely managed to fall asleep and only slept for a few restless hours before I woke to the faint sound of my door clicking shut.

CHAPTER SIXTEEN

That was what I thought it was, at least. I snapped my eyes open and listened intently, yet all was silent. Even if a monster loomed over me, I wouldn't be able to see it. Why was there no light? Oh great, I hadn't lit the fire. Getting up in the morning for sparring was going to be a bear.

I let my heart slow its pace as I realized I had probably been dreaming. Why had a dream scared me so badly?

I heard something again, a small shuffle next to my bed. My abruptly woken muscles wanted to freeze and play dead rather than face the unknown intruder, but I reached slowly and silently for my short swords on the ground next to me. My fingers brushed against a sheath, and I reached my other hand silently around to take the sword out without being detected. My bed made the tiniest squeak as my weight shifted, and that was when I heard a growl very close to me.

Somebody grabbed my wrists to keep me from getting to my short swords and a second person had a hand over my mouth before I could scream. I tried to break free by jerking my whole body to the side, but they were far too strong to squirm away from. Then I felt something brush against my shoulder that meant it was all over.

165

Arm spikes.

"Quit moving!" one of the Escalis hissed. I felt a blade come into gentle contact with my neck and I froze, struggling to take short breaths through my nose and stay calm enough to think.

"Let's kill her now." This second whisper was interlaced with a growl.

"Not until she tells us how they got out of the Breathing Sea." I recognized this terrifying sharp voice as the Escali from the bridge — the more lithe of the two monsters who kept tormenting my life. "And I have other questions for her."

Well I didn't have any answers! I caught them by surprise this time as I jerked my pinned arms in front of my face and rolled to the side, straight off the bed. The sword cut into my neck, but it wasn't deep. The grip the Escali had on my wrists had been relaxed enough to yank free, and I was away from them as soon as I hit the ground.

"She's mine!" a snarl came from the more aggressive of the two.

I backed up to where I knew my wardrobe stood and squeezed in next to it to hide. Where were my short swords? I needed something to defend myself with! I hoped they could see as little in the dark as I could, because knowing the layout of my room was my only advantage. I considered screaming again, but I couldn't bring myself to let them know where I hid.

"She can tell us later!" The Escali searching for me grabbed me by the shoulders and threw me with his unnatural strength into the wall.

I screamed but found myself back in my bed. The two were on either side of me now as I thrashed and threw my covers off, bolting upright.

"Allie! Calm down!"

"You're alright!"

These voices were different and I froze to snap my head to either side. Terry on my left. Michael on my right. My neighbors.

166

"It was just a dream," Terry said. "We're the only ones here."

"No no no, not a dream," I said, swinging my feet off the bed and standing up to check around my room for danger. Everything looked the same as when I had gone to bed, but it couldn't have been a dream. It had been too real for that. Unless...

"You scared us both to death," Michael said, his hands shaking in his night clothes.

"It was the thistleweed fever," I replied, sitting back onto my bed. "It all looked so real. It must have been because I was asleep." My thoughts were disjointed from the confusion and rude awakening, but I knew the fever must be to blame. "I'm so sorry."

I could see both of their relief that I wasn't being attacked. Terry asked, "Do you want us to stick around for a little while?"

"No, I think I'm alright," I said, finally feeling embarrassment creep into my cheeks. "Thanks for the offer though. And thanks for coming to help me. I'll see you guys tomorrow."

After they left, I lay back down and took a deep breath, the thrill of fear still fresh in my chest. When I finally began to doze off, my dreams were strange and vivid. The Escalis dragging me outside, a fight between them and a group of others, a horrible black falcon, teeth biting into the back of my hand, running, stumbling, back to the Dragona's caves. They wanted what I knew, and I knew for a brief moment what they wanted. The dream-Escalis forced me to drink something horrible and burning, and I sat straight up with another shriek.

This time only Terry came to my room to make sure I was alright. I wasn't alright. "It was real," I told her. "I know it was real. I need you to take me to Anna."

"Allie, you just had the thistleweed fever," Anna said as the wakeup trumpet began to sound through the hallways. "I'm sure that's all it was. You're still recovering."

"I know I had it, but I hadn't seen anything weird all evening. And I'm telling you, this was real. Look at this!" I held my hand up, where teeth had ripped into the back of it. The marks they left were in the shape of a symbol, one that looked strangely like it said *Everarcs*.

"Allie, they're teeth marks. You have teeth. I know you're afraid right now, but this doesn't mean anything. The Escalis don't know where the Dragona is, and have even less knowledge about how to get inside."

I tried to argue my point to her. We had just had the Eclipsival at the Dragona, and the Escalis had surely seen, heard, and smelled exactly where we were. When Anna told me we had mages keeping an eye out for the Escalis all through the Eclipsival, I reminded her of the Escali who had just found me down by the lake. When she called that a fluke and reminded me that he was now dead, I left.

This was horrible. The Escalis definitely knew where the Dragona was. Anna needed to take that seriously! Who else could I talk to? Sir Darius?

The details of my dream started to slip back to me through the emptiness. Somebody had helped me. I couldn't remember who, but I just had a nagging suspicion it was Archie. With no evidence whatsoever, I was convinced.

He had brought a group with him too, so he must have known of the danger ahead of time. I knew I shouldn't be back to my theory that he was an Epic, but I was. Premonition was just one more power he had used that I needed to add to my growing list.

It even made sense with Sir Avery's resentment of Archie. These family issues Archie spoke of were probably just father and son issues. What could Archie have possibly done to become so estranged?

My feet carried me unthinkingly to Sir Darius's study, and I pounded on his door, which he opened in the midst of pulling on a warm cloak.

"I was just about to leave, Allie. We can talk later."

"Wait, I just have one question," I said, as he grabbed a bag from the nearest table.

"Anna has already told me of your suspicions. We can talk later."

"Then I just have one thing I need to ask. When you recruited Archie to come to the Dragona, where did he come from?"

Sir Darius scowled as though I wasted his precious time. "You're asking the wrong person. Anna was the one who brought Archie to the Dragona. Not me."

Sir Darius leapt into the air, and I flipped around in the direction of Archie's room. I hadn't misheard anybody. Archie had, without any doubt, told Anna that Sir Darius had recruited him. And apparently vice versa as well.

This needed to end. Either Archie needed to tell me what was going on, or I needed to involve Anna and Sir Darius to find out.

I heard running footsteps behind me and whipped around in paranoia, only to see Liz. "Come on, we need to talk," she said, leading me off.

"Where are we—"

"Shh. We'll talk in a minute."

What I think Liz actually meant to say, was *we need to walk,* because she took me straight to my room without another word. I sat down on my bed as she closed the door, and I motioned for her to go ahead. She had my full attention.

Liz tried several times to say something, but never made it past one word before deciding there had to be a better way to say it.

"I..." She sat next to me. "I listened in on one of Anna's conversations, and I heard what you told her."

"I know it sounds crazy, but it was real, Liz."

"And I believe you, but that's what I've come to talk to you about. See, I need to warn you about something." She stumbled on her words, nervous to say them. I moved over to sit with our shoulders touching, giving her encouragement.

"Calm down Liz. It's all ok," I said, although I could feel my own breath increasing in anticipation.

"Anna is worried you might be right. What if it really was the Escalis and not the thistleweed fever?"

"She doesn't believe me," I said, noticing Liz shaking.

"She just doesn't want to believe you." Liz threw her arms down and declared, "They're going to run a blood test on you and hope you've still got a hint of the fever. There."

"Hey, that's not too bad," I said, so relieved that I had to let a laugh escape. "You scared me, Liz! From the way you were talking, I thought something horrible was coming." I stopped talking when I saw sympathy in her eyes mixed with horror across the rest of her face.

"Do you know what a blood test is?" she breathed.

"No."

She held out her hand and pushed the sleeve back to reveal the skin of her forearm. Several deep scars ran from her wrist to her elbow.

"They take a knife, Allie, and they run it all the way up your arm," I could feel the color draining from my face, "they have a mage who can tell exactly what's in your blood, but they won't tell you what's happening until it's over." She quickly looked up to see my reaction and it was apparently what she expected. *Mortified.*

"I'm sorry," she continued quickly, "it's just that the first time they did it to me, they just grabbed me from behind, and I was so scared. I thought they were going to kill me."

I lost myself in thought for a few seconds, which Liz broke with more talk.

"Please don't be mad at me. I had to warn you —" she trailed off mid-sentence as I pulled her into a hug.

"I'm not mad at you. Thanks for telling me."

170

She looked around nervously. "Just *please* don't tell anyone. I'm dead if they find out I told you. In fact, I'm dead if they find out I was listening outside the door."

I laughed. "I won't tell, I promise." She hugged me back and then jumped off the bed.

"I guess I'll talk to you later then," she said, appearing confused as to whether she should be sad or happy. "Have a good life." She was out the door and gone before she had to decide.

Great. Just great.

I got lost trying to find my way to Archie's room, only to find it empty, and nobody in the Wreck had seen him. I didn't know what to do with myself.

Leaf. I would go visit him. He wouldn't be the one to surprise me with this blood test, and maybe he could take my mind off the situation. I crawled out of the Wreck entrance and set off toward the hatchery, ready to draw my short swords at the first sign of an Escali.

Of course I wanted to know whether I had imagined the Escalis in the Dragona, and I was immensely glad Liz had forewarned me of the blood test, but that knowledge couldn't get rid of my anxiety. They could at least warn me before they cut my arm open! How stupid. All of this was stupid. Stupid Escalis, stupid war, stupid magic —

"Hey Allie, are you ok?" Archie was unexpectedly next to me, matching my fast pace. I was glad to see him, because I was getting my answers. Right now.

"No, I am not. Archie, last night with the Escalis, you were there, weren't you? You helped me?"

He searched my face, probably to guess at how much I knew, then said, "Yes."

"What happened?" I exclaimed. "How did you know they were coming?"

"I... Listen, I need to tell you something."

171

I had never seen Archie so nervous. He kept glancing about and didn't walk with his usual light step.

"You should have more than one thing to tell me!"

"I do..." Archie took precious time to find the right words as we walked, making me want to explode as the trees began to thicken around us.

Wait, I didn't even know where we were going! What was I doing, walking alone with this stranger? Did I even know anything true about him?

Archie was just as entangled in thought as Liz had been, so he didn't notice as I stopped. A gap grew between us as I thought quickly.

We were somewhere close to the lake and definitely out of earshot of everyone back home. From a pile of rocks near my feet, I reached down and withdrew one weighty conversation starter. *Here went everything!*

I hurled it at him, and two things happened at once that finally made sense. First, the rock stopped just short of hitting him as it rebounded off an invisible barrier — yet *another* power for my now undeniable list. Secondly, I startled him into snapping around in an instinctually defensive stance, his teeth bared in a snarl.

This wasn't Sir Avery's son.

He was Prince Avalask's.

Everything from time to my beating heart instantly stopped. Neither of us moved. Neither of us spoke. The entire forest had been muted, except for the one snapping twig I heard behind me, where I had just come from, accompanied by the very quiet and controlled breath of a predator. The next time my heart beat again, it was only to pump fear through my veins, just to make sure I knew my beloved life had reached its conclusion.

The only direction I could dash was toward the lake. The only movement Archie made was a tiny shake of his head while his eyes told me, *don't do it.*

Of course, I bolted. I had to hurdle a moss eaten log, scramble up a crumbling embankment, and tear through a thicket of briers, all without any plan. Ok, I would get to the lake, stand with the water behind me, so nobody could get me from behind, pull out my short swords, and try to defend myself.

I wasn't nearly there yet when another Escali simply stepped in front of me. No way was I fast enough to veer around him, and I skidded through a pile of rotting leaves in my attempt to change direction.

Archie collided with me from behind and I tried to throw him off. He grabbed both of my short swords and discarded them, a betrayal that stung like the death of another friend. He wasn't about to let me go anywhere, and attempted to pin my arms to my side, saying, "Allie! Listen to me. I promise you're going to be—"

"Shut up and let go!" My throat constricted and breathing became painful as the truth sank in. I threw my weight against his arms to escape his grasp. When that didn't work, I combined my writhing with kicking and punching, throwing in a few elbows and knees. He was careful not to let me bite him, and my thrashing was apparently unimpressive because he even began to speak to the Escali as I tried to break his tight hold.

"You agreed you wouldn't show yourselves," Archie said, and I saw that his plural use of the word was justified as two Escali women approached us as well, bows drawn just in case.

The male growled, "Izfazara said to step in if you didn't have the situation in control."

"I do have it under control!"

"No, you don't," I snarled, finally sinking my teeth into one of his arms. Izfazara — he was the Escalis' king. How much trouble was I in?

The Escali said, "We needed to intervene. Somebody's already out looking for her."

"What? How?" Archie exclaimed, finally jerking his arm out of my teeth. "We've hardly been out here five minutes!"

"I don't know how they've realized she's gone, but if you listen, you can already hear them."

Even I stopped resisting just long enough to hear a lone voice in the distance, fading as though travelling away from us. "Allie! Please, you have to come back. It's not as bad as I made it sound. Just pretend I never told you anything." Why did it have to be Liz?

The Escali said, "We all know how badly this plan will fail if they use the resources of the Dragona to find her. We'll take care of the girl calling for her, and—"

"NO!" I screamed. "LIZ—"

Archie clamped a hand over my mouth, and no amount of wriggling or writhing could free my voice. He exclaimed for me, "No no no, leave her alone."

The Escali scoffed and twirled a twig absentmindedly between his fingers. "Getting rid of this lone searcher will buy you time."

"We've already got plenty. Look, we're leaving right now. Please, just leave her alone."

Archie took a few backward steps toward the lake to prove that we were, indeed, leaving.

I heard the deep voice of another Escali behind me, saying, "You could at least use some help."

Archie peered around behind us and said, "Ekvid! Yes. If Ekvid stays with us, can the rest of you leave? We'll be fine."

The Escali in front of us, who appeared to be the leader, contemplated the idea, then said, "We'll stay in the near vicinity. Remember, you're in a hurry."

Each of the Escalis, save the one behind us, retreated back into the trees. I couldn't hear Liz anymore. Archie must not have been able to either, because rather than try to keep me silenced, he released his tight hold.

All I could do was slump to the ground to finally let the due shock flood through me. How could he do this? I had trusted him *so much*. I was glad to be sitting, because the wave of hurt crashing through my chest was making me dizzy.

The one thing I could do right now was keep myself from crying. I wouldn't give Archie that satisfaction. Plus, I had no need to cry when I could be angry about all the realizations I was too late in reaching.

It was no wonder he had shanking family issues with Sir Avery!

"Allie…" he said, but I simply shook my head to tell him to stop. "Allie, look. I'm really sorry about all of this, but we need to move."

In the most accusing, hurtful tone I could come up with, I told him with all sincerity, "You are dead to me." To my surprise, he flinched and stooped down to look me straight in the eye.

"I know you mean that too. But if you don't get up and walk, we're going to have to carry you."

"Don't you touch me."

I crossed my legs, grabbed onto a few sturdy roots in the ground, and waited for him to do something.

"Allie, we really will carry you." His voice was challenging, and then he made to follow through when I didn't move.

"I'll walk," I said as he got too close. I stood up — still feeling mildly faint and disoriented — and ordered my feet to move.

I walked slowly, trying to buy time. I only stole one glance at the Escali who had come with us, just long enough to see his thick eyebrows set over small cloudy eyes. We were headed toward the lake, but I had thought we were closer than we were. After a few minutes of slow travel, I heard voices in the distance. They were calling for me too.

Archie and Ekvid heard them as well. Before they could silence me, I made another break for it and yelled back, "HELP! ESCALIS! I'M OVER HERE, ARCHIE'S A TRAIT—"

Archie caught up within a second, stuck his hand in my mouth, and I bit down hard. I was sure it was hurting like a nightmare, but he didn't take it out. I tried again to wrestle myself away as he tightened an arm around my middle, but Ekvid grabbed both of my feet and the two of them picked me up like a sack of flour to be hauled to the lake.

They arrived at the edge where they set me down and Archie wrenched his hand out of my mouth.

"Please don't start yelling!" he said quickly, "Just give me a minute and let me expl—"

"HELP!" I screamed, "I'M OVER HE—"

But before I could finish, Archie and Ekvid grabbed my shoulders and threw me through the air, into the drenching deep.

CHAPTER SEVENTEEN

I crashed into the algae-ridden lake water with the full force of their throw, and my momentum didn't halt until I was several cubits under.

So this was how dying was going to be? Fine, but I wasn't going to sink without a fight!

I kicked out hard with my feet and tried my best to swim upwards to no avail. I wasn't a decent swimmer by any standards. Did Archie know that? That I was capable of drowning in a shallow pond? I *might* have enough breath to last me until I breached the surface, and then I could make enough noise to catch the attention of someone nearby.

The lightheaded sensation began to kick in and my lungs began crying the same word over and over again. *Drowning, drowning!* I was almost there, only a little ways left, and finally I surfaced.

I breathed in the air and let one waterlogged cough escape, pulling my short hair from my eyes, and then I saw Archie jumping in the water and swimming toward me. I instantly forgot about yelling for help in my rage of yelling obscene curses at Archie.

"YOU FILTHY—" I was cut short as he grabbed me and pulled

me under. I tried to kick him but the water slowed my attacks into ineffective blows.

He pulled me deeper and deeper until I couldn't possibly get back to the surface.

I truly tried to strangle him as we descended, but still, we went deeper. I couldn't hold my breath any longer, but I wasn't going to let it out before Archie did. That would be letting him win.

Why he hadn't left yet to head toward the surface was a mystery to me. I didn't stand a chance of ever making it back to breathable air. The other Escali was swimming down behind us. *Right, because Archie really needed his help.*

I hadn't realized it, but we had turned into a small underwater tunnel, and then I understood what was going on. We were headed for an underwater cave.

My lungs decided to collapse, and I breathed in a mouthful of water that stung my nose and forced me to cough all my remaining air out as well. Seconds later we broke through into a dry pocket where I could breathe again. Archie hauled me onto solid ground while I coughed out water with such force that my eyes teared up and I could feel the pressure of blood reddening my face.

"Are you alright?" he asked. He had brought me to a completely barren cave, save a few rocks situated in the now lapping water.

"YOU DIRTY BACKSTABBER!" I half cried, breaking free of him to clutch a large boulder in the water. "IS THIS WHAT'S GOING ON? I'LL JUST GO MISSING FOR THREE MORE DAYS AND YOU'LL SEND ME BACK HOME WITH NO MEMORY OF THIS? OF YOUR TREACHERY? AND THEN YOU'RE GOING TO PRANCE BACK TO THE DRAGONA AND PRETEND TO BE MY FRIEND?" I looked him in the eyes to find him smiling as I ranted, as though my panic amused him.

I flung both of my arms wide open, and a magic I didn't know I had inside me took control. I held my hands up to see each glowing brightly, throwing light everywhere. My eyes glowed too, illuminating my vision. My entire being was filled with magic, and I took no time in aiming it all at Archie and unleashing.

He threw up some sort of magic barrier in between us to stop my attack — a shield that kept my siege of white crackling energy from touching him. *Shanking Epic!*

The other Escali was standing to the side of us, not knowing what to do, so I took away his options before he could choose. Letting up on the barrage of Archie's defenses for only a second, I sent a flash of brilliant destruction toward the Escali, knocked him into the wall opposite, and watched him crumple. Archie took full advantage of the moment, leapt onto the boulder next to me, and twisted my left arm behind my back. My palm was facing out — not smart on his part.

I lurched forward to pull him off the rock, then launched myself backwards, slamming Archie into the cavern wall. I tried again to break away from him. His hold was too tight so I shot all my power through the left hand still pinned behind me, knowing it would cripple him as soon as it hit — but it never did. He had put up that shield between us, which absorbed most of the onslaught, but redirected some of it back toward me.

It felt like the shock after building up too much static, but like that shock had been multiplied by every grain of sand on the beach. I fell forward a step and gasped as I tried to get a hold of myself again. My nerves had been fried.

Archie let me fall to the ground and then backed away, shaking, to lean against the wall as if it was the only thing holding him up. I brought myself slowly up to see him on even terms, both of us unstable and out of breath.

"So what happens now, Allie?" he asked as he shuddered and eyed the glow of my hands.

"I don't know," I whispered, but my voice wasn't my own. A strangely ethereal tone made it sound menacing, and my strength was already returning to my limbs. Archie slid down the wall to sit on the ground and flinched when I raised my hands again. I crouched down next to him. "What's the matter? Don't like the disadvantage?" He laughed shakily.

"I knew something like this would happen. Could you stop glowing for a second and talk?"

"No!" I said, stepping back. I rubbed my fingers together, feeling energy buzz between them. "But *you* are about to explain everything to me."

Without any warning signals from Archie, every muscle in my body suddenly refused to move, and I was stuck with one arm frozen out in front of me. *No.* How was this fair? I finally found my power, and even that was useless now? No! I would find a way to break free of this new magic.

From behind me, a new and deep voice of confidence said, "The power of destruction, Allie. Impressive."

I saw Archie relax slightly into the wall, and I knew instantly he wasn't the one using this power — which meant the Escali behind me could only be one. *The* Prince Avalask. Even if I could move, I would have been too terrified to actually turn around to look at him. I could not acknowledge that I was in the presence of the monster of our age.

"Allie, I need you to hold this for me," Prince Avalask said. All I saw of him was his arm, draped beneath a black fur sleeve, reaching from behind me to place a tiny golden stone in my hand.

I shrieked as soon as the pebble dropped onto my palm. It began to steal everything from me. My brightly lit eyes dimmed as the magic I had so recently found was absorbed into the stone. I tried to drop it or even shake it off, but I still had absolutely no ability to move my arms or any other part of my body.

Not only was my magic energy leaving, my real energy was being taken as well. I felt sure I would have collapsed to the ground if I wasn't fully immobilized. I was at least on the verge of losing my vision and consciousness.

I heard fingers snap behind me, and the stone disappeared from my hand. I had no glow left in my eyes, and hardly any life either. I swayed in and out of reality, but still heard most of Archie and Prince Avalask's conversation.

Prince Avalask, still out of my sight, was telling him, "Your opinion doesn't matter to me right now. Head the Humans off. Tell them you saw her taken. She and I will have words, and she's all yours as soon as you're back."

Archie began to argue with him, but Prince Avalask threw me somewhere new where I couldn't hear what was said.

The tiny cell I landed in was dead silent, except for the tiny snaps of a burning torch. It cast a gloomy flicker on nothing more than a wooden door with bars across the top and a hammock hung straight across the room.

I kicked the door and ripped the torch off the wall to hurl it furiously to the ground. I stomped a foot and then shivered — my leather clothes slimy and dripping onto the floor while my sopping wet hair stuck to my face. I was absolutely too exhausted to be throwing a fit. Finally I was alone, and one thing above all others needed to happen.

I lay down on the hung mesh, curled in on myself to keep warm, and covered my face with both hands, hopelessly pulling in a stuttering breath. I finally released the sob of anguish that had been building since the day I had woken in the woods as a broken soul, and I let my tears fall through the hammock onto the floor.

Everybody has to die sometime, I told myself. I think I might have fallen asleep and woken again. I wasn't positive.

Except I'd be lucky if the Escalis simply killed me. I knew that wasn't their intention. The Escali king needed something from me. The Escali Epic was going to get it.

I couldn't dedicate my mind to that stress right now. I had to assess the situation.

My hands weren't bound — that was good — but my short swords were still gone. I reached out for the magic I had used against Archie, but I couldn't access it. My hands were so frozen I couldn't even move my fingers, and my whole body shuddered to keep warm as my wet clothes refused to dry. I got up strenuously from the hammock to grab the torch I had thrown and hold my hands over it. They felt immediately better as the heat sank in.

I could hear somebody approaching outside, so I threw the torch back into its socket on the wall and pulled my legs in to my body to stay warm as the door opened. My heart sank and burned as Archie stepped quietly inside, but I was too cold and tired to inform him of the rotten things he resembled.

He had a blanket with him, which he quickly tossed onto me. "I have to talk fast because Prince Avalask thinks I've already left. I'm sorry, Allie. I know it's cold down here." He talked like we were still friends.

"I hate you," I muttered as loudly as my voice would let me.

"I know you do, but not forever I hope." He pulled the blanket around my shoulders. I would have shrugged it off if I wasn't shivering.

"So what now?" I whispered.

"Well, right now I have to go, and you'll have to stay here for a while. I need to get back up to the surface before anyone notices I'm gone."

"And what will you tell them when you get back home?" I could feel anger returning, but no magic accompanied it this time.

At least he was honest, telling me, "I haven't decided yet. I'll probably tell them you were kidnapped by Escalis, and I saw the whole thing but was too far away to stop it. Or they may just think you ran off after Liz told you about the blood test."

"You can't pull this off." I wanted to scream. "I'll get out of here, and I'll tell everyone. We'll see what Anna and Sir Darius do to you when—"

I was interrupted as an Escali came through the door and growled upon seeing Archie. "You're not supposed to be here."

"I know. I was just leaving. Just thought I'd come say 'bye' before I was gone. Allie," Archie looked directly at me, "I won't be back for a while, but you'll understand once I am. You're going to be alright. I promise." I didn't respond, so he turned to go, leaving the door open.

The Escali watched him depart and then turned his attention to me. "I have a question to ask you."

"I'm not going to tell you anything," I spat. I had a plan forming in my mind, and my strength seemed to be coming back at a good rate.

The Escali let out a deep laugh at my reaction, further infuriating me. "I'm not about to torture you. Do you have any idea why you're here?"

I glared at him in silence for a second and then jumped off the hammock and raced toward the open door.

I underestimated the Escali's reflexes, and he was as fast as lightning in slamming the door shut before I could get to it. I looked into his piercing, foggy eyes, and he asked again, "How much do you know about why you're here?"

"How about this," I said as I backed away from him, "let me list all the reasons for you on the fingers of *one hand*! One, Escalis are evil. Two, Archie's a traitor. Three, I probably know something you want to know. But I can tell you right now, I will never—"

The Escali growled to himself and then opened the door and left, closing it behind him. Nothing was making sense — except that I needed to get out. With him gone, I wrapped the blanket around my shoulders and pushed and pulled at the door — pushed and pulled at the *wooden* door, and then wondered how long it would be until somebody would be along to check on me. The longer I sat wondering, the less time I would have to make something work.

I pulled the torch off the wall and stuck it under the wood, hoping it would eat quickly. Obviously I knew the door wouldn't shoot up in flames, but I didn't expect the fire to consume *quite* so slowly. As wood charred away I would move the torch to a different area of the excavation, then pull as much of the burnt area off as I could before moving the torch again. It was burning my hands, but I didn't take much notice. I wished I had the magic I used against Archie again — it would definitely make things faster.

The hole in the door was almost to the point where I could try to squeeze through when the Escali came back, accompanied by two others. He was angry and irritated by the damage I had caused, and relieved I hadn't succeeded. The other two found it funny and were trying to suppress laughs. I hoped my mischief got him into trouble.

"We are here to escort you to Prince Avalask," he said, wiping the smile from my face. "If you'll follow me." He opened the door, then stepped aside and motioned for me to follow. I absolutely did not want to, but it was inevitable with the three of them there, so I might as well face the prince with a little bit of dignity. I stood up and walked out of the cell behind the Escali as the other two walked silently behind me.

The Escali in front spoke, but I was too busy contemplating my fate to listen.

Prince Avalask could probably violate my mind in a heartbeat, know everything I knew, and see anything I had ever seen... He would know the location and layout of the Dragona, everything I had ever heard from my friends, the best ways to infiltrate — Wait... wouldn't he already know everything from Archie? Yes, so I was back to the original question. What did they need me for?

If I used to know something of importance, I should probably be glad I couldn't remember it anymore. Whatever my old secrets were, at least I couldn't be tempted to tell them to the Escalis now.

The cave grew larger, and our walk came to an end outside a pair of spectacularly carved obsidian doors running twenty cubits up to the top of the tunnel. The engravings in the black glass depicted great battles, gleaming heroes, and Escali kings through their bloody triumphs, all highlighted by the small amount of light filtering through from the other side of the door. I wished I could have stayed and looked at it longer to put off the coming encounter, but one of the Escalis pushed the thick glass open and the four of us entered.

While terrifying, it was simply amazing. Lining the enormous hall were pillars of black obsidian, all of them reflecting light as though the sun shone from the middle of the room. It housed a throne at one end, sitting on which was Prince Avalask with all his might and power. The hall must have been designed so large for a reason, because walking down its length with an Escali on each side and one behind me was a blow to my morale. Such a doom walk would be a blow to anybody.

The Prince wore a dark fur robe that swept to the floor, had icy green eyes set into his battle-ready face, and long flowing hair, so dark that simply calling it black wouldn't do it justice. It was an unnatural shade of midnight, as I had once been warned.

No fangs though.

We approached the base of the throne and the three Escalis around me kneeled. When I didn't, I got a hand in the back of each knee that made me.

"You may leave now." The Epic's voice rang through the hall, and the Escalis stood, bowed, and then started their return walk. I was on my knees and defenseless, and I set my shaking hands on the stone floor as panicked discomfort flooded me. As soon as the door shut, I was back on my feet and sorting through my options. If Prince Avalask was anything close to Sir Avery, I knew options were impossible to come by.

"Come here," he said, standing up.

"Actually, I'd rather not," I replied, backing away. I didn't make it far before my feet stopped working and I couldn't make them move despite all effort.

"Allie, my goal isn't to force this on you," he said, releasing his hold. I darted to the side and jumped behind one of the massive pillars, promising myself I wouldn't plead with him. With my back pressed to it, I could hear him laughing to himself from the other side. Then the laughing suddenly stopped.

I chanced a glimpse around the corner but jumped when he appeared right in front of me.

"Just tell me what you want," I demanded, wishing my voice sounded like I had control.

"I only want to talk," he said, raising a hand to my face.

"No, you shanking don't!" I felt my magic from before flood back into my body, readying to save me. The instant I shot a stream of raw power at him, he had a shield like Archie's up to protect him, but his seemed to cost him no effort.

"As I said before, very impressive," he commented, "but I don't have the time to deal with your games right now." My hands went suddenly numb, and although they still glowed white, I couldn't move my fingers or use them at all. Prince Avalask put a hand on my face and I felt the same serenity as I had with Sir Avery. Warmth tried to seep into the crevices of my mind, but I retaliated with mental stabs of power, keeping it away from all that was vital.

Feeling returned to my fingers as I distracted him on the mental playing field, and I shot at him from the palm of my hand as soon as I could. He withdrew from my mind to shield himself before my magic hit, and I saw a flash of irritation cross his face. Pain shot into my hands to immobilize them this time.

"You need to stop being foolish and listen," Prince Avalask growled, his words drenched in more magic than sound. They compelled me to stop fighting, even though my life depended on staying strong.

"Let me go, and I might listen to you!" I said, not sure if I could resist a second command from him.

"Fair deal. Let me into your mind, and I'll let you go."

I shook my head and growled, "Likely."

"I'm not trying to attack you. Just to communicate. Why can't you ever make things easy?"

I glared back and said, "You make it sound like we've met before."

"Once or twice," Prince Avalask said with a frightening chuckle to himself. "Tell you what. How about I let you go, on the condition you come back?"

"I..." I paused... "don't understand."

"I let you go now, you find your answers, and then you come back and we'll pick up where we left off." I knew he wouldn't just let me go. What was the catch?

"And it's that simple? I get to walk out those doors right now?"

"Yes, because I have places I need to be, and not much time to waste. But if you do leave, you have to return, and you can't contact any Humans while you're gone. Don't even try to get close, or leave messages, nothing. I hope I've made it apparent that there is no place you could go that would be safe from me if you broke our deal."

"What answers am I supposed to be looking for? And what am I supposed to find when I can't talk to anybody?" I felt like I was suddenly contaminated. If I *did* talk to anybody, it would be the end of both me and them.

"You can talk to Archie. He has your answers."

"I don't want to talk to Archie."

"Then you'll have to stay here, and we can continue—"

"Ok, fine!" I leaned away from his magic filled hands. "How am I supposed to find him?"

"Don't worry, you'll find him." He made another wave of his hand and everything around me disappeared, replaced by trees, earth, and sunshine.

I instantly knew where I was. Behind me was the trail from

Mizelga's cabin to the Dragona. I could even see where Archie had run off and killed the tama cat. My mind reminded me of the inhuman concentration on his face when he had smelled it, like he was driven by a predator's instincts. *How had I not noticed?*

A tiny snap sounded next to me, and both my short swords fell into the underbrush. I could barely believe it, but I dug them out of the bushes, put them on, and walked to the path. The entire emotional spectrum raged in my mind, but above the rest was a strong sense of confusion. How was any of this happening?

The way home was apparent, so I started down the trail at a running pace I could maintain until I got there. I had time to think about what I would do when I found Archie. I had the time, and I probably *could* have thought about it, but I didn't really want to.

I came out to the field where I had been walking with him earlier in the day, but remembering that I couldn't be seen by anyone, I retreated into the trees and continued toward the Dragona under their cover. I wasn't sure if I would try to defy Prince Avalask or not. I didn't fancy the thought of him hunting me down, and I believed he would do it. Was there a chance Sir Avery would protect me from him?

Distant movement caught my attention, and I looked back up the mountainside to see Archie running down.

He was completely unaware of me, and I wanted to keep it that way. I grabbed the closest tree, pulled myself onto the lowest limb, then climbed to the next. As long as he stayed on the trail, he would come close enough to be ambushed. I could see him muttering to himself as he kept up the pace, and I edged out of sight behind the trunk to wait for him.

He finally passed right underneath me, and I jumped down with both my swords drawn. As soon as my feet hit the ground, Archie drew his own and whipped around to meet me.

CHAPTER EIGHTEEN

swung with more strength than ever before, and
though he parried me, both swords crashed into the rocky hillside,
releasing a shower of sparks in every direction. Archie's blade
broke on impact, leaving him with only a handle and a jagged scrap
of metal. He held up the stub of his sword and gave me his
expression that said *really?*

"Now I'm going to need a new one—"

I took the opportunity to shove him backwards into a tree and
hold my sword to his throat. "I want to know what is happening
and why!" I demanded.

"I thought Prince Avalask was telling you!"

"Prince Avalask? He told me to hunt *you* down and ask *you!*
What is going on? No, just answer this. Is he your father?"

"What?"

"Prince Avalask!" I shouted, making Archie hold his hands up
with a grimace to brace himself. "Is. He. Your father?"

"No! Holy life, no." He met my eyes and began to understand,
"Is that what you've suspected this whole time? You thought I was
the new Epic?"

"I thought I could trust you! What is going on? Mages can't have
more than one power! Escalis don't have any unless they're Epics,

189

and I've *seen* you using more than one. Who are you? Are you one of them?"

"In case you haven't noticed, Allie, I don't have any arm spikes. And I only have one power. Just the shield. Plus, I'm pretty sure I'm bleeding all over your shiny little knife there, which an Escali wouldn't do." I flicked my eyes to the sword at his throat and saw red, Human blood flowing onto the blade.

"If you're not one of them, then how could you betray us?" I asked. I lowered the sword, but grabbed his shoulders and rammed him against the tree one last time.

"I haven't betrayed you." He took a step away from the tree, but kept his hands apart in a gesture of peace. "I'm trying to help."

"Help? I thought you were sane! I can't believe this is happening."

"I know this isn't making a whole lot of sense, but I'm really not the bad guy here."

"I can't believe this is happening," I repeated, keeping a tight hold on my swords.

"Allie—"

"So you've been spying for the Escalis?" I brandished one of the blades as I spoke. "That's been the answer this whole time?"

"Not... Not *really*. I've been going back and forth, but I'm not doing anything wrong—"

I stuttered, "Nothing, *what*? Nothing— nothing wrong? What are you— Escalis are violent, aggressive, unreasonable, and they'll use whatever you tell them to kill us all! People are murdered on a daily basis, and you're helping to do it. They want us dead just because we're here, and I don't even want to start on that rogue king they've got. Izfazara has got it in for all of us. I just can't believe... I can't believe you don't get that."

"None of that is true," Archie said calmly, taking very slow steps around me. "The Escalis aren't even the ones who started the war.

We're in *their* territory. If they had come into ours, if they tried to take over Tekada, you can't say Humans wouldn't—"

"We wouldn't have killed them in cold blood!"

"The Escalis aren't killing in cold blood—"

"So what about the Escalis who chased us out of Treldinsae? Are you going to tell me they didn't want to kill us?"

Archie stopped when he got to a rotted stump and sat back against it to explain, "No, ok they wanted to, but they were a special circumstance."

"*Special circumstance?* They were both—"

"That's completely different. The two of them are particularly evil. You can't judge the whole race based on them. They happen to dislike us more than the rest of the world," he said in agitation.

"Us? Who's us?"

"You and me, but mostly me... It's a long story."

I simply gaped. He was causing more questions than answers! Where did I start? I could barely think past what I knew to be true. Escalis were evil. I could at least get that straight with him.

"Then what about the ones in my room, I *misheard* them saying they wanted to kill me? They really just wanted to talk?" Answer *that* Archie.

"Those were the same Escalis from the bridge, Allie, and I'll tell you again that they're wicked. They took you from the Dragona, and I don't know why. They weren't supposed to."

"You don't know why? Well how fortunate I escaped—"

"Allie! I'm the one who helped you escape!"

"And how did you do that, Archie? How did you know they were coming for me?"

Archie exhaled exasperation and replied, "They were clearly going to hunt us down after they chased us from Treldinsae. Escalis don't let prey escape. Ever. So I grabbed some friends to help defend both of us."

191

At least he hadn't used another power to sense the Escalis in my room. Maybe he wasn't an Epic after all.

"Well it's your fault they knew where to find me. You gave them the Dragona's location."

Archie scoffed at that accusation and said, "Quit acting blind. The Escalis know exactly where the Dragona is. That wasn't my doing."

"And throwing me in the lake wasn't your doing either?"

"No… that was me… I didn't want to, but I didn't have any other choice. I can explain why, but you won't like it." Archie sighed, "Are you ready for the hardest part of this?"

"Hmmmm, something harder than finding out your best friend is in league with your greatest enemy? Sure, how much worse can it get?"

"You'll be surprised." He looked around at everything but me. "I'm not really sure how I'm going to say this…" I could see on his face that he knew I would never believe him. "Ok, you know how you lost your memory and had to start all over?"

"Yes. I'm aware."

"Well before that, you used to do what I do. You used to bring information back to the Escalis, but still lived at the Dragona with all your friends. You led a secret life just like I do now. We've just been trying to get you back, Allie. Remember the first time the Escalis tried to contact you in the woods? That was right after we first realized something was wrong with you—"

"And then you showed up right after," I finished his thought in disbelief. I wouldn't have considered my first encounter with the Escalis as them trying to *contact* me, but that was beside the point.

"Those first two who jumped me said I had something to atone for," I said.

Archie smiled slightly as he replied, "You and I always have something to atone for. It comes with the job. We're in trouble all the time for breaking Escali rules while we're keeping cover."

It couldn't be. Had I really led a double life? Was I such a scoundrel that I actually went behind my friends' backs and—

"Escalis really aren't evil," Archie stated again. "Aggressive, yes, but not unreasonable. This whole war is ridiculous. If we didn't have a stupid king and such a desire on both sides to get revenge, none of this would be happening."

"What, this war is our fault now? They're raiding our cities and killing anyone they come across—"

"And Humans are doing any different? Neither side is taking any initiative to end it."

"You can't end something with an enemy you can't talk to!"

"Can't, or won't?" Archie pressed.

"Neither! You expect us to get within shouting distance of those murderers?"

"Exactly! If you came across an Escali who wanted to talk—"

"I wouldn't be able to. We don't speak the same language."

"Don't give me that, Allie. You know Escalira."

"No, I don't. I just found my power, and that's not it."

"I'm not saying it's a power. Escalira is a language you remember from your past, the same way you knew how to speak the Human language when you woke up. You understood the first two Escalis who tried to contact you, remember that?"

"They were speaking Human—"

"I guarantee they weren't. The ones in the woods just now weren't speaking Human either. And look at this," he pulled out a scrap of paper and unfolded it. It was my name, the one I had written on the chore chart before Archie ripped it out and rewrote it. "Look at it Allie. You wrote it in Escalira." I briefly glanced at the paper, and sure enough, the symbols didn't look like Human writing even though I could read them easily. "You were writing *everything* in Escalira," Archie said with a hint of exasperation. "If only you knew how many times I had to come behind you and redo your messages."

193

"Ok," I threw up my hands, unsure of how to dispute such evidence, "so what if that is what I used to be? I'm a different person now. Maybe losing my memory and starting over was a good thing. Maybe I'll actually have some loyalty in this life!"

"Loyalty to what?"

"My people!"

"And what if your people aren't always right?

"You're saying yours are?"

"Not always, and I don't always side with them either. I take the side of whoever is making more sense at the time."

Even if he wasn't an Escali, he referred to them as his people. "Some loyalty you have!"

"I help them both, Allie—"

"You can't have loyalty to both! You have to pick one, and you have to pick the right one. There isn't anything that the Escalis have that I would side with—"

"What about the fact that the Escalis are willing to negotiate and end the war? The fact that the Humans are invading *Escali* territory. Places that have been Escali for a thousand years are now under attack by Humans. People need to realize very fast that Izfazara is willing to negotiate, but none of his successors are. If this war doesn't end soon, it never will."

"We're not the ones who are unable to negotiate—"

"Really? You just said yourself that you can't be expected to get within shouting distance of those murderers. If an Escali got within three miles of the Dragona, you're going to claim it wouldn't have a dragon sent out to hunt it down?"

"Well, no—"

"And who won't negotiate?"

I stopped to think for a second… I knew I had reasons for hating the Escalis, but Archie was somehow… *Making sense?* I almost felt like listening to what he was saying. Not quite, but almost.

"Did you know the Escalis really could take down the entire Human existence in a matter of weeks? The Dragona is an especially easy target, fooling itself into thinking it's hidden. The only reason the Escalis haven't killed us is because Izfazara is one of the fairest kings the Escalis have ever had."

"Fair?"

Archie took a deep breath, seeing I wasn't convinced by anything he was feeding me. "Allie, we really used to be friends before any of this happened. We were friends before you thought I betrayed you, but we were also friends back before you lost your memory — back when you were on both sides like I was. I'm not lying to you. Even if you choose never to come back to us, I just want you to know the truth."

"You're right that I'm not going back. I'll never serve the Escalis, Archie, not when they kill my people every day. How could I? And how can you? How can you sleep at night?"

"I don't. And I end up having to make decisions nobody should ever have to make. It's not always fun, but if you could understand how many lives I've saved in the process, and how many you've saved in the past, you would get why I still do this. Sometimes, if you help one side out enough, the battle's over before anyone's dead."

I thought about that for a second... The situation was a lot bigger than I had thought. This wasn't just about Archie and me — it involved everybody in the war.

"So..." I said, unsure of where to go from there. "How does all of this have to do with kidnapping me? All that trouble just so you could convert me back into a spy with you?"

"Not exactly," he said, once again choosing his words carefully. "See... You were about to be discovered... Your former life was about to be discovered at least, because of the blood test... And, it's just..."

"What are you talking about?" His prolonging was irritating me.

"Look at my neck. Do you notice anything?" he asked. I saw nothing but the blood from where I had just cut him. I looked a little closer and noticed —

"The cut I just gave you is gone," I said. Archie raised his eyebrows but didn't add anything. "Archie. Who. *Are you?*"

"I'm half-Escali," he said. "My father was Human, my mother was Escali. Healing quickly isn't a power I have, it's just a genetic ability. It's the same with my sense of sight, hearing, and smell, and you might have noticed how much faster and stronger I am than everybody else."

I didn't reply due to a loss for words. There was nothing left to say.

"But that's not all," he added, watching me carefully. "I'm not the only one at the Dragona with this heritage. There is another —"

I didn't want to hear him finish; I had a pretty good guess who. I picked up one of the jagged remnants of his sword and cut open the flesh of my palm before he could go any further. He stopped talking as I watched the red blood flow from my hand. Nothing happened at first, but then the skin started to grow itself back together and the cut began to disappear.

Archie said nothing as my heart stopped for the tenth time of the day.

I was an Escali.

I *am* half Escali.

The enemy I had grown to hate — I'd become. I'd always been. Now it all made sense.

Archie remained silent, waiting for me to speak first. It took me a while. I was thinking about everything he had said, breathing harder with each thought. Could I really have been on the wrong side before I lost my memory? I didn't even know which side was the wrong one anymore. What he had said actually made some sense. *It shouldn't make sense!*

196

"I didn't know half-Escalis existed," I finally said to break the silence.

"Nobody does. If Humans knew about us, they'd probably be a little more on the lookout."

"Where are your arm spikes?" I asked.

"I broke them off so I could blend in at the Dragona. So did you."

I heard my name being shouted in the distance. I could see Archie's worry that I would shout back or try to escape to them, but I had no intention of doing so.

"I can prove what I'm saying is true," he said quickly.

"Can you really?" I asked. "I'm sick of not knowing."

"Yes, all I need is a little trust, and we'll go back to the mountain. Can you give me that?"

I had to return anyway for fear of Prince Avalask, so I might as well have somebody I knew with me. I could go with him, see what he had to show, then return to Prince Avalask and still keep my loyalties in the right place...

"Lead the way," I said. Archie was visibly relieved and stepped onto the mountain trail to begin climbing.

As I started after him, I could still hear the sounds of my friends calling. I was betraying them in every way, and they were still out trying to find me.

CHAPTER NINETEEN

We had only covered a small distance before I decided I needed time to myself to think everything over. Too much to take in all at once. Too much dread in having to go back to the Escalis' lair and see Prince Avalask again.

As we ascended the trail, the voices calling for me died out. I began trying to make my footsteps as quiet as possible so that when they disappeared altogether, maybe Archie wouldn't notice. A large branch loomed over the trail, and I grabbed it to pull myself up. I didn't even look to see if Archie had noticed. He was smart enough to understand that I needed some time alone.

I climbed to the topmost branches and sat on one near the trunk, sturdy enough to support me. From where I sat I could see the Dragona, the vast expanse of our cedar forests, the lake… My mind wandered to my recent encounter with the lake…

How could any of it be true? I pulled out one of my swords and cut the palm of my hand again, just to be sure. It hurt, stung, bled, and then healed itself within a minute. No wonder I was about to be discovered, if someone tried to cut my arm open for a blood test and saw *that*, they wouldn't know what to think. I tried to think of a time when I had been wounded, or simply bled for more than a few seconds. I tried to find evidence that maybe the entire thing was an elaborate setup, but I couldn't think of a single injury that had ever stuck around.

I quickly checked the back of my hand, but found that even the carved symbol from earlier in the day had disappeared without a scar. I recalled when I had smashed my knee in my first encounter with the Escalis. Was the aggression I witnessed really just part of their culture? Maybe. And then my knee had been completely better only a few hours afterward. I remembered the scrapes all over my body from pulling myself out of the Breathing Sea, but they had quickly disappeared as well. Michael had been covered from head to toe in scratches while Archie and I had only seemed to sustain damage to our clothes.

So assuming I was… *half-Escali…* could I still stay on the Human side? I knew they wouldn't accept me if they ever found out. It was surprising the Escalis did, because they seemed so hostile toward everything. Why would *they* accept someone who was half enemy?

Maybe Archie was on the right path, trying to end the war, but what could one person do? I was starting to question everything. Archie wasn't stupid by any means, and if he really believed his actions had an impact...

As I thought through our conversation, a falcon swooped in and landed on a branch to my left. It was grey with flecks of a darker shade all over its face, and its feathers reflected the sunlight. It leaned over, head-butted my arm, and then cocked its head to the side.

"You can tell Archie I'm on my way," I told it, but the bird's gaze remained unbroken. It head-butted my arm again and resumed staring at me as though it understood everything. Of course I was imagining it, but I liked to think something might understand.

I knew I had to climb out of the safety of the tree. Not much of my mind had cleared, but I felt ready to come down. Once back on the ground, I looked up the trail to see Archie waiting for me. He understood I needed the time. I didn't even wonder anymore how he knew me so well, he just always had.

"So... I met your bird up in the trees. It's... pretty," I said awkwardly as the falcon flew down from the canopy, landing on his arm.

"Who, Flak?" He gave it a dead mouse he had produced from nowhere. "Flak's not my falcon. She's yours." She took off from Archie's arm and stretched her feet out to land on mine. The talons were sharp and strong as she held tightly.

"She's mine?" I asked. I went to stroke her feathers, but she didn't seem to like it, so I stopped.

"Yes, but she's been helping me recently. You know, all falcons are smart, but Flak is really something else. She's the reason we were able to get you away from Sav and Gat, because my friends wouldn't have shown up in time without her. "

"Well... thank you," I said to her. She seemed content and took off into the trees, leaving me back on the ground. I was jealous. I wished I could just fly away and leave everything behind. "Let's get going," I said as I jumped ahead of Archie and started climbing the hill again. It only took him a few strides to catch up with me.

"I have to warn you about several things before we get there," he said.

"Do tell."

"Ok. Well the first thing is basically who we are. You might hear someone call you a Tally. Talliendra means 'half' in Escalira, so that's just what we're called."

"I asked you what that meant before! You told me that was what the rest of the world called Humans."

"I lied."

"So there are more like us?"

"Only a few. Escalis look down on us because we're part Human, but we usually have information they want, so they try to treat us well at the same time. It's complicated."

"Yeah, but it makes sense," I said, pausing for a second to think about the word *Tally*. "I feel like everything I know is wrong now. What all have you lied to me about?"

Archie didn't have to think hard about his answer. "A lot."

"Name the times — since we're being honest now. I want to know everything you've ever told me that wasn't truthful."

"Allie... In complete honesty, I don't think I can name them all."

"Try."

"Alright then... Where to start... First would be on the first day you met me at the Dragona. I pretended I didn't know you when I definitely did. I also told you I couldn't read the map, when I actually could. I wanted to tell you everything that first night, at the Eclipsival, but there were just so many people nearby. I decided to wait.

"And... I lied and said I didn't have a power when I have a shield that protects me. I used it to keep everything in the Breathing Sea from smelling me and Michael. We would have never made it out otherwise. And remember that time outside my room when you hit me in the ankle? I pretended to be injured for a few days, but it had actually hit the shield, so I didn't feel it at all."

I nodded, eyes fixed straight ahead. "I actually noticed that one too. You forgot to limp a couple different times over the next couple days. That was one of the reasons I thought you were an Epic."

"I'm glad I'm not. Life is complicated enough as a Tally. I always told you that I got good at sparring because of my friends. That is half true because the practice helped, but the agility and natural talent comes from being half-Escali. That's the only reason you and I stand a chance against the Escalis in a fight. Not a good chance though, which is why I grabbed my friends to help me at the Dragona."

"Explain to me what happened, Archie."

"I grabbed the other Tallies as fast as I could, knowing we were about to have trouble, but you were gone by the time we got to your

201

room. We caught up to you and the twins outside, and you were completely out of it by then. I probably should have stayed with you after we got you back to your room, but I left again because I thought we might have a real chance of killing Sav and Gat."

"Who?"

"They're the ones with hair as black as Prince Avalask's. The ones from the bridge who were also in your room. And from the description you once gave me, I'm pretty sure Sav is the one who destroyed your memory and carried that little girl off."

"And tore that poor woman's throat out," I mumbled.

"I know. We both have a hundred reasons to hate them. Treldinsae also wouldn't have been such a disaster if not for those two. That was another time I was trying to tell you who you were. I couldn't believe my luck, that you and I would be in an Escali city with no other Humans around. And while we're talking about lies, I didn't find those sasperan arrows just lying outside of Treldinsae. I brought the stunning arrows in my bag so we wouldn't have to kill any Escalis. Then I convinced Michael to bring his bow along before we left."

"Was one of those arrows reserved for me too?" I asked. "In case I tried to run away?"

Archie looked uncomfortable. "I didn't want it to be, but the thought crossed my mind. None of that mattered though, because I had no time to tell you anything once Sav and Gat found us. They probably smelled us, the devils. I'm not saying I think it would have gone well otherwise, telling you who you were in the middle of Treldinsae, but we wouldn't have lost West if Sav and Gat hadn't chased us into the Sea."

"Why didn't you stop them? If you're on their side, they might have listened to you."

"No, Sav and Gat don't listen. They're the ones who took you from the Dragona, remember? They don't care."

"Do you know what they want from me?" I asked.

"No. I can explain a lot about your past, but I don't know everything. I just know you used to keep more secrets than a dead man, and many of them weren't yours."

"What about Sir Avery? What secrets did I know that have him so worried about me?"

"I have no idea. I can only tell you that Sir Avery has never had an issue with you living at the Dragona, whereas the rest of us were warned never to go near it. If I hadn't been there for the sole purpose of helping you, I have no idea what he would have done to me. Whatever you used to do for him, or used to know, I know he valued it highly. Even enough to let me stay."

"I'll bet it's related to what those two Escalis want from me..."

"I'm sure it is. And if you ever see them from a distance, Allie, run. Or if you get the chance to kill one of them, take it. They're more dangerous to us than anything else." I had never heard Archie speak with so much loathing. "Prince Avalask is their older brother, but they aren't like him. They're purely evil, justifying all they do with beliefs of Escali-supremacy. They view Tallies as rotten scum since we're a mix, and even though they constantly try to wipe us out, we can never kill them because they're royalty. Their father is next in line to take the throne, and we'd be dead if we tried."

"So then if Izfazara *and* their father died, would one of them —"

"Yes. They're twins, but Sav would be the one to try to take power. He's the cunning brother. Gat just likes to break things."

"Could it really be any worse than it already is?"

Archie coughed in disbelief. "Izfazara is *nothing* compared to those two. If Sav became king, Tallies would be exterminated, and Humans would probably be enslaved. Izfazara uses Tallies all the time. We're valuable to him, whereas Sav and Gat already try to kill us on sight. Oh and if you ever see their black falcon, Gyr, you can kill him too. He's almost as bad. Just don't do it if Flak's around."

"Alright then. I understand that they don't like Humans, but we still have half of their blood. Doesn't that matter to them?"

"Yes. We're worse than Humans to them. Anybody involved with the enemy is fair game to Sav and Gat."

"Even other Escalis?"

"My sister was full Escali, and they had no problem taking care of her."

I was distracted enough to stumble into a fern as he said so. How horrible. "Holy life, I'm sorry."

"It's in the past. I don't really like talking about it." He frowned and stopped.

"We just passed the place," he said, backtracking a few paces before veering off the trail. He steered through bushes in no apparent direction, startling a small hiding rabbit. Archie instinctually reached to his side as it scampered away, but had nothing to grab.

"Sorry about breaking your sword," I said.

"Naw, if it's breakable, it's not a sword I want to put my trust in. I can get another one. If you had broken my Escali sword, then we would have had a problem." We stopped by a large hole in the ground, which was apparently another entrance to the Escali world. Archie jumped in and I followed after.

We descended and made several turns before reaching a polished, grey stone floor with pillars supporting a massive ceiling. Vines were woven throughout the pillars, so thickly that the stone ceiling was barely visible. Blooming blue flowers on the vines lit the entire room, illuminating several large paintings on the walls.

Archie walked comfortably by the arm-spiked monsters who passed us, but every one of them set me on edge. A few of them drilled me with questioning gazes, either because I had bare elbows or because I was showing fear. I knew the latter was a horrible weakness to display among Escalis, so I held my head high and pretended that the sight of them didn't terrify me.

As soon as we reached an empty corridor, I sat on a protruding piece of the wall that seemed bench-like. "With this life I used to lead… Did I save a lot of lives doing it?"

Archie leaned against the pillar nearest me, and answered, "Tons. You were the best of any of us at getting information and using it. I know for a fact that you once hid a whole village from a surprise attack, and I've seen you smuggle survivors out of enemy territory — on both sides. You had one of the most secret and important jobs in the world, until you forgot what it was."

"But I'm still half-Escali, a hybrid of the two worst enemies in the world. I don't know if this could get any worse."

"Being a Tally isn't that bad. We get the best abilities, the best friends, we don't have to grow old, we don't have to live as aggressively as—"

"We don't grow old?" I stopped him.

"Well, not as fast as normal people. Didn't I mention that?"

"No, you—" I stopped talking when an Escali walked over and joined us. Even if they weren't as bad as I had always imagined, I still wasn't comfortable being so close.

"Archibald. Cruldor requests you immediately," he said to Archie in Escalira. Archie answered accordingly.

"I'll see him later. We haven't been here hardly any time at all."

"The council is requesting you as well. I would advise to not keep them waiting," the Escali said, and this seemed to change Archie's mind.

"What am I supposed to do with— Hey, Tresca," he got the attention of a striking Escali woman. I couldn't tell if it was the shape of her face or her thickly slanted eyebrows that made me think of a wolf, but I would have bet my life she had the killer instinct of one. "Could you take care of Allie for a while? She just got here and isn't quite sure what to think, but I have to go."

"So this is the Tally I've been hearing about," she commented in Escalira. I wasn't sure if I could speak well in a language other than my own, and I didn't want to try.

"Yeah, this is the one. Could you please take her? I have to go talk to the council."

"Yes," she answered, showing more teeth as she spoke than I did when I was angry. "I understand the importance. You may leave."

"Thanks," he said to her, and then turned to me, "I'm sorry, but I've got to run. I'll be back before you know it." He still spoke Human when he was talking to me, which I appreciated.

"Ok, well, have a good life then," I answered. He dashed off and I was left standing next to the Escali who had delivered the message and the dangerously attractive one who was now in charge of showing me around. The spikes on her elbows were still ominous, and when she started away in a different direction, I was hesitant to follow.

"My name's Tresca," she said as I caught up. "What would you like me to show you?" Her tone of voice was almost... *Normal.* I thought Escalis were all about growling and snarling when they talked — it was weird to hear a conversational tone. I decided to try Escalira.

"I don't know," I replied, finding it easy. I felt like I was talking normally, although the language itself was harsh and demanding. "Where did Archie have to go in such a hurry?" I asked.

"You are being accused of treachery, and he has gone to the council in your defense."

"*I'm* being accused?"

"Indeed. It shouldn't take him long either, since he knows what he's doing. Archibald should be able prevent you receiving the death sentence."

I laughed nervously, knowing she wasn't joking. Tresca was anything but subtle.

Without asking for my input, she decided, "We'll go to the Tally caves. Perhaps you can find your way around there."

"Sure, that would be great." I hadn't even thought of the fact that I probably had my own room here. I probably had all my own stuff too.

I followed Tresca down a few more tunnels, all of which were lit by glowing blue flowers, and I realized how very lost I was. We made a right turn, right turn, left turn, right turn, and I was fairly sure I wouldn't be able to find my way out from wherever we were. The most interesting cavern we passed by was a very large space where Escalis younger than me played some sort of team sport. I didn't know the rules and only witnessed a few plays, but I had to admit I envied the way they slammed each other into walls and fought as a team to keep the opposition from advancing. Not that I could ever be talked into playing with them.

Distance grew between us as the game distracted me. When I looked back up to see where Tresca had gone, I found a group of Escali children in front of me, led by one arrogant one who seemed more aggressive than the rest. Even as children they were frightening. Their eyes only had a slight fog to them, but the arm spikes were well on their way to becoming lethal, and their slightest movements were still quick and precise.

The one in the lead regarded me with condescension and took a bold step away from his friends. "Hey, Tally," he addressed me in a cocky tone of challenge. "My sister tells me your kind got the most timid qualities of the Human race. Tell me, if I didn't have six friends with me right now, would you even be brave enough to fight me?"

I only needed to glance over this kid half my age to know how to deal with him. "Listen up, you little brat-wad," I startled him by grabbing both his shoulders and pulling him dangerously close to my face. "I don't care if you have twelve friends behind you — I will tear you apart in front of all of them if you ever talk to me like that again. Understand?"

He nodded quickly, and two of the other kids behind him immediately stepped forward to retrieve him from my grasp. "We're really sorry," one of them said.

The other said, "It won't happen again, Talliendra." Ten seconds ago the whole lot had regarded me with scorn. Now I had their respect. Order established.

I strode straight past the group of kids without looking back and rejoined Tresca. She had a thin grin of approval on her face, and said, "There was one correct way to handle that situation, and you did it well. Perhaps you won't be such an outcast among us."

I said nothing in response, but wondered if that was the way things went around here. Tallies were accepted, but only as outcasts.

We came upon a beautiful silver archway that lined the inside of the tunnel. Across the top in elegant Escalira was the word *Talliendra,* and down the sides were beautiful carvings of what appeared to be words, but had no meaning. Not to me at least. Tresca had evidently already seen it before and didn't slow to marvel as we strode underneath. We rounded a corner and saw Archie coming from the other direction, looking for us.

"I thought I might find you down here. Have you found your room yet?"

"No," I replied.

"You're almost to it. Over here," he said, pushing one of the round wooden doors open. I stepped in to see less than I expected. It was just a small cave similar to the prison cell I had recently occupied. One hammock swooped across the room with a few blankets piled on top, a bow leaned against the wall behind it, and a deep rounded chest sat next to everything, holding what I guessed to be my belongings.

"We'll probably have to cut the lock off," Archie said to an old fashioned latch, flaked with rust.

"Wait. I might have the key." In high hopes, I pulled my necklace up from beneath my jerkin, and the lock sprang open as soon as I turned. Finally, something had gone right. I lifted the lid and saw a large assortment of remarkable possessions. Archie sat down to help me pull everything out while Tresca stood distantly by.

First came a large sword, lying on top of its sheath and running the length of the chest. Its blade was gleaming silver, and its hilt was handsomely golden. Intricate dragons were engraved down the blade, and each side of the guard looked like an angel wing. I put it back in its sheath as Archie pulled out a beautiful white quiver with a couple of arrows inside.

"That's dragon skin," Archie said as he tapped on the scaly exterior. Each clink sounded like tapping on glass, yet it was durable like leather. I pulled one of the arrows out to see a sasperan tip, and I was extremely careful to not touch it.

"Is that one of the unending quivers?" Tresca asked from behind me.

"I don't know, what's that?"

She took the quiver from me and pulled all the arrows out. They were sasperan tipped, so she carefully set them on the floor before reaching her hand back into the quiver and pulling out an entire new set of arrows from its depths.

"Whoa," I leaned toward it, although the idea of a bottomless quiver didn't appear to be new to Archie. She set the new group of arrows on the ground and reached in once again to pull out a whole new set. The latest set had regular broad head tips instead of sasperan. She reached in again but came up empty handed.

"That's all there is at the moment, but it only holds as many as you put in." She handed the quiver back to me, and I reached my hand into the bottom, which was exactly where it should have been.

"Huh... So how do I get them back in?" She took the quiver back from me, put in the first group of arrows, and then took the next bundle and shoved them in on top of the first. She handed it back to me with a look that said I was ignorant for not figuring it out myself. "You two have fun sorting through the rest of it. I'm leaving."

She didn't mean, *I'll leave in five seconds' time;* she was already on her way out, and I hoped she heard the "thank you" I called after her.

We continued pulling all sorts of things out. I had a couple sets of Escali clothes, a real dress made of thick green and white fabrics, a large bag full of coins, a box that rattled around but had no apparent opening, and lastly an iridescent bracelet with tiny stones that were dominantly foggy white but reflected flecks of every other color when the light hit them.

"So Archibald..." I said as I examined the bracelet.

Archie grimaced. "I hate that name. Don't ever use it. It's terrible."

"Whatever you say, Archibald."

"I know one you don't like either, so if it's a war you want to start—"

"Such as what? I don't even know what Allie's short for."

"I don't either, but I know how much you hate Allie the Tally."

"Alright, fine," I said, setting the bracelet down. I hated the name already. "We can call it a truce."

"Sounds good to me."

I smiled and looked into the chest to make sure we hadn't missed anything, but what I saw made me look again. We had hit the bottom, but it wasn't as deep as it should have been. I could see a hole in the wood where a knot had existed, and I peered into it to see what I had expected — the chest had a false bottom.

Archie hadn't noticed anything — he was still trying to figure out how to open the box which lacked an opening. I decided I'd check it out later when he wasn't around. Footsteps started coming down the tunnel as I threw a couple things back in the trunk.

"Izfazara now requests your presence." Archie and I looked up to see the same messenger from earlier.

"Already?" Archie put the box down. "Alright, I'll be there as soon as I can." The Escali nodded and left. "Holy life," Archie muttered in frustration. "I'm sorry I can't be here as much as I was hoping on your first day back."

"That's ok," I told him, "I have something I need to do too." Archie watched me inquisitively, clearly waiting for the rest of the explanation. "I told Prince Avalask I would go back to see him after I got some answers." My stomach felt uneasy just mentioning it. Archie noticed.

"You look worried."

"A little bit. I was being difficult last I saw him, so I doubt I'm his favorite person."

"You don't have to worry. He understands."

"Yeah, I know."

"Are you... afraid?"

"No," I scoffed. "But, I don't know... He was trying to get in my head when I saw him, and I don't want him in there," I admitted, feeling weird. I hated feeling weak. Archie put his arm around my shoulders, which was strangely comforting.

"I'll come with you."

"No, you have a king to talk to."

"I said I'd get there when I could. He can wait. Plus, I doubt you know the way to Prince Avalask's hall."

"Not in the slightest."

"Then it's settled," Archie said, helping me put a few of the contents back into the chest.

CHAPTER TWENTY

We arrived at the giant obsidian doors to Prince Avalask's hall, and I froze as Archie made to push them open. "Don't you have to… knock or something?" I asked.

"It's Prince Avalask. He already knows we're here."

The doors swung open of their own accord as if to reinforce Archie's statement. "Allie!" Prince Avalask called from the other end of the hall. "It's been a while. I'm glad you came back to see me."

My stomach, throat, and mind suddenly twisted into permanent knots that might never unravel. Archie had to grab my hand just to persuade me to enter.

"Will you stop with the dread? You're making me sick to my stomach too, and I'm all the way over here." Prince Avalask disappeared and reappeared right in front of us, making me jump. "We're not enemies, and I'm not going to hurt you."

"Then what do you want?" I demanded, possessing just enough pride to keep from fleeing.

"Only to help. I can't give your memories back, but I can show you some of mine about who you used to be."

I wrapped my arms across myself and said, "I'd rather just not." I didn't want to expose my mind to him, or to anybody. "What could you know that's of value to me?"

Prince Avalask said, "This sounds strange, Allie, but I knew you before any of your friends did. I know all about your list of tally marks, and I can even show you memories of the first few hashes you put on there."

Before I could even ask, Archie interrupted, "Now isn't a good time. Not with everything else she's trying to take in."

I had to breathe out a short sigh, because *of course*, Archie knew about my list of tally marks. "What would you show me?" I asked Prince Avalask.

"It's nothing," Archie insisted. "You'll be happier not seeing it."

Although I appreciated Archie's concern, I asked, "Who do the first hashes represent?"

"On the saved side, a few of your friends," Prince Avalask said. "On the death side, your parents. Which would you prefer to see?"

"My parents."

"You really don't want to," Archie said, almost pleading.

"I really do," I replied. I had been waiting on answers for too long to let them get away. "Show me."

Prince Avalask touched my face again, and without fighting him, I fell into a vision more vivid than reality. I could sense emotions and thoughts, I could see colors more vibrantly than I ever had, I could feel the weather affecting the air in the area, and I was able to see through walls into the landscape beyond. It was a small taste of how Prince Avalask perceived the world.

Through my heightened senses I saw a scene taking place outdoors, yet inside the walls of what appeared to be a city. A large crowd of people — Humans — had gathered as though waiting for a show to start on the elevated stone stage.

Small curiosities stood out to me. The women wore dresses, a style I knew to be from our homeland across the ocean. Banners of

King Kelian had been draped from walls and windows, whereas I had never seen one before. The anxious murmur from the crowd also had a slight accent. This had to be Tekada.

A hidden door opened from the wall, revealing the purpose of the event. An Escali with light hair was being dragged out by four strong men, bound in ropes and looking positively worn.

I could sense every emotion in the area, and while almost everybody exuded shock or excitement, a small pocket of mortification stood out among the crowd. I was able to see the faces of two women exchanging glances, their fear setting them apart from the rest. A little blond girl stood on her toes next to them, trying to get a better look. She was an unmistakably younger image of me.

Though both of the women had the same brown hair, the one with the big tummy and beautiful complexion stood out. My mother had features that were distinctly mine. The man she was standing next to, however, didn't resemble me at all. He had darker hair and he looked... He looked like Liz.

"Everybody gaze upon this wretch from Kelianland!" A hook-nosed man shouted from the front. The Escali didn't say or do anything. "Not only was he caught in our territory, but he seems to have corrupted one of our own. This woman knows who she is and has one chance to step forward of her own accord." The speaker looked straight to my mother, but I was no longer with her. I could sense my own upset mind being shepherded away from the danger by the other woman. Little-me didn't know what was going on, but she knew it wasn't good.

"I am the one you're looking for," my mother said as everyone around her turned to gawk. Emotions went wild — the man next to her was overwhelmed with shock, the Escali in the front was terrified, and the overseer was triumphant but confused.

"Where is your daughter?" he demanded.

"Not born yet." She touched her tummy while meeting his gaze.

"You lie!" he hissed. "They are both abominations!"

"This child she is carrying is mine!" the man next to her defended.

"Even on the slight chance that is true, the first daughter isn't! Who in this crowd is harboring her? They will speak now or face the consequences of treason!"

My younger self knew what was going on by that point, and kept quiet as she looked up at the woman gripping her hand. The presence of fear was immense, but the woman committed herself to silence.

"I don't know what child you're talking about," my mother said calmly.

"The one who was born four years ago, yet looks like she's eight! This is your last opportunity to bring her forward!" Everything was silent while everybody waited for something to happen. "So be it. Sir Avery, show us where she is!"

I felt something else in a higher dimension of thinking. Thoughts were being projected through the air toward each other, while nobody could hear them but the two Epic receivers.

Don't do it, Avery, you know this isn't right — It isn't for me to decide — It isn't for your king to decide either! Kelian is misleading all of you, and you know it — It's my responsibility to follow what he says. Don't you dare try to interfere. — You know I will — Your people don't want abominations among them either — Then consider her mother — Her mother is a traitor — She did nothing wrong! — I can see as well as you, but it isn't my decision!

"Sir Avery!" the man shouted again to an open spot on the stage. Sir Avery broke off his mind-conversation with Prince Avalask to become visible, and everybody gasped. "Show us where she is!" he repeated. Sir Avery hesitated but reached out to touch the minds of everyone in the crowd. He looked straight at little-me, but Prince Avalask materialized haphazardly in front of the Human Epic and blasted Sir Avery into the wall. Sir Avery recovered quickly and countered with a wall of ruthless fire, springing into action with inhuman speed.

The entire crowd screamed and scattered as lightning struck around the two Epics, dark clouds forming over their battle. Two Escalis and a Tally climbed up and over the walls with bows drawn, searching the commotion. The Tally was clearly the leader of the rescue, there to help me because of our similarities. They climbed into the crowd as I saw my mother run and jump onto the platform with the Escali.

In the widespread panic, nobody noticed her withdraw a knife from the folds of her dress to cut him loose. One of the Escalis ran to help her while the other ran straight for me to take me from the second woman. The overseer was also on his way over to me.

There was no confusion left about which little girl they were looking for once the Escali had me in his arms, but the overseer wasn't about to let him go. He got to the Escali and hit him over the head with a block of demolished cement, dropping him straight to the ground.

The woman who had taken me tried to stop the hook-nosed man as I bit and kicked at his legs, but he threw her down and picked little-me up. A ferocious growl resonated off every wall, coming from the blond Escali my mother had cut free as he spotted me in the hands of the overseer. The Escali leapt over the heads of everyone left and knocked the man down, catching me in the same movement. He set me on my feet but then was distracted by the king's soldiers lining the ramparts and aiming bows down at the scene. The overseer jumped back up and threw a rope around the neck of the Escali, pulling him back from me.

I heard my mother screaming as the overseer tried to strangle him, and little-me had latched onto his back, sinking teeth into him. The archers on the battlements held at the ready, watching the commotion play out, but the overseer's assault ended when the

Escali thrust his elbow back and sent an arm spike through his stomach.

It wasn't a victory, but rather a cue for the archers to take aim and fire. The Escali jumped over little-me to block the assault, and though I was fine after the arrows finished falling, he wasn't. He hadn't lost a drop of blood, but something about the arrows left him unmoving. My mother tried to get over to us, but her way was blocked by the king's soldiers who had been called to action, preventing her from going anywhere.

Another volley of arrows launched toward both me and my mother, but Sir Avery and Prince Avalask broke apart long enough for Sir Avery to shield my mother and Prince Avalask to deflect the arrows intended for me. Prince Avalask blasted the wall next to me apart before Sir Avery returned to battle with him, causing him to leave me. Little-me was overwhelmed and looked at the Escali lying on the ground next to her. I could sense that my small self vaguely knew him.

I had lost all track of the Tally until he ran over and grabbed little-me in one arm. He jumped onto the rubble of the demolished wall and sprinted away from the commotion. The archers turned to get him before he was out of range, but he was too fast. Little-me threw a fit as the Tally carried her out of danger's reach. She didn't want to leave her family.

King Kelian's soldiers began to nervously close in around Sir Avery and Prince Avalask, having already disarmed my mother. I could sense Prince Avalask realizing it was over, and he broke away from the Human Epic, disappearing and reappearing next to the Tally and my younger self.

He grabbed them both, and the three vanished, ending the vision.

Prince Avalask's hall was back. I felt numb, and Prince Avalask hardened his face to hide the emotions he had relived with me. I didn't know what to think.

"What happened to them?" I asked, dumbfounded.

Prince Avalask's hand shot to his head as though he felt some pain we couldn't. "Ask Archie. He'll tell you." Prince Avalask disappeared and I turned my eyes slowly to Archie. He couldn't have looked any sorrier.

"It's not like it's your fault," I said to him as I sat on the smooth obsidian floor, leaning against a pillar.

"I'm still sorry. You and I actually had a conversation once, about the things we wished we could forget... I wish he wouldn't have shown that to you."

As I reflected bitterly on the memory, Archie sat next to me. He let us fall into silence, waiting for me to talk. "You know what I need?" I looked at him. "I need an enemy. I need someone I can blame all of this on, someone I can hate eternally."

"Wouldn't that be nice."

I stared at the ground, knowing my blame and wrath had no target. "So... what happened to them?"

"Are you sure you want to hear about it right now?"

"I'm sure. I want to know."

Archie took a deep breath and clenched his open hand into a tight fist, as though telling me what happened would hurt us both. "Well... Your father died on the spot—"

"So that Escali was my father?"

"He was. Sara — your mother — lived to give birth to her baby, but we were told she died in the process. Liz's father wanted nothing more to do with the mess, and he left."

"So the baby she was carrying at the time was Liz?"

"Yes. Fully Human, but sent to Kelianland anyway for being a mage," Archie said, sighing. "And then the other woman with your mother was given ten thousand years of Time for treason..."

"Of course."

"Then Prince Avalask brought you here, where the rest of us eventually joined you."

"Right." I gazed at the ground dejectedly. "You know what I think? Both sides can go ahead and blow each other into oblivion. It won't hurt my feelings."

Archie was quiet for a second. "I used to feel that way too."

"What changed your mind?"

"Family. You wouldn't want Liz dead."

"Liz is the only exception."

"No, she isn't. You wouldn't be detached if something happened to Terry or Michael, and what about Leaf? You weren't alright after we lost West either."

"So there are a *couple* of exceptions," I grumbled.

"And then everything gets more complicated. You start making friends with Escalis and you don't want anything to happen to them either. So then what do you do?"

"That's when you go out, live in a cave secluded in the woods, and just let everything play out."

Archie laughed lightly. "One of our Tally friends, Robbiel, tried that. You should ask him how it went." Archie looked at the ceiling as though a new thought had occurred to him. "Do you want to come meet them?"

"The other Tallies? I think I've had enough sulking for now, so yes."

"Believe me, if they can't get your mind off this for a while, nobody can."

Chapter Twenty One

We walked, and each time we passed an Escali in the narrow corridors, I felt just a little less alarmed. "So… they're more similar to us than to Escalis, right?" I asked. "Because Tresca was… more civil than I was expecting, but talking to her was a little dry.

"Yeah, I'm pretty sure the other Tallies have more of a sense of humor than anyone you've ever met." He smiled to himself. "You're going to love them."

I knew we had arrived when we reached a white marble door mounted in the wall, so I stopped.

"I have a question," I said, preferring to stall for time rather than admit I was afraid to enter.

"Really? You have a question? Out of everything happening, you only have one question?"

"I have lots, so maybe we should go one at a time. Those powers we were both using when we were fighting in the cave… Have we always had those?"

Archie grinned and I saw a hint of admiration. "I've always had mine, but I've never seen you shoot lightning before. Congratulations on finding your gift."

"I can't use it *now* though. It only works when I'm freaking out about something. And is that what it's called? Lightning?"

"I don't know, I've never actually seen someone do that. I think Prince Avalask calls it destruction. And just give it time. You'll be able to use it when you want. It takes practice."

He was about to grab for the door, so I hastily asked, "That shield thing you were using to protect yourself, can you use that whenever you want?"

"Yeah, I've had my magic for a while, so I've had plenty of practice. Here, try to touch my hand." Archie dropped his hand from the door and held it out to me instead. I was strangely nervous about trying to touch it, but I tried. As soon as I got close, I was slightly repelled, and when I tried to push my hand closer, a strong force simply wouldn't let me. When I looked closely, I could see a faint golden shimmer along the otherwise invisible barrier.

"Can you make it stop?" I asked.

"Sometimes I can," he frowned in concentration, "but it's hard."

"This can't be right," I said as the barrier remained in place. "I've touched you before."

"You've touched me *once*, the time Sir Avery attacked me and destroyed my every defense. The catch is, nothing can touch me, but it doesn't keep *me* from doing anything." He moved his own hand and touched mine.

"That's... weird."

"Allie?" A girl with long dark curls pushed the door cautiously open. She may have had the lightest skin I had ever seen, and it made her beautiful.

"This is Karissa," Archie said. Karissa put her finger on the tip of her nose as her eyes questioned me. I had no idea what that meant, but I did the same and she nodded as though I had just acknowledged something significant. "Well, come in! We've missed you." She pushed the door open as wide as it would reach.

I took a slow step through the doorway as Karissa told Archie, "It's good to see you," and gave him a hug. Bitter feelings boiled up within me when he hugged her back, and I found I didn't want to swallow my jealousy back down. Archie was the only person I knew in this world of Tallies and Escalis, and he was not allowed to like someone else when I needed him.

They broke apart, and I moved on to see that Karissa was one of six friends in a room with four long walls, a high ceiling, and a fireplace. One of the six sat on the top of a large pole in the center of the room, and along the wall next to me was a table of food, plates, and utensils.

The girl balancing on the pole jumped off and landed next to Karissa.

"I'm Nessava," she said, grabbing my hand to shake it wildly. Stray strands of hair fell in front of her large eyes and teeth, and I immediately knew I liked her.

"I'm going to go, Allie," Archie said as I glanced at Nessava's elbows. All of the Tallies in the room had arm spikes about half the size of Escalis', but just as sharp and deadly. "I'll see you later."

Of the two guys who stood across the room, the shorter one with the square face said, "Archie, you're leaving?"

"Yeah, I'm supposed to speak with Izfazara. I probably shouldn't keep him waiting."

"That's too bad. We were just thinking of stealing Robbiel's book and setting it on fire." A dark haired boy looked up from his book, raised his eyebrows just enough to let us know he wasn't impressed, and went back to reading.

"Save it for next time I'm here, and I'll help."

Archie turned to me once again, "I probably won't be back for a while. If nothing else, I'll just have to see you in the morning."

"Okay, have a good life," I said. Archie bid farewell to everyone and left.

"So is it true?" Nessava asked at once. "Can you really not remember anything about us? You had no idea you were even a Tally?"

I shook my head with a hopeless smile. "Never did a stray thought come across that idea."

"We all wanted to come help you, you know," Karissa said. "It actually turned into a giant fight between all of us — but doesn't everything?" Nessava nodded as though truer words had never been said, and Karissa added, "We eventually let Archie do it since he's the only one able to hide his thoughts from mind mages. None of us would have stood a chance entering the Dragona."

"It's just... Wow..." Nessava mused. "I can't believe you have to start all the way over. You can't even remember that time Karissa put a giant spider in your bed?"

"I thought we were past that," Karissa said. I laughed slightly and then shuddered at the thought. *I would kill somebody if it happened again.*

"Soooooo," Karissa restarted the conversation, "I'm guessing you'd probably like to know who everybody is?"

"Yeah, I really would," I replied.

"Well, over there, reading the book," she pointed to the dark haired boy absorbed in a giant novel, "that's Robbiel. And the one working on the fireplace, her name is Celesta." This thinly-built girl had wispy brown hair and was working with the tiniest chisel and hammer to carve out an intricate pattern around the fireplace. I walked closer and saw an assortment of tiny, sharply-angled shapes.

"That's amazing," I told her.

"Thanks," she said without looking up from her carving.

"Now, those two boys over there talking," Karissa pointed to the corner. The shorter one, who had been talking to Archie, had eyes very similar to Archie's and a smirk I wasn't sure I trusted. The tall one had his arms folded. "The tall one with the deep voice and dark hair is Jonnath, and that stupid irkbat next to him with the sandwich is Emery."

Emery didn't appear to have heard her, but as soon as she had moved on to show me the next thing, he peeled his sandwich apart and hurled it across the room.

It hit her white fur coat and she turned around to glare at him furiously. She pulled the piece of bread off to reveal an awful stain, and Emery only started laughing as Jonnath joined in the mockery.

I looked to see how tightly Karissa clenched her jaw, beyond livid. Her anger was justified, of course. I would have reacted entirely the same — all until she shook her dark curls from her face, reached to the food table next to her, and grabbed a handful of knives.

"Last straw, Emery!" she shouted, hurling one after the next with amazing force and speed.

I gasped, but Nessava nudged me. "Don't worry, this is normal." Sure enough, Emery jumped out of the way and the knives buried themselves in the wall behind him. He laughed even harder. Without wasting a second, Karissa launched herself across the room in an attempt to tackle Emery, but he stepped to the side and I thought she was going to crash into the wall. She stopped in plenty of time.

Emery retreated to the other side of the pole, and Karissa went after him. They circled each other, and Emery said, "I get Jonnath!"

"I get Allie," Karissa spat back.

"Wait, get me for what?" I wanted no part in the madness. *Not at all!*

"You're on my team," Karissa said.

Before I could object, Jonnath had already pulled the knives from the wall and thrown one so fast that I couldn't see it. My hand flew up to cover my face, and through some miracle, I caught it before it buried itself in my flesh. I dove behind a cabinet to avoid the next one and heard Emery call, "I get Robbiel —"

And then Karissa responding, "I get Nessava!"

"I'm not playing!" Celesta announced before anyone could take her away from her carving.

Nessava joined me behind the cabinet to give me the battle strategy while I tried to comprehend what was happening. *Knives!*

"Don't go for Emery, that's Karissa's job," she said. "We just have to get Robbiel and Jonnath. And watch out for Robbiel, the one closing his book right now. He's a speed mage."

Nessava dragged me to my feet, out from behind the cabinet as Robbiel and Jonnath finished exchanging words and pulled out their knives. I didn't realize the four weapons were aimed at me until they were already in the air. I dodged two, caught the third a hairs breadth from my stomach, and was relieved to see Nessava snag the last out of the air before I lost a foot.

I hated to admit it, but I was having fun. In some weird sort of way.

"Aim them at Jonnath," Nessava whispered as I felt the knives ripped from my hands by Robbiel, who returned them to his side of the room in less than a second.

"I'll get him next time," Nessava muttered. I had barely processed the fact that my hands were empty when I had to help catch the round of knives thrown at Nessava. Robbiel immediately ran at us, but Nessava jumped out to knock him to the ground. They both hurtled into the table behind us, knocking it over in a loud clang of breaking tableware and utensils flung across the floor.

We were all distracted when Karissa finally caught up with Emery and they both smashed into the side of the fireplace, shattering Celesta's masterpiece. She began cursing them in outrage, but when words weren't getting the job done she picked up a stick from the fireplace, with the end still burning, and joined in the fray. Emery quickly grabbed the fire poker as he got up, forced to defend himself from Celesta. Karissa darted to the overturned table and wrenched a leg off to serve as her weapon.

225

I almost forgot that Jonnath was still out to get me as Nessava scuffled with Robbiel, but I had the knives and he didn't. I threw them as hard as I could across the room, but he caught each easily. Instead of throwing them back, he kept them, and looked as though he was about to approach. Hand to hand combat, huh?

I grabbed the two knives Nessava had dropped, then dove back behind the cabinet, out of sight. Celesta, Emery, and Karissa were still battling it out by the smashed fireplace, each one fighting the other two.

I jumped out from behind the bookshelf and ran at Jonnath, faking like I was going to stab, but then didn't. He moved to block my attack, but instead I dove past, turned around, and threw the knife at him.

What had been a game suddenly turned wrong as he failed to catch it and it hit him in the back. Everybody stopped what they were doing to help Jonnath as he fell to his knees bleeding.

"I'm so sorry. I'm really sorry," I said as Robbiel yanked the knife out. *How could I have let that happen?*

Emery slapped me on the back. "Don't be sorry. That was a good throw."

"A good throw?" I demanded.

Jonnath reached his hand out and shook mine. "I'll be ready for that next time," he grumbled, his deep voice making him sound like a bear.

And then I saw it — the wound was already almost gone. I knew we healed fast, but I didn't know it was *that* fast.

"You know, I think that's the best battle we've had in a while," Robbiel said.

"Yeah, ruined my fireplace though," Celesta said.

Emery scoffed and said, "You were having fun."

Celesta frowned sourly, then broke a smile and said, "I guess so." Her words made all of us laugh, and it almost seemed like I hadn't just stabbed my friend in the back... literally.

226

"It's getting late," Karissa said simply, "I'm going to bed now."

"Yeah, I'm turning in too," Nessava agreed.

"Sounds good," Jonnath said, wincing as he stood.

I found my way back to my room, happy to crawl onto my hammock and wrap up in a thick blanket among the clutter that I'd clean in the morning. Seeing my old friends really had gotten my mind off everything for a while. They were all slightly insane, and I had probably been a large part of the madness back in my old life.

Now, finally alone with my thinking time, I had the chance to fully examine the situation.

It was a strange concept, being a Tally. I liked the other six of us — if that was all there were — but it was just so bizarre. How could any of it be true?

I thought about my mother as I closed my eyes. She had been so strong. She must have really loved that Escali to face the consequences of having a daughter with him, and I wished I could remember more about her.

Archie had mentioned something about not growing old, but I had obviously grown older since whenever that vision had happened... That would have been about thirteen years ago because it was right before Liz was born. That was a crazy thought. I certainly didn't look as though I'd aged thirteen years.

Someday Liz would grow up and look older than me. Maybe it wasn't the worst thing, but what would she think? How was I going to tell her about... my situation? *I was a Tally.* I was half-Human, and I was half-Escali.

Which side *was* I on? I couldn't be on the Escali side — it was the wrong side. I opened my eyes and looked around the black cave, imagining the Escali walls in the dark. *The bad side, the evil one!* And yet... I had been working for the Humans and the Escalis before everything went wrong. What made this side the bad side anyway? I must have been somewhat of the same person before I lost my memory. If I had chosen to help both sides out back then, then I must have had a good reason…

Morning came very differently than at the Dragona. A trumpet didn't call through the tunnels to wake everybody up. Instead, Nessava came running by each of the rooms shouting the wake up tune.

I laughed as I rolled out of my hammock and realized that unlike the Dragona — frigid if I forgot to light the fire — it was comfortably warm. I heard Nessava's voice as she ran past the door again, and I got up to start the day. Usually I would have changed clothes, but I didn't have any normal clothes with me, and I didn't want to wear the Escali ones I had found. Oh well.

I had decided in my sleep that maybe this was the right course of action. I wouldn't ever do anything to hurt my family at the Dragona, and maybe being in such a unique position meant I could help out in some way. What if I could end the war someday? Obviously it wasn't a likely concept, but who was in a better position to try?

The first thing I had to do was get back to the Dragona with a very good excuse as to where I had been. I picked up my stuff, threw some back in the chest, and stood as Nessava pushed my door open to make sure I was awake.

With eyes squinted in resentment of the day, Jonnath plodded down the hall past Nessava who was still shouting. She flung open the door of the room next to mine, bolted inside, and continued yelling the wake up tune, possibly even louder. I ventured over to see her swinging Karissa's hammock violently back and forth while Karissa covered her face with both her arms and groaned.

"Get up, get up!" Nessava yelled at her.

"Ok, ok!" She got out of her hammock and stood up for a few seconds before jumping right back in it and trying to go back to sleep.

"You're hopeless!" Nessava threw her arms up and left the room defeated.

Karissa continued to make swatting movements with her arm even after Nessava had gone, but looked up when she heard me laughing. "I'm getting up." She strenuously rolled from her hammock.

"Not a morning person?"

"Oh, who is?" she barked. She walked out the door and glared fiercely at Nessava, the enemy.

Nessava gave her a big smile in return and exclaimed, "It's hunting day!"

"You make me get up, but you're letting Archie sleep in?" Karissa griped as she pointed to Archie's closed door.

"I forgot he was here." Nessava then busted Archie's door open, yelling the wakeup call again.

"Gahhhhhhhhh!" We heard from across the hall. "I am bolting my hammock to the floor, Nessava! Then what will you do?"

"That is not a bad idea…" Karissa mumbled as she stalked off. I grinned to myself as Nessava walked out, followed by Archie who tried fiercely to rub the sleep from his eyes.

"Are you even awake?" I asked. Nessava skipped after Karissa and Archie set a hand on his doorway to stay standing.

"No. I had to meet with another Escali after Izfazara, so I only got two hours of sleep." He let out a big yawn. "But." He pointed at me and yawned again. "We did come up with a plan for getting home, which we need to start on right now."

"I think it can wait. You should get some more sleep."

"It can't wait, and the lack of sleep will help make this convincing. You should have stayed up all night too."

"So what *is* the plan?"

"I'll tell you on the way. We need to get up to see Krelaran." Archie started walking through tunnels, still half asleep. I wondered if he might be lost.

"Another Escali?" I asked.

"Yes, one who is going to taint your magic. Anna will make both of us take blood tests the second we get back, and we can't have our half-Escali genes knitting our arms back together in front of her. Once we taint it, our magic won't work for a day or two.

"Getting back won't be fun either. You already used the "I escaped" excuse last time, so we can't use it again. Since the Humans don't think that Escalis know where the Dragona is, a couple Escalis will drag us straight through the sparring field where everyone can see us. They'll help us escape our *captors*, and we'll be safely home."

Archie knocked on a door in the wall, and a tall blond Escali had both of us come inside. We sat down in chairs, facing each other, while the Escali left us alone.

"What are you so deep in thought about?" Archie asked me.

"All this secrecy," I replied, thinking hard.

"You aren't going to tell anyone about this when we get back, are you?"

"I don't know. I'm considering it."

"Allie," Archie shook his head. "We can't. They won't accept us. You saw what happened in Prince Avalask's memory."

"But that was different. That was on Tekada. People at the Dragona are more understanding."

"People at the Dragona accept magic. They don't accept Escalis. I can tell you now that Sir Darius's entire family was killed in this war. If you tell him you're a Tally, you're going to get a one way jump to the top of a cliff."

"You're probably right," I admitted. "What's our story going to be?"

"We'll say we were out talking when the Escalis showed up. They chased us up the mountain where we spent all night trying to lose them. We'll say that in the morning the falcons showed up and

230

found us. We got caught and dragged back down the mountainside, where we were then rescued."

"And you're sure we'll be rescued?"

"Yes. The Escalis will make sure we're rescued. We'll both get blood tests, but nobody will see our half-Escali abilities since we're tainting our magic right now. Everybody will be confused, but hopefully we'll be able to return to normal life."

The Escali who had left came back into the room and bluntly said, "This will hurt." It was still weird to hear them speak. Everything about this situation was disillusioning.

"Allie, talk to me so you don't have to think about it," Archie said, taking my attention away from the apprehension. "I already did this last night. It really does hurt."

I felt every muscle tense as I asked, "What do you want to talk about?"

"Tell me what our story is when we go back. What are we claiming happened?"

"You lost me on that one. I think I'll just follow what you say."

"That will work for most of the time, but you have to know—"

"Gah!" I screamed when Krelaran touched my hand. All the blood from my fingertips to halfway up my forearm boiled, and it didn't stop! I gripped my wrist with my other hand and pulled it close to my body, but nothing made the pain subside.

"Allie, tell me what the story is," Archie pushed as I clenched my teeth and tried to block it out.

"I don't care what our story is!"

"It'll be gone in a second. Talk to me!"

"Umm, oh holy life, we were out talking, and, and, Escalis came, and they, they chased us up the mountainside, and, then—" I just wanted to rip half my arm off. My eyes watered and—

"Come on, tell me the rest," Archie pressed.

"And, gahhh, and we eluded them all night, until, until morning when... When..." The pain finally started to ebb away in my arm and I could feel my fingers again. "Shank!" I exclaimed as I shook them out and quickly wiped my eyes.

"That's when the falcons came and we got caught and dragged down the mountainside," Archie finished for me.

"Exactly."

"Thanks Krelaran," Archie said, standing up. I followed suit and as we walked out the door the Escali nodded gruffly to us, handing Archie a leather satchel right before closing it.

"I hate this," I said, massaging my hand as we traversed more tunnels. I didn't even care to ask what was in the bag.

"I'm sorry. It's about to get worse too."

"*Worse*? What now?"

"Not right now, but when we go back. The plan isn't to walk back to the Dragona, but to be dragged there. It'll be most convincing if we're injured when we show up."

"How injured are we talking?"

"I don't know. The Escalis who are taking us back won't know we're Tallies, so it could be bad. They think you and I have been given false information, so they're supposed to get us to the Dragona in one piece, then drop us off and run."

"I guess we might as well, since this is one of the few times we'll actually be able to bleed. Let's make sure people see it."

"That's the spirit."

I had no idea how the combination of turns we took got us back to the big marble door, but they did. We walked in to see everybody sitting around, their grogginess preventing another war from breaking out.

"What's in the bag?" Robbiel asked as Archie sat down.

"We're going back today, the story being that we got captured and dragged down the mountainside."

As Archie pulled out a length of rope, Emery asked, "So you need somebody to tie you up?"

"Yes."

Emery grabbed the rope in the middle, incinerating the spot where his hand touched. *Were all Tallies mages?*

"I'll do yours then," Karissa said, taking the other half of the rope to tie around my wrists. I couldn't have gotten it off with days to try, and she left about four cubits extended, which I coiled and held in my hands.

"What's the point in tying yourselves up now? Might as well do it when you get to the base of the mountain," Robbiel said.

"We just got our magic tainted," Archie answered. "We'll be scratched up pretty badly by the time we get there."

Several of my friends grimaced at the thought.

"What's in the bag?" Celesta asked, pulling a smaller bag from the satchel on the ground. She turned it upside down, and a tiny golden pebble rolled onto the table.

"I am not touching that," I said, remembering the underwater cave when Prince Avalask had handed me something very similar.

"Well, I guess that's up to you," Robbiel said. "But Archie has gone a night without sleep and it's going to show. It will make more sense if you're both just as exhausted and hurt."

"Plus, you only have to touch it for a few seconds. I can make sure you let go of it before you lose consciousness," Karissa offered.

Yeah... I would be able to handle it. I'd probably be no more tired than Archie already was.

"Ok," I agreed.

"So just pick it up, and after a few seconds, I'll pull it off you." I looked at the pebble, and really, *really* didn't want to touch it. I finally reached out and grabbed it, and before I could even think, it started draining. I felt like I hadn't slept in one day, two days, three days—

"Karissa!" somebody shouted. She pulled it off as I fell over backwards and fought to focus my vision. I lay dazed, listening to the muted sounds of movement and yelling.

"Aren't you supposed to know what you're doing?"

"I do know! I counted to four; three to drain the magic, one to drain the physical energy. I'm the expert in anatomy around here, and that's what you're supposed to do."

"Yeah, except that Archie *just* told us they had their magic tainted and don't have any magic energy."

"She was just supposed to be tired, not unconscious!"

"I'm not unconscious," I mumbled. I wasn't sure who was saying what.

"Maybe not right now." Someone grabbed my tied hands and hauled me to my feet.

"Nice job, Karissa. She'll never make it down the mountain," someone else said.

"I am really, truly, sorry," Karissa said to me.

"Naw, it's fine," I said sleepily, "I'm still good enough to go."

"Good enough to go?" Archie asked incredulously.

"Yeah. If I sleep it off, it'll be too late for our story to make any sense. We've put in too much effort to call it off now."

"Tranaka's here for you two," somebody else said, pushing the marble door open to let an Escali in.

Archie said. "Last chance to back out, Allie."

"I wouldn't go. You look like Karissa does in the morning," someone advised.

"Nope, I'm ready," I insisted, walking to the door with my eyes half open.

CHAPTER TWENTY TWO

I might have even liked Tranaka if he would have just *slowed down*. I felt like an ant in a chariot race — I just couldn't keep up with them. The miles of tunnels we had to cover didn't help either, nor the possibility that I may have been sleepwalking through half of them.

Finally we got close to the surface and Tranaka took hold of the ropes to look like he had led us up. I felt like a dog. I decided on impulse that I would just try to be strong for as long as I could, and when I crashed, I would just have to crash. I stood up straight, opened up my eyes, and followed Tranaka into the fresh air to meet our captors.

They were both Escalis, (obviously,) very tall, (most of them *were* rather tall,) and looked like they were eager to leave (I *really* felt tired).

"Remember what I said about how to treat them," Tranaka said as he handed my rope to the one with dark hair and blue eyes, and Archie's to the blond one with the flat face.

"That shouldn't be a problem," the blond one said in Escalira, grinning toward the other. Tranaka bowed to each of them and then returned to the tunnels. "We'll have to stay off the trails to avoid further complications," the blond Escali told his partner. Obviously he was in charge.

Archie edged over to me and whispered, "Remember not to respond. They don't think we can understand them."

"Hey!" the Escali yanked on Archie's ropes, "I bet they were thinking they'd get to talk the whole way over, huh? Let's separate them." He marched into the trees, pulling Archie behind him. The one holding onto me started walking and then nodded to me to walk with him instead of dragging me behind.

Even without being dragged, I stumbled and fell enough to scrape myself up nicely. It was strange to be bleeding for more than ten seconds, and the scratches I was accumulating stung brutally. I had never noticed such inconveniences before.

I tripped over something and came down hard on a sharp rock in my side. "Stop waiting for it!" the blond one yelled. My Escali pulled on the ropes more to help me up than to drag me, but I could barely stand anymore. I was crashing a lot sooner than I had expected. We jumped over a creek, and I collapsed on the other side. He dragged me through the dead leaves a little ways, and though I could feel little tiny rocks cutting into me, there was no alternative. I couldn't get back to my feet.

He stopped and sat on a log next to me as I lay panting. I glanced over to see the other Escali tie Archie to a tree before coming over to sit next to mine. I closed my eyes to just listen to them talk.

"I can't do it anymore."

"Can't do what?"

"I can't keep dragging her along like this. Something's wrong with this one."

"Something's wrong with all of them. But I can guarantee that if the roles were reversed, *it* would be dragging *you* right now."

"I would therefore be very thankful if it let me sit down for a few minutes to have a break."

The blond one flicked his eyes several times from me to the other Escali. "You're growing soft," he let the other Escali know. "As soon as your little break's over, we can switch Humans. You won't feel as bad about dragging the boy."

"No."

"No? What do you mean—"

"I won't."

"Tral. Give me the rope."

"No."

I looked to see the blond jump to his feet, an act of dominance, and the second Escali rose right after him in one rapid movement. They were having some sort of standoff right there, their lips pulled back into snarls and eyes locked aggressively.

"Why are you defending it?" The cruel one demanded.

"Because you see an *it*, and I see a girl. She's still young, and probably hasn't committed any—"

"Even if we hadn't been *ordered* to be rough with them, do you not care about avenging your brother?"

"His death wasn't her doing."

They were both quiet long enough for my focus to wane, and then I heard, "You are unbelievable." I refocused just long enough to see the blond one untie Archie from the tree and head off again. "You can do whatever you want with yours, but I'm treating mine as we were told."

I closed my eyes, and didn't open them until I felt a slight pulling on the rope. I expected to look up and see the Escali trying to drag me off again, but instead, he wrapped the extension loosely around my hands before he picked me up and carried me.

I felt happy, awkward, grateful, tired, safe, and scared all at the same time, along with guilty that Archie was still stuck with the devil up ahead of me. I was usually too proud to let anyone see me cry, but sleep deprivation rendered my pride irrelevant, and I felt silly as tears began to spill. I hated to be doing it, so anger quickly joined the other overwhelming emotions.

The Escali didn't know what to do with me when the tears started. He held on tighter and tried talking to me, saying that everything was ok and I would be fine. I didn't even realize I had fallen asleep until I woke to the sound of them arguing again.

"We can't just walk across the field," my Escali said as he continued to carry me. "They still think we don't know where their city is, and we can't let them know differently."

"We can't release them here either. They'll suspect something if we make their escape easy."

The dark haired Escali stopped where I could see the sparring field, and suggested, "If we get these two to fight us, they'll attract the attention of those Humans across the field."

This intrigued the other, who stopped as well. "I guarantee if we throw the girl around, the boy will fight us."

Archie glanced over and made eye contact with me. He tilted his head to the side just a fraction, to ask if I was up for it. I gave him the slightest nod back.

"Look at her, she's not in any condition to be thrown around," the one holding me said.

"She's awake now at least. Look, I won't hurt her too badly. Just enough to get the other to respond and draw everyone's attention."

My Escali thought about it for a few seconds, then set me down and traded ropes with the flat-faced one who immediately started walking along the border of the trees and the field, just out of sight of everybody sparring.

We got fairly close when the blond one turned sharply out into the field. He jerked on my rope so hard that I flew out in front of him, landing on my shoulder in the grass. He yanked me back toward him and then pulled out a knife, only to be hit in the side by a flying tackle from Archie, who had somehow gotten his ropes off. They growled and snarled as they struggled in the grass, and the Escali came out on top in time for me to jump on him, strangling him from behind with the ropes on my hands.

Dark-hair pulled me off him, pinning my arms to my sides as I snarled as well. I kicked, yelled, definitely got the attention of everyone in the area, and then somehow managed to wrench myself free. I bolted forward to knock the ugly blond off Archie, and then Archie joined me in trying to pummel him.

Everyone from sparring dashed across the field to help us, and the Escalis realized their cue to leave. The nicer one grabbed us both by the hair and threw us off to either side of his friend before he helped him up and they bolted.

"Allie? Archie? Are you ok?"

I collapsed to the ground in exhaustion. *Did I look ok?*

"Somebody go get Anna, now!" I only closed my eyes for a few seconds before I heard a man next to me talking, warning me about something.

"GAHHHHHHHHHH!" I screamed as he dug a knife into my forearm and ran it down.

"Yeah, I know, I know, I'm sorry." I opened my eyes to see Anna in front of my face. "Somebody bring Archie over here," she said. Somebody pulled Archie over and set him next to me. The man who had stabbed my arm pulled out a clean knife and grabbed Archie's wrist.

"Oh, no no no no no no," Archie said as he looked the other way. I didn't watch either, but I heard him gasp.

Without warning, Anna pushed two hands to my arm, and I stifled my next scream as she scorched it with searing heat. She did the same to Archie and then quickly began wrapping our arms in bandages.

The man said, "She's still got enough thistleweed fever to cause hallucinations. Neither of them are being tracked by the Escalis though. They're clean."

239

I hadn't noticed my eyes droop closed, but I heard somebody say, "We should get Allie up to the healers," and I realized they had already helped me to my feet. Sleep walking felt good but not nearly as glorious as crashing onto a bed minutes later.

Was there anything better in the world than sleep?

I woke in a cave with two rows of beds — the medical branch of the Dragona, where I had once dropped Michael off. A lantern threw shadows off everything in sight, illuminating Liz in the bed next to mine. I couldn't imagine what was wrong with her. She looked fine.

Upon moving, I realized I was bandaged in several places. I was exceedingly sore with a lasting pain I had never experienced before.

I turned back over, more carefully this time, and stared at the flickering shadows on the ceiling. How strange, to be lying in a bed and not wondering about the mystery of my life. I finally knew.

Liz stirred and opened her eyes. She saw me and said, "Finally, Allie." She got to her feet. "Did you know you've been sleeping for a whole day?"

"An entire day? That's got to be a record or something. What are you in here for?"

"For you, of course." She didn't speak with her usual excitement. "It seems like you have to be guarded every minute of the day, doesn't it?"

"So that's what you're here for, guarding me?"

"Somebody has to."

"You know Archie was with me just this last time, right?"

"Yeah, he's already told us the entire story. Archie can't protect you like I can though. Have you heard the news?" She raised her eyebrows, but her eyes just looked dull to me.

I shook my head, grimacing as the thoughtless movement provoked my injuries. "What's the news?"

240

"I'll show you." She picked up a glass of water from the table next to her and stared at it with her full concentration. Nothing happened at first, but then condensation began collecting on the outside of the glass, and a very thin layer of ice crystallized across the top.

"Liz," I exclaimed, trying to sound as happy as possible and wincing from the effort, "you found your magic."

"Yeah," she answered, barely smiling at the glass in front of her. "It's not a lot right now, but I've already met my main instructor. After sparring in the morning, he'll start training me to be deadly. And there are two other ice mages here to help me too." Liz didn't have anything else to say on the matter, a disinterest which concerned me. Instead, she asked, "So... what happened?"

I sighed and stared at the ceiling, making sure I had every detail of our story consistent before repeating it. I told her about how the Escalis chased us, and we eluded them all night, but their falcons found us in the morning, and they caught us. She kept an intense gaze on me as I spoke, and I grew uncomfortable as she peered, as though figuring something out.

"Is... everything alright?" I asked.

"I don't know," she replied, "because something here... *isn't* right."

I gave her a cross between a smile and a frown to let her know that was a silly assumption. But... What would happen if I told her about Tallies? Nothing good, surely.

She went on slowly, "Not many people believe you about the Escalis in your room, Allie, but I do. And that means that you miraculously escaped them, only to arrive back home, get taken *again*, and then escape *again*."

"Anna saved me from an Escali at the lake too. We can't leave him out." I smiled, trying to bring humor to the situation, but I didn't even draw a hint of laughter. This new version of Liz set me on edge.

"As your sister, Allie, I know you haven't told me everything."
I stared at her long and hard. If she could read me half as well as I
could read her, she would know I was hiding something.

"Why don't you tell me what's going on?" Liz pressed,
convinced further by my silence. "I won't tell anyone."

"You promise? No matter what it is, you absolutely promise?"

"Of course."

"Ok," I said with my very best sigh of giving in. Liz stared
intently, no longer watching for deception. "That dream, I know it
was real. The details don't make sense to me, but I remember
somebody helping me to escape the Escalis. I don't know who, and
I don't know how many, but somebody came to help me."

I told her this insignificant part because I knew she would see
the truth in it, and hopefully it would end her doubts about my
honesty.

She did believe it, but then she concluded, "So somebody strong
enough to fight the Escalis knows who you are and is helping you.
You know it's nobody from the Dragona, because they would have
come forward to back your story. So who could it have been?"

"It's another mystery," I said, instantly wishing I had kept my
mouth closed. I wasn't getting myself anywhere but deeper, and
we were treading too close to the secret I was supposed to be
keeping.

"Are you even half as worried about this as I am?" she asked. *I
wasn't acting worried enough.*

"Of course I'm worried, but what will worry fix? Brooding just
makes everything worse."

"Maybe so, but you're acting like you don't care. You won't be
able to figure anything out if you never put a single thought
towards the matter."

"But I don't have any thoughts. You're the creative one. Give me
some of your ideas."

"I would," she sighed, "but all of my ideas are impossible."

"I know the feeling." My head felt like it was being squeezed, and I was glad to still have the bed beneath me as a sturdy support.

"You should go back to sleep," Liz said, noticing my distraction.

"Believe me, I want to, but there's too much to do. I'll sleep later." I tried to get up, but Liz wasn't going to let me.

"Whatever it is can wait." She pushed me back down, and I was astounded by her sudden strength, or more likely, how weak I was with my half-Escali abilities suppressed.

"Where's Archie?"

"Anna's talking to him. I'm not really sure where he is."

"Why isn't he in here too?" I wondered, realizing something was amiss.

Liz hesitated before she said, "I think Anna wanted to talk to him as soon as he woke up."

"She could have done that in here. What's going on?"

I didn't expect a straight answer from her, so I was surprised when I received one. "Anna thinks the same thing I do — there's more here than we're seeing. She wanted to talk to you both separately to find the missing pieces, things like the guardians in the woods who were left out of the story. Why did you leave them out anyway?"

"It didn't seem important. And nobody believes me anyway," I said vaguely.

"Anna might. And she'll have an easier time investigating this when she knows everything. You need to tell her what you think happened in the woods."

"No, I do not."

"Then I will."

"You can't. You promised you wouldn't."

"I promised I wouldn't tell her what you said. I didn't say anything about writing it down on a piece of paper and giving it to her."

243

"Liz, you can't do that." I wasn't sure I liked new-Liz at all. Maybe if I was still old-Allie, I would have been better at weaving lies she would believe. Was that what I wanted though?

"Why shouldn't I tell her? I'm just trying to help."

"Because... Well..." Why wasn't I able to tell Anna the truth? Because if Anna knew somebody had helped me, somebody strong enough to fight Escalis, it would bring up too many questions. Who aside from mages could stand against an Escali? If she used the resources of the Dragona to find out, they would uncover the truth. That wasn't any reason to give Liz though, and I couldn't think a new one up. "Ugh, my head hurts," I said in complete honesty, due to the mixture of a crazy trip and my irritation with Liz.

"Yeah, you need to get more sleep."

"Goodnight," I said as I put my head on the pillow and clenched my teeth together. I wasn't sure what would happen when Liz told Anna about the Tallies in the woods, but it wasn't going to be ideal.

CHAPTER TWENTY THREE

I woke up determined to not let anything get me down. Not being tired, not the scratches and bruises all over, not the wound running along my arm, not the idea that life was changed forever, and definitely not the fact that I could now be charged for treason. Ten thousand years of Time were not on my mind. I was going to be optimistic.

On one good note, I was already feeling some of my normal strength return. Some.

The medical wing was still empty, and I felt well enough to walk, so I simply left. I was on my way to the Wreck before I could even stop to think of how much I didn't really want to be there. People were already starting to leave from breakfast — off to do whatever the day had in store for them — and I didn't feel like talking to any of them.

I sat alone to eat something quick, feeling like a danger to everyone around me.

"Where are the rest of your friends, Allie?" The hollow and whiney words came from behind me, and I knew from the sheer confidence in Jesse's voice that he had brought friends. "Did you get them all killed too?"

Without turning around, I said, "Go away. I don't want to deal with you right now."

"Of course you don't," he said, sitting next to me, setting his cup of tea down to make himself at home. Two of his friends seated themselves as well, or possibly his brothers, judging by what seemed to be a family nose.

"Fine," I said, not wanting the fight after I had, admittedly, threatened his life. "I'll move."

"Oh no, don't do that," he said, reaching out as though to stop me, *accidentally* knocking his tea over and spilling it all over me. I shrieked and jumped up, shaking my arms to try to get it out of my scratches and cuts. My skin screamed at me to make the burning go away, and my eyes filled with water.

"My deepest apologies," Jesse said as he stood and watched me clamp my arms tightly against myself. I could read in his eyes and on his smirk that this was just the beginning of what could be a long line of accidents.

"Jesse!" I snarled. "Get away from me before I kill you."

"Oh come on, Allie, what are you going to do? I didn't *mean* to—"

A growl rumbled from my own throat as I shoved him away from me with as much force as I could. Being a normal person, it probably would have been the beginning move to a fight, but being me... he of course flew back into his friends and crashed into both table and chairs, drawing the attention of everyone in the Wreck. They saw me with my flushed cheeks and fiery arms while Jesse tried to stand, dazed from hitting the table and sending chairs clattering to the floor.

I left the site in a rush, instantly on my way back to my own room. As I walked through the tunnels, trying futilely to convince myself back into optimism, I ran into none other than Anna, who was exactly who I wanted to talk to. I was going to be in trouble as soon as she found out — maybe I could get somewhere productive before she heard.

"Allie, shouldn't you be in bed?" she asked. *Did I still look so bad?*

"No, I'm fine. I want to get back to work today. Where am I supposed to be?" I hoped my eyes weren't watering too much. She took a second to observe my appearance.

"You signed yourself up for combat dragons for this entire week."

"Excellent!" I said, turning to leave. *Optimism!*

"Allie."

"What?" I turned back around to face her. *Had Liz already gotten to her?*

"I haven't had the chance yet to talk to you about recent events." *Maybe…*

"I —" my answer was cut short when one of Jesse's friends ran through the connecting tunnel without even seeing us. *That was the way to my room!*

"What's his hurry?" Anna asked.

"Well, I just threw Jesse into a table a few seconds ago…"

Anna squinted critically at me before asking, "*Why?*"

"He spilled hot tea on my arm," I said, tensing myself for the scolding of a lifetime. My arm still stung.

Anna rolled her eyes and said, "Jesse has needed to be thrown into a table for quite a while now." I breathed a small laugh of relief. "Listen though, there's something I need to tell you. I want you to know this isn't your fault in any way, and you shouldn't blame yourself —"

"What's the matter," I asked, feeling suddenly sick.

"I need you to pack your things. You have to go."

"Go? Go where?"

"To Dincara. Allie, we've never had an Escali come near the Dragona, and in the past few days, they've been here two, maybe even three times trying to catch you. I don't know if they have some

247

way they're tracking you, and I don't know what they want you for, but if any more show up, they're bound to figure out that this is where we're training our mages. We can't risk keeping you here if they've got some way of finding you."

"I have to leave?" I asked, dumbstruck.

"Not permanently," Anna answered, seeming genuinely sympathetic. "And we may all be joining you in Dincara before you know it. They're expecting an Escali attack soon, so while you're there, you can help Sir Darius give the Dincarans defense suggestions and coordinate how we might help them."

I was still speechless. "I have to leave?"

"We've got a dragon ready to fly you over as soon as you pack your things." Anna nodded with a look that might have been encouragement before she left. I rubbed a few of the stinging scratches on my arm and started back to my room in a daze. *This was too much.*

When I neared my bedroom, I found the door ajar. I took a deep breath to calm myself, and warned, "Get out of my room, or I am going to kill you."

"That would be a shame," I heard Archie respond from inside. I walked in, closed the door, and sat on my bed, utterly defeated.

"I have to leave," I said.

Archie leaned against the wall with his arms folded across his chest. "I heard," he replied. "I asked Sir Darius if I could come with you, but he wants me to stay."

"I have to go by myself," I stated aloud. I stood and started grabbing things I would need to take to Dincara. I was already wearing my short swords, and I didn't need extra clothes because the stuff I was wearing would last me for a while.

I picked up my oldest piece of parchment with its haunting array of tally marks. I wasn't ready to add West to the list yet, so I put it back beneath my pillow.

"When do you have to leave?" Archie asked.

"Right now," I said, trying not to feel upset. "Although it sounds like you may be joining me soon. The Escalis may be attacking Dincara, and it sounds like the Dragona may lend a hand for the battle."

"I'll definitely see you soon then. Dincara is important. If they're attacked, half the continent will show up to defend them. I'll be sure to be there."

"Thanks, Archie. And tell Liz," I said, looking around to make sure I hadn't forgotten anything, "that I said bye, and congratulations again on finding her magic."

"I will."

"And I'll see you in Dincara."

The flight to Dincara gave me time to calm down about the situation, and the gusts of wind in my face helped keep my emotions from boiling over. Things really weren't as bad as they had initially seemed. After all, I would get to come home after a while, and somebody had to go represent the Dragona in Dincara anyway. It might be nice to have the time to clear my head.

I had seen maps, and I knew where the fortress was, but it was still a sight to see when I arrived. A ring of eight giant turrets circled a massive central tower, as tall as the one we had built during the Eclipsival with ice. Thick walls ran between the eight battlements, and the surrounding moat was wide enough to make the fortress look like an island in the ocean. One bridge connected Dincara to land with a giant stone recreation of a spider above the main gates, and its gated harbor in the back opened up to the ocean.

Dincara stirred as everyone turned to watch me fly overhead and land inside. I jumped off the dragon and nodded to a man who had come to greet me.

"I assume you're here from the Dragona?"

"Yes."

"If you'll follow me, I will introduce you to our commander. I apologize, but it is a bit of a walk."

"Walking is fine."

The entire fortress seemed to be built so unknowing attackers wouldn't have any idea where to go once they entered. The stone grounds surrounding the central spire were flat and wide open, the space occupied by vendor's tents and people walking between them. We had to circle around the massive pavilion to get to the entrance of the tower because it faced the harbor to prevent easy access.

I could hear the echoes from the breezy day resound through the gigantic stronghold as I stepped inside, and I glanced back at the impressively sized ships docked in the harbor. I felt like I was no more than the smallest and most insignificant of creatures beside them.

We passed door after unknown door in the walls as we climbed to the very top. It was a ridiculous feeling to be out of breath by the time I reached the spire, but everything was much more tedious without my Tally magic. *I hated it.*

We entered to find a respectable old man reading through papers at his desk. He had aged well, with deeply set eyes that spoke of experience, and he actually stood to acknowledge my arrival.

"You have impeccable timing," he said, looking out over the ocean. I wondered if he could tell time by the tide. "Sir Darius will be here any minute. And what's your name?"

"Allie," I told him.

"Allie, have you been to Dincara before?"

"No," I said, not wanting to waste his time by explaining why my no was really a *maybe.*

"Then you don't know me. My name is Sir Laud. And Allie, we keep receiving report after report," he gestured to the stack of papers on his desk, "that we're about to entertain the assault of a lifetime."

Sir Darius appeared across the room from us, and I was glad he was here to speak for the Dragona. All I wanted to do was avoid the battle altogether.

"Perfect," Sir Laud said upon his arrival. "Now that I have you both here, we can explore this fortress and solidify your resolve to stand with us."

Sir Darius bowed quickly to him and said, "We're eager to see the defenses Dincara has in place."

"We'll start right here then. Let me tell you what we plan to do with the moat," Sir Laud said, holding up a silver goblet filled with clear liquid. "This is only water right now, but one of our alchemists made a discovery a while back." Three tiny grains of sand rested on the tip of a knife he carefully lifted, and he tilted it until the grains fell into the water. "If you were to dip even a finger in here, you'd lose half your hand." It bubbled into green froth and white vapor spilled over the edges. "We're going to dump it into the moat, so anyone who falls in won't be coming back out."

I tried to imagine how terrifying Dincara would look when the moat turned into bubbling green death, and realized Sir Laud was heading for the door.

"We can jump wherever we need to go," Sir Darius said, but Sir Laud only shook his head.

"I fear I have so few walks left in this life, I would be loath to lose one." He stopped in the doorway for just a moment, as though he wasn't sure how many more times he would see it. "And most of what I have to show you is in this tower anyway."

Sir Darius glanced to me before we followed, as though he didn't understand why anyone would want to walk anywhere. But I understood.

Once out on the spiraling staircase, Sir Laud took us room by room from the top of the tower to the bottom. The first room, filled with swords from King Kelian, gave us a good laugh because Escalis couldn't be cut. Sir Laud just wanted to throw them off the battlements, hope they hit something, then tell King Kelian how crucial they had been.

The second room had maces and weapons that would actually damage our opponents. Rooms three, four, five, six, *and* seven were filled with armor. Eight and nine were filled with bows and quivers of arrows. Sir Laud said they were a type of arrow that could cripple an Escali, but that they only had enough for each archer to take three arrows.

That was why the next room on the staircase had been stuffed full with stacks and stacks of —

"Thistleweed?" I said, seeing the enormous piles of spikey green and red leaves.

"Beautiful isn't it? It works the same on an Escali as it does on a Human. They'll be entirely delusional, and done for the rest of the battle."

"How do you know it works on Escalis?" I asked.

"We've run a couple tests."

"Oh," I replied, pushing the thought from my mind.

"In the next room down we have a few people with immunities working furiously to get all the thistleweed onto arrowheads. We'll have enough by the time of the battle to be sufficient." As he said this, a woman walked through the door, nodded in respect to Sir Laud, grabbed a few glovefuls of leaves, and left.

Sir Laud opened another room to show us barrels stacked corner to corner and all the way to the ceiling.

"This is another of our valuable discoveries," he said, pulling the top off the nearest.

"It's... water?" I ventured at the unknown liquid.

"No, not quite. We call it antiwater. Normal water extinguishes flames. Antiwater kindles them. I would give you a demonstration, but I'll refrain because we might possibly destroy the tower."

"Flaming water?" Sir Darius asked.

"Explosive, even. It will come in handy in several places. If you come outside, I will show you a few."

We neared the entrance with the stone spider suspended in its web above the bridge, and I noticed that the bridge connected to the fortress at a lower elevation than we stood. The stone walkway plummeted ahead of us, and when we got to the edge I saw that the entrance to Dincara was a walled off pit. Ladders and ropes around the edges allowed people to climb out, and a door opposite the iron gates led inside.

"This part of the defense has always been a pain," Sir Laud remarked, looking down upon the scene. "That door down there leads to the living quarters around the central tower, but you can't get to the tower from this entrance. We always have to hoist any shipments we receive onto the main level and carry them to the back of the tower. Now those tedious efforts are finally paying off.

"That door below will seal shut, and with all the ropes and ladders gone, not even an Escali will be able to climb the face of this wall. This is where the main defense will be, where the archers can easily hit their targets and mages can drop boulders on their heads. And how many water mages do you have?"

"We have six at the moment," Sir Darius replied.

"Six will be perfect. We can place them around the edges of the pit and have them spray water in along with the alchemist powder."

"We could also put a combat dragon above on either side of the pit, just in case the Escalis end up making it over," Sir Darius suggested.

"Absolutely. How many of these dragons do you have?"

"Three."

"That will leave one more to put on the bridge, which you need to stand on to truly comprehend." Sir Laud grabbed one of the ladders into the pit and lowered each foot quickly onto a new rung as though he had been climbing them all his life.

We followed him out to the middle of the bridge, past people coming and going. The sides didn't have any rails or measures to prevent falling, and I peered over the edge to see the long drop that ended in the water.

Sir Laud said, "With the alchemist powder in the moat and the harbor gates closed, the Escalis will only be able to reach us by way of the bridge."

"Is there something special about the bridge?" I asked, hoping we weren't relying solely on our archers to make it an obstacle.

"Look at these beauties," Sir Laud said, pointing out two pipes that connected the sides of the bridge to the walls of the fortress. "You can fill the pipes with antiwater from inside the walls, and then the entire bridge will emit flames when anyone tries to cross."

"That sounds... effective," Sir Darius said as I pulled my toes over the grated stone walkway where flames could leap up to incinerate anyone trying to cross.

"It has to be. The bridge is the main defense, right before the inside pit. If we can put a dragon out here, then it can kill off a number of Escalis before we start lighting the flames underneath them. Then between flame bursts we'll have the archers shooting multiple volleys, plus anything else you can throw at them to keep them back. It'll take a miracle just for them to get across the bridge."

"I had no idea that Dincara had this kind of thought in its defensive design," Sir Darius admitted. "And you can expect the Dragona's full support to defend it."

"Excellent," Sir Laud said, clasping Sir Darius' hand in thanks. "I think I may sleep well at last. When can I expect the Dragonan mages to begin arriving?"

"Within a day, perhaps two."

"How many are coming?" I asked Sir Darius, worried about which of my friends might end up in the fight.

"The kids under twelve will be sent to hide with the kids from Dincara for the duration of the battle. The rest of the Dragona will be in attendance," Sir Darius answered.

"*Everyone?*"

"We all fight together Allie. We live together, work together, fight together, and we die together."

"Spoken like a true Dincaran," Sir Laud said approvingly. "We also survive together, and we all embrace victory as a whole."

"And this is a victory I finally feel confident in," Sir Darius said. "I'm going to return to the Dragona, and I'll send word for when our reinforcements will arrive."

"I can't wait to hear from you," Sir Laud answered him.

Sir Darius jumped and disappeared, presumably back to the Dragona, leaving me alone on the bridge with Sir Laud. No new travelers came or went from the fortress anymore.

"Tarace, would you kindly show Allie where she will be staying?" Sir Laud asked to thin air. "I think I can walk to the tower by myself unharmed." I shouldn't have been surprised to hear thin air answer him.

"If you say so." The source of the voice materialized, and I saw a young man appear next to Sir Laud. His short brown hair seemed motivated for messiness in contrast to his clean-shaven face. I had to wonder how long he had been there. "The living quarters are this way," Tarace said, motioning for me to follow.

We left Sir Laud on the bridge, preoccupied, and entered back into Dincara under the massive stone spider at the gates. Instead of climbing back up the walls to the upper level, we entered through the door in the pit, which led into the stone halls underneath lit by the lanterns and barred windows.

I attracted attention as though the Dincarans could tell I wasn't one of them — every last one of them could tell.

"So… do you know much about the battle?" I asked.

"A thing or two," Tarace replied, turning back to me as we walked. He had eyes between green and brown, and I could tell by his smirk that he probably knew everything about the battle.

"What do you think our chances really are?" I asked.

"Well, if the Escalis send four thousand of their own, as we've heard they will, and we get all the allies who have promised to come, we'll have their numbers tripled. And this is the best place we could ever choose to have a battle, so I have to say our chances are pretty good."

"Do you guard Sir Laud while you're invisible? Is that how you know these things?"

"You could say that," he said, seeming to find this question funny too. If I had to guess, I would say he was probably important and I should know his name.

He stopped outside a door that looked exactly the same as the rest along the wall. "You can stay in here as long as you are in Dincara," he said, pushing it open for me.

"Thank you," I said, walking into the small, bland space. I hoped not to call it home for too long.

CHAPTER TWENTY FOUR

I didn't get to know many Dincarans, but I had them figured out as a whole. They seemed to be one large family who shared a fierce pride in being Dincaran. The city even had its own crest — a large spider over the words *loyalty to the death* — so nobody would have to associate themselves with King Kelian's starred emblem of Tekada.

King Kelian took the brunt of almost every joke and criticism, actually. I had known he was widely disliked, but people at the Dragona seemed to care a lot less about him than the Dincarans, who had to deal with his men docking in their port on a weekly basis. Their dislike for the king was another thing that brought them so close.

Of the people I *had* met, Tarace was the only one who came back to check in on me. Although he was a mage himself, he hadn't grown up at the Dragona and therefore wanted all the input I could give him. As we talked about every type of mage I could remember battling in sparring, Tarace came up with unique ideas to incorporate their gifts into his defense plan, and I learned even more details about Dincara's strategies.

Of course, I wouldn't betray his trust by repeating anything, regardless of the fact I was a Tally. The Dincaran sense of loyalty was contagious.

Mages from the Dragona started arriving two days later. I was eager to see my friends again, but at the same time, I didn't want them anywhere near the coming battle. The first wave to arrive consisted of people I vaguely knew, and none of my close friends. It was getting dark outside before the next group was supposed to arrive, and I was sitting in what might be called my room when somebody darted in and closed the door.

"Karissa?" I asked, confused by her arrival. She was wearing long poufy sleeves to conceal her Tally arm spikes.

"Hey," she replied, glancing around for something. "You don't happen to have that sand you used to talk about, do you?" she asked, grabbing my bag to rifle through it. She found Mizelga's box before I could answer her. "Never mind." She dumped the entire container out in front of the door at eye level, and then pulled on the handle to make sure the sand held it securely shut.

"What are you doing?" I asked, bewildered as she took off her own bag and began searching through it.

"We have to leave, right now. Where's Archie?"

"He's back at the Dragona—"

"Good, hopefully Robbiel and Jonnath have already found him."

"What's going on?"

"Izfazara is about to finalize the battle plans, and if we wanted any say in them, we were supposed to say it hours ago."

"Then why didn't you?"

"They don't want to talk to us. They wanted you, Archie, and Corliss, but the three of you are impossible to find."

"If we're so late, why did you just shut us in here?" I asked, pointing in bafflement at the sand in front of the door.

258

"We're not leaving that way," Karissa said impatiently, finding what she'd been looking for. It looked like nothing more than a stick to me, but she held it as though it was important. "We're going to set the flare off so Prince Avalask knows where we are, then he'll get us out of here. We have to keep the door blocked so we have a safe place to come back to."

"What if somebody tries to come in while I'm gone?"

"Emery's outside watching. He'll keep everything under control," Karissa answered. I didn't know what she did next, but the stick in her hand ignited suddenly into a blinding light that seared my eyes.

The next thing to happen was the sensation of everything around me leaving and being replaced by a new scene. I was underground once again, but definitely not in the Dragona. Karissa wasn't with me anymore, and of the four Escalis who were, I recognized three.

I had just missed the tail end of an argument between Prince Avalask and Sav, while Gat leaned against a wall in boredom. A fourth Escali looked up from a massive table of strategy, where a map of our continent had been painted across the surface. Older than the three brothers, but with the same unnatural shade of black to his hair, I knew he had to either be their father or the king.

"You're late," the eldest Escali said to me, a statement, rather than the snarling accusation I would have expected.

I refused to avert my gaze, for fear I might look ashamed. "I didn't know I was supposed to be here until just now." I couldn't help but notice the deeply etched lines around this leader's eyes, as though years of this war had taken their toll on him.

"An empty apology," Sav, the twin with the spiked hair, said from across the room. "The plans have already been made. If she wanted her say, she should have been on time."

"I might have been on time if somebody had taken the initiative to tell me there was a meeting!" I snapped back. My uncouth reply seemed acceptable among Escalis, and the eldest motioned for me to come closer and join them.

"Why are you here by yourself?" he asked as I strolled over, giving the impression of confidence.

"Was your other Tally friend caught?" Sav mocked.

"No, we were separated." I disliked Sav more every second, but Gat was the one who set me on edge, leaning wordlessly against the wall. His crossed arms were thicker than my legs, and he watched me with calculating eyes, giving me the feeling that I was still being hunted.

The Escali who was clearly in charge handed me a large rolled scroll. "Look this over, and see if it looks right to you."

Sav maneuvered himself around the table to whisper furiously to his elder, while I undid the scroll.

My jaw dropped.

It contained aerial views of Dincara, floor-plan layouts, and multiple side views, so detailed, I was sure somebody had sat for days at each angle, painting what they saw. Everything was recreated flawlessly, from the harbor to the top of the central tower.

"How *does* it feel?" Sav asked me, leaning across the table between us. "Knowing that you're about to lose everyone in a day's time? Knowing that *I'm* personally going to—"

"Nobody says you're going to win," I replied, keeping my head high.

Sav sneered and said, "You're still under the impression that your information is accurate. You're expecting a force of *four* thousand to attack?" He dropped his voice to a barely audible whisper. "We're sending sixteen."

"That's enough, Savaul," said the Escali at the head of the table. Sav immediately straightened and fell silent.

I looked at the scroll in my hands and felt numb. *Sixteen? Sixteen… Thousand?* Even with all the ingenious defenses Dincara had, it could never hold off sixteen *thousand* Escalis.

"Is that true?" I asked the leader of the four.

"Yes. Sixteen thousand are preparing to leave, and you're here because I expect you may know something about the Humans' defenses that we don't."

"Their intent is to destroy Dincara and everyone in it, right?"

"Yes. No less than the Humans attempted in Treldinsae."

"Then I won't help. You can find someone else." I rolled up the plans, dropped them on the ground in front of me, and every eyebrow in the room jumped to higher ground.

I thought I caught a grin on Prince Avalask's face as Sav hissed, "This is just like you Tallies. You expect the world from us and give nothing back. Every one of you is filthy and ungrateful —"

"They found another of the Tallies," Prince Avalask interrupted Sav's rant and waved his hand, making Archie appear. Archie took in the situation for only a second, and I heard a deep growl emanate from Gat at his arrival.

"What's happening?" Archie asked me, sensing the tension.

"I was just letting them know that I refuse to help destroy Dincara," I answered, glaring deliberately at Sav and then stepping on the plans I had dropped. Sav snarled and turned to Archie.

"This is your chance to bail her out, Tally. You can tell us what you know, or she's dead."

"I don't side with you," Archie responded, instantly furious. "If she's not going to tell you something, then I'll be shanked if she doesn't have a good reason."

I told him, "They're planning to slaughter everyone in —"

"Sounds like a good reason to me," Archie agreed, further angering Sav.

"You don't understand who you're —"

Prince Avalask shouted over top of us, "Fight each other on your own time. I have greater tasks to tend to."

"Feel free to tend to them," Sav said, breaking his glare away from us. "We're done here."

A guttural snarl resonated across the table, and the brothers fell silent again as the respected figure said, "Savaul! This meeting will be over when I say it is. Understood?"

"Yes, Uncle," Sav bowed to him then sent another threatening look our way. I could no longer question who this was. We were in the presence of King Izfazara.

"Surely we can find an agreement between us," the king said to me. "We really do need whatever insight you can offer."

King or not, I still replied, "As long as you're planning to kill everyone, I won't be helping."

"Is that so? Perhaps we can change your mind."

"You can try," I stated boldly, but I felt fear run through me. *I might have just pushed him too far.*

"Pick up the plans again," he said.

"I already saw all I need to know."

"So you think. Take one more look."

I picked them up and unrolled them again to glance briefly, but the pictures had changed drastically. The views from every angle of Dincara were the same, but they looked like they had been painted this time in the middle of the battle.

Realistically painted flames licked up from the bridge, but nobody stood on it. Instead, Escalis hung over the side to avoid the fiery danger, and those who were close to the fortress appeared to be breaking off the pipes that fueled the fire.

The water underneath simmered green from the alchemist powder, and it looked as though a few people from both sides had met their demise in the moat. Escali archers were taking out the Human archers on the battlements; boulders were falling through the air into the entrance pit, but the Escalis were stacking them so they could be climbed; armed Human ships in the harbor were being overrun as the harbor gate burned; dragons were being slain on the pavilion; fighters were being taken down outside the main turret; and almost every detail of Dincara's defenses was perfect.

"Did we leave anything out?" Izfazara asked.

"Yes," I responded hastily, trying to give the impression that they had missed a lot.

"We need to talk for a second," Archie said, pulling me off to the side and then dropping his voice low enough that only I could hear. "How much are they missing?" he asked, looking at the plans in my hand.

"Barely anything," I whispered, peering closely to find anything omitted. The details were intricate enough that I could see the arrowheads used by the archers on the battlements, and they weren't wrapped in thistleweed or marked with Kelian's seal from Tekada like they should have been. The drawing accounted for the two dragons next to the pit, but was missing the one on the bridge as well as those that would be flying over once the Dragona joined. I also spotted that they had missed the water mages who would be around the pit. Everything else, however, seemed perfect.

"Is there any chance at all that we can win?"

"None. Not with sixteen thousand Escalis and plans like these. They know everything."

"Then in the interest of everybody living, we have to make some kind of deal. Follow my lead?"

"Ok," I agreed, hoping Archie could come up with a miracle.

"How much value is there in what Allie knows about the defenses?" Archie asked Izfazara.

"There is none," Sav quietly advised. "We know the majority of it. We can do without the rest."

"I place high value in her information," Izfazara said with his eyes only on us, as though Savaul's input wasn't worthy of his attention. "If it means the difference between one hundred of our own casualties and two hundred, I'll never be able to live with myself if one of my family is among that difference. Yet, I do get the sense that you Tallies want something in return?"

"Yes," Archie answered. "We don't want you to kill everyone in Dincara when you take it."

"Really? And what would you rather?" Izfazara asked. "What am I supposed to do with… How many Humans will there be?" he asked me.

"A lot," I responded defiantly.

"And what am I supposed to do with *a lot* of captives? Let them go so they can rebuild a new fortress elsewhere? Put them to work as slaves?"

"What if you used them as a message?" Archie suggested. "You could send them back to Tekada as a warning to King Kelian that you don't want to be messed with. It gets them out of your way without killing them, and it conveys how much power you hold. Maybe Tekada will think twice about sending more people after receiving a warning."

"We could do it," Prince Avalask said, giving me the feeling he was on our side. "Our new flagship, *Shadow's Doubt*, is being completed as we speak. She's built to travel against the trade winds, and is strong enough to pull several loaded ships with her."

Savaul said, "We owe these Humans nothing, least of all mercy."

Izfazara replied. "We don't have to owe it to give it. We never have."

"It sounds as though your decision already stands," Prince Avalask said.

Sav intervened, "It will cost more of our own lives to capture that city than to destroy it, even if we do have the advanced information. These Tallies have their own agenda, and it is ignorant to strike deals with them!"

"I disagree," Izfazara answered. "If the cost of saving our own lives is simply sparing the lives of others, then I see nothing ignorant aside from you." Izfazara then turned to Archie and I and asked, "Is it a deal then? If we capture the fortress instead of destroying it, will you share your knowledge?"

I looked uncertainly at Archie and then at King Izfazara. I thought of all my friends and how life would be if they were gone within a few days. Nothing was worth that. *Nothing.*

I could be loyal, or I could spare the lives of everyone I knew.

"It's a deal."

Guilt overwhelmed me after I pointed out the spots they had missed on the maps, answered a few questions about numbers, then described the inner layout of the central turret. Half of me insisted that I had done what was right, that saving my friends was worth the guilt. The other half was twisting and pulling and nagging inside me, telling me I had betrayed everything I stood for.

I had no idea how I was going to update my list of tally marks after this battle. I would have no idea how many lives were lost and saved because of me. Most would be on the saved side though, and that was what mattered.

I expected to be up all night, pacing and contemplating, but when Prince Avalask sent Archie and me back to my "room" in Dincara, I was startled by violent pounding on the door.

"Come on, Allie. You can't block me out of your room!"

"That's Liz," I whispered. "Help me get this sand off the door."

Archie wasn't much help since the sand refused to move for anyone aside from me, so I had to get every single grain back into the box myself.

Liz thundered against my door with both fists, and then kicked it furiously, reminding me she was my sister.

"Just a second Liz," I told her through the door.

I tried to pull it open, but I must have missed a grain or two somewhere. It wouldn't budge.

"Let me do it. We'll find them later," Archie whispered as Liz shouted back, *"Are you deaf?"*

I stepped aside and he forced the door open, creating three tiny holes in the wood where I had missed a few grains. Liz stood fuming in the doorway with her arms folded and her feet planted in a wide stance to keep anyone from getting past her.

"You could have at least said something so I knew you were in there! What were you... Never mind, I don't want to know," she stopped when she saw Archie behind me, and I felt my cheeks turn red. Unfortunately, I couldn't think of any better explanation.

Blotchy red spots crept into Liz's cheeks too, and she stepped back from the doorway, fixing her eyes on the ground to keep angry tears from escaping. *Oh no.* This was jealousy. I was with someone else when she needed me. "I was just coming to check on you..." she said, tucking her chin close to her body as her lower lip quivered furiously. "I can go."

This was the dirtiest guilt-tactic in the book, but I took the bait without hesitation. She drug her feet as she turned to leave, and I only exchanged a quick glance with Archie to see his eyes saying *go go go,* before I left him behind.

"I'm sorry, Liz, I didn't know you were here yet."

"I guess I should have figured that when you didn't come out to greet me. You sure found Archie quick though."

I sighed, having no explanation that would sound both believable and non-incriminating. "Come on, it's just you and me now," I said, wrapping an arm around her shoulder to pull her into a left turn. "Dincara has something like the Wreck where we can get some food, and I want to hear all about what's been happening at the Dragona."

I got the feeling she wanted to stay mad at me, but the need to talk was greater. She took her time, but her rigid shoulders relaxed as she started telling me about the Dragona's speeches and preparations for the coming battle. I was also glad she didn't mention West as we grabbed and ate dinner. Liz was far from alright, but being able to talk without her sobbing on me was a relief I needed.

As I filled my plate with food for a second time, I glanced back to our table to see Archie in my spot. Liz was clearly giving him sour answers as he tried to talk to her, which tore at me more than it should have. I couldn't have them fighting right now with everything else going on.

And so I took an immense amount of time to fill my plate.

By the time I looked back to the table, Archie was messing up Liz's straight black hair like she was his little sister too. To my relief, she threw her arms defensively over her head with a smile as she spoke to him. *Dang*, Archie was good.

I stepped into a side corridor to give them a few extra minutes and sat against the wall to eat, alone with my thoughts. Just me, my thoughts, and two low voices speaking down the dark corridor, sounding so distant that I wondered if my half-Escali ears were the reason I could hear them.

I couldn't help my curiosity, and I found myself setting my plate down so I could sneak closer.

"I can't let you dump antiwater all over the spire." It was the muffled echo of a voice I recognized. Tarace. "What if someone accidentally triggers an explosion? We can't have our leader going up in flames halfway through the battle."

"I will only be consumed in flames if someone opens the door," Sir Laud's calm voice answered him. "That's the only thing rigged to set it off. And I will *only* unlock the door if we lose the fortress. So stop fretting."

"But I can't let you kill yourself," Tarace said, and even from a distance I could hear the struggle a voice has to overcome with heartbreaking words.

Sir Laud replied, "A death by fire would be a kinder fate than falling into the Escalis' hands, especially if the explosion kills the commander who's come to rip my throat out."

Their voices faded and I turned back around, gritting my teeth together. If Sir Laud had the spire rigged to explode in the event we lost the fortress, then he truly was living his last handful of hours right now.

Should I tell him? Was it on my shoulders to let Dincara know their information was wrong?

I needed to talk to Archie, because this did feel like my responsibility.

Liz and Archie ran into me right as I emerged from the dark corridor, and Liz said, "We wondered where you had gone. I think I'm ready for bed."

I could see on Archie's face that he wanted to talk to me too, but I had already agreed to let Liz sleep in my room, and we sure couldn't talk with her around.

Liz yawned and Archie said, "We can talk tomorrow," giving me the feeling he had an idea to get us away from her.

A knock at the door woke us early the next morning. I closed my eyes for a second, remembering that I was on the stone floor because I had given Liz the makeshift bed, then I jumped up to open it.

"Good morning!" Archie greeted me as Liz rolled over to see who it was. "I was wondering if you both wanted to come for a walk?"

I squinted my sleepy eyes at him. *A walk?*

"A walk where?" Liz groaned.

"Into the woods, just to take a look around."

"Sure," I agreed, realizing this would be the time to talk. I looked back at Liz. "Do you want to come?"

"Out in the woods? No. And you shouldn't either, Allie, after what… seven kidnap attempts?"

"It's ok, we'll be armed," Archie joked, holding up his sword.

"You two have fun." Liz rolled back over and closed her eyes.

"Ok, we'll see you later," I said.

I heard her mutter, "But not too much fun," as I pulled the door softly into its latched position.

I stretched my back and whispered, "You didn't have to come so early."

"I didn't know how else to get rid of Liz. And we don't have to go into the forest, but we're getting out of the fortress at least. Can't be too safe with what we have to talk about."

We walked out into the entrance pit and crossed over the bridge without any issue, but when we got to rocky land, Archie stopped and jerked his head to the side, startling me.

"Somebody just brushed against my shield," he said, scanning the empty bridge in confusion. There was no one else in sight.

"Are you sure?"

"I'm positive."

"Maybe it's Tarace," I suggested. "He walks around invisible a lot of the time."

"Tarace?" Archie repeated. "You've hardly been here any time at all, and you've already met Sir Laud's son?"

"I knew he was important," I muttered.

"Well, it's no good talking with someone invisible around," Archie said. "We could go down to the ocean front. Then we'll see footprints in the sand if he comes close."

"Brilliant, let's do it."

When we got down to water, we were both disappointed to see that the waves broke on jagged and sinister rocks. Despite the disappointment though, it was a beautiful view of the ocean without a cloud in sight. Dincara was huge and majestic to our right, then a giant cliff lined the left side of the inlet with a waterfall spilling over its side.

"Let's go this way," Archie said, walking along the rocks away from Dincara. It reminded me of the last time I had followed him alone — I had ended up thrown in a lake only to have my entire perception of the world changed. Something about that crazy thought made me laugh.

Archie turned around. "Are you coming?"

"Yeah, I'm coming."

I was relieved to see this was nothing like the last time once we stopped next to the waterfall and nothing out of the ordinary happened. The spray from the rocks felt good in contrast to the already hot sun.

"I'd like to see anyone stay invisible in all this water," Archie said, pleased by the spot he had chosen.

"We're going to get drenched." I laughed as the water started soaking in, noticing the sunlight glinting off the mist in a rainbow. I sat down and watched as a fish jumped from the water, landing with a splash and disappearing.

Archie sat next to me and looked out at the same beauty I saw. "I can't believe the battle is tomorrow," he said.

"I can't either... Archie, should we tell them what we know? About how many Escalis are coming?"

Archie sighed and said, "I already did. They needed to know."

I didn't press for the details. I just said, "Thanks for getting it done."

I wished so much, with everything I had, that time could stop right then so I would never have to face tomorrow. I wished so hard, but I knew it wouldn't happen.

"Do you think we made the right choice, Archie?"

"By giving them the information? Yeah. They did seem disappointed with the amount you had though. We got the better end of the deal by far. Did you leave anything out?"

"No, they had everything else right."

I twitched my lips a few times, then bit them and clasped my hands in my lap. "What if we die?"

"We won't die, Allie."

"There's no guarantee of that. It could just be an accident, or part of the siege..."

Archie threw a rock in the water. "You know... You will always live wherever you go. Not because you're a Tally, but because you're always living. If you aren't, then the only way you're going to know is by looking around and finding that you're in a better place. Then it won't matter anymore." I thought over his logic and found that I liked it. "Thinking of that keeps me from being afraid."

I looked up as a shadow passed over us and I saw my grey-freckled falcon swoop down to land on a looping root next to us.

"Hi, Flak," I said. I reached out to stroke her feathers, but she hopped away, not wanting to be touched.

"Are you scared?" Archie asked.

"Yes."

Flak moved close to me again, but I didn't try to pet her.

"Of which part?"

I shrugged uncomfortably. "I'm not so afraid of dying, but of getting hurt, losing somebody, seeing life change forever... Are you scared?"

"Yeah, a lot more than I'm letting on."

Just as I noticed how thoroughly the waterfall had drenched me, trumpets blared from atop Dincara.

"That means we have to get back," Archie said, standing up. I stood too and wrung the water from my tied-back hair. Another fish jumped between waves, catching Flak's apt attention and making me smile.

"It feels like this is the end," Archie said.

271

"It does," I agreed. We hugged before we had to leave and I realized that Archie was completely dry because the water had been hitting his shield. Well, he *had been* dry. He wasn't anymore.

"Sorry about that," I said, stepping back.

"Naw, don't be," he grinned.

When we got back to Dincara, lines of people stretched in every direction to grab armor, weapons, and assignments. The first place we had to go was the line assigning each person to a different area, and Archie and I both ended up on the forward left battlements, overlooking the bridge. We found where to get bows and arrows, and then we had to listen to extensive instructions on how to proceed when time of the battle arrived.

Liz found us eventually, holding a helmet and armor in her arms.

"Where are you going to be?" I asked her, my heart fluttering in anticipation.

"On the ships, helping to shoot the ballistae at any Escali lucky enough to make it to the backside of the pavilion."

"Well, as long as you're far from the front lines," I replied, not feeling any more comfortable.

As everybody finished getting assignments and gear, Sir Laud stepped into view on the walls. The silence he received was almost unreal, and the reverence that everyone held for him marked his as an exceptional leader. "Dincara," he addressed everyone with a smile. "For nearly fifty years, I've watched this fortress become a home, a safe haven, and a symbol of defiance for everyone on our continent. And now, looking out among you, I see more than just Dincarans come to defend it. I see every last one of the Dragonan mages, quite a few warriors from Tabriel Vale, I'm also seeing a lot of blond hair and blue eyes from the northern cities, Lakama, Terrinatel, Keldrosa, Glaria... I've always been secretly jealous of those northern looks myself."

272

A nervous chuckle swept through the crowd.

"It's good to see the men and mages we can count on when the day of the battle comes. We come from different places and hold many loyalties, and just as long as none of those loyalties are to Kelian, we should be fine. Otherwise, there's a bridge leading out of the city — feel free to jump off before you get in our way."

Everybody laughed again, this time a bit louder. These Dincarans fiercely loved their leader, and it was infectious.

"Dincara has always been the strongest Human fortress on this continent — our symbol of strength in this war torn land, and an unflinching reminder to the Escalis that we're here. However, the truth of tomorrow's battle has now come to the fore. And... We won't be able to hold our city."

A surprised murmur resonated off the walls, and I exchanged a nervous glance with Archie.

"The Escalis understand this to be our center of strength. They know it's where we receive our supplies, and they know it's our symbol of defiance, which is why they are coming in numbers greater than we can handle. The original reports consistently assured me that a force of four thousand would attack. We could have handled the initial numbers, but they've changed. The Escalis are now sending sixteen thousand, and they'll be here at noon tomorrow."

The outburst of talk was instant — fear and alarm, surprise and sorrow — people only quieted down again when Sir Laud held out his hands so he could speak.

"I won't force anybody to stay. In fact, you're all free to leave through the escape tunnels when the kids go. There is no shame, no guilt attached, but you may not leave until I have finished speaking.

"Personally, I've gone through our options and I only see three. Fight, flee, or forfeit. I also personally feel that I have worked too damn hard to do either of the latter! I may have to stand by myself at those gates, but the Escalis will still have to go through me. This is my home! I'll fight because this is where my son was born and raised. I'll fight so the Escalis don't have free reign over me — I'll fight because I am Human and will not be driven by their demands! I'll fight because I am Dincaran, but most of all, I'll fight because this is the legacy I want to leave. The next time they attack a Human city, I want them to fear what they will find. I want them to fear the Human spirit. It's what separates us from them.

"Tomorrow I ask that you stand wherever your heart calls you. If that happens to be at home, then go. If you choose to fight with us tomorrow, to die with us tomorrow, then treasure this moment. Look at each person around you and make amends with your enemies, share hugs with your friends. This is the last time we will all be together. Tomorrow we fight not for me, not for Kelian, but for each other. We fight for the future, and we fight for the hope of all. We are not outcasts. We are Human, and we are all brothers."

"And before you decide whether to stay or go, I'll ask you this…"

Thousands of bated breaths left Dincara dead silent.

"What legacy do you want to leave?"

Chapter Twenty Five

Whenever I looked over the side of our archers' tower, I found a long, straight drop to the crashing water which put an extra knot of anticipation in my stomach. I wished the sky was still midnight-blue and that the sunrise hadn't killed the stars watching over us. I wished I could focus on the tall man in command of our battalion, drilling everyone with the meaning of each trumpet call. Yet I just found myself staring out at the combat dragons on either side of the pit, eerily silent and still.

Nobody had left Dincara last night. Even the kids had to be coerced after their leader's speech.

Our prep-talk included the word "courage" more often than not, and I had the feeling that our leader was convincing himself to be brave as much as any of us. And yet, for all his talk of bravery, courage, honor, and sacrifice, I could still see his heart freeze in fear when the first Escalis stepped out of the forest.

Everybody knew to expect immense numbers but could never have anticipated the shock of seeing sixteen thousand Escalis closing around Dincara. They filled in the space between the trees and the bridge, and the fact that we couldn't see the ones behind the forest cover made the swarm seem endless.

It was obvious to me and everybody else that we didn't have a chance, and I knew without a doubt I had done the right thing by convincing them to spare our lives. We all would be dead otherwise.

"You ready?" I hadn't even noticed Archie appear next to me.

"Definitely not," I replied.

"Now would be a good time to get ready."

"Yeah, I know," I groaned, brushing my hair fretfully back from my face. "I'm working on it."

Two trumpets sounded from above, signaling to prepare, so he returned to his post as archers all over Dincara stepped up to theirs. Many were on the lower decks of the battlements, aiming through gaps in the stone, while quite a few lined up along the fortress walls. All the Escalis had arrived and were preparing to rush across the bridge. The level of tension inside the fortress was mounting and then we saw a single Escali come forth, taking slow and purposeful strides across Dincara's great walkway.

An entire city held its breath as the Escali neared the main gates, jerking his attention and gaze rapidly in every direction. He shouted something for all of Dincara to hear, but I couldn't even catch it with my Tally ears. I couldn't hear his declarations, but I had no problem seeing his bared teeth as he spat them.

I heard a shout from one of our own down at the main gate, and then saw at least eight arrows fire at the Escali on the bridge. His superiors howled in anger from across the water as he fell to his knees, and then the entire Escali army bellowed roars of outrage. A horn sounded from somewhere within the Escali ranks, and the assault began.

It didn't start with an angry charge of warriors.

Only six of their soldiers broke across the bridge in a surreal sprint until flames erupted underneath of them, scorching their feet. Their preparation for this obstacle was instantly apparent as all six leapt off and dangled from the edge of the bridge. They waited for the fire to subside, all except the Escali who had been in the front. He had launched himself forward and landed on one of the pipes fueling the bridge. He was undoubtedly attempting to break it, but was knocked into the water below as our trumpet calls ordered us to open fire. One splash into the green, and he was gone forever. Every Escali clinging to the edge of the bridge was either killed by arrows or knocked into the water, and so we successfully kept the first wave from causing any damage.

And when I said we, I meant the archers around me. I aimed poorly so my arrows wouldn't cause me more regret.

The fire subsided, and another wave sprinted toward the gates as the next batch of fuel was piped into the bridge. We had less luck with this group of Escalis. Two of them were able to jump and land on the left pipe before we could shoot them, and they both immediately pushed against the bridge with all their might to try to break the duct loose. The combined strength of the two Escalis was enough to wrench the pipe from its intended socket before they were shot and fell to certain death. The antiwater that was supposed to be fueling the bridge began draining into the moat, and the right pipe was the only one left to kindle the bridge-fire.

Flames burst up from the grated bridge again, and the Escalis waited for them to subside to make their next run. The Escalis in this new wave made it up to the last remaining fuel pipe despite Dincara's efforts to shoot them down — however, they found it more sturdy than the other, and they couldn't break it loose. They resorted to pulling out tools and weapons and punching gaping holes in the pipe instead.

The bridge flamed up one last time, effectively annihilating that wave of Escalis as they either burned or dangled from the edge of the structure to be picked off by the archers. The entranceway was overrun as the bridge took an immense amount of time to collect any antiwater from its one damaged source. It probably wouldn't be spouting fire for the rest of the battle. Barely a dent had been made in the Escali ranks as hundreds swarmed into the pit and a whole new wave of archers opened fire on them.

The cue was sent to start releasing boulders, and mages levitated them out to fall into the pit, killing or injuring those who weren't yet hit by our arrows. A different trumpet call announced the arrival of dragons overhead, who swooped down and incinerated those trying to climb onto the main square.

Our rampart received the order to fire a volley, and we wiped out half the regiment on the bridge, knocking several into the water, never to resurface. More Escalis eager to get in on the action were quick to replace the fallen, and they flooded into the entrance pit where those who had survived the falling boulders were dragging themselves out.

The horn sounded for the archers to ready for another volley, along with three long notes signaling the water mages to commence.

Frothing green water came in from above, and the Escalis in the pit screamed in shock and agony as it splashed and burned into their skin. But the result wasn't that they stopped, rather they climbed up the sides of the pit as fast as they could and came face to face with the combat dragons on either side. Raging flames erupted from the dragons as they were released from their trances, reflecting their hatred toward the world and everyone in it. Escalis who had just climbed up the walls either had to jump back down or be burnt to death.

The horn sounded to release another volley of arrows, but the Escalis on the bridge were now equipped with shields and very few of them suffered hits. Curses came from the archers in both battlements, but the voice of one man rose above them catching everybody's attention.

"LOOK TO THE HARBOR!"

The *Shadow's Doubt* was burning down the harbor wall, eager to bring another mass of Escalis in through the back. She was plagued by fire arrows, but shook them off like water down a bird's feathers. She was almost through.

We were drawn back to attention with the horn sounding to fire again. The archers around me knocked more off the bridge, but not enough to make a difference through the Escalis' shields. The bridge was no longer an obstacle for them, but the pit was. They couldn't climb up past the dragons, the door to get inside Dincara was sealed shut, and the water being constantly poured in was mixing with the alchemist powder and burning them.

Most of the Escali forces still stood waiting to cross the bridge, but they now had a contender on their own side of the battle. An aerial formation of nine dragons had taken to swooping over their ranks, jet-streaming fire and carrying mages who could do much worse. I had never seen such a trained force, able to instantly turn and maneuver together as though they shared thoughts. All nine dragons jumped into the sky as one to avoid the Escali's arrows, then plummeted back down with maws of fire, darting sharply to the left to avoid all predictability, then lurching back into the sky.

The unit swooped over the bridge, and the power I had often seen blasting opponents across an open field was used to knock entire groups of Escalis into the moat beneath. One mage always seemed to lead the group, and his power was one of crackling white destruction. It was the same energy I had seen glowing in my own hands, and he was using it to cause ruin upon countless Escalis. Lines of them crumpled as the squadron wreaked havoc with each pass.

A thought occurred to me that never had before. *We might not lose this battle.*

I didn't know what the Escalis did, or how they did it, but a roar resonated across the entire ocean as the moat burst into flames. We all ducked down to avoid the blistering fire filling the air, but it burned down in haste so the flames only licked menacingly on top of the water. The next Escali to fall in looked to be falling into a pit of lava, flaming most brightly where the antiwater continued to spill.

The archers on our battlement got back to their feet and were about to fire when we had to dive down again and avoid arrows the Escalis had launched up at our turrets. They didn't fire them one volley at a time, but kept a continuous stream coming, pinning us down.

The arrows suddenly stopped pelting the sides of the battlement, and when I peered over the edge, I saw why. The gigantic stone spider that lived over the entrance to Dincara had jumped onto the bridge and begun knocking Escalis into the water. I had no idea what had brought it to life, but it was an amazing force to be reckoned with. Several Escalis jumped onto its back, but it had eight swift and flexible legs that could pull them off while striking at any others close by.

I jumped in surprise as somebody pulled at my shirt from behind and I turned around to see —

"LEAF! What are you doing here?!"

"I snuck over in an empty barrel. I'm going to help defend!" he said.

"No," I said harshly, "you're going to get out of this city right now."

Archie ran over to us when he saw. "*Leaf!* You're supposed to be with all the other kids!"

"I know, but I wanted to help, and look," he said as he pulled out a very worn dagger, "I even got a sword to kill the evil Escalis!"

I heard a great splash and glanced quickly down to see the spider disappearing into the flaming water below. *Shanking life.* "Leaf, that won't save you," I said in exasperation, feeling tears of worry in the corners of my eyes.

"Come over here," Archie pulled Leaf over to the edge where he could look through the gaps in the wall and through the cloud of smoke to see the multitude of Escalis in the pit, on the bridge, climbing the walls, and those who were shooting down the aerial squadron on the other side of the bridge. Three of the dragons had been brought down already, and we watched a fourth crash into the Escali ranks. Those remaining were still grouped around the lead mage with my power.

As Leaf's eyes took in the battle and began to widen in fear, light exploded in the middle of the pit, announcing the appearance of Prince Avalask. He hovered over the battle for no more than a second before his outstretched arms used an amazing force to rip the entrance door out of the wall from a distance. He hurled the entire doorway at one of the combat dragons above the pit, killing it instantly.

Sir Avery was on him in seconds, and the ensuing battle between the Epics became a blur, taken up into the sky, where the clouds darkened and stray fireballs and thunderbolts came hurtling down at the rest of us. Archie turned Leaf to face him and I could sense his frozen shock at the magnitude of the situation. He was suddenly not so eager to be involved.

"Now listen to me," Archie bent down until his face was level with Leaf's, "Allie's going to take you down to the escape tunnel, then you're going to get away from this fortress as fast as you can. There will be no arguing whatsoever. Got it?"

Leaf nodded quickly.

"I can't believe this is happening," I mumbled to Archie before I grabbed Leaf's small hand.

Archie took my other in a quick grasp, tight enough to kill a small animal. "I'll see you soon," he said.

I nodded wordlessly and he let go. I turned with Leaf to dash down to the escape tunnels.

The descent of stairs seemed immense as I heard crashes and screams outside the walls. We reached the end of the stairway and started across a long corridor, only to violently startle the mob stationed to guard the archer's battlements. We hurried past, but stopped momentarily as a voice called out to us from the group.

It was Jesse's hateful tone, asking me, "Where are you going?" and thinking himself entitled to a response. I turned around and stopped for a moment, just long enough to cover Leaf's ears and tell Jesse in a less than pleasant tone how much I cared about what he wanted to know. Then I proceeded on towards the tunnel entrance with Leaf in tow.

We rounded a corner in the hallway just as a huge smash sounded behind us and another of the *impenetrable* doors was busted down. The sounds of outside's battle clearly filtered into the fortress through the breach, and the din of the guard we had just passed echoed loudly off the walls. The Escalis were advancing quickly now that Prince Avalask had broken them in.

Leaf was considerably slower than any Escali, and I began to worry that we might not make it to the tunnel before they caught up to us. Finally though, we rounded the last corner and flew into the room with the trapdoor, which I wrenched open for Leaf. He jumped down onto the ladder, and I quickly wished him luck and told him I'd see him when the battle was over. I slammed the door shut, and then tore back out into the hallway to rejoin where I could.

I didn't have to go far. At the first corner, two people smashed headfirst into the wall in front of me, both trying to inflict as much pain on the other as possible. I jumped in without hesitation and tried to pull the Escali off a man I didn't recognize. The man was, of course, dazed by the collision with the wall and passed out within seconds, leaving me with an angry Escali.

I jumped back and pulled out my short swords, not to attack with obviously, but to defend myself. The Escali turned toward me and either didn't recognize that I was a Tally, or was really good at not showing it since he pulled out his own bladed staff and struck so fast that I almost lost my head. I would have lost some sort of limb in the next few seconds if not for my Tally reflexes. Before he struck again, somebody grabbed me roughly from behind and held a dagger to my throat. "Drop the swords," she growled.

I did and saw that further down the hall, the battle wasn't going much better. The one who had been about to kill me growled at the loss of his prey, and my captor dragged me backwards around the corner, away from him. She opened a door and threw me inside, slamming it shut again so we were alone in a brightly lit room of book shelves.

"Are you trying to die?" Tresca growled. I felt sudden relief when I saw her.

"Thank you," I said. Another crash sounded outside, making the walls rattle and dust fall from the ceiling beams.

"You don't leave the room until this is over," she commanded, sheathing her dagger. "You're far from being out of danger."

"What danger am I in now?" I asked. I had no intention of remaining with her, but I wondered what could be worse than the already dire situation.

"Savaul and Gataan are here, and you have to pretend you're a captive until the bitter end. I know them, and they won't pass up the chance to accidentally kill you before this is over."

"Who says I'm going to be the captive? Our side could still pull through and hold Dincara," I said. Tresca raised her eyebrows at me.

"We'll probably have the entire fortress in another ten minutes. The *Shadow's Doubt* has already docked and your forces are falling. They did well preventing us from entering, but they can't match us in battle now that we're in." Another blow outside shook more dust off the ceiling and two books toppled to the floor in a rustle of pages.

"So what now?" I asked restlessly.

"Now we wait," she said. "When the fighting dies down, we'll go back out, and you can be a prisoner along with everyone else."

"I can't stay in here," I said as another yell from outside penetrated the wall. "What am I supposed to do? Pace?"

"Pace all you want. Pace a hole in the floor, but I'm not letting you leave to get yourself killed."

I tried that for a couple minutes. I tried pacing, I tried looking at the books lining the walls, but I couldn't do it. I needed to know what was happening. I needed to be involved! What if we weren't losing after all?

Tresca was scanning through the titles and had her back turned to me, so I made my way slowly toward the door and silently turned the knob.

"What will leaving here accomplish, Allie?" she asked without even turning to look at me.

"I don't know, but more than standing patiently will!"

I wasn't sure if she would let me go, so I opened the door and darted away from the library. The hallway ahead was empty, but I could hear sounds of a skirmish somewhere off to my left. I headed in the direction of the noise, but I couldn't find anybody. I stooped and picked up my swords, which were still on the ground, and then the commotion I had been hearing suddenly stopped. I had no idea whether that was good or bad.

Every corner I rounded filled me with dreadful anticipation, but I still found no one. I decided I might as well make my way back to the archer's tower and start there. I walked cautiously, but the lack of noise on the way was disconcerting. Maybe the fortress had been taken. It was horrible not to know.

I found a barred opening in the wall that looked into the pit, and quickly pressed my face into it. The battle hadn't gone well in my absence. The remainder of the Escalis were now crossing the bridge unopposed and either climbing the sides of the pit to access the rest of Dincara, or entering through the gaping hole in the wall where Prince Avalask had extricated the door. Gigantic boulders littered the pit along with dead Escalis and a slain dragon. A group of about fifty Humans were on their knees in the middle, more so than were dead, but they were certainly unable to fight any longer. With a sunken heart I stepped back and turned around, violently startled to see Tresca had come up behind me as silently as falling dust.

"It's over, let's go," she said, holding the tip of her sword to my heart. I took a deep breath, swallowed my pride, and then dropped my swords on the ground at her feet.

She marched me out to the pit and sat me down with the group of Humans already there. We were left to listen as the Escalis took the remainder of Dincara. Nobody could bear to look at each other.

I could do nothing apart from bite my lip and wring my hands together behind my back as the shouts, clangs, and panicked voices echoed from the tower where I'd been stationed. The tower where Archie was still stationed.

I had no idea if the Escalis had reached Liz yet.

With my head hung low, I found myself whispering, "Please be alright. Please be alright." More than anything I just wanted a hand to grasp right now, the bone crunching grip of somebody who could understand and share my overwhelming anxiety.

Time truly seemed to freeze in that misery. I waited an eternity to find out what was happening, and only at the end of that eternity did the Escalis finally bring another group of Humans to sit with us in the pit. After what felt like years, they marched in another small crowd. However, the only person I recognized so far was Jesse.

He clearly had tears in his eyes, and he coped by hissing through a sob, "Why did you have to survive?"

"Stop talking," one of the Escalis told him. I didn't realize until later that he wouldn't have understood the Escali, but he stopped talking all the same.

I looked around to see who else I knew, and as they escorted in another group of captives I saw Archie, to more relief than I have ever known. He didn't seem to like being put on his knees one bit, but I managed to get his attention.

'Liz?' I mouthed to him.

He shook his head to say he hadn't seen her.

I dug my fingernails further into my palms, and then told him silently, 'Sav and Gat are here.' He frowned to say he couldn't understand me. "Sav," I whispered aloud—

"And Gat?" he finished my thought, looking to the ground in worry.

He asked me something in return, but I couldn't tell what. Before he could repeat it, the Escalis made everyone get up to relocate so they could fit more people into the enclosed area. I immediately moved over next to Archie, and he whispered, "Did you see Sav and Gat?"

"No, Tresca told me they're here."

"Maybe we won't run into them."

"They're going to be looking for us."

"Nobody's looking for us. Everybody's been killed or captured."

"What?" I replied, confused by his answer. That wasn't what I had been saying.

"There is no rescue coming, because everybody's in the same boat right now," he continued.

I stared at him for a second and then realized what he was doing. Jesse was next to us listening intently, so Archie had changed what he was saying for Jesse's benefit. He couldn't just save it for a less important time?

"But what about the people back in Tabriel Vale? They could do *something* to help," I played along impatiently.

Sure enough, Jesse turned to me. "Nobody's coming, Allie," he said, "just give it up!" then he blazed away from us as though trying to distance himself. Archie and I were both glad to see him go, but realized we couldn't risk talking with people around us. When the Escalis forced us to sit again, we did so silently.

The worst news was that we had lost the battle, and a lot of lives with it. The good news, which I tried to dwell on, was that so many people had been captured alive, the Escalis couldn't even fit them all in the entrance pit. The Escalis had hauled the dead combat dragon into the moat in an attempt to make more room. They had also stacked the boulders up for easy access to Dincara's main outer level, but we still had more Humans alive than the entrance area could contain. Most of the Escalis were now discussing what to do with the survivors. They had a large variety of opinions, most of which disregarded Izfazara's decision to keep everyone alive and well.

"That's Gramsaf, Izfazara's brother, and the father of Sav and Gat," Archie whispered, pointing to the leader of the Escali force, who was giving instructions to the Escalis near the shattered main gate. Among the group I spotted Sav's jet-black hair, but Gat wasn't with him. I pointed it out to Archie, and we both ducked as far from sight as we could.

"Probably off killing survivors," Archie muttered.

The Escalis around Gramsaf split up, and each went a separate way into the crowd, getting everybody to their feet again to move them. In the commotion of standing, whispering, and fretting, somebody tapped me on the shoulder from behind and I turned around to see the last person I desired.

"Your group will follow me." Gat's words were deep, gruff, and to the point, as though he wasn't a fan of language. His black falcon, Gyr, had been perched on his arm, but took off at the sight of us.

"Sorry," Archie said furiously, stepping in front of me. "We don't speak your stupid language."

"I'll make it clear for you. From here over," he put his arm in between us, "comes with me." He put his hand on my arm for effect, and Archie grabbed Gat's wrist in a flash while one of the younger girls nearby yelled, "Stop it, you're going to get us killed!"

"You should listen to her," Gat peered wickedly at Archie. I felt sick.

"I'll be okay," I said as Archie's thoughts whirred almost visibly, trying to come up with a solution. He suddenly let go of Gat and acted as though he wasn't there.

"Ok, keep yourself safe," he said to me.

"I... will," I stammered, taken aback by his unexpected change of mind. He pushed away from us into the crowd, leaving me with Gat who seemed as confused as I was. Groups of people around us were being directed to climb up the boulders onto the upper level. Gat waited and waited, probably for Sav to show up. When the last of the groups climbed to the upper level, and we were the last ones remaining in the pit, Gat demanded the same of us.

I hoped to lose him by climbing quickly up to the plaza and disappearing in the hustle, but I had no such luck. Gat tailed me closely. He was actually directing our group back to the shipyard like he was supposed to, where all the Humans from Dincara were being loaded onto their own ships. A few Human vessels had already launched into the bay and were just waiting on the rest to leave the dock and join them.

I spotted Liz just as she saw me too. Yes, my heart grew immediately lighter, but I wished I hadn't seen her because she surreptitiously left her own group to join mine.

She said, "A girl in that other group thinks they're probably sailing the ships out to sea to sink them. Get rid of us and our ships all in one."

"Yeah, maybe. Liz, I think it might be best if you pretend you don't know me," I whispered, eyeing Gat ahead of us.

"What? Why?" she asked. Why did I always think I could hear suspicion in her tone now?

"It's just..." there weren't many ways to explain without explaining everything. "I might be in more danger than you are, and I don't want anyone to know we're related." There. I said it.

Gat turned around and saw me talking to her, which sank my heart even further.

"Well I don't care," Liz said, "I'm not going to abandon you if you're in trouble. What kind of a sister would I be?"

"Be quiet, Liz. Please." Not that it mattered anymore. Gat had seen us.

We came nearer to the ships, where one was obviously not Human in any way. The *Shadow's Doubt* was made of a deep red wood and polished to perfection. The mast held lines of beautiful white and golden sails, making the Human ships next to it look worn and weary.

As our group approached the ship we were meant to board, Sav showed up next to Gat with the black falcon on his arm, whispered to him, and they both veered off in a different direction from everyone else. We were headed away from the ships, back toward the bridge, and out of the crowd's sight.

I hoped somebody would see the twins redirecting our group, but nobody seemed to notice. As soon as we were around the central tower and hidden from view, Sav and Gat both stopped and turned to us. *Turned to me* in particular.

"Tell the rest of them to go," Sav said. "We only want you."

I obviously couldn't respond with everyone else around. I silently matched each scoundrel's stare and said nothing.

"They can go or we can kill them. Your choice," Sav said. Everybody was focused on me and confused. *Shanking life!* This would be the end my secret. It didn't matter anymore.

"You guys can go," I said without taking my eyes off Gat's malicious face. Nobody moved.

"Liz, just take everybody and leave."

"I'll stay with you," Liz said with bold determination. Everybody else was of the same opinion — not wanting to leave me by myself. I could only see one option left to keep the rest of them safe, and I was going to take it.

"Liz, please go," I whispered, meeting her frightened gaze and glancing right behind her to the entrance pit that separated us from the bridge.

"Not without you."

"I'm going to miss you Liz — have a good life!" I took two steps to gain momentum, leapt into the entrance pit, landed with a roll, and then took off across the bridge at a speed that could only be matched by Sav and Gat. It took them hardly a second to see me making a run for it, and they sprinted in pursuit, leaving everyone else behind.

I turned into the forest as soon as I was across the bridge and trees whirred past as I dodged in and out. Sav cut off to one side and disappeared while Gat continued on my heels. I realized I didn't have a plan, and my run couldn't go on for very long because they were faster than I was. So much faster, and I wasn't even headed in any particular direction.

Improvising became the strategy as Gat and his predatory sprint closed in. A massive cliff on my right dropped abruptly down to the bay where the boats were preparing to leave, but the water was too rocky to jump into. Dense underbrush and unending trees impeded my view to the left. Up ahead would be the river that turned into the waterfall seen from Dincara, but the Escalis might not have realized that yet. I had an idea.

I pushed my legs vigorously to make it to the river, and Gat was almost even with me by the time I got there. One tree stood on the bank, and I changed my course to head straight for it. Without slowing down, I got all the way to the riverbank and grabbed the trunk to stop myself. Gat hadn't realized the river was there and tried to stop, but was going too fast and slid down the bank. He turned around to come back, but I was already far ahead of him, running back towards Dincara.

I knew I didn't have long before Gat caught up, and Sav could be anywhere. I needed to take the opportunity to hide from them.

Nowhere seemed safe enough. I looked back over the edge of the cliff and saw six of the ships in the water already, the Human ones being towed by the *Shadow's Doubt*. Its mast was so tall that it almost broke even with the plane of the cliff. If I timed a jump just right...

No time to think it through — I saw Sav closing in from the side, so I ran straight for the cliff and jumped over the edge. I hadn't factored in the fact that the ship was *moving*, so I almost missed the mark and barely managed to grab the mast, landing my feet on the sparkling white ropes holding the sails. Success!

Yelling came from behind me, and I heard Sav exclaiming, "She just jumped!"

Gat swore loudly in Escalira and then started shouting, "She's on the boat! She's getting away on *Shadow's Doubt*!"

Sav lowered his voice so I couldn't hear him, and I saw both figures start running along the cliff line, racing the boat. It wasn't over yet.

I climbed slowly down the mast, lucky that the ship was gigantic so I could stay inconspicuous. The entrance to the cargo hold was visible from where I was, and easy to get to, so I dashed for it and ducked inside, shutting the door behind me. All the light in the hold came from the slots in the entrance and a couple holes in the sides of the walls. Even with my Tally eyes, I could barely see a thing.

I descended a set of stairs until I felt my feet hit the floor. A couple steps forward and my shoulder brushed the side of a large crate, definitely big enough to hide behind.

Rough Escali voices clashed above, and I heard a cascade of water rejoining the ocean as something sopping wet was hoisted onto the deck.

Sav's unmistakable laugh reached me over the thuds of footsteps, and he said, "We're fine. We just didn't realize what time the boats were leaving."

"Did your group of Humans get on a ship?" someone asked.

291

"Yes, yes," Sav answered, "They're all in the third one."

"Alright. Go get yourselves dried off. It's a long trip and you're soaked."

"Right, we will," Sav laughed again and a few other Escalis chuckled before going back to their work.

It only took a couple seconds before I could see the silhouette of Sav's face at the slotted entrance, and then he whispered, "She's down here."

Gat appeared right next to him and growled, "I smell her," then wrenched the door open.

CHAPTER TWENTY SIX

maneuvered myself behind the crate and crouched as Sav grabbed Gat, yanking him back. "*Are you sane?*" he whispered.

"You want to leave her down there?" Gat asked, as though he wanted his brother's approval.

"Yes, I do. It's darker than a cave — she can ambush us with anything she finds. But think, it's six days until we touch land again. If we go down there *then —* "

"Then it'll be easy," Gat finished his sentence. "But anyone getting supplies down there will see her."

"She's smart enough to stay out of sight. And there's Human stench everywhere, so I doubt anyone will notice hers."

"Ok," Gat said, backing out of the hold and shutting the door once more. "I'll take first shift."

"Alright, just call if you need help. Remember, you can't kill her yet. She still knows something we need." Sav walked off and Gat's silhouette planted itself outside the door. There wasn't much to do then besides sit down and watch him.

Darkness fell, by which time I had retired to looking out one of the knotholes in the wall to watch the ocean. Two full moons lit the sky and cast reflections off the frothy water, completing the ominous feeling. I saw Sav come out and trade places with Gat in the night, but everything remained silent otherwise. Morning couldn't be too far off.

I almost drifted off to sleep when a small bird started singing and woke me again. It was the part of the duskflyer's song that I heard Archie whistle every once in a while, and I liked the tune of it. It continued singing and repeating until I pulled myself together and realized what it was.

I cautiously moved to the other side of the hold and peered around. "Archie, where are you?"

"On the other side of the wall," came his muffled whisper.

"How did you get there?" I wondered, pressing my ear against another tiny knothole in the beautiful wood. *That would be on the outside of the hull.*

"I am hanging... from a rope," he said, straining his voice. Forgetting all that was going on, I had to laugh quietly.

"Do you know that you're barely out of Sav's sight?"

"Yeah, I got this rope from right behind him."

"Why didn't you strangle him?" I asked quite seriously.

"I would have if Gat wasn't so close by. Do you have a plan for getting out of here?" he asked.

"Not really... Would it really be such a bad idea to get the other Escalis involved and get those two into trouble?"

"Yes, bad idea. They're royalty, and the Escalis up there don't know who you are. If you got caught... It's just a bad idea. And anyway, my hands are starting to hurt, so let's figure out how this is going to work."

"What do you have in mind?" I asked.

"I want you to use that magic you have to blast a hole in the back of the ship."

"I would love to, but it doesn't work like that. I can't just use it when I want."

"When *can* you use it?"

294

"I don't know... When I'm really scared, or angry about something."

"*And you're not now?*"

"I said I didn't know! Believe me, I would use it if I could."

"Alright, well that's the end of that plan. I'll come back in a while when I think of something, or when you think of something."

"Ok, don't leave me here too long," I said, wishing he could stay.

"If they come in after you, I'll be right there."

"Thanks."

I heard Archie's feet touch the hull of the ship as he climbed back up, and then I was alone again. As hard as I tried to stay awake, I couldn't do it. In one moment, I was trying to keep my eyes open, in the next, I was being killed in my dreams — killed in many ways, and then I found myself waking to hear an Escali descending the stairs.

I was behind a crate, so although the Escali had a lantern in his hand, he didn't see me. He stacked the lantern on top of a barrel, picked the barrel up to bring above deck, and I breathed again once he was gone.

Morning came, and I spent the entire day thinking things over, waiting to hear the duskflyer whistle from Archie again. It was too much time to think. I wished I had something else to occupy myself.

About halfway through the day, as Sav waited outside, I heard him whispering. I was curious because nobody else was near him, and I moved slightly closer, only to hear that his words were directed at me. He was goading, obviously trying to make me show myself. As transparent as his intent was, I could still feel the anger growing inside me with each word.

"It won't be hard to find the city's escape tunnel either," he whispered. "As soon as we get back, Gataan and I plan to follow it and find where your cowards fled to before the battle. I'm sure Dincara's children will love to see us. I have such great plans for them." He paused in thought, and I tried to back off so I couldn't

295

hear him, but his next words drew my attention. "That's always where you fail, Tally, trying to protect those Human kids. I wish you could remember the shame of losing the Epic to me. You sacrificed everything you knew to hide your secrets, but you had already shown us where she was. I'm sure we'll get those other secrets from you soon."

I grabbed tightly to a crate as I tried to steady my breathing. *The new Epic was a she?*

I lost my memory protecting our new Epic, and now Sav had her?

"And what a pity that you can't recall the fun we all had just a few weeks ago, before your Tally friends showed up. I can tell you why you don't remember anything. Come up here and I'll tell you *all* about it."

The edge of the crate splintered under my grip, and I slowly released my hand, watching the remnants fall. I didn't like being confused. Sav knew what happened to my memory, and I wouldn't be above strangling him to find out.

Sav leaned back as though thoroughly relaxed, and continued on. "What else is there to talk about?" he pondered slowly. "I met a few of your fellow mages in the battle. The one with the orange hair in particular, she was intriguing. She almost had me at one point, but was too slow. She only left a couple of burns on my arms when Gataan got her from behind. They're gone now, of course, and her flames stopped burning quite so brightly once she realized everyone in the room was at our mercy."

I didn't want to hear any more, but couldn't convince myself to stop listening.

"And we were merciful too. We gave her the option to beg for their lives. We were both slightly surprised when she did. Yet… not as surprised as she was when we didn't keep our word," Sav chuckled at the memory. "You should have seen the looks on their faces when we killed her anyway. Gataan—"

I heard a vicious snarl escape and then realized it was mine. I was momentarily blinded by rage, but then realized that I wasn't blinded at all — my hands and eyes were illuminating the entire hold. I aimed at Sav through the grated door, but before I unleashed my magic on him, I heard a tiny voice in the back of my head urging me not to.

It won't kill him, the voice advised. Maybe it wouldn't. I didn't care. *Gat will come running.* That didn't matter either. I could blast him out of my way as well. *Then you'll attract everyone on the ship and you can't handle all of them.* What was the alternative — sit here with my magic and do nothing?

I remembered what Archie wanted me to do. Though I wanted to cause Sav as much pain as possible, I forced myself to turn around and unleash my wealth of power on the back wall. The wood splintered and disintegrated, ripping a large hole in the exterior, much bigger than I needed.

I heard Sav shouting for Gat behind me, and a general commotion above as everyone came to investigate the sound of destruction. I whistled a very hurried version of the duskflyer song before I heard Gat's snarl behind me, and I bailed off the ship.

The moment I hit the cold ocean, I heard yelling from every deck.

"One's in the water!"

"Escape!"

But above all was, "Shoot it! It deserves to drown — shoot it!"

I dove under the water as several sasperan and thistleweed arrows pelted the surface, and then I watched as they floated to the top. I resented being underwater almost as much as being shot.

I was able to stay under as the Human ships passed by me, but I needed air. I *really* needed air. My plan was to surface, take a breath, and then dive again, but as soon as I breached the surface an arrow pierced through the water and buried itself in my left arm. The cheers and congratulations to the Escali who made the shot weren't as loud as my scream when it hit. Through the pain, I realized what I would have to do to live, and it was going to take all my willpower.

I relaxed my legs and arms and floated motionlessly on top of the water as my blood seeped into the ocean. The arrow in my arm had been laced with thistleweed, and I thanked the moons that I had already had the fever and was immune to it. Immune or not though, it was an awful pain, and my eyes watered uncontrollably. I closed them, didn't move, didn't make a sound, and the Escalis on the ship fell for it. They didn't shoot any more arrows, and I heard their voices growing farther and farther distant.

I stayed that way after I ceased to hear them, and didn't even move when I felt something gently touch my injured arm. I did however open my eyes and see—

"GAH, SHANKING LIFE, ARCHIE!" I shouted as he jerked the arrow out.

"Pain's over!" he said, quickly holding up both his hands in apology.

"Pain is *not* over!" I howled as the saltwater rushed into the wound and I clamped my good hand over it with all the strength my cold fingers could muster.

"Give it a minute, and it'll be gone."

"Right, let me just *give it a minute*. Be careful with that arrow, it's got thistleweed on the end," I snapped.

"Thanks," he said, turning and throwing it as far as he could. "At least it wasn't sasperan. We would probably both be dead."

"Why would we both be dead?" I asked irritably.

"I don't think I swim well enough to get us both back to land. I don't know... Maybe I could do it if—"

"How far is land?"

"After that long on the *Shadow's Doubt*, several miles at least."

"Several miles!" I tried to kick him under the water, but ended up crushing my foot when I hit his shield. "I hate swimming!"

"Well that's hardly my fault." He backed away from me in his treading. "I'm not the one who chose to hide on a moving ship."

"But it was your stupid plan to bail into the water. Now we have to swim for *miles!*"

He laughed through a disbelieving frown. "You're right Allie, my apologies. I should have found a way off the ship that didn't involve water. I just don't even know what I was thinking."

I tried to stare him down, but the amusement on his face made me break into a reluctant grin. I looked away before he could catch it. "It'll be a long swim back if you're mad at me the whole way," he said, disarming the situation. "Can we call a truce?"

"I guess," I said, getting rid of the smile before facing him again. "It's not as though it's your fault... I'm just angry in general, I suppose."

"I figured *that* when you blew a hole in the back of the Escali flagship."

"Yeah... I'll probably be in trouble for that too, won't I?"

"We're Tallies. We're always in trouble. What got you angry enough to use magic?"

"Sav. He and Gat killed Anna, and he had the nerve to sit there and tell me about it."

I saw Archie's jaw drop. "I can't believe they got her."

I realized my arm had stopped hurting, and I let go of it to see the wound almost healed over. "They have our Epic too. That's how I lost my memory. I was trying to protect her."

Archie gaped. What else was there to say? I didn't want to speculate about the horrors she had already faced if Sav had her. I said, "We should probably start swimming. We can talk while we go."

We started off with slow strokes, but neither of us mentioned the horrible idea any further. Actually, neither of us said anything for close to an hour, so I had full concentration on my dislike for the water and the royal twins.

The swim wasn't as bad as I initially predicted. I wasn't sure if travelling with the wind was helping or not, but I tried to convince myself that it was. I fooled myself several times into thinking that I could see the cliff line of Dincara in the distance, but I knew we were still too far out.

We kept moving forward until the lack of conversation almost killed me. "I hate swimming," I said again, not ready to talk about the Epic situation.

"Do you know why?"

"Because it's a pain?"

"That's one reason. It's actually because we're Tallies though — Escalis can't swim well. If we were Human, this would be a whole lot easier."

"That explains why Gat didn't jump into the water after me. He sounded ready for the kill when we were on the ship."

There was silence again, save for the sound of the wind and waves, so I cut it short before it became overwhelming. "Do you think Leaf is ok?" I voiced the first question that came to mind.

"The escape tunnel only had one direction. I'm sure he found his way out."

"But where is he now? Do you think maybe he's trying to go back to the Dragona?" I worried.

"Hopefully not. He should know that nobody would be there. Maybe he found the other children once he got out…"

"I hope so. And I hope they get far away before Sav and Gat go looking for them."

The sun was sinking fast, and its light was on the verge of being smothered when I saw the outline of a mountain in the distance. I let out a cry of relief and Archie cheered at the wonderful sight. I couldn't wait to get to the beach and be done swimming! I planned to collapse and fall asleep as soon as I landed.

I kicked my legs harder since we were on the last stretch, and it ended up being the hardest part of the journey. The waves were breaking on a beach I didn't recognize, and as soon as I got close they tumbled up and over me, crushing the air from my lungs. I fought my way back to the surface, but the next wave pushed me under. The battle was hard fought, but I was able to struggle my way up to breathable air eventually. I had barely started coughing up the water when the next one hit me, and then it was suddenly over.

I felt sand brush against my knees right before I tumbled onto the beach and hacked uncontrollably, crawling onto dry land while heaving water from my lungs. A forest had sprouted at the edge of the beach, but I couldn't see any recognizable landmarks. Archie pulled himself from the tide and collapsed onto the sand as well, breathing heavily. My coughing had ceased, but my muscles complained about the journey. I felt like going to sleep for the night right there with sand sticking uncomfortably to every part of me.

A shadow passed over in what little was left of the light, and I looked up to see the black falcon. I could almost feel glee radiating from it, having found us.

"Get out of here!" I picked up a rock and threw it at him, on my knees now. He swerved around it and then let out his piercing screech. Archie jumped to his feet and ran over to me. "And take that too!" I threw another rock.

"We need to get out of here," he said.

"I'm way too tired to go anywhere. Plus, what's he going to do? Go get Sav and Gat? It's not like they can swim here!"

"No they can't, but they're probably already on their way in one of the smaller boats, and we don't need Gyr telling them where we are."

"All the more reason for you to help me throw rocks and take him out!" I threw another one, which missed again.

Another screech echoed, but from over the water this time. A grey mass as fast as an arrow slammed into Gyr and sent him flying into the trees.

"FLAK!" I shouted as she straightened herself and Gyr darted back out to attack her. They collided in hideous shrieks as they bit and clawed at each other, trying to stay airborne. "GET HIM FLAK! Tear him to pieces!" I shouted as torn feathers blew away from their scuffle and drops of blood peppered the beach.

Flak somehow got the upper hand as they both hurtled to the ground, and Gyr crashed first before he could shake her. Archie and I ran over as Flak jumped up and left Gyr lying in the sand. Before we got to him, he desperately tried to take flight, but one of his wings was dragging the beach.

"So do you want to kill him or do you want me to?" I asked as Gyr glared hatefully at me. Flak instantly jumped in front of him and extended her wings as though shielding him.

"It doesn't matter whose falcon he was. He's still a falcon. We can't kill him." Archie replied.

"Can't kill him? *Of course not!* Ok, so we'll tie him up and take him with us." Flak seemed to be ok with that. She left Gyr and jumped onto my shoulder, digging her talons in to stay up. I didn't even care. She had just saved us both. She head-butted me and closed her eyes as I looked at her injuries. She had lost many precious feathers, but her wounds were thankfully superficial.

"I'm at a loss for string," Archie said as he checked his pockets, "do you have any with you?"

"I do have this," I pulled my tied key from my neck and undid the knot.

"Perfect," he said as I handed him the cord and tucked the key into my pocket.

Gyr voiced his opposition to having something tied to his leg, and he bit and clawed until Archie was bleeding, but finally done with the knot and already healing from the scratches.

302

"Where are we?" I wondered at the unfamiliar beach.

"Not Dincara."

"Flak probably knows," I reasoned. She didn't acknowledge me, as she was too busy having some sort of face off with Gyr. They had both locked gazes with each other, and neither moved until Gyr tried to launch himself off the ground and attack her. The assault would have been successful, except he was cut short by the tether holding him back. Flak took off, let out a screech, and flew into the trees without looking back.

"I hope that meant to follow," Archie assumed as he picked up Gyr's tether and made to follow her into the woods. Gyr would have nothing to do with it, and chose to hang upside down from the leash while Archie carried him. Archie apparently didn't care either and just left him that way, held an arm's length away. I followed them into the towering needle-trees, and we were on our way home.

CHAPTER TWENTY SEVEN

It took a Tally's pace to keep up with Flak as she soared through the trees, yet she still had to stop and wait for us every once in a while. After swimming half the day and running half the night, I felt hot and sticky all over with the exception of the tip of my nose, which was doomed to always be cold. My muscles began rebelling as my lungs started giving out from the stress. I didn't know what had kept me going so long, but it was almost gone.

A sliver of the largest moon began rising into the sky when Flak finally stopped and perched herself on a tree. I was relieved to stop at last. Ecstatic might have been a better word. I coughed and doubled over, ready to collapse. Nothing was worse than seeing Archie — who was merely breathing hard — look at me to make sure I was ok. *Sorry that running fifty miles kills me!*

Archie left to hunt down some food while I built up a small fire and kept watch over Gyr. Needless to say, Gyr hated me.

It obviously took some skill for Archie to catch two rabbits in the time before he came back — especially in the dark — but they couldn't finish cooking fast enough. Flak brought a dead mouse for Gyr, but he refused to eat it so it lay forgotten on the ground.

I should have been more worried without any weapons close by, but strangely, I wasn't. I didn't expect anyone to happen by in the day after the battle, and in truth, Archie and I could probably kill a tama cat or a wolf with our bare hands.

We fell asleep quickly next to the fire — at least I knew I did. Its warm glow was small and sleep-inducing until I woke later on, freezing after it had gone out. I was never going to get back to sleep through the shivering, so I moved over next to Archie to steal some of his warmth.

"Archie, put your shield down before I freeze to death," I chattered. Archie rolled over to put an arm around my shoulder, and with him beside me I fell back asleep and didn't wake up again until it was morning.

I had no intention of waking with the sun, but Flak bit my fingers in impatience. I was on my side with Archie still next to me, asleep with his arm still on my shoulder, and I was entirely too comfortable and exhausted to move. I opened my eyes a fraction to glare at Flak. *We had barely gotten any sleep at all.* She bit my smallest finger, eager to go, but this time she bit hard.

"Ok, fine! I'm getting up." I set my hands in the dirty pine needles that were still warm from sleeping on them, and I pushed myself to my feet, only to lean against the nearest tree and close my eyes again. It was good enough for Flak at least, who moved on to Archie.

I opened my eyes to watch as she poked at him and he tried to ignore her. When she bit at his hands, he tucked them underneath himself, and when she pecked at his arm, I heard him mumble, "I'm not getting up, Flak, and you can't make me."

Flak thought otherwise and batted her wings maniacally in his face while screeching, her talons dangerously close by. Archie threw his arms up to protect himself, but Flak grabbed one in her vice-like grip and tugged wildly.

Archie rolled onto his knees to get away from her, his woken glare emanating murder. Flak deflated and took off into the trees, giving us no time to wake up, yet expecting us to follow.

I ran quickly to keep from losing her, and Archie caught up to me a minute later with Gyr hanging once again from the tether.

"I want to know who told that falcon she could be in charge," Archie said loudly enough for both Flak and I to hear.

"I think it was a self-appointed position," I replied. "Worse things have happened."

"Worse things are going to happen if we don't get back to the Dragona soon," Archie said, peering up at Flak mutinously. Flak screeched in response but kept flying, high above the trees. I didn't press the matter — we were both on edge from a lack of sleep.

We didn't see the welcoming peaks of the Dragona through the dense cedars until we were practically there, several hours later. The entrance to the Wreck was the closest to us, and I picked up my pace to reach the overhang into the caves I called home.

I didn't know what I was expecting, but I wasn't expecting what I found. There was... silence. Dead silence. No people, no laughing, no games being played, none of the constant chatter that had always been present, no life, no joy, no smell of cooking food, nobody doing the cooking, no friends, no *welcome backs*... just... silence.

Archie entered behind me, but didn't say anything as we both took in our surroundings. Halfway played games remained on the tables with chairs still pulled out around them. It looked like people had been in the Wreck ten minutes before and simply disappeared.

"Is anybody here?" I asked, my voice echoing off the desolate walls. Only resonance answered me. I glanced at Archie uncertainly, somehow hoping he could make things better.

"Let's split up and look through the main tunnels," he suggested. "There has to be somebody here."

"Ok," I said, feeling my heart beat anxiously. "Right, we'll find somebody."

We took separate ways, running down the main tunnels trying to find somebody. Trying to find *anybody*. I called out as I ran and I could hear Archie's voice echoing in the distance, looking for people too, but it was an ultimately futile search. I got to the very end of the main tunnel to see the sparring field deserted, fake weapons abandoned on the ground, the wind blowing by hollowly. I turned around and started slowly back to the Wreck.

That couldn't be it. That could not be what was left of home. How could home be empty? I felt my throat constricting into a knot and broke into a run to keep it from consuming me. I got back to the Wreck before Archie and couldn't hear his voice in the distance anymore, so I sat on the edge of a table and let tears roll silently down my cheeks. I didn't allow any sound to escape, because I couldn't bear to hear it echo off the walls. As I tried to comprehend the situation, to let it sink in, something clattered to the floor on the other side of the Wreck, creating an awful, resonating racket.

I stood quickly but couldn't see anything over the tables, so I cautiously approached the clamor. I didn't have my short swords, but it turned out I didn't need them. I only found Leaf's favorite tiny red dragon hunkered defensively, shooting a jet of flame at the fallen pan. Red whipped around when he heard me behind him, then squeaked and tromped over. *What was he doing in the Wreck?* Were all the dragons loose?

I scooped the scaled baby into my arms and he squirmed to nestle against me, warming the hands I hadn't realized were cold. His contentment helped to offset my hollowness.

Archie stepped into the Wreck, and his blank face reflected that the emptiness affected him as well. Neither of us could bring ourselves to admit the entire mountain was vacant. Instead, Archie said quietly, "I need to take a walk."

"I'll come with you," I said, also keeping my voice low.

I had never noticed how loudly footsteps could echo. Like annoying little drums, pointing out how silent the rest of the world lay.

"Should we even stay here?" I asked as we wandered aimlessly through the cold and colorless tunnel-rock. Red had gone to sleep in my arms.

Archie shrugged and snapped himself out of a blank stare. "Some people might trickle back here eventually. If we do leave, maybe we should wait a while first."

"Where would we go?" I asked. The Dragona was the only home I wanted to know. "Would the other Tallies take us in?"

"Of course. Actually, they'd be thrilled for us to come back."

I heard the faint sound of voices and froze with a step still in progress. Archie stopped when I did.

"I heard something," I whispered.

On an equally soft note, Archie said, "Let me stop by my room. Then we'll check it out."

We arrived quickly at his door, and he said, "Stay here just a second. I'll be right back." He stepped inside, closing it behind him.

"Really, Archie? You *still* have secrets you're keeping from me?" I whispered.

"No," he said, emerging seconds later with short swords for me and his own Escali sword, which I had never seen in person. "It's just a mess." I couldn't hold back a laugh as I took in the beautiful engravings on the silver hilt of his Escali sword, prominently showing a falcon over all else. I wished I had the time to look closer, or to take the sheath off and see the blade.

I set Red in Archie's room, and we took up a quick pace to get to the Wreck, where the voices were far too loud for anybody trying to sneak around. They spoke Human too.

Relief overwhelmed the knots of stress in my chest when I stepped inside and saw Liz among the twenty returners. I took my hand off the short swords I had been so prepared to use and trotted quickly to her. Since she had her back turned, talking to several people, I slipped in among them without her noticing.

She spoke about the future of the Dragona, wondering if anybody else was going to come back, and if they didn't, worrying about their fates. The way she talked made her sound so much older, like she had suddenly been forced into adulthood. A sad revelation, but maybe one that was necessary.

She was halfway through a sentence when she noticed me, a thought that would never be finished because of how quickly we grabbed each other. Our wordless hug brought no tears but filled me with intense relief.

"I don't know why I ever worry about you anymore," she said, pulling away from me to make eye contact. She may have been forced to mature recently, but I still knew how much she needed me. "Did Archie make it back too?"

Archie joined the circle of people as well, saying, "It came close at times, but we lived." Liz gave him a less welcoming greeting, in the form of a kick in the shins. Archie jumped back before she could make contact with his shield, then had to dodge her again before she could shove him.

"You need to stop running off with Allie and leaving me behind!" she shouted, breaking her illusion of control.

"What makes this my fault? I don't see you kicking Allie!"

Liz turned and kicked me as well. "Stop leaving me!"

"I'm sorry," I said, pulling her into another hug. She punched me in the stomach before hugging me back.

"I didn't think you were coming back this last time. I don't know what I'll do when you don't. You have to stop leaving me!"

"I'm sorry Liz. But I always come back, don't I? And it looks like the group with us made it out of the city?"

"Yes," she said, pushing me off once more. "The Escalis chased you, so there was no one left to guard us. We ran. And you *still* beat us back here. You and Archie, I swear…"

"Believe me, we did our fair share of running too," I said, shooting an exhausted sigh Archie's way, which he shrugged off. "How many of the people with you are mages?"

"Three," she said. "We only have *three* people who will know what to do to keep this place alive. Eight are from Dincara, and three are from the northern cities."

Every one of them were men except two female mages from the Dragona. The three from the north were tall and fair skinned with blue eyes.

"My name is Gin. My brother and I are from Keldrosa," the tallest of the three said.

The other Northerner didn't mention his name but said, "I am from the snows of Lakama."

"Are you all staying at the Dragona?" I asked hopefully. With such a minimal amount of people, we would barely be able to keep the place up.

The Dincarans agreed they would be staying because they had nowhere else to go, and the mages already called this home, so they weren't planning to leave. Gin and his brother said they'd stay, but the other Northerner had a family to return to in Lakama, so he'd be leaving in the morning.

"Hopefully more people find their way back to the Dragona as well. We're going to need all the help we can get," I said.

"Is there really nobody else here?" Liz asked.

Just as I replied, "Nobody," a large girl appeared across the room, and those from the Dragona relaxed.

"Oh good life, there are people here!" Although relieved to see us, Terry's eyes were clearly swollen and reddened.

"Is everything alright?" I asked as we migrated to her and she sat momentarily.

"*Is everything alright?* No, it isn't. Sir Darius and I were put on the same ship, so when the Escalis were above deck we started jumping people back and forth to the shore. I was back on the ship when the Escalis got it figured out, but when Sir Darius jumped back in, they hit him over the head, and I think… I think they killed him. I took two more people out, but I was afraid to go back."

"It's alright," I said, seeing the stress in her eyes. "How many did you get off the ship?"

"Sir Darius got fourteen, and I got fifteen plus myself. All but five of them will come to the Dragona, but only ten are actually mages. I couldn't bring anybody else."

"Ten mages is more than we have," I answered her. She stood to leave, antsy about staying in one place too long.

"I'll go tell them that there are people at the Dragona. If we all set off tonight, we should be here in a day and a half, maybe two."

"You aren't going to jump them here?"

Terry's desperate laugh showed us her exhaustion. "I'm too tired to jump anybody but myself." She leapt forward and disappeared.

"We should get rooms for everybody," Liz said to me.

"We can do that," I said, glancing to Archie because I couldn't help notice most eyes in the room on me. I think I had just accidentally taken charge, and Archie just had that tiny smirk in the corner of his mouth that meant he was impressed.

Nobody really owned anything to move in, so rooms were claimed quickly and without chore.

Hardly half an hour passed before I was able to retreat to my own. I wasn't about to fall asleep with all that had been going on, so I looked around my room and found my list of tally marks, a quill, and an ink well.

I sat down on my bed flipped my list over several times, then set it beside me. My room didn't feel right anymore. My cave walls hadn't changed while everything else had. It wasn't fair.

I got up and left my room to find a better spot, but my feet ended up taking me to the Wreck. In the past, the Wreck had been the one place I could find someone to talk to at any time of the day or night. Now it was desolate. I wound between the tables, then climbed outside where the night air felt pleasantly cool on my skin and in my lungs. A second moon had risen to light the sky, giving me more than enough light to read by. I lay down in the grass and grabbed my list and quill.

Deaths that were my fault.

I finally dragged a line of ink across four others, giving West his spot as number fifteen. Someday, I would find out who the other fourteen were.

Lives I've Saved.

I had a few thousand tally marks I needed to fit onto this page, but I found myself distracted by thoughts of what was to come. Surely Sav and Gat were on their way to the Dragona in pursuit of me. I probably shouldn't stick around because I was endangering everybody. Yet, if I were to leave, I would be leaving the Dragona even more shorthanded than it already was. And I couldn't abandon Liz.

I looked up at the stars and pondered my recent choices, not sure I could keep making them. I had saved thousands of lives in Dincara. Traded my loyalty to save them. I hadn't changed my loyalty though, had I? No, surely not. I had made the decision in Humanity's best interest. But it had also been in everybody's interest.

I flattened the parchment on my legs, *Saved* side up. Instead of covering the page in an indefinite amount of ink, I wrote one line across the bottom. A conclusion I hadn't come to lightly, but one I finally decided I believed.

It's worth the trouble.

I heard the scrape of boots climbing over stone, and I turned to see Archie emerging from the Wreck as well. Flak flew from his shoulder to land next to me.

"What are you doing out here?" I asked before he did.

"Getting out of my room. I couldn't sleep with Gyr being such a deranged crow. Why are you out here?"

"I'm just thinking about things."

"And I see you brought your list," he said, sitting in the grass next to me. "What are you thinking about?"

I exhaled and replied, "Everything. Right now I've got my mind on the battle and our role in it. And how many times we might have to play that role again. And how we can possibly keep the Dragona up with this many people. I still don't know what Sav and Gat want from me, and I wish I could just silence my thoughts for a little while. Get a good night of sleep without all the hopelessness, you know?"

Archie pulled up a few blades of grass and said, "Nothing's hopeless."

A cool breeze blew by and I heard a duskflyer begin singing in the distance, its song a low whistle in the wind. I brought my eyes up to the immensity of stars, swirled throughout the sky, and said, "You know, I used to spend hours every night, just thinking. Trying to remember who I was, then putting myself in danger when nothing else helped... I don't think I'm going to try anymore."

Archie smiled and said, "It never really worked, did it?"

"No, but that's not why I'm stopping. I think... Well, I used to think that finding my memories would define me. I would have a background, make the decisions that the proper Allie would make, and I could be the person everybody used to love."

Archie nodded and said, "They didn't even know the real you though."

"They didn't. So all that time, I was trying to live up to an old lie, a mask I put on for everyone else. And I think it was all a waste of time anyway, because having those memories wouldn't have changed the decision I made about Dincara. Memories or not, I'd still be determined to find this Epic girl, and that's what I want to define me."

"I think that's always defined you," Archie said with a smile, "trying to protect everybody around you. That's how you were before you lost your memory too."

Warmth overwhelmed my heart because that tiny drop of information meant oceans to me. I was exactly the same person I used to be.

"I'd really just love to have a conversation with my old self, more than anything, to find out what she knew."

"It would be amazing to find out how you ended up defending Sir Avery's daughter."

"And I'd love to know what Sav still wants from me."

Archie clenched his jaw and his fists at the thought of the Escali he hated, and I fixed my gaze on a soft patch of grass near my feet. Archie took a slow breath before saying, "Sav and Gat will keep hunting you until they get what they want."

"They already have our Epic. I don't know what other secrets could be nearly as valuable." Archie set his hand on mine, and I lifted my eyes from the dark ground to meet his reassuring gaze.

"Don't worry, Allie. We'll find out."

THE END

THANK YOUS

Here's the problem with a world of friends who help each other… I sit down to write my thank yous, and I don't know how to make the page count less than that of the book. Thank you, thank you, thank you to everyone I have ever known, because your stories inspire me and your support is what keeps me writing.

Thank you to my family for, you know, putting up with me and feeding me and everything while Secrets of The Tally was being written. You guys rock.

Thank you to Robbie, Karissa, Corie, and Madison for being my first readers, and to Jordan for being the first one to sit down and pick the entire story apart over a cup of mint tea.

To my mom, Hannah Dye, Hannah Richard, Matt Frye, Shell Adams, Katie Reed, Laura Abbott, and Jessica Colvin — thank you for the long hours spent critiquing and editing. And special thanks to Lauren Loftis who almost ended our friendship over the description of a fern in Chapter 1.

I had upwards of forty people read Secrets of The Tally before it was released, but Caleb and Josiah hold the record as the only beta readers who guessed Allie's identity before she did.

I was also inspired by more teachers I can count, starting with Mrs. Cooper in 5th grade, who had the super power of making every subject fun. I started Secrets of The Tally the summer after her class and never looked back. Skip ahead nine years, and I had a long-finished manuscript I wanted to publish and a professor named Osiri, whose lectures were all about dreams and goals and entrepreneurship. I can say without doubt that without his class, I wouldn't have flown to New York to meet with publishers and I would never have won the PNWA literary competition because I would never have entered. Sometimes all we need is that nudge.

Many thanks to everybody who supported me on Kickstarter to get our first print run off the ground — especially Thomas and Cody who loaned me their house and came out to do all the Kickstarter filming. We were climbing trees and steering bikes through the living room to get those shots, and it was *fun!*

Thank you to Ginger Anne London for the incredible cover art, and for all your support since the day I met you.

And thank you to YOU, dear reader, for picking up and reading a book without the seal of a large publishing house. It is my goal and dream to be a full time author, so if you liked this story, please please please consider writing a review for it on your favorite book-finding platform (Amazon, Goodreads, a blog somewhere), and hand it off to one of your friends to read.

See if they're able to guess the Secrets of the Tally.

Pronunciation Guide

However you pronounce these names in your head is perfectly acceptable, but for the sake of resolving those inevitable arguments, here's how I imagine a few of the harder ones.

Dincara – Din-car-uh

Dragona – Druh-go-nuh

Escali – Ess-caw-lee

Escalira – Ess-caw-lir-uh

Gataan – Gat-ay-an

Izfazara – Iz-fuh-zar-uh

Nessava – Ness-uh-vuh

Ratuan – Rat-yue-awn

Savaul – Suh-vall

Shadar – Shuh-dar

Tarace – Tare-iss

About The Author

My name is Halie, and I love to spend time in magical worlds filled with characters who inspire me. I started writing Secrets of the Tally when I was twelve years old, and I never stopped. It's been fifteen years since I very first set pen to paper to write Allie's story, and now writing and selling The Secrets of The Tally Series is my full-time career.

All four books in my series have been made possible through Kickstarter funding, and I couldn't be more grateful for my amazing support network who buys their books several months early so I have the money up front to print them.

Being a self-published author is a crazy job, and I love it. I'm a one-woman show who's in charge of writing, editing, formatting, production, artwork, sales, marketing, scheduling, accounting, finance, shipping, and logistics. I have more spreadsheets than any one human being should ever own, and I spend my weekdays running this crazy book-business while most weekends are spent meeting readers and selling/signing books in person.

My absolute favorite part of my job is when people connect to my stories the same way I have. It's the best feeling to have readers seek me out, needing to discuss their favorite characters and events.

Stay up to date with the series at www.secretsofthetally.com!

THIS BOOK FUNDED BY
KICKSTARTER

(And 161 Backers)

Stuart Pollock
Kathryn Reed
Gerald Mickelsen
Linda Kramer
Annette Oppenlander
Sophie Ascaso
Colleen McInnis
Amy Fewkes
Sam Peilow
Lexi Ray
Dan Neal
Karissa Neal
Noelle Zimmerman
Shell Adams
Yuliya Leonidova
Caleb Palmquist
Jasmine Vasion
Kevin DeVine
Klancy Shriver
Maria Scaramella
Arturo Anguiano
Sue Boucher
Kaitlyn Hort
Casee Callaghan
Cameron Kockritz
Jenn Donner
Lauren Loftis
Eilidh
Ashleigh DeBuse
Amy Keough
Mackenzie Greene
Hanna Badger
Corie Burck

Aaron Burck
Laura Panek
Genevieve Showalter
Matthew Wensley
Will Massart
Tressa Holcombe
Brynnan Fink
Joshua March
Darian Cummings
Hazel Smith
Stephen Simmonds
Allison Adams
Dan Spindler
Evelyn Sabbag
Adam Lazaruso
Louisa George-Kelso
Lindsay MacKay
Tina Fewkes
Sarah Ann Richards
Brian Davidson
Lani Schmidt
Molly Wakeling
John Almirall
Kari Burkett
Jordan Emery
Taryn Harmon
Alison Crofton-
    Macdonald
Tatiana Schwiering
Matthew Anderson
Madison Keezer
Anna Reorda
Allison Dulin

Rob Steinberger
Hayley Swanson
Michelle Tran
Sarah Brewer
Laura Adams
Cody Nelson
Ashley Falter
Kat Steinberg
Molly Diamond
Shah Kulsoom
Kayla Carlile
Jamie Pacton
Ren Bettencourt
Jen Stiles
Janessa Darr
Kendra Waters
Ariel Maras
Alexandra Lucas
Lisa B. Martin
Dean Fewkes
Wendy Fewkes
Alissa Maley
Iain Donoghue
Jennifer Chi
Kyle Schmidt
Matt Frye
Sandra
Michelle Lustig
Ashley VanRiper
Chelsea
Nadia Lustig Frye
Tyler Schroder
Unity Yule

Terrana Cliff
Chyna Wagoner
Susan Sperling
Nicole Hall
Ellen Boucher
Scott
Scott Freisthler
Wade Holter
Kayla Koontz
Anisha
Israel
Brody Gandy
Jessica Colvin
Erica Hamby
Katie D
Maegan Murray
Kayla Palmer
Amber Monroe
Sara Privatt
Jody S Shriver
Jonna Davis
Adelaide Lang

Kathy Carlsen
Thomas Stoneham
Karen Harmon
Kenton Webb
Evelyn Taylor-Nelson
Stephanie Burtt
Jarrod Swanson
James LaFave
Patricia Pollock
Chad Bowden
Mark Urlacher
Matthew Johnson
Nico Morales
Kristján Björn
    Snorrason
Emily Brinkman
Brandon Williams
SchizoTyler
Kristina Emmons
Kenny Hitchings
Mikayla Pena
Brandy Jo Grampp

Michael Graves
Alexis Guse
Bushra Zaman
Jill Gibson
Kevin Hassett
Michelle Faber
Haley Bellows
Devon
Holly Dye
Matt Kmetz
Amy Tanton
Luu Le
Kirsten Lane
RJ Lancaster
Lorin Robertson
Nina Venables
Brian Jaynes
Curtis P
Andrea Nelson
Cherry Taylor
Kathy Lucore